MW00451426

MONSTER
HUNTER
MEMOIRS

FEVER

To purchase any of these titles in e-book form,
please go to www.baen.com.

MONSTER
HUNTER
MEMOIRS
FEVER

Larry Correia &
Jason Cordova

MONSTER HUNTER MEMOIRS: FEVER

This is a work of fiction. All the characters and events portrayed in this book are fictional, and any resemblance to real people or incidents is purely coincidental.

Copyright © 2023 by Larry Correia and Jason Cordova

All rights reserved, including the right to reproduce this book or portions thereof in any form.

A Baen Books Original

Baen Publishing Enterprises
P.O. Box 1403
Riverdale, NY 10471
www.baen.com

ISBN: 978-1-9821-9293-8

Cover art by Alan Pollack

First printing, October 2023

Distributed by Simon & Schuster
1230 Avenue of the Americas
New York, NY 10020

Library of Congress Cataloging-in-Publication Data

Names: Correia, Larry, author. | Cordova, Jason, 1978– author.
Title: Fever / Larry Correia, Jason Cordova.
Description: Riverdale, NY : Baen Publishing Enterprises, 2023. | Series: Monster hunter memoirs ; 4
Identifiers: LCCN 2023026711 | ISBN 9781982192938 (hardcover) | ISBN 9781625799333 (ebook)
Subjects: LCSH: Secret societies—Fiction. | Monsters—Fiction. | Hunters—Fiction. | LCGFT: Monster fiction. | Fantasy fiction. | Novels.
Classification: LCC PS3603.O7723 F49 2023 | DDC 813/.6—dc23/eng/20230612
LC record available at https://lccn.loc.gov/20230267118

Printed in the United States of America

10 9 8 7 6 5 4 3 2 1

To Toni, for being an amazing editor.

MONSTER HUNTER
MEMOIRS
FEVER

CHAPTER 1

I knew we were screwed when the Akkadian sand demon erupted from the ground and tore our point man's head off.

Unsurprisingly, things had gone poorly after that.

The boys and I had been tracking the demon for days. Some Egyptian general had summoned it in a plot to assassinate the Egyptian president. As plans involving malevolent beings often do, the play had gone awry. Anwar Sadat was still alive, the general dead, and the summoned monster was off on a rampage. I didn't know all the details, just nine men and me had been tasked with tracking down and destroying the vile creature before it made its way into the civilian populace of the Sinai.

Legally, my unit didn't exist. The Kidon was a special section of the Mossad—the Israeli intelligence agency. If any of us were captured on this side of the border, Israel would disavow us and deny involvement. Which made sense, all things considered. Our two countries were still reeling from the most recent conflict and peace was tenuous at best. Being a woman, I really didn't want to get taken prisoner here.

Something had to be done about this demon, though. The Egyptians hadn't been able to handle their mess, and they knew we had the best anti-monster specialists in the region. So diplomats had talked in secret, concessions had been made, and the Egyptian army had looked the other way long enough for us to

1

cross the border. When it comes to ancient demons devouring their populace even the most stubborn nations can temporarily set aside their differences long enough to ask for a favor.

It wasn't the details of this mission that left me feeling uneasy. This sort of clandestine operation was the Kidon's bread and butter. I'd been feeling troubled lately, plagued by dreams that I needed to return to a place that I'd not been for a very long time. Decades, actually. I was here instead of home for good reasons, so I'd pushed those premonitions aside and focused on the mission.

But I couldn't shake the feeling that something bad was going to happen.

The dawn was a cold one. Typically, February remained warm during the day and got chilly at night, but with the cloud coverage and light rainfall overnight, the temperatures had actually dipped down enough for even Gideon to complain. Given that he'd spent his childhood in northern Italy before returning to Israel for *Aliyah*, that was an impressive feat.

We were on foot, sore, tired, and almost out of food. There was supposed to have been an airdrop for resupply the night before, which didn't pan out. We were out of fresh water, and were using purifying tablets in our canteens, filled with water from a small spring where I hoped the arsenic content wasn't high enough to kill us quickly.

The group had just rotated our duties at sunrise. Since I had the best eyesight I'd been on point when the light had been at its lowest. As the sun began to lighten the sky, Haim ordered a switch-off and Shmuel had taken the lead. I'd gone back to rear watch, which was far more taxing than it sounds. Point was simple—you watched for signs of ambush, tried not to step on any mines, and hoped you got off a warning cry before you died. Bringing up the rear meant a lot of walking backward, always checking behind the team, and making sure the tracks we left wouldn't be too easy to find. And fighting off my natural urge to wander off and explore on my own. Sometimes my instincts make it hard for me to be a good team player.

The odds of anything human attacking us here were slim but not zero. We'd just finished a shooting war, after all. Lots of under-the-table politics later and now we were wandering our sworn enemy's countryside doing them a favor, but since it was a secret favor, there would still be plenty of people around who'd shoot us on sight.

Cold, hungry, utterly exhausted, and thus distracted, of course this was when the sand demon erupted from the ground and killed Shmuel.

It happened so fast the kid didn't even have a chance to be alarmed. One second Shmuel was standing still, looking up toward a ridge with a curious expression on his face, and the next his head was flying toward us. His body crumpled to the ground as his head landed at the feet of Haim, our team leader.

"Shit!" Haim shouted as he looked down at the confused expression on our dead comrade's face. The attack had been so sudden that Shmuel had died without even knowing why.

With wings unfurled, the sand demon cut an imposing figure. Carved in a male form, eight feet tall, horned, with skin the texture of sandstone, he cackled with glee as his forked tongue licked Shmuel's blood off his claws. He eyed all of us before the demonic gaze settled on me in particular.

"Half-breed."

"Motherfucker," I agreed, and triggered a short burst from my Galil, striking him in the chest with several 5.56 rounds.

They were good shots. Too bad demons are *tough*.

The rest of the Kidon reacted a bit slower than I had and started shooting, but the demon had already unleashed his terrible magic.

Wings spread wide with a violent crack, and the sand around us went flying. I moved, trying to avert my eyes as the visibility suddenly dropped to near zero. The cold and damp vanished in an instant. The air turned bone dry so suddenly that it sucked the moisture out of my mouth.

My friends were pulling down their goggles, trying to protect their eyes. Haim started bellowing orders. I could hear Faud and Gideon moving to flank the monster while Yehuda and Eli kept shooting where the monster had been. Nobody else had an angle. Without a clear visual, they'd hold their fire. It was one of the many tough lessons our team had learned while hunting monsters: confirm, then destroy, because friendly fire isn't.

No goggles for me. I just squinted and blinked away the grit and pain, and was able to track the demon's shape through the impromptu sandstorm. He was moving to the left, toward where

Faud and Gideon were running. I shouted a warning. Uncertain whether they heard me over the howling wind, I went after them. They were between me and the demon so I couldn't fire.

The already blistering sandstorm was growing worse by the second. Stinging particles were hitting hard enough to lacerate exposed skin. Even I was mostly blind now, and when I got to where I thought the demon should be, he was already gone. Somewhere to my left I heard Haim cry out in pain. Someone fired a single shot, which was quickly followed by a curse. It sounded like Yehuda but I couldn't be certain. Then all I could hear was the howling wind and sand beating the keffiyeh over my ears like a drum.

I'd never experienced anything like this. There was so much sand in the air it was like trying to walk underwater. It was growing harder to breathe by the second.

A heavy blow to my pack sent me sprawling to the ground. As I rolled away I caught a faint glimpse of the demon through the tearing dust, and it looked like the thing was smiling down at me, razor-sharp fangs white in stark contrast to the golden skin.

Before I could get up, he kicked me in the ribs. The air whooshed out of my lungs from the force of the blow. I was lifted off the ground a few feet before landing hard on a pile of rocks. One of the sharp ends stabbed me in the thigh, piercing the skin. It wasn't super deep, but it *hurt*.

Somehow, I kept hold of my carbine. I clutched at the stab wound with my free hand and tried to get to my feet. Even over the now-hurricane force winds the demon made sure I could hear his condescending tone. I hated magic like that.

"Weak. I expected more from your kind."

The wings continued their flapping motion, each beat kicking up more and more wind and sand.

"You interest me more than these others, half-breed. What is one of your kind doing *here*?" The summoned creature sounded offended, as if something like me didn't belong on his continent, and to be fair, I *was* pretty far from the land of my birth.

I brought the Galil up and fired it one-handed, peppering the demon's torso. The demon retreated through the storm as though he were a part of it. Still, I managed to hit him at least three times, so I definitely got his attention.

I was wounded, sure. A quitter? Never.

The demon returned on the wind. Claws sliced through my arm, laying open the skin.

Rage began bubbling in my chest as the demon danced away once more, laughing. There were other cries of pain as the demon flew about, tormenting my friends. He was doing hit-and-run attacks while we staggered around blind and confused. He was toying with us.

Another hand grabbed my arm, only this one was human.

"Let it out!" Haim shouted in my ear.

"No! It's too dangerous!"

Haim knew what he was asking for. It was what had gotten me assigned to this very special unit to begin with. Haim always pushed for me to use my bestial side on missions more, because he had more far confidence in me than I did, but there was no way I could afford to let it out.

Only the maddening wind had gotten to the point we could barely stand. The demon wouldn't need to kill us because we were about to get blown away. Someone shouted a warning followed by the heavy staccato of machine-gun fire ripping through the air. The demon roared with laughter. Whoever had fired had missed, and badly.

Haim had to shout directly into my ear. "This demon is stronger than expected! If you don't, we'll all die!"

"We can't risk it."

"Let it free. That's an order."

Rarely had I ever let the *nagualii* out of its cage because when I did, I was nothing but a passenger in a vehicle of violence.

"I'll take responsibility for whatever happens, Chloe."

We were getting our asses kicked and time was running out. I reached down within my soul, found the caged animal part of me, and opened the prison door. The change began immediately. The drumbeat in my chest doubled in time. Smoke spread through my brain as the *nagualii* began to take control.

The sand demon reappeared and grabbed hold of me, wearing a triumphant look as his razor-sharp claws dug into my soft flesh. However, his expression changed to one of surprise as the *nagualii* roared defiantly, and I bit the demon on the face.

I could smell it, thick and heavy.

Fear.

The foul monstrosity was afraid of me. To a normal human

nose it would have smelled like nothing but sulfur, a stench typical with demons and their like. Only I could smell the underlying garlic under the brimstone. It was the scent of a predator who suddenly realized a more dangerous threat had arrived.

And it was delicious.

I was past the point of no return now. The monster within was totally free.

I'd been blinded by sand, but now my entire awareness was clouded by something different. Smoke, thick and black, boiling off an obsidian mirror. The drumbeat grew louder.

I was barely aware that my body changed, ripping free of my clothing. I was a spectator on a disjointed fever dream, catching glimpses here and there as monster battled monster. Claws tore. There was the foul taste of demon blood in my mouth.

The *nagualii* was enraged. The demon, terrified. There were no more taunts from it now. Only a vain attempt at survival.

The demon had been right. My kind didn't belong here. But that punk shouldn't have disrespected royalty.

The sand annoyed the *nagualii*. Stung our eyes. Got in our nostrils and burned our lungs. So we stopped the wind, sinking claws into the demon's membranes and violently ripping off one wing, and then the other. The demon screamed, until we reached down his throat to yank out his steaming guts, then kept on tearing.

Then I saw nothing but black. Thankfully.

Until a human voice screamed in agony.

The *nagualii*, lost in the bloodlust, had turned and bit what had been perceived as a new threat. Red-hot human blood filled my mouth, and it had been a *long* time since I had tasted that, only that was a flavor you never forget.

The smoke cleared and I recoiled in disgust as human reality came rushing back.

The *nagualii* didn't care for my feelings. The beast continued to rip and tear, luxuriating in the screams of the dying. Ribs cracked and popped. Blood sprayed everywhere as the *nagualii* howled in triumph. I could only see bits and pieces through the falling sand, but what I did see shocked me to my core.

Stop, I begged the monster. Only she ignored me, because I had kept her locked inside for so long, a prisoner of iron will and self-control. The primal needs of the beast had been ignored.

I only called upon our power when my own life was in danger. She was angry at my selfishness.

I felt someone trying to pull me off the man whose neck I'd been gnawing on. The *nagualii* lashed out and blood sprayed from a torn throat.

I fought to regain control of my wicked half. My vision shifted. The *nagualii* screamed in frustration, the cry of the jaguar hurting my throat. Control was returning, but the *nagualii* was fighting hard to stay in charge of our body and I didn't know if I could win.

I saw Haim, and begged, "Kill me," through disfigured lips and fangs. The monster finished my statement with a savage roar. She wasn't going away easily this time. I hoped Haim could see the raging inferno struggling for control and put me down.

Something cracked against my skull. Staggered from the blow, I turned to see Jacob holding his rifle. He raised it a second time and brought the steel butt plate crashing down on my temple. I fell to the ground with a crack in my skull.

With neither of us driving now, the *nagualii* slunk back into her prison, sullen, but contained at last.

My body was fully human again, and I lay there, bloody and naked on the sand, surrounded by shredded demon body parts. Shame welled up within me. For the first time in decades, I'd let the monster out, and good men had died by my hand. I waited for the bullet to come, the one that would end my existence. It would be justice. I deserved it. There was no denying what was to happen next.

Only no killing blow came. There was no merciful end to my disgrace.

Mission complete, my friends tied me up and carried me back across the border.

My name is Chloe Mendoza. I am both a monster, and a monster hunter.

CHAPTER 2

A solid bump jarred me from my nap. Rubbing my eyes, I looked around the first-class cabin in some confusion. It was dark outside, though there was a dim light from the cockpit area. Last I remembered, the sun had still been up. Falling asleep on an airplane always leaves me hazy. The businessman in the seat next to me lit a cigarette, which was annoying. Still, it was better flying these days than it used to be. Fewer people smoked on planes nowadays, not since the new jumbo jetliners came out. Pressurized cabins and cigarette smoke didn't mix well.

Covering my mouth as I yawned, it finally dawned on me that we had landed.

The last time I'd been here it had been called Candler Field. They'd renamed it the William B. Hartsfield International Airport a few years ago. Atlanta, Georgia was still a few hundred miles from my ultimate destination, which meant I still had a long ride ahead of me, but someone from Cazador was supposed to be picking me up so at least I wouldn't have to drive myself.

I'd been somewhat surprised by the warm reception I received when I had made the phone call to Monster Hunter International. It had been a *long* time since I'd worked with them. We had parted on good terms, but I was sure nearly everyone I knew from back in those days was either retired or dead. I hadn't even known who to ask for. Yet there'd been no hesitation from the

9

receptionist once I identified myself as a former employee. She had patched me through to "the Boss" and wished me luck.

It turned out the man in charge of the family business now was Raymond Shackleford III, who had once been one of the toughest kids I'd ever met, and who now sounded like a rather confident, mature adult over the phone. His father, Ray the Second... now there was a man I was pretty sure nothing on this planet could have beaten in his prime. If I were trying to kill him, I'd wait until he was old and crippled. Then I might have had a chance. *Might.*

Despite remembering me—and knowing all about what I was—Ray had agreed to talk about employment opportunities. Which was good, because I didn't really have anywhere else to go. I'd given him the brief rundown of what I'd been up to since I'd last been in the US, but I'd left the details of why I was leaving Israel vague. During my trial, Haim had kept his word and accepted full responsibility for freeing the *nagualii* and the resulting deaths of our teammates. While the IDF was furious about what happened outside Taba, the Mossad had declared I'd been following orders. The fact that this had led to the deaths of two Kidon members was beside the point. I wasn't getting executed as a traitor, but I was no longer welcome. With my official government employment terminated, as a supernatural noncitizen I was no longer exempt from bounties there, so I had to leave the country immediately.

Things like me were useful to have around until we weren't. At least they'd paid me well, though.

It wasn't the Boss who would be picking me up at the airport, but rather his new Director of Operations at Monster Hunter International, a recently returned Vietnam veteran by the name of Earl Harbinger. I wasn't familiar with the name. Ray told me that Earl would fill me in on what was new at MHI, as well as get me brought back up to speed. I didn't really think the Shacklefords would be so welcoming. Granted, Ray knew about my family history and abilities, but those weren't necessarily positives.

It was well known that I was a skilled Hunter, though. In certain circles I had a bit of a reputation for getting the job done. More importantly, Ray knew how quickly I could adapt to just about any situation. He'd been a relatively inexperienced Hunter when we'd helped the people in a small village outside San Antonio deal with a skinwalker. Ray had been enthusiastic, and smart for his age, but he would've gotten killed that time if it wasn't for me taking a haunted spear for him, and the Shacklefords weren't the kind of people who forgot things like that.

Except Raymond Shackleford the Third was still a pragmatist, and he'd done a few days of research before calling me back to make the job offer. I'm sure he had all sorts of sources, because even in secret organizations like the Kidon, Monster Hunters talk to other Hunters about monsters. The cynical part of me figured Ray wanted me back just so he could make sure I was still the same person and hadn't given in to my other half over the ensuing years. It's easier to kill something you didn't have to go and hunt down first.

I shrugged that dark thought off as the flight attendant opened the door to let us off. Nice thing about first class—board first, disembark first. I didn't have any luggage save for a small bag I'd picked up in New York City after getting deported. It was a leather knockoff with an "I♥NY" logo on the side. Cheap tourist crap, but I kind of liked it. Plus, it was large enough to hold my spare dress and a few toiletries I'd picked up during my sudden departure from Israel. The less I dwelt on that incident, the better my psyche would be.

One thing I'd immediately noticed during the flight from London to New York was the jarring change in clothing styles. In Israel, the people there were what could generously be called "fashion backward." It wasn't as though we were too worried about keeping up with the latest styles in the middle of surviving multiple wars, and when I'd left America it was still coming out of the Great Depression, so I'd not had a lot to compare us to. Until I'd landed in London, that is. Everywhere I'd turned there were women showing way too much leg and midriffs, wearing hip-hugger jeans that left little to the imagination. I didn't think of myself as a stick in the mud, but clothing here seemed too flamboyant, colorful, and sometimes downright weird.

I deboarded the plane, nodding politely to the stewardess in the really tacky uniform as I descended the portable stairs. For some reason, Braniff International had them dressed in a sort of mock spacesuit uniform. It was polyester and pain. I felt bad for the stewardesses for having to wear that outfit.

Pausing at the base of the stairs, I looked around and was shocked by what I saw. This place had grown *a lot* since 1942.

The wind was strong but the air was warm. Spring in Georgia usually meant lots of rain, but I couldn't see a cloud in the sky. The moon was high above, a fingernail crescent, thin and faint. I held my bag close as I followed my fellow first-class passengers down to the tarmac and into a terminal.

There were people waiting, holding signs with names written on them, to pick up travelers. The one waiting for me didn't need a sign, as he was a very good friend who I'd been led to believe had died long ago.

He had the same lean build to him, sandy blond hair cut close, and a smooth-shaven face which hadn't aged much, maybe a few years, in spite of the decades that had passed. There were just a few extra wrinkles around those icy blue eyes. He looked like a tough, fit man in his thirties, the same as when he'd departed for England to fight the Nazis in Europe. Seeing that face, it felt as though we had just said our goodbyes the day before. He still had that toughness about him, a cocky swagger that suggested he was far more capable than first appearance.

Ray Shackleford Jr.—who I'd been told was dead—waved. So I did what was only natural and returned the greeting.

I was confused. The Boss had said a man named Earl was picking me up, not *him*.

When I'd left, only a handful of us had known how unique he was. Tough, sure. He had a certain *je ne sais quoi* about his demeanor, which set most people back on their heels the longer he stared at them, and that was because this man was a werewolf. And not just any old werewolf, but the only one I had ever heard of to get that under control enough to earn an exemption from the government's bounty system, the Perpetual Unearthly Forces Fund. I knew he had earned a silver PUFF Exempt coin—just like mine—and we'd even earned them in the same war.

"So *you're* Earl Harbinger?" I asked, curious.

"Yep." He nodded, which confirmed my suspicions. When you're the kind of thing that ages slowly or lives an abnormally long time, it's handy to change your name every so often. The name change was a brilliant idea, actually. Something I would have considered if not for the fact that the deportation papers given to me by the Kidon were under this identity. It's hard to get a legitimate new passport when you look twenty but your birth certificate says you're a hundred.

"You're looking pretty as ever, Chloe."

"Thanks . . . Earl."

"No more luggage?"

"This is it," I said, holding up my "I ❤ NY" bag.

It was an awkward reunion, but the Shacklefords had never been big on emotional displays. So I just followed him out of the terminal, and into the parking lot to a pickup truck.

"You've aged well," Earl said as he—always the Southern gentleman—opened the passenger side door for me.

"So have you," I replied, feeling a little uncertain. "Which is, frankly, kind of a surprise."

"Eh. I'm taking aging gradual." He went around to the driver's side and got in. "It looks like you're not aging at all."

"Trust me, I'm not immortal."

"I believe your pop is supposed to be, though."

That was low. Was he trying to provoke me? "Thirty years ago you knew I didn't like to talk about that. What makes you think that's changed?"

Earl just grunted at that, started the engine, and got us out of the parking lot and onto the road.

"I was told you'd gotten killed," I told him.

"What is it the kids say nowadays? I had to *reinvent* myself." Earl shook his head sadly. "The government drafted me again."

"For Vietnam?"

"Yeah."

"Multiple terms? That's against the PUFF exemption rules."

"We both know when it comes to folks like us the government makes the rules up as they go along."

Something about him was off and unsettling now, and there was a bitter anger in his voice I'd never heard before. I didn't know what it was. He hadn't been like this thirty years ago. Then again, my own powers hadn't really started to bloom until I'd had to fight Hitler's monsters. Maybe werewolves got surlier over time? Or worse, what if he'd always been this dangerous and I was only now picking up on it? He'd always left me feeling a little uneasy, but now it seemed worse. It was a sobering thought.

We sped along the highway in the old truck heading southwest. One thing that had changed since I left the States, there was a national speed limit now, which apparently Earl did not

care about in the least. We passed Union City in a hurry and
blew past a state trooper hidden by the side of the road. However, he didn't even flip his lights on as we went by. I glanced
over at Earl curiously.

"He already stopped me on the way in." He sensed my questioning look. "Got lucky. He knew who I work for."

"That good or bad?"

"I didn't get a ticket."

Earl drove so fast it actually made me nervous. Israeli driv-
ers weren't as courteous as Americans were, but then again there
weren't as many. Wide-open country roads tended to teach driv-
ers to respect the road—especially since one never knew when
their car would run face-first into a Holstein. Crazy speed was
a problem we really never had to deal with while navigating the
narrow, winding roads of Haifa.

"So now that you're somebody else, your son is the Boss,
not you?"

Earl chuckled. "It's more of a family business partnership,
but he's the one who's officially alive. And honestly, the kid is
a better leader than I ever was. My boys have come a long way
since you knew them."

"So what do you do, then?"

"Us old-timers come in useful...for the experience. And upon
occasion to rip the head off something beyond what the regular
folks can handle."

"Which one did you hire me for, then? The experience? Or
the head ripping?"

He didn't answer.

There was a tension between us. Not that I blamed him for
it. I was a *nagualii*, after all—as far as I knew, the only PUFF-
exempt one in the history of the list's existence—and we'd not
spoken in a couple decades. Plus, my kind and his traditionally
didn't get along too well.

I've got a gift for reading people. Some of the more recent
arrivals to Israel spoke about auras, but there is something to
that, and I think my heritage gave me some insight into people's
true nature. This was an honorable man, but something in him
had changed since we had last seen one another. I couldn't put
my finger on what, though. He was sharper than before, balanced
more on a knife edge. Now I had the odd feeling he had slipped

off that knife and was trying to climb back on, costs be damned. It was the strangest sensation...and I hated it.

"There's sandwiches and some beers in that cooler if you want some."

"They fed us on the plane. How's the monster business?"

"Solid," Earl said as the pickup truck fairly flew down the highway. "MHI is expanding. How was the Middle East?"

"Eventful." I wasn't deliberately being evasive toward my old comrade. These sorts of things just came naturally now. I coughed, embarrassed. I was back in the United States. I could afford to trust those around me a little more than I had while overseas. "Actually, I was doing pretty well, up until a few weeks ago."

"I heard."

"How? It didn't make the papers."

"You know how it is. Hunters talk."

"I don't trust newspapers anyway. Over there, it's nothing but propaganda and gossip rags."

Earl actually smiled at that. "It ain't much better here."

"At least you don't shoot your reporters when they report bad news. Yet."

"How'd you like working for the Kidon's Supernatural Monitoring Unit?" Earl asked as he changed lanes and blew past a small yellow Datsun. "Is Haim a good boss?"

I glanced over at him, scowling. He was just showing off how well-informed MHI was. My association with a secret government assassination team should have been a better kept secret, yet Earl just dropped it into our conversation as casually as someone taking out the garbage...or the Kidon would a terrorist. It was irritating, but a good reminder that I was amongst equals now and couldn't underestimate any of them.

"That's classified." I'd like to figure out who was leaking and plug it. Preferably with a large-caliber bullet. Haim could thank me later.

Earl grunted before lighting his cigarette. I waved the smoke away from my face. Frowning, he rolled down his window and blew the smoke out. "Forgot you don't like smoke."

Everybody smokes. I was used to it, but I didn't like it. Smoke was one of the sacred symbols of my father, and the haze reminded me too much of what happened to my mind when I let the *nagualii* take over. "It's fine." Then I changed the subject. "Ray said John died. John Libal, remember him? The chemist."

"Went on to be a team leader. A science project gone bad got him. White Sands. 1961."

"He was a good man. What about the really tall guy, Oscar Kolbinger? Hell of a shooter."

"Wights," Earl answered. "A pack of them up in Boston. Way back in '57. Tore him to shreds, but he took them with him when he blew the building."

"Oh. Tobias Redfeather?"

"Zombies."

"Zombies? Really?" I was incredulous. "Redfeather, that tough bastard, got killed by *zombies*? He must have died embarrassed."

"These weren't the slow ones we used to see," Earl explained in defense of our dead teammate's honor. "Haitian voodoo priest created some faster ones somehow. A horde of them got Redfeather in New Orleans. His son worked for us for a couple years too, but he got drafted and killed in Vietnam."

"Eric Meske?"

"Actually Meske left MHI, invested all his bounty money, and started up one of those newfangled computer companies. MicroTel or some such thing. He got superrich, lived like a king, and died wrecking his Ferrari in a race."

"Oh," I said as that all sank in. Nobody from our old team was around anymore. That was the sad nature of being half immortal.

We didn't talk much for a while, but were making good time, had reached the middle of nowhere countryside, and would probably be in Cazador well before midnight. Except I suspected our arrival might be delayed.

MHI had become the gold standard when it came to monster hunting. The Shacklefords had always been careful, ever since Bubba Shackleford founded the company in 1895. One thing that had been beaten into my head during my own newbie training was that you always verified what you were dealing with. Assumptions led to dead Hunters. I knew what was coming next, but just because I understood the why wouldn't make it any less annoying.

MHI was still the best, and I was currently an enigma to them, and thus a potential threat.

"So, going to test me now, or pull over to the side of the road and do it?" I asked.

Earl gave me a look that was a combination of annoyed and amused. Even though his name had changed over the years, he'd apparently kept the dark sense of humor.

"Pulling over would be safer, in case you get angry and try to eat my face. It's hard to fight and drive at the same time."

Coming from anyone else I'd be insulted. "Rude, but understandable."

Earl parked the truck on a deserted side road and killed the engine. I sighed into the silence. "Time to talk about the proverbial eight-hundred-pound gorilla in the room?"

"More like hundred-pound Aztec demigod in my truck."

It was nice of him to lowball a girl's weight like that. "Thank you."

Whether I liked it or not, Earl lit up another cigarette. Or maybe he did it specifically because he knew I didn't like it. "Your last employer, what with them being Jewish and all, you'd think that whole demigod thing wouldn't sit too well with them."

"It's complicated. Let's just say the Kidon's the sort of place that still works on the Sabbath. They filed me under the same category as lycanthropes."

"But you ain't."

"I'm kinda unique."

"You're an oddity, and oddities make folks nervous. Because of that rarity, nobody really knows exactly what a *nagualii* is capable of. You've got a good record with us, but it's been a long time since you've operated here in the US. People change. People who are only half human can *really* change. There're some nasty rumors about how your contract ended."

"I'm an open book." Well, at least as much as someone from a clandestine hit squad that sometimes employed inhuman creatures could be, but Earl knew how that world worked all too well. "Ask what you need to ask."

"The Boss and I talked it over. There's some worry you might not view humans as . . . well, *human*."

"I did spend years killing lots of them."

"Me too. Except yours spoke Arabic while mine spoke Communist. Only MHI aren't soldiers."

"MHI's glorified pest control."

"Exactly. Bloodthirsty supernatural pests, and that's a public service. Accent on public. Listen, Chloe, people like us, there's always a worry that those of us who've made the PUFF Exempt list before will start to slip and view humans, not as equals, but as prey, or less, like cattle."

"Or they're a flock of sheep and we're... wolves?" I asked pointedly. A cheap shot, true.

Earl just grunted and smoked, ignoring that. Werewolves had it a whole lot worse than I did. My blood was downright calm in comparison. Here I was, judging the guy for being grumpier than I remembered, but by werewolf standards he was the all-time champion of self-control.

"Is it me your son is concerned about going feral because of my experiences? Or somebody else at MHI?" That was really cruel, and I immediately regretted saying it. "I get it," I assured him. "I give you my word, I'm pretty fond of mankind in general. I don't think of myself as different most of the time. I can't change my heritage, or where I come from, but I can make the best of it. Your curse is different than mine. You've got to fight yours all the time, and every full moon, it takes over no matter what. I have to invite mine in, and believe me, I do *not want* to do that."

"How's that working out for you?"

"I killed some teammates by accident last time I let the *nagualii* free," I admitted in a quiet voice. I glanced over to see his reaction but Earl's eyes were on the darkened road, so I figured that was his cue for me to keep explaining. "An Akkadian sand demon ambushed us. We were losing badly. I was ordered to change, and only did it under protest. I beat the demon, but before I could get the *nagualii* chained back down, I'd attacked two of my friends. Good men died because of me."

"And they kicked you out because of it?"

"I was a liability. They didn't put a bullet in my brain, so that was nice of them."

"Why'd you go there to begin with? You aren't even Jewish."

"I converted."

"Huh..."

It had seemed like the right thing to do at the time. "In my defense, I don't claim to be good at it."

"Hell, you never struck me as particularly religious at all. Which is kind of funny, all things considered."

Sure, I wasn't exactly stringent about doing all the things I was supposed to, but that was more out of laziness, distractions, or thoughtlessness than some kind of coherent secular philosophy. I made commitments. I just wasn't good at sticking to all the hard ones.

This was harder to explain than I thought it would be. "Toward the end of the war, I helped liberate a death camp in Poland."

"I didn't know that." Earl had been over there too, drafted by the same organization, only I'd never run into him during the war. There had been several special task forces, each with its own clandestine missions, using supernatural beings as operatives, some of us more voluntary than others.

"Liberating a death camp's the kind of thing that sticks with you." Which was the biggest understatement of all time. "After my term was over and the special task force granted me my PUFF Exemption, I could've gone anywhere, only I felt like those survivors would need help getting started over, so I stuck around. I ended up escorting some to Jerusalem. And when word got out what I really was…I made myself useful. Never truly accepted—or trusted, it turns out—but useful."

Earl mulled that over for a time, his cigarette dangling precariously from his lip. "I respect that. The monster scholars at Oxford claim all *nagualii* crave war and conflict. Seems like you found a good place to find an endless supply of both."

"Academics are full of shit. The only thing I crave is a day at the beach." One cleared of luskas, though. Obviously. "I had a purpose, and I felt needed. I tried to belong to something bigger and more important than I am. Okay? Isn't that what you're checking up on, how well I fit in with humanity? Well, there you go."

Earl might not believe me, but unless things had changed a lot over the last thirty years, it wasn't like MHI ever had a shortage of conflict, so he knew I'd be useful here too. "You said you could go anywhere, so why here? Why ask for your old job back?"

Now this was the hard part. "You once told me a good Hunter trusts their gut? Their instincts?"

Earl didn't say anything. Sensing this was both acknowledgment and agreement, I continued, and there was no use trying to lie to someone like him.

"For months, I've had this feeling that I needed to be back on this continent. Dreams, premonitions, whatever. This general sense of worry and pressure has been growing. Just nagging at me. But I ignored it. I had a life, you know?"

"Being here puts you closer to your...family."

"I'm an orphan."

"Any chance these *feelings*"—Earl said that particular word with distaste—"are from your monster side?"

"Maybe. I don't know. All I do know is that I need to be here. If I'd listened and come back when I was supposed to, two of my friends would still be alive."

Earl tossed the butt of his cigarette out the window. "That's bullshit. They might have lived, or every single one of them would've died because you weren't there to fight a demon for them."

"You don't understand."

Which was when Earl gave me a very weary look that told me he understood *exactly* how I felt. "You being miserable about what might have been won't bring them back. People like us don't get that luxury. Move on and save the ones you can. You good with that?"

I looked him in the eye and said, "Yeah. I'm good with that."

I had a supernatural gift for reading others, but this man could stare right through you straight to your soul. He was a frightening judge, but after a minute he turned the key and started the truck. "You're a tough, scary dame, but I think you're alright."

"Dame?" I asked, arching an eyebrow. "Seriously? Do people still use that term?"

"You were still using 'bully' a lot in 1941, so you've got no room to talk."

What a way to come back home, I thought as the engine started up. Soon enough, I was watching the mile markers fly by once more.

By the time we reached the compound outside Cazador, I was in a bad mood. Neither one of us wanted to talk anymore. Things had changed enough between us that we weren't as comfortable around one another like when we had been working together back in the old days—and we hadn't been too comfortable then. I didn't think it was me, so I assumed something really bad had happened to Earl.

It was hard being a freak of nature in an orderly world, but there were ways you could exist legally. Americans and Israelis weren't the only governments using certain monsters to do their bidding. I'd heard rumors the Soviets and Chinese were doing it too. If you were supernatural and not a complete psychopath, it was a great time to get a real job and not have to live out your days hiding in a cave. Of course this only worked for those of us who could keep a lid on it. There were a lot of things out there that could never be tamed. But as I had recently demonstrated, employing monsters is like playing with fire, and sometimes people get burned.

As we pulled up to MHI's front gate, I noticed the changes immediately. There were a bunch of new buildings surrounded by a fence, the top of which was covered in razor wire to help discourage any entrepreneurial individual from trying to climb over it. There was also a warning sign on it. Looking closely, I saw the lightning bolts and blinked.

"Did someone try to attack the compound or something?"

"Or something." Earl stopped and got out to unlock the gate.

I rolled my window down and listened to the hum from the electrified fence.

"Not worried about frying the deer?"

"They learn," he said as he unlocked multiple padlocks with a ring of keys from his belt.

"Cruel."

"They don't like the sound more than the actual shock. We're probably gonna have to get rid of the electric fence, though. It's a pain in the ass to maintain. Biggest problem is the kudzu keeps growing onto it and shorting it out."

"Kudzu? Is that a kind of monster?"

"The worst." Only Earl didn't elaborate as he got back into the truck.

Gone was the rickety wood building where the main headquarters had been. Now it resembled a fortress, all concrete, with reinforced doors and narrow windows. There were prefab buildings around it. I began to wonder just where I was going to stay.

"Ray said he wanted to meet with you before you turn in." Earl pointed toward the largest concrete building. "Come on."

The lights were on but the main reception area was deserted. Reasonable, considering it was almost midnight during the work week.

Raymond Shackleford's office was on the second floor of the new building. Well, it clearly wasn't that new, but it was new to me. This had all been part of the old firing range when I was last here. A lot of newbies, including me, had spent a lot of hours on that range learning to shoot. Considering how much MHI trainees shot, this place's foundation had probably been built on brass.

I paused at the big door with the Boss's name stenciled on it.

"You nervous? Think about how *he* feels." Earl was clearly amused. "The last time he saw you he was a kid with really confused feelings about the pretty scary monster lady."

"It sounds creepy when you put it that way, Earl."

"Don't worry. My boy grew up, found himself a good woman, got married, and had lots of kids. He's been running this joint since my brother Mack passed away, and doing a better job than either of us ever did."

Earl opened the door for me and I'll admit I was surprised when I saw Ray for the first time in decades. I remembered him as a gangly kid, but standing before me was a tall, broad-shouldered man who was *really* good-looking in spite of his age. Grey at the temples with a lean face, and eyes almost as blue as Earl's. There were a few scars along the impressive jawline but otherwise he was one hell of a recruiting image for MHI. The Shacklefords had good genes, I guess.

"Chloe Mendoza." Ray shook his head in disbelief. "You look the same as the day you left."

I grinned. "You got taller."

"And greyer and fatter." He smacked his stomach, though there wasn't really any flab on it at all. "Have a seat." As soon as Earl and I were both on the plush, oversized red leather chairs, Ray asked, "So?"

"She's good," Earl answered. "She was getting frustrated, and I thought she was going to punch me a few times, but she's alright."

"We pulled over so . . . *Earl* here could try to provoke me into losing my cool and fly into a rage."

"Goes without saying," Earl replied casually as he shook out another cigarette. "But you think I'm gonna let somebody we ain't seen in forever stroll into our secured headquarters without at least a little questioning? Especially someone who is a PUFF-applicable creature? I had to make sure you were still you, Chloe."

I reached down the top of my dress and pulled out my PUFF Exempt coin, which I always kept attached via a silver chain around my neck. "I earned this. Same as you."

Earl snorted as he lit up. "You wouldn't have ever gotten a chance to earn that coin if I'd put you in the ground like I was supposed to. The *Federales* asked us to shoot on sight. You're lucky I decided to talk first."

"You're lucky I was feeling talkative back."

"Enough, you two," Raymond said in a manner that suggested he was used to being listened to around here.

To be fair, Earl and his team could've killed me. The reports had called me a menace, and MHI had rolled into the dusty little Mexican town expecting a vicious Aztec monster. They'd ended up with a new recruit instead, which had been lucky for me. I'd done some hand-to-hand combat training against Earl afterward. I'm tough, but I'm certainly not werewolf tough.

Ray sat on the edge of his desk. "I'm sorry, Chloe, but we had to make certain we weren't inviting in something that was just wearing an old friend's face. We're more paranoid than we used to be. We have to be. MHI is on a lot of radars these days."

I stuffed my PUFF Exempt coin back down my top and scowled. I hated anyone questioning my worthiness . . . probably since I'd been doing that a lot to myself over the last few weeks anyway.

"It's getting tougher to keep what we do secret, and because of that the government's constantly breathing down our neck. I need people who are dependable, solid characters. We're not the freewheeling gunslingers we used to be when you were here before. The times are changing. The sixties were a time of turmoil for this business, and since we hit the seventies information keeps moving faster and faster. Monster hunting isn't as simple as it used to be. It's just as dangerous as it's ever been, only harder to keep things off the news."

"Believe me," I grumbled, "I understand keeping things clandestine."

"Indeed. Which is one reason your call intrigued me. The company is currently expanding. I've got lots of men who can kill monsters like you can't believe. I've got a handful who can do it without drawing the eye of the media and the wrath of the Monster Control Bureau."

Of all the skills I'd picked up working for a secret assassination squad, I hadn't realized public relations would be the biggest draw on my résumé. That was not what I'd signed up for. I didn't want to do that job. The pragmatic part of my mind was counting my money. If I was frugal, I could probably stay unemployed for the next twenty years before I'd need to work again. Raymond almost certainly didn't know my financial situation. Normally someone my age would have a pretty absurd retirement fund, but I wasn't the best investor.

I did have that one security deposit box in Zurich I could always sell the contents of, though the reappearance of a Fabergé egg that had been missing since the war would draw some unwanted attention, especially since it was one of the magically cursed ones. Though I would have to take off the demon-summoning runes with an angle grinder first, it'd still fetch a nice bit of spare change.

"When Earl was poking around to see if I hated mankind now, and I said no, I didn't mean that I wanted to go out of my way to talk to more of them."

"We've got lots of shooters." Ray picked up an ashtray off his desk and tossed it to Earl before he left ash on the nice chairs. "I've got an abundance of recent hires with solid combat experience. Monster activity is up, which means there's no shortage of survivors and witnesses in the know to recruit from. What I need is older, wiser heads until we get more men up to speed."

"I am *not* leadership material."

"I wasn't thinking team lead, but second. Think NCO. People who can soothe hotheaded authorities while dealing with testosterone-laden Hunters fresh off a kill. People who can talk their way out of an argument with the likes of the MCB without infuriating them, and are easy on the eyes."

"Someone who can pretend to be a harmless stewardess for days of a tense standoff until she can get all the hostages out of the way before snapping three hijackers' necks," Earl stated flatly.

I was aghast. *How did he know about that operation?*

Ray spoke up, "By the way, Haim assures me that what happened a few weeks ago wasn't your fault, you had an exemplary record before that, your removal was political rather than tactical, and I'd be an idiot not to hire you back. He sends his love, wishes you well, and this conversation never happened."

My old commander reaching out like that made me a little teary eyed, because that's the sort of conversation that could get a Kidon member executed. "What never happened?"

"Exactly. On that note, I'll cut right to the chase. I'm not making this job offer because of your bloodline, but rather your experience. What you are stays as secret as you want it to from your fellow Hunters. I'd prefer for you *not* to use it, for the safety of my people, and the peace of your mind."

Ray had never seen the *nagualii* in action, but Earl had, and more than likely told him all about it. "I can agree to that." I looked over at Earl to see if he was going to add anything about what I'd told him, about how I'd felt prompted that I needed to return to this continent, but he said nothing. "The less I have to acknowledge my background, the better."

"Well, that settles the matter, then. I spent my day arguing with moronic congressmen on the phone and I'm tired and want to go home. I'm satisfied for now." Ray looked over at Earl, as if there was an unspoken question between them.

"We've got the latest crop mostly through," Earl confirmed. "Instructor?"

"Not teaching newbies..." I muttered.

"Only while you get acclimatized," Ray assured me in a manner that suggested there'd be no arguing over it. "Sounds good. We'll figure out your team assignment after this class is through."

"Please tell me your guest rooms are better than before." I stifled a yawn. "I'd prefer a bed over a blanket on the floor." I jerked my thumb at Earl. "Unlike him."

The Boss laughed at this. Things might not be back to the way they'd been long before, but at least the uneasy tension was diminished slightly. "Out the door, take a right. Fourth door down on the left. There isn't a number on it or anything. If there's filing cabinets in there, you've gone too far. We'll put you in a teaching role while we get you up to speed, then decide where to send you. Any preferences?"

"Texas?"

Raymond nodded. Clearly he'd expected as much, as that had been my adopted home state. "Anywhere else?"

"Not New Orleans?" I answered after giving it some thought. Something about the place had given me the creeps back in the day.

"Welcome back, Chloe."

CHAPTER 3

I spent the next couple of weeks teaching. It turned out the biggest challenge to instructing a bunch of monster-attack survivors in monster lore so they could become professional monster killers was convincing them that they actually needed to listen to the wisdom of someone who looked like a petite Mexican girl younger than they were.

"You don't seem like most of the teachers here, you dig?" one of the recruits attending my class pointed out as we were going over various demons and their archetypes. "But you talk like you've seen all this scary shit personally."

They'd already been here for a couple of months. Every other instructor was a tough guy with obvious experience and the resulting swagger. Earl had introduced me to the recruits as an expert in monster lore who had recently been a consultant for the IDF. Appearances can be deceiving, but I didn't look like much of a fighter, and I looked too young to be a convincing academic.

My pride told me it was time to establish dominance.

"I've seen a fair bit. What's your name?"

"Wall. Kimpton Wall, ma'am."

He was a good-looking guy, young, fit, and would probably have a very western All-American athlete feel to him if he was cleaned up, only his hair was too long and shaggy, he was too young to grow out anything but a scraggly, unrespectable beard, and was wearing a beat-up military field jacket.

"What sort of monster got you recruited, Wall?" I asked, figuring I could lord it over him because I'd probably fought one of those already myself. Odds were good, mostly because I'd been around for so long, and done this on multiple continents.

"*Yakseya*," he replied after a moment's hesitation. "I killed one while in Cambodia."

"By yourself?" I asked incredulously.

"It had already killed everybody else in my squad, so yeah."

So much for establishing dominance because that was actually rather impressive. "Okay, wow," I muttered approvingly. "And you walked away with all your limbs. Nicely done."

"What's a *yakseya*?" the blond girl in the back asked, curious. "It sounds Italian."

"Sri Lankan demon." There were only a couple of female recruits out of the entire class. Melanie Simmons was the nice, yet pretty one, who struck me as kind of ditzy. I knew she'd survived a blood-fiend attack, but I had no idea how, unless it had eaten her sorority sisters and then been so full that she'd been able to run away.

"*Yakseya* are nasty, mean things. Their true origin's unknown, but probably extradimensional originally, though they've established a few breeding populations across Asia. Because the *yakseya* are Earth-born and apparently not summoned or unholy, blessed water doesn't usually work with them. They walk most normal injuries off. Or if you know a good pujari—a Hindu temple priest, that is—they're very effective at destroying a *yakseya* for some reason. So the *yakseya* hate them and will go out of their way to kill a pujari. The one you fought in Cambodia, was it near a temple?"

"The ruins of one. Came out of nowhere, took out my entire patrol. Napalm doesn't do much to them either," Wall added, his tone quiet.

"No, they're pretty fireproof. How'd you kill it?" I asked, genuinely curious. The Kidon had fought one once that had stowed away aboard a cargo ship anchored off the coast near Haifa. It had been fast, deadly, and extremely pissed off at us. I'd like to say that we kicked its butt, but to be honest the battle pretty much ended indecisively. We'd lost a man, only blew one of its hands off, and ended up having to retreat and sink the ship to drown it. So I'd call it a draw.

"I set a trap with dynamite. A lot of dynamite. Used myself as bait. Then I took his head with a Ka-Bar after I blew his legs off."

"Smart. An M67 fragmentation grenade will only annoy a *yakseya*. When in doubt, use more boom," I added for the benefit of the class. "Good job, Wall."

"Thank you, ma'am."

So much for putting a cocky trainee in his place... but I had to remind myself a good teacher doesn't teach to stroke their own ego, they do it to help others reach their potential. And Earl had seen potential in all of these, or they wouldn't be here.

I'd slid into the role as an instructor easily and found I kind of liked it. I had more knowledge about the subject than most Hunters. My upbringing hadn't exactly been a normal one, then I'd worked for MHI—mostly in North America, but we got around—and then in the Middle East. The IDF had run into some really weird stuff over the years I had been there and the Kidon were the ones best equipped to deal with it. In the oldest region of civilization in the world, all sorts of creatures dwell in the shadows.

Plus, I liked to share that knowledge. Being an instructor suited my personality, and in this sort of environment I could actually talk about some of the crazy things I'd done over the years... and if I was careful, do it without revealing too much about myself. I'd even managed to condense down what I thought were the most pertinent Monster Hunter tips into a list, and I wrote a couple more of them on the board every day. Kind of like those motivational posters people put up in normal office spaces. I needed to compile those, because maybe Chloe's Monster Hunting Tips might be useful to somebody someday.

These particular newbies were smart and had very flexible minds, which was the one trait the Shacklefords had harped on forever. It's hard to fight some sort of abomination when you freeze up at the horrific monster eating some innocent person in the middle of the street. Hunters had to just kind of roll with things, and not get trapped by their preconceived notions.

On a personal level, I was rather thankful for that philosophy, because it was how I'd ended up working for the Shacklefords instead of getting murdered by them. A lot of other hunting companies would have just seen me as a really nice paycheck. MHI recognized that not everything that had a bounty on its head deserved it.

"Ms. Mendoza." Another trainee politely raised his hand,

like this was an actual respectable school setting, and not the
Shackleford Home for Wayward Homicidal Maniacs.

"Just call me Chloe, Alex."

"Cool." Alex Wigan was a blond, blue-eyed, super-fit kid who
looked like he could have been in a recruiting poster for the
Germans during World War II, so it amused me when I found
out he was Jewish too. He was one of the youngest newbies but
struck me as one of the sharpest. "On the *yakseya*, silver bullets? Yes or no?"

"Uh . . ." That was a good question. "Silver is often poisonous
to creatures like that, but I honestly don't know."

"All I know is that he laughed at the bullets from my M-16,"
Kimpton said.

Alex had been one of the only students to actually take notes
the whole time, and now he was checking them. "You said that
silver tends to work better on things originating from other
worlds and shapeshifters."

"*Most* shapeshifters," I corrected. Just touching silver would
harm Earl. It didn't do anything to me. I hadn't confided in anyone else at the compound about my heritage just yet. Part of my
wishful, hopeful side liked to imagine that these kids would be
okay with it, but if word got out that MHI hired monsters—PUFF
exempt or not—all sorts of business contracts could potentially
dry up. Good or evil, we oddities get lumped together in the
minds of the customer. "Shapeshifters are a *really* big tent with
a lot of possible origins and types."

Alex noted that down too, only he didn't seem happy about
it. I suspected he was the sort who liked to have everything
neatly categorized.

MHI training was grueling. They spent their days running,
working out, training in hand-to-hand combat or with edged weapons, shooting *a lot*, and their only quiet time was in classrooms
like this getting blasted in the face with a firehose of information.
At the end of the day, most of them just went to bed early or sat
on the couch watching something brainless on the newbie dorm's
television set, mentally and physically exhausted. Only not Alex
Wigan. When the training day was over, he was hitting MHI's
archive to find another book or diary to read about monsters.

Glancing at the clock on the wall, both hands were almost
at twelve. It was time to break for lunch. After, we'd all hit the

range. The boys were quietly taking bets on whether or not Melanie would have another "hot brass in bra" incident like the other day. "Well, that's about all the time we have to talk about the endless hordes of hell today, kids."

A few days later was the company "beauty pageant," as some of the other experienced Hunters liked to call it. The Shacklefords just called it graduation day. It was an exciting time, with team leaders from all over the country coming in to take a look at the remaining recruits to fight over who got which one.

This graduating class was actually larger than normal, which was nice since the company was expanding. MHI's hiring standards were strict and the washout rate was high, yet this group was beyond normal in their capabilities. Even Earl had to admit that this was one of the better classes they'd ever had. Most had made the cut. He'd only had to dismiss a few as unacceptable. Those received nice severance checks and were sent on their merry way with a warning about not speaking to anybody about this world, because that tended to draw visitors from federal agencies who really enjoyed permanently silencing witnesses.

As the team leaders arrived, I realized that I didn't know a single one of them. I really had been gone a long time. So I kept to myself and observed, knowing that one of these would probably be my new boss.

After Raymond Shackleford gave a motivational speech—professionally speaking, it was rather stirring—it was interview time, and the recruits were shuffled off to talk to the various leads to see where they were going to end up stationed around the country. Sometimes it would be based on regional knowledge because locals were always valuable, and other times it would be decided based on a team needing a particular skill set.

During that, I got summoned to the Boss's office. Raymond looked pleased with himself and Earl was chain-smoking cigarettes, which usually meant he was seriously irritated about something.

"So you've decided what to do with me."

"There's a couple things came to mind," Ray answered.

So I'd finally get my assignment. I'd talked with some of the Miami crew the night before, and they needed people. While I wasn't sure about joining a team whose primary job was hunting luskas, the idea of lying around on a beach, sipping drinks was appealing. Sandy beaches and mai tais versus luskas? It was too close to call. Plus, the eye candy in Miami was to die for. Literally. Luskas, though. Gross.

Just as long as it wasn't somewhere cold. I *hate* the cold. Blame it on my roots, but I don't handle snow.

The odd thing was, I'd be okay staying in Cazador. I had enjoyed training the new recruits a lot more than I thought I would have. I never really thought about how much knowledge of monsters I had to pass on until I tried it. With what MHI already knew coupled with what I'd picked up around the world, these new hunters would be going out to their teams better prepared than ever. It made me smile, knowing the knowledge I'd passed along might one day save their lives. Plus, unlike a lot of Hunters, I wasn't addicted to the action. I'd be content here, taking a peaceful break. And it wasn't like I couldn't afford the pay cut of not constantly collecting on bounties.

"I could stay here."

"You could stick around, be on call in case my team needed you in an emergency. You've got the patience and personality for teaching the youngsters."

"*But...*" Earl said.

Ray sighed. "But headquarters staff makes up Team Cazador, which means being ready to roll and support another team anywhere in the country in twenty-four hours. That's Earl's team."

"It ain't personal," Earl assured me.

"What for—oh..." I quickly figured it out. A werewolf and a *nagualii* on one team? That would certainly attract the government's attention. We were allowed to exist. It didn't mean they liked us hanging out together. The attention would be more hassle than it was worth. I coughed and shook my head. "Never mind, then."

"I've got something better for you anyway," Raymond stated.

"Someplace warm?"

"Yep."

"You know me so well."

"I figured if I sent you to Minneapolis my life might be in danger." Ray went over to where there was a map of the US on his office wall. There were pins in it showing where each of the regional teams were based. He pointed at the west coast, which was suspiciously bare, with a lone pin in Seattle.

"MHI hasn't had much luck in California."

I'd never been there. "They make it sound nice in the movies."

"It's a big state, with a large and growing population, lots of money and excitement, deep history, much of it bad, with a few giant cities and a whole lot of countryside between them for all sorts of nasties to hide in, not to mention a huge number of immigrants, transients, and bums to feed on, all of which means lots of monster activity...activity which we should rightfully be the ones handling and getting paid for."

"So why haven't you?"

"We're the best, but we ain't the only company who does this. MHI started in the South and expanded outward, but we got outcompeted west of the Rockies. The California market has been cornered by Golden State Supernatural for a long time."

"Who?"

"Buncha assholes," Earl grumbled. "Governor Reagan was friends with the owner so they got all the municipal contracts."

"Sometimes connections win over skill. Sad fact of business," Ray agreed. "Only recent events have opened up an opportunity for us to station a team there again."

"Reagan quitting to run for president?" I'd been reading the newspapers.

"More like Golden State Supernatural bit off more than they could chew awakening an eldritch being among the redwoods, a bunch of their employees got massacred, and the company filed for bankruptcy."

Now *that* hadn't been in the papers.

"I don't want to be a team lead," I stated. Being a team leader was like herding cats, and I was way more catlike than most Hunters.

Earl snorted. "You won't be. We're promoting one of the shooters from New Orleans."

"I need you to back him up. This will be his first time in charge of a team. He's killed about one of everything, but he's not the most...cultured individual."

"Marco is a goon," Earl said. "But he's got potential to be a good leader if cooler heads can coach it out of him. You know more about monsters than he does, you're easy on the eyes, and you're far more diplomatic than he'll ever be."

"Flattering."

"Just calling them as I see them. You'll need to establish a base somewhere in LA, but be aware, the Monster Control Bureau is getting crueler about keeping witnesses silenced there. They've got a regional director who thinks a permanent silence is the best one. You'll deal with the Feds so your team lead doesn't get MHI in more trouble."

Lovely. Joining an existing, functioning unit was one thing. Starting a team from scratch was a whole different challenge. "Where are you drawing the team members from?" I asked, though I had a sinking feeling I already knew. It wasn't as though we had a ton of experienced Hunters with nothing better to do at the moment, and there was this perfectly good newbie class just sitting here...

"I've got you one Hunter from St. Louis, ten years on the job, precision rifle specialist, and one from Chicago, with two years in. Tough kid, came up on the other side of the law and all the skill sets that entails." Then Earl trailed off as he looked toward his son to break the bad news I already knew.

Raymond offered me a smile. It reminded me of a used car salesman sinking his clutches into an unwary buyer. "Pick three from your class today to take with you to get started. We'll send you more as we have them."

"Oh, come on," I protested. "Three newbies on a brand-new team is setting us up for failure."

"All your excess experience will average it out," Earl assured me.

"I can't afford to pull anyone else right now," Raymond countered before relenting somewhat. "I'll give you first pick, though."

"How long do I have to decide?" I asked.

"The duration of this meeting, and I've only got a couple smokes left in this pack," Earl said. "Everybody else is waiting."

"That's hardly any time at all." Whining was embarrassing, so I gathered my dignity and bit the bullet. "I can do it, but shouldn't I discuss this with my new team leader first? Or, you know, actually meet him?"

"Team building isn't his thing. You know them better than he does."

"Fine. If I get first pick, Benjamin Cody." That one was the obvious standout in the class. A decorated war hero, six and a half feet of solid muscle, had a brain like a steel trap, and was one of those men whom leadership just came to naturally. Provided Cody survived long enough, he had future monster hunting legend written all over him.

"First pick, *after* Ben. I should have clarified," Ray said apologetically. "He's already promised to New Mexico for the mad science boys. There's educational requirements for the government contract there. Did you know he was almost finished with a degree in physics or some such thing before dropping out to enlist?"

"Nice bait and switch, Ray. Alright, then I want Kimpton Wall on my team."

"Why?" Ray asked, curious. "He's got a chip on his shoulder and issues with authority. Just so you know, he complained to me about how there was no way some, I quote, *little girl* had fought so many monsters."

"Bingo. He was the first one to be openly suspicious of me and wasn't afraid to call bullshit when he suspected I might be exaggerating my knowledge or lying about my background. I'll take the honesty."

Ray nodded. "The boy is currently rather disillusioned, but personally I see having issues with authority a trait that all patriotic Americans should share. Done. You've got Wall."

"Then Alex Wigan."

"Clever lad. Did a brief stint in the Navy. Ran into a dip on shore leave in Rota, then almost got himself murdered by the MCB because he was too excited to shut up about finding out monsters were real. If we hadn't found him and made him a job offer he'd probably be at the bottom of the ocean with cinder blocks tied to his ankles."

That wasn't hard to imagine at all. Whoever the Monster Control Bureau couldn't intimidate into silence, they'd ruin the credibility of, and when that didn't work, they went for more permanent measures. The US government did not mess around when it came to keeping the existence of monsters secret.

"Alex is a nerd, but he's genuinely passionate about the subject. Guys like that never stop thinking. Their brains are constantly churning. I like having someone I can turn loose to let them find solutions."

"Alright, you can have Wigan."

Earl chuckled. "He'll be happy to go to California. He told me he likes to ride one of them *surfboard* things."

"For the third, give me Carlos Alhambra."

Ray shook his head in the negative. "You can have Simmons."

"Melanie? The bubbleheaded cheerleader? What did I ever do

to you, Ray? You're sending us to California, which has a big Spanish-speaking population, and Carlos is fluent in Spanish."

"So are you. Carlos is from Massachusetts, while Melanie's the only recruit we have this time from California. She knows more about the place than the rest of you put together, and most importantly, her uncle is the Orange County sheriff. We get their contract to handle supernatural events and that gives us a head start on negotiating all the lucrative municipal contracts that Golden State will be defaulting on."

There was a lot of money to be made off of local contracts. They pay to keep you on retainer, then when they have an issue, you handle their monster problems quietly, and get paid again by the Feds for the PUFF bounty on whatever it was you had to kill. If it wasn't for the constant potential for violent death, it would be a great business model. Ray certainly had me there.

"Come on, Chloe," Earl said. "I thought you ladies would be in favor of sticking together—female empowerment and all that feminist equality stuff they're always going on about now."

"I can lift one end of a Volkswagen off the ground, so I don't get too worried about being anybody's equal. This isn't a girl-power thing."

"Good," Earl said. "Because your rifleman is actually a riflewoman."

"As long as she hits what she aims at, I don't care. On the other hand, Melanie seems sweet. She's genuinely nice, but..."

"She's a bleeding-heart do-gooder," Ray agreed. "But don't underestimate her. She's smarter than she looks and has got potential."

"We done, then?" Earl asked.

"I guess." Which was when I realized that they'd plowed ahead so fast I'd never even agreed to go to California. Yet another demonstration that the Shacklefords had always been masters of negotiating deals.

"Talk to Russ at the armory to gear up," Ray told me. "We'll wire money to buy the rest of the supplies you need once you find a base of operations. We've got a few suggestions from local contacts, but you'll need to scope them out and pick the best one. Then start making friends."

"Build contacts, establish contracts, let the local MCB office know we're there." I sighed. It sounded like I was pretty much the team lead in all but name and paycheck.

"Be careful of the competition out there. With the big dog in the area dying, upstart companies might try to come in and poach contracts and bounties. If any of GSS's decent employees lived and want a job, send them our way, but odds are they'll form new start-ups. Home base, the Los Angeles area, is big and chaotic, but you'll also have the entirety of California and western Arizona. Probably as far as Tijuana, maybe even some contracts farther south in Mexico. Las Vegas will also be on your list, since it's only a few hours to drive there, and that's probably the next place we'll stand up a team. But in the meantime, you okay with Mexico?"

Great, I thought. *My old stomping grounds.* "I'll make it work."

"Oh, by the way," Earl was grinning now. "Your team lead?"

"Yeah?"

"You'll like him. Probably. His name is Marco Moss. Goes by Rhino."

"Why?"

"You'll see."

Marco was a giant of a man, taller and wider than anyone I'd ever met. If I didn't know any better I would have suggested he was at least half ogre, but Earl assured me we were the only two PUFF Exemptions in the company.

Marco's hands were large enough to completely envelop my head. I know this because later on he tried one night while drinking. Well, he drank, I drove. He also had the sunny disposition of a rhinoceros with a tooth infection. Hence, "Rhino." I called him Marco when I was speaking to him. Pretty sure he appreciated it more than the nickname.

I mean, he didn't come out and say it, but it was there. Beneath the glower and the frown. Oh, and the scars. God, the scars. I don't think there was an inch of exposed skin on his arms or face that wasn't scarred up somehow. He'd seen and killed it all, and most had taken a good chunk of flesh in return.

Within a few hours of meeting him, I could tell exactly why Ray had assigned me to be Marco's second-in-command.

For starters, Marco seemed to think there was no reason to elaborate when a simple "yes" or "no" would do. The man simply didn't volunteer explanations at all. He'd give orders but getting him to explain the why behind them was worse than pulling teeth. I hoped he'd get a little better as time wore on, because it was a long drive from Alabama to California.

Asking around to the other experienced Hunters, it turned out Marco was very accomplished indeed. If a human being could theoretically pick up a gun, then Marco could shoot it well. Rifles, shotguns, machine guns? Obviously. Grenade launcher? Yes, please. Somebody claimed to have watched him fire two separate shotguns simultaneously and nail both ghouls he was aiming at. He was almost inhuman with firearms. Give him a knife and he'd probably end up cutting his own pinky finger off. He could manage the stake part of vampire killing well enough, but he was lacking in the chop department.

Those same Hunters who praised the man as a badass tended to give me a surprised look when I asked them about Marco getting promoted to a leadership role, and ask, "Marco Moss? Are you sure?" Which I didn't take as a good sign.

Ray had flown all the members of our newly formed California team in so that we could get to know each other and start planning. He had set up the big meeting room at headquarters with various maps of the state, including the San Francisco, San Bernadino, San Diego, Oakland, and Los Angeles areas. Seeing it all laid out like that really put into perspective that we were just a temporary bandage to be slapped onto a logistical nightmare. At the same time it was beautiful, unorganized chaos, and actually made me a little excited at the prospect of being on a true MHI team for the first time in a very long time.

It was a huge area to cover, but the thing people need to keep in mind about monster activity is that it ebbs and flows. Sometimes an area will get crazy, and business will be booming. Others, it will be quiet, and a team will spend a lot of time twiddling their thumbs. With monsters being a government mandated under penalty of death level secret, a lot of times there could be activity right under your nose and you wouldn't even know about it. A huge part of our job would be building the network necessary to know what was really going on, so when we got word something supernatural had sprung up, we could move on it fast.

It would be an interesting team dynamic, that was certain. Four men and three women—one of whom was a PUFF-exempt creature from mythology. Thankfully, neither Ray nor Earl brought up the *nagualii* in the room.

Ray provided the introductions. He talked up Marco, which was easy, because he was intimidating as hell. He introduced me as someone who'd consulted to the IDF on monsters before coming aboard, but left the rest of my history vague, and made it sound like this was the first time I'd worked here. Thanks for that. He also made it abundantly clear that I was his pick to be second-in-command, and that if anybody had an issue with that, too damned bad. Nobody said a word.

Up next was Justin Moody, our Chicago transplant. A former Marine who had done two tours in Vietnam, until he'd encountered a hob in the jungle. The encounter had landed him in the hospital with a wicked chest wound, and a deep hatred for all forest folk. MHI had recruited him a few years ago. Ray left it at that for the official introductions, but since I was responsible for making this team work, I'd done some asking around.

Justin had grown up a poor Black kid in the roughest neighborhood in Chicago. His home life had been awful. Even his old teammates couldn't tell me a thing about his family because Justin *never* talked about them. What they did know about his upbringing suggested the same tragic story I was hearing about a lot of American cities now: poverty, drugs, gangs, and plenty of senseless violence.

He hadn't joined the Marines willingly. A judge had given him the ultimatum: enlist or do time. Only Justin had taken to it, loved it, and probably would have made a career out of it if he'd not gotten himself nearly clawed to pieces.

The last experienced Hunter that Ray was giving us was Lizz Yarborough. She was shorter than I am, which is impressive, since I'm not big. Lizz was downright petite, but she had a chip on her shoulder that more than made up for lack of height. She'd gotten mauled by a mutant catfish down in Florida and had nearly lost her leg, which was her introduction to this world. Despite the gruesome injury and pretty interesting scar—I quote, "Damn thing was shaking me like a rag doll, so I popped it in the head five or six times with my pistol, then stuck my hand in its gills and strangled it"—she had been recruited afterward and been on our St. Louis team for nearly a decade, making her the longtimer after Marco. Well, and way after me, but I was a super longtimer, and that was none of their business.

Lizz warned us she wasn't fast because of the old leg injury, she was too small to wrestle anything, don't expect her to lift anything heavy, oh, and she was an absolutely terrible driver who should never get behind the wheel, however . . . she was a *really good shot.* And when she had claimed that, Earl, Ray, and Marco had all nodded in agreement, having seen her in action.

Ray testified, "Lizz once plugged a running werewolf in the dead of night with a Winchester Model 70 from the observatory of the Gateway Arch at just shy of seven hundred yards, killing it instantly with a silver bullet through the cranium."

"Ayup. Not my longest shot in the field, but that is the company distance record on a lycanthrope," she bragged.

Lizz would do just fine on our team.

Mostly I stayed quiet during the *get to know you* portion, and evasive whenever anybody got curious about my background. The newbies—Kimpton, Alex, and Melanie—knew me from training. The experienced ones would accept me off of Earl vouching for me. I was riding his reputation. That wouldn't last; before long I'd have to prove myself competent. Once everyone seemed to be warming up to their new teammates—except for Marco, because nobody had ever accused him of being warm—the Boss cleared his throat.

"None of you have ever been a part of a new team starting up, so listen closely." Raymond Shackleford the Third had been around the block a few times and knew the score. He was an expert at quieting Hunters down with nothing more than a glance with those ice-blue eyes. "You'll be starting almost from scratch. We have some contacts in the northern parts of the state thanks to our team out of Seattle catching the occasional case there. However, southern and central, you'll have to start slowly and build as you go. Local sheriffs may or may not be read in on the supernatural. That'll all depend on who the Monster Control Bureau has needed to brief. Tread carefully there. You make contact with somebody not read in, they'll think you're nuts, and when word gets back to the MCB they'll be furious. MCB regional headquarters are in Sacramento. I want you to avoid that office. They'll still be sore they ain't collecting kickbacks from the now-defunct Golden State Supernatural and will probably try to squeeze money out of us instead."

Earl pointed toward the map of the biggest urban area. "Your home base will be in the LA basin, because it's got the highest levels of activity. Get established there first, then worry about the rest."

"There's an MCB office there as well," Ray warned. "They're very good at manipulating the local media and keeping things quiet. I'd rather you build a relationship with them than the ass-kissing parasites in Sacramento. Active cases take priority over networking. I'm fond of long-term profitability, but I really hate innocent people getting preyed on. Once you're settled, start making friends. We've got a list of counties, cities, and big companies that Golden State had contracts with to handle their monster problems. I'll give that list to Chloe to prioritize and figure out the best way to approach them."

Great. Now I was doing door-to-door sales too.

"The sooner you accomplish these things, the sooner you will be making large sums of money. Listen to your team lead. Marco has the experience to get you through. If things get to the point where you are unable to handle them, he'll call me. Marco knows his stuff. Listen to him and you'll survive long enough to spend all that hard-earned money. We'll take the next couple of days to plan and iron out details, then some of you will fly out there to arrange accommodations, while the rest of you drive your equipment across the country. I expect Team Rhino to be fully up and running within a month." And the way Ray said that left no doubt that we had better not let him down.

Even Marco picked up on that tone. In an organization full of tough, accomplished, professional monster killers, there were some men we all still looked up to. Nobody wanted to disappoint this man. "We won't let you down, Mr. Shackleford."

"Got it, boss," I agreed.

The rest of the team said so too.

Earl looked around at all of us and seemed to approve. "Good hunting."

CHAPTER 4

Three weeks later, we'd acquired a base of operations where our team could be kept away from prying eyes. Following Raymond's advice, we'd picked a facility in Pasadena for a good price. The Gasparyans were an Armenian family who ran the business in the front of our building. They were "read in" about the supernatural, as they say. I'm not certain what their monster encounter had been, only that they were of great assistance to the US government and were granted asylum here soon after. They ran a little restaurant that served the best Mediterranean food I'd ever had outside of Lebanon. Their spit-roasted chicken was great, but their falafel and tahini were to die for. Rafi Gasparyan could do things with food that no mortal man had ever accomplished before—and do it without costing a fortune, thanks to his wife, who actually ran the business. With four kids, and a fifth on the way, they were living the American Dream. The Gasparyans were good people.

Behind their restaurant was a warehouse that was perfectly suited for us. Relatively private and out of sight, it had a large area on the first floor for a machine shop, which Rhino seemed happy about because he loved tinkering on our guns and cars. The one downside was the walls weren't soundproof enough for an indoor range. However, the Mojave Desert wasn't too far away, so we weren't going to suffer for a place to practice. There was a second floor that served as our offices, and a space for a bunkroom for those times when someone had to sleep here on-call. There was a private driveway so we wouldn't bother the Gasparyans' customers, and plenty of parking for our personal vehicles.

It was the perfect setup. I was glad the Boss recommended this one in particular.

By this time Rhino and I had a good grasp of who could do what, and everyone had begun to settle nicely into their role. Melanie had already reached out to her uncle the sheriff and gotten a positive response, and he had passed our information along to a buddy of his at the Los Angeles County Sheriff's department, and another at the California Highway Patrol. Most big police agencies usually had someone with some monster experience, or who had been briefed on it by the MCB—along with all the corresponding warnings about keeping monsters secret or else. It was hit and miss, with the MCB being so haphazard about who they would let in on the secret. In general, assume a big agency will have one or two senior staffers in the know. Smaller departments, probably not.

Sheriff Robert Simmons turned out to be a gold mine when it came to contacts, because the man seemed to know just about *everyone* in law enforcement, and even had a cordial relationship with the local MCB office, which was rare.

As much as I was still hesitant about how Melanie would perform as an actual Hunter, her connections had already paid off big time. Golden State Supernatural—or GSS as they put on all their vaguely worded invoices so those bills could be explained to auditors as something benign—had done a decent job discreetly handling monster problems so the local police wouldn't have to, but their rapid collapse had left a lot of people hanging. Into this sudden vacuum steps MHI, a family-owned company with eighty years of experience handling cases around the world.

Luckily, contract negotiations were not my team's responsibilities. Marco was bad at talking to people. As for me, even though the country seemed to have lightened up since I'd left in 1941, most police chiefs and CEOs still wouldn't take a woman talking business seriously. We could occasionally make friends, but MHI's official negotiator was Leroy Shackleford. I didn't know him, but apparently he was a silver-tongued charmer, part heroic Monster Hunter, all salesman. He handled most things with a long-distance phone call from Alabama, but if there needed to be any in-person meetings, Leroy would come out here to wine and dine them. The idea of Marco trying to do that made me giggle.

A few of us rented apartments in the area, some cheaper than others. Not everyone, though. MHI's base pay was good, but it wasn't like my team was collecting our own bounties yet. That's when the real money would come rolling in.

In between moving in and training, I had my teammates go out in pairs, cruising the streets, purposefully getting lost in order to find their way back to the shop. It was a neat trick I'd picked up overseas. You figured out faster routes that way instead of relying solely on maps, and you learned about the shortcuts and unusual one-way streets that weren't always labeled on the maps. Pasadena was *rife* with one-way streets, so knowing where they were and which direction they went was a bonus. All this driving around town was a huge pain because of the gas shortage and waiting lines at the stations, but worth it because we needed to get to know the area fast.

One interesting thing I discovered about Melanie: the girl *never* got lost. It was eerie. Drop her anywhere in the city and she'd find her way around. She had an unerring sense of direction. Then while we were out practicing in the desert, I had to admit that she was actually a pretty good shot too, though she had a propensity for wearing tops that showed off her cleavage and suffered from "brass in brassiere" a few more times. Still, a decent shooter. Maybe I'd been wrong about the pretty bubblehead? Time would tell.

Despite not being in the valley proper, traffic here was still awful. The smog was horrible. Pollution from the Ports of Long Beach and Los Angeles made the air taste like oil. Fortunately, we arrived in the middle of March, so the temperature only managed to get up to about 70 degrees for the first few weeks. It was almost pleasant. Much nicer than Alabama. Unlike the South, California didn't make you feel as if you were walking and breathing soup when it got hot. Well, except for the smog. And the food was much better than anything within a hundred miles of Cazador, though everyone's fashion sense…ugh. Hideous.

The saving grace for the entire region was what the locals called the Santa Ana winds. Every so often these powerful winds would kick up and blow all the smog out into the Pacific Ocean, leaving the San Gabriel Valley with blue skies. This was pretty much the only time you could see both downtown Los Angeles and the San Gabriel Mountains at the same time. With the smog gone and the skies clear, the basin that held Los Angeles and the surrounding cities were quite beautiful. Picturesque, even. I bought a new Canon F-1 and snapped a lot of photos while wandering around lost. Some of which I had framed and put up in my apartment. It was expensive getting all that 35mm film developed, but I could afford it.

Getting lost on purpose was a good way to get to know your area of operation, and we started spreading out farther. One day I was out with Justin, and we had found ourselves driving around a rough neighborhood in south El Monte. The locals here were predominantly Mexican, which meant I fit in fine, but Justin was catching a lot of angry looks.

"There sure is a lot of racial tension in this city," I said.

"A brother driving around with a *chica* is asking for trouble."

"We're coworkers, not boyfriend and girlfriend."

"Explain that to the *cholos* over there," Justin said as he came up to a stop sign and a group of young men on the corner started doing the aggressive head bob and arm spread his way. It was the middle of the afternoon, so I doubted anybody would randomly shoot at us, but then again, half this city had been rioting and on fire not too long ago. The *cholos* looked ridiculous, wearing hairnets and long-sleeve collared shirts buttoned only at the neck, and khaki pants. As bad as some modern American fashion was, these guys were definitely worse.

"Bad neighborhoods are the same everywhere: Stick with your team, hate everybody else." Where I had been living those kids would be Palestinians, Kurds, or Druze. Minus the hairnets.

"I know. The music and accent are different here, but same story where I came up. I know how people be." Justin kept both hands on the wheel and very specifically kept his eyes forward as he muttered, "Which is why if they wanna start some shit I've got an AK-47 in the back seat."

"We're just here for the monsters, Justin."

Ignoring the hairnet hoodlums, he turned the car right. "You say that, but next time we do this, you can see what it's like and we'll cruise through scenic Watts instead. You dig?"

"I hear it's nice in the spring." We made it only a hundred feet before I saw something that shook me to my core. "Stop the car. Stop!"

Justin hit the brakes. I jumped out with my camera in hand, not believing what I was seeing.

The entire side of a Mexican market had been covered in a giant, colorful mural. Calling it graffiti cheapened it. This was religious iconography. It was a mishmash of Aztec and Mayan influences, and much of it was wrong, but it got a few very specific things right, and seeing *his* sacred glyphs so brazenly displayed out in the open like this filled me with rage. Even though his influence shouldn't reach into these lands, this had clearly been created by worshippers. This was trespassing, plain and simple.

"What's that painting of?" Justin asked, still in the driver's seat, obviously confused by what I was staring at.

"The invisible and the darkness, ruler of the north, and lord of night," I muttered.

"Say what?"

"Nobody," I spat as I raised the lens to my eye and snapped a picture of the mural to analyze later. Alex would probably add it to his files and thank me.

The hairnet kids from the corner had seen me get out and were approaching. Their cat calls grated on my ears. Justin saw them coming in the rearview mirror and nervously said, "We'd better scoot, Chloe."

Except I wasn't in the mood. As they drew closer, I turned toward the boys and hissed in Spanish, *"Cross me and I'll eat your fucking hearts."*

I was so angry at the presence of the mural that a touch of the *nagualii* crept into my voice. It cut right through their swaggering *machismo* and caused all of them to take a nervous step back, probably subconsciously reminded of old tales their *abuelitas* had told them when they were little, about things that were best not to mess with. What lived in darkness was nobody's friend.

"Bruja," one of them whispered fearfully and crossed himself. That kid must have had the gift of sight or a really stern *abuela*.

The obvious leader raised his hands defensively. "Sorry, lady, we don't want no trouble."

I got back in the car and closed the door. "Drive."

Justin did. "Holy shit. You scared the hell out of them. What'd you say?"

Taking a deep breath, I composed myself before responding. "I told them if they kept being rude I'd tell their *abuelas*."

"What'd you take a picture of?"

"I like street art. It's different. Just keep going this way, I think that'll get us home."

We kept driving in silence, because Justin was smart enough to recognize I was deeply troubled about the mural but didn't want to talk about it. He turned on the radio instead of trying for more awkward conversation and the familiar notes of "Brand New Key" came on. Lizz loved the song and hummed it all the time.

I'd told Earl and Ray I was willing to go into Mexico if this job required it. Why not? The old ways were mostly dead. The odds of me running into anyone from the Court was low even in Mexico...I certainly hadn't been expecting to find their sign on this side of the border.

Times were changing, and not for the better.

It was in the middle of the day a few weeks after getting settled in the new office when we got our first callout. Something big and red was trapped within an old Spanish-mission-style house out in Covina. Cute town, used to be known for its orange groves. Marco decided we needed to do a full team evolution to show just what we were capable of.

We didn't even leave anyone to answer the phone in case of an emergency. We didn't have enough business yet to justify hiring a secretary, but Lizz had purchased a marvelous device called an answering machine to record our phone calls for us while we were away. So it was all hands on deck for the maiden voyage of Team Rhino.

Intel was sparse. The monster was trapped in a house. MCB agents had already secured the location and intimidated the witnesses, as usual, but they weren't about to clear the house. Some local police had it surrounded and had evacuated the neighbors, but the MCB wasn't letting the cops get close enough to get a look either.

The street was blocked off with roadblock signs when we arrived. Once we told the sheriff's deputy manning the entrance into the small suburban neighborhood we were MHI, he let us through. He didn't even know what MHI was, but orders were orders. As soon as we were through they closed the road behind us.

It was pretty simple to figure out which house was the problem one. There was a gaggle of police officers crouched behind their cars, all with their guns aimed at the house. A few of them were armed with pump shotguns but most only had revolvers.

Melanie, Lizz, and I were in the first car and stopped on the street a few houses away. Rhino, with the rest of the team, pulled up quickly behind us, his massive Ford Econoline van spewing noxious fumes. It amazed me that thing managed to survive the drive across the country. Justin, Kimpton, and Alex jumped out of the back of the van, every one of them looking a little green, either from this being our first mission together, or the exhaust from Rhino's van.

While I walked over to the police, everybody else started gearing up.

"You MHI?" the one wearing sergeant's stripes asked, probably wondering why he was talking to me instead of one of the men. Not unfair, but still a little annoying.

"That's us."

"What's an MHI?"

"The answer to your problems, which I heard was something big, red, and furry?"

The sergeant had clearly been expecting Marco to be the head of our merry little band of miscreants, which, technically he was, but I don't think the big man had the vocabulary for it. "Something like that. We got the noise complaint, but when my men knocked, whatever kind of animal they've illegally got in there started raising a fuss and tearing the place up so they retreated and called for backup. I called animal control, only then the Bureau of Land Management people showed up and took charge."

BLM? That was a new one. It was clear the sergeant was not having a good day. I decided to take it easy on him.

"Where are they at?"

The sergeant breathed a sigh of relief and pointed off to the right, where a tall blond woman dressed in a blue windbreaker and black slacks was standing. Which was a surprise to me, because the last time I'd dealt with them, the Monster Control Bureau had been very old-fashioned and didn't normally allow women out in the field.

"You with MHI?" the woman asked as I approached. Seeing my nod, she continued. "Agent Erin Beesley."

"Nice to meet you, Agent Beesley," I lied. She didn't offer me her hand, which told me the feeling was mutual. MCB always disliked private organizations like us. I figured it was mostly because we got paid like robber barons while they worked for peanuts. "I'm Chloe Mendoza."

"They put you in charge?" she asked incredulously.

"No. The giant one with all the scars is in charge." The cops were far enough away they wouldn't be able to hear us. "So you're pretending to be BLM today?"

"We are." Earl had warned me that the modern MCB liked to travel around with a stack of fake credentials, so they could butt into any local incident, take over, and then cover it up. "This will be written up as illegal animal trafficking in the police reports and newspaper. Understand?"

"Understood. Part of my job is making your job easier. MHI looks forward to establishing a good working relationship with the MCB in Los Angeles."

Agent Beesley snorted and rolled her eyes. Apparently that wasn't the first time a Hunter had tried to feed her that particular line of bull. "You private-sector types are interchangeable to me."

"What've you got for us?"

"Something you can't kill," she stated as she looked back at the mission-style house.

I chuckled darkly. "With enough flamethrowers, I can kill just about everything."

"No, I mean, you're not *allowed* to kill it."

My customer-service face must have slipped and let my confusion show because the Fed sighed and explained in a very condescending tone, "Under the cryptozoological protection rules, the *miniwatu* is an endangered species."

The Endangered Species Act was a relatively new law that Monster Hunters were still trying to figure out. There were two versions: the public one and the secret one, with the secret one only being applied to natural creatures that fell under PUFF guidelines for keeping the knowledge of their existence away from the public, but not actual supernatural creatures that we were still allowed to blast on sight. The difference between the two was one for the lawyers to argue about.

"I don't even know what that is. Mini what now?"

"*Miniwatu* were hunted to near extinction back during the French-Indian War. Something about their horn curing impotence or something, I don't know. They've only recently begun to climb back up in number. With one of these, it's a catch-and-release policy. Fish and Wildlife will fine MHI into oblivion if you kill it."

"Seriously?"

"Which means no flamethrowers." Her smile was smug and condescending, which suited her pinched, narrow face. I could already tell she was going to be a joy to work with. "Besides, I don't want to put out a call to the fire department here in town. They want nothing to do with this sort of stuff. Subdue it unharmed, and once that's done another agency will transport it out of the area."

I sighed. This was going to be one of *those* calls. My opinion of the east San Gabriel Valley was already beginning to slip. It had looked so promising too. "Anyone inside? Other than the *monster* I'm not allowed to kill?"

"Not that we're aware of."

Oh, this is going to be so much fun. I pivoted on my heel and practically stomped over to where the rest of the team was busy loading guns and getting dressed.

MHI didn't have any kind of uniform. Ray had talked about investing in some kind of anti-monster armor to be issued company wide, but what was available on the market was just too heavy, hot, or awkward. We'd just picked up some surplus flak jackets and dyed them black. They were heavy and left our arms exposed, but they were good for protecting the body from teeth and claws. I'd heard some Hunters were paying for custom chain-mail shirts now, but I'd never seen one. Thick leather gloves protected our hands, and everyone wore steel-toe boots. Some of the guys wore helmets. I didn't like to since they interfered with my peripheral vision and hearing. Plus, the *nagualii* part of me hated anything covering my ears.

Justin and Kimpton were carrying AK-47s. Marco had a Remington shotgun loaded with silver pellets, which cost a fortune but were very, *very* effective against some types of monsters. New Orleans PUFF payments must have been better than I thought. Melanie and Alex had Colt Commandos. Lizz had her trusty scoped bolt action. And I had to ruin their fun by saying, "MCB declared we can't kill it."

"What kinda bullshit is that?" Marco asked. "It's a monster, ain't it?"

"If we shoot it, MHI gets sued. We've got to capture it unharmed."

My team was baffled. Especially the newbies, because this was not something they'd been trained on. I certainly hadn't told them anything about this in class, because back in the old days we probably would have just thrown a bunch of dynamite through a window and called it a day.

"Are you shitting me?" Justin said, with a look of disgust clearly evident upon his face. "Shouldn't all monsters be killed?"

"That's arguable," I said, trying not to be prickly about it, as none of them knew my little secret. This wasn't the time to get into a discussion about PUFF Exemptions and monsters who simply wanted to be left alone. "Point being, this one needs to be bagged alive."

"What is it we're supposed to be capturing?" Lizz asked.

"A *miniwatu*, whatever the hell that is. It's an Endangered Species Act crypto-something." *Stupid MCB...*

"It's what certain Indian tribes called a giant horned beaver," Alex immediately said.

The kid could remember just about everything he ever read. I forgot what I had for breakfast by lunchtime. "Native to the Missouri River Valley. Dark red fur, almost purple, one eye, single horn...okay, I get that reference now. Sheb Wooley wrote a song about one, once. Big hit in the fifties."

"Seriously?" Melanie asked.

"They probably don't eat people, though. Or fly."

I had no idea what song they were talking about, as the musical selection had been rather limited where I'd been during the fifties. It wasn't like Alex was ever wrong, though. I think he might even have one of those so-called photographic memories. "We're a long way from the Missouri River."

Alex shrugged. "Someone probably got it as a kit, thinking a baby beaver would make a cute pet. They're born without horns, so someone not paying attention could have missed there was something wrong with it. Probably spazzed out when it grew bigger than a dog. They top out at around two, three hundred pounds. Herbivores aren't usually dangerous, except when cornered."

"Like this one that's trapped inside a house?" Kimpton asked pointedly.

"Yeah...I wonder who owns the house?" Alex mused.

"Why?" I felt silly, asking all these questions. I was supposed to be the knowledgeable and experienced second-in-command, not some newbie.

"Someone is trading in exotic animals. The Fish and Wild-life people will probably want to investigate when we're done capturing it."

"Do we even have tranquilizer guns?" I asked. I couldn't remember any being listed on the equipment inventory, and even if we had some in one of the still unpacked moving boxes back at base, we certainly didn't have any here. "Where's the nearest zoo? Maybe we can go and borrow theirs?"

"No time," Marco grunted. "We're supposed to be the pros who handle this kinda thing. It don't look good going around begging for equipment. If we don't do this job right now, it looks bad on all the other contracts we're working on." Apparently that meant the decision had been made. "It don't sound too big. Hell, I'm three hundred pounds. Let's do this."

"*How?*" I asked. Because that was the kind of thing an experienced second-in-command should ask when your boss has decided to go wrestle a giant beaver.

Alex scratched his chin thoughtfully. "Well, according to the lore, they're nocturnal. Right now, it's napping probably. Get some rope and we can probably just tie it up and get it into a van for transport. Logically, the longer we let it wake up, the harder it'll be to catch."

"MCB said they'd handle transportation." I cast an evil look in Agent Beesley's direction. She wasn't paying attention, focused instead of chatting up one of the local sheriff's deputies.

"So what's the plan, Rhino?" Justin asked, looking at our team leader.

"Rope in the van," he grunted. "We go in. Two on front, two on back. Take it down quick. Let's go."

I blinked. As far as plans went, it felt a little light on any actual planning. Earl had warned me this might happen, so I expanded for the rest of the team.

"Justin, get the rope from the van. We'll go in the front door at Rhino's signal. Try to stay quiet until we find the monster so we don't spook it. Alex, you and Rhino grab its front legs. Justin and Kimpton will grab the back. I'll take overwatch on the front door. Flip it over, hog-tie it, and try not to hurt it. Protect yourselves, but for the love of God don't shoot it. We can't afford the fines, and I'm pretty sure the Boss would kill us."

"What about us?" Melanie asked.

Melanie was physically fit, but not nearly as strong as any of the guys. Lizz was tiny and would probably just get squished.

"Melanie, stick by me so we can help if we're needed. Lizz…"

"I'll stay here and guard the guns. Good luck with your mutant."

Everyone nodded at this and went into action. That was good, as despite Earl vouching for me, I still wasn't sure how much they trusted my experience. I looked over at Rhino but he seemed unconcerned about his lack of communication, or me taking over. I'd talk to him about it later. I didn't want our leader feeling like I was usurping his authority. Right now, I needed to focus on surviving an oversized red beaver with a horn on its head.

We moved into position, only now without all our machine guns, which the local cops seemed rather disappointed about, as they still thought the thing in the house was a grizzly bear, and that would be a heck of a show. The house was styled to look like a Spanish mission. There was no monster visible through any of the front windows.

Rhino stepped back away from the door and looked ready to put his massive size-thirteen boot to it. I put my hand on his shoulder to stop him, pointed at the door knob, and made a twisting motion with my hand. He reached out to test the door and found it unlocked. He didn't seem pleased by this. My guess? Rhino hated doors and really wanted to kick that particular one open to show it who was in charge.

We went in quietly.

The really interesting thing about single-story house designs in Southern California is the waist-high walls scattered around, which served to separate the rooms while still keeping it looking like an open-floor plan. The owner had clearly put a lot of work into remodeling. It was a shame that most of the living room had been destroyed by the giant angry beaver.

The living room area was clear. No sign of the *miniwatu*, save for a chewed-up sofa and pillows. Rhino and Alex began to move toward the kitchen, which was just inside the front door and to the left. Kimpton and Justin stayed back a bit, while me and Melanie stayed in the entryway. There was a long, narrow hallway just off the dining room, and when I noticed the dark wood paneling was covered with red hair, I motioned for their attention and pointed that way. Our team of intrepid beaver wranglers started down the hall.

"It smells like beaver piss in here," Justin said.

"How do you know what beaver pee smells like?" Alex asked.

"Call it an educated guess, wise guy."

While they searched, I inspected the living room. It was a product of the era, complete with thick shag carpet and tables that were brass and glass. The wooden television box took up one whole wall, but it was basically two big cupboard doors on either side of a relatively small screen. There was a stand for records, and one of the legs had clearly been gnawed on. The kitchen was filled with avocado-green appliances and floral print wallpaper where the dark wood paneling ended. The dining room table looked vintage compared to the rest of the setup, except it had been scraped with beaver teeth too. All in all, it was a very strange combination of money and tackiness.

Lizz would have loved it. From what she'd bought for our office so far, she seemed to be really into modern design and ugly furniture.

Justin came out of the closest bedroom, shaking his head. *Nothing.* Rhino led Alex toward the back of the house where there appeared to be doors for two more bedrooms back there. Kimpton poked his head into one, then came back out and signaled for me to come look.

"Stay here," I whispered to Melanie.

"What if it tries to run past me?" Considering this was her first real hunt as a professional Monster Hunter, she was understandably nervous.

"Don't get run over." Then I walked over to Kimpton.

"Trophy room," he said quietly. Since it was the home of somebody trafficking in illegal animals, when Kimpton had said trophies, I'd expected animal heads and antlers. Only when I peeked inside there were bowling trophies everywhere. Most had been broken and were on the floor from the beaver chewing on the shelves, though the ones higher up remained untouched. There was a partially chewed leather bag with a black bowling ball in the corner.

"Whoa," I muttered. "Serious bowler."

"Master bedroom was clear, just a bed with a dresser," Justin stated as he came up to us from behind. "No closet, bathroom is a mess. Single guy, midforties would be my guess. No signs of a live-in girlfriend or anything. No pictures on the walls."

"I wonder where he is?"

"Maybe the beaver ate him?" Justin suggested.

"Alex said they don't do that."

"A book of unknown reliability told Alex that," Kimpton responded.

I put my finger to my lips and shushed them.

Rhino poked his head into the last bedroom before quickly backing away. He circled with two fingers before pointing into the room. Our target was inside.

With five of us in the hallway, it was rather cramped, but I shuffled forward to take a look. "If that thing's only three hundred pounds, I'm a ballerina," Rhino whispered.

The creature was probably double that weight, and taking a nap on the smashed remains of a futon. Kimpton had been right about the accuracy of Alex's book, because when they had said the *miniwatu* was big, it hadn't really clicked in my head as to just *how* big the thing would be. I'd seen all manner of monsters in my life, but seeing a sofa-sized horned beaver sleeping in a makeshift nest of ruined sheets and partially chewed bowling trophies was something else entirely. I blinked and rubbed my eyes. The tail was wider than the *miniwatu*'s body and looked particularly sturdy. Something told me I did not want to get hit by it.

"So much for our *everybody grab a leg* plan," Justin said when he looked inside.

Alex, of course, was super excited. "The tail is special, according to the Arikara Indians. When a *miniwatu* swims in the waters of the Missouri River during a full moon, the wake the tail leaves behind is filled with precious metals which drop to the river bottom. They believe this is how gold gets into their river."

"You really need to get a girlfriend," I said. He looked at me, hurt.

After all of us except for Melanie had gotten a glimpse of the slumbering beaver, Rhino ordered, "Get ready to bag this thing."

"Anybody else ever rope livestock before?" Kimpton asked. "No? Really? Okay, easy-peasy. Back legs first, then tie it off on the front. Watch that tail. If it panics, it's probably going to start bucking."

"I got this," Rhino said, taking the rope out of Justin's hand. Making a quick slipknot, the big man crept around the makeshift nest to get behind the *miniwatu*. I motioned for everyone else to hang back. The room was small, barely larger than the master bathroom. If this was going to work, Rhino needed the space. Kimpton bailed to the living room, while Justin stayed close to me.

The moment the nylon rope wrapped around the back legs of the *miniwatu*, the thing absolutely spazzed out.

Well, the *miniwatu* might not be able to fly, but they can jump really high when startled, much to our surprise. It also moves far faster than anything that large should. Oh, and the tail? Just like a beaver, except the *miniwatu* swung it the way Hank Aaron would a baseball bat. Believe me when I say that this critter hit a home run.

Rhino had absolutely no warning before the frightened beaver's tail slammed into his flak jacket. Our very large team leader's body left a very impressive dent in the wood paneling after he bounced off it.

"Grab it!" Rhino shouted as he immediately got back up.

Credit to the team, they sure tried.

The nylon rope flexed but didn't break, which was good for our purposes. However, it did allow the creature to get one of its hind legs out from the lasso almost immediately. In the living room this wouldn't have been a problem. In the tight confines of the miniscule bedroom, however, this proved to be a huge issue.

The *miniwatu* made a horrid sound which nearly shattered all of our eardrums. It sounded like *"QwikqwikQWIKqwik!"*

"I got a leg!" Justin shouted, and then, "Oh shit!" as it turned out he didn't.

The terrified giant beaver kept jumping and spinning, trying to escape its attackers. Unfortunately, six hundred pounds plus of angry beaver monster thing had nowhere to go and responded with the grace and agility befitting an animal half the size of my car.

The *miniwatu* pivoted again, this time bringing its flat, heavy tail into play. Alex tried to grab the makeshift lasso but the beaver was having none of it and was bucking like a fat weird-looking bronco, just as Kimpton predicted. This time it ran directly into Alex.

The poor kid didn't even have time to move out of the way before the angry beaver knocked him down. Alex was maybe just shy of 180 pounds and was immediately squished as the *miniwatu* landed on him. The *miniwatu* scrambled over the downed hunter and bolted for the hall and freedom. Rhino, still holding onto the rope, was jerked halfway across the room as the beaver ran for the door.

The damn thing was fast, considering its size, and I only just managed to get out of its way. "Angry beaver! Angry beaver!" I shouted. "Incoming! Melanie! Close the front door!"

She did and then wisely climbed on top of the big wooden TV to keep from getting nailed by the agitated beaver, which was now bounding in circles around the living room, still dragging Rhino, who was shouting, "Grab the beaver by the horn!"

"What the fu—" Kimpton started to ask before he was bowled over by the six-hundred-pound-plus *miniwatu*. Justin, thinking quickly, jumped on its back. He almost got a good hold around the monster's neck before sliding back a little. The *miniwatu* was frightened, desperate, and really fat. Justin had absolutely no chance. Spinning rapidly, the giant beaver flung off Justin, who went over the decorative wall to land in the kitchen. Something in there broke when he hit it and suddenly water was spraying *everywhere*.

"QwikQwikqwikQWIKQWIKqwik!" the terrified monster screamed as Kimpton took his chances and jumped onto the *miniwatu*. Somehow he'd avoided getting injured when the beaver had run over him. Unfortunately, the creature wasn't as stupid as it looked, and must have been starting to catch on that we had no idea what we were doing, so it reached up with a front paw to drag Kimpton off its back. It hooked his flak vest, and then the *miniwatu* slammed him onto the now-wet carpet. Thick claws stuck in the flak jacket and the beaver looked down at the Hunter in annoyance. It opened its massive mouth and the large, orange-stained buck teeth were inches from Kimpton's face. The creature bellowed a challenge. "QWIK?!"

"It's gonna eat him!" Justin shouted in alarm.

Suddenly, a very pissed-off Rhino let go of the rope, jumped up, and bellowed a challenge at the beaver, before lowering his massive shoulders and tackling the damned thing. Mass versus mass, Rhino should have lost, but I don't think the monster had been expecting that and got bowled over, sparing Kimpton from finding out if Alex's hypothesis about *miniwatus* eating people were just folk tales or not.

Rhino and the beaver crashed into the remains of the couch. Promptly rolling over, the beaver thumped Rhino's legs with its tail. We all heard the *snap* of a bone and the big man cried out in pain.

The giant, soaking-wet beaver was *pissed* now. Scratching and kicking at the increasingly soggy carpet, the beaver began to slap the downed Rhino in the head and shoulders with its heavy tail. *Thud! Thud! Thud!*

I picked up the nylon rope and pulled hard, and luckily nobody else noticed that I was a whole lot better at it than Rhino had been, actually managing to drag the beaver out of thumping-Rhino range. Well, the *miniwatu* sure noticed, and now it turned its horn my way, and that beady little eye was staring right at me.

Before it charged me, Melanie distracted it by throwing some vinyl records at its face, so the beaver retaliated by smashing the thick glass of the TV beneath her with its tail. Kimpton had managed to scramble out of the way, but got clubbed on the backswing, so now he was stuck under the monster again.

I was about to say to hell with the MCB and the Endangered Species Act, and to tell everybody to just pull their pistols and shoot the damned thing, when Alex stumbled into the living room, holding up a ratty old bedsheet in front of him like a shield.

I did a double take when I saw Alex, because getting trampled by the beaver had knocked one of his boots off and its claws had shredded his pants. There were some things about my team I was not ready to know just yet. Like, for instance, Alex's tattoo on his upper thigh, and just how high the tail of the shark in question went.

"What are you doing?"

"I'll use this sheet." He was out of breath thanks to the *miniwatu* knocking the wind out of him. "I'll throw it over its head!"

"It ain't no fucking *parrot*!" Justin called back from the kitchen. "That only works on birds!"

"What are you still doing in the kitchen?" I asked, grabbing the nylon rope and snaking it around the beaver's hind legs. It was too busy being angry at Melanie and her vinyl rain to even notice. I managed to get the rope knotted before the tail slapped it out of my hands. Nylon is slick when wet, turns out, but can still rub the leather fast enough to generate heat. I yelped in pain. "Quit messing around and help!"

"I'm trying to find a carrot or something in the refrigerator!" Justin replied loudly.

"A *carrot*?!" I called back, incredulous. "This is *not* a rabbit! Shit. Kimpton, watch that horn!"

Kimpton had realized it was now trying to gore him before I had and managed to catch hold of it with his hands. The *miniwatu's* gnarly teeth snapped closed next to his face, but the horn was pointed safely away. However, it was a still attached to a wriggling, angry, now sopping-wet beaver trying to crush the man.

"Try the damned sheet!" Kimpton shouted as the *miniwatu* used its weight to press down into the Hunter's chest. The giant beaver's tail was smacking the wet floor in irritation, splashing everyone in range. The horrid smell emanating from the wet *minwatu* was almost as bad as the wet shag rug—which, it turned out, had a lot of dried beaver poop on it.

Alex tossed the sheet over the beaver's head and let it settle, like he was making a bed. The sheet partially covered Kimpton and for a moment I thought he was a goner. Surprisingly enough, as soon as the sheet went over the *miniwatu's* head, the monster immediately calmed down. It continued to grunt and make noises, but the frantic thrashing ceased.

Kimpton pulled himself out from beneath the placid creature, practically swimming through puddles that had accumulated on the carpet. We all remained there, breathing hard, kinda shocked by the sudden quiet, and waiting for the beaver to change its mind and go back to trying to kill us all.

After a moment I said, "Well, that worked surprisingly worked well." The room smelled absolutely horrible, but the *miniwatu* seemed placated for the time being.

"Is Rhino dead?" Alex was clearly concerned as he looked over at our team lead, who was lying on the floor, unmoving.

"He's breathing." Kimpton crawled over to where Rhino lay and checked out the big man.

Rhino moaned as he lay there. He looked like shit, and smelled even worse. "Did we win?"

"I think so, boss." Justin came out of the kitchen, holding a large clump of overripe carrots and a head of lettuce. He staggered over to the massive shape of the *miniwatu* and knelt down next to it. Lifting the corner of the sheet a few inches, he quickly shoved the carrots and lettuce under. All of us could hear the giant horned beaver make some snuffling noises and then happily munch away on the produce. Since it seemed happy blind and eating, we hurried and tied the rope around all of its legs and neck. Now all we'd have to do was pull it tight and our beaver wouldn't be going anywhere.

"How are you not covered in water and beaver shit?" Justin asked Melanie.

"I didn't get thrown into the kitchen or roll around on this scuzzy carpet." She was still safely standing on the broken TV and seemed happy to stay up there.

Rhino groaned as he rolled over, wincing at the pain. "Everybody else okay?"

Alex had an embarrassed expression on his face. The *miniwatu* had practically barreled through him. It was amazing he hadn't busted any ribs. "I think so."

Everybody else agreed. They were beaten up, but in one piece.

I took off my glove and held up my hand. It was slightly red. "I got rope burn."

Rhino winced as he looked at his leg, which was pointing in a very awkward, obviously broken direction. "Well, ain't this some bullshit."

The man was *tough*.

"Do we even collect PUFF on this thing?" Kimpton asked. "We're not dogcatchers, you know."

"Well, the county will pay us. As for a PUFF bounty, I don't know. I never even heard of this thing before today." I looked to Alex, who shrugged, which meant probably not, because if it had been on the bounty tables he probably would've seen it and remembered. "Well, shit."

Considering the badass nature of our job, Team Rhino was off to a rather ridiculous start.

CHAPTER 5

Once the *miniwatu* was secured inside the Fish and Wildlife minivan and sedated by a very unhappy game warden, we were able to get Rhino to the hospital. After much debate and questioning, the sheriff's deputy directed us to a small, physician-owned hospital nearby in San Dimas that was practically brand new. I stayed behind with Kimpton while the others drove Rhino to the emergency room in our team lead's van.

Agent Beesley smiled coldly as I approached. She was standing by her car, smoking a cigarette. *Be professional, be professional*, I continuously repeated the mantra in my head. It had been a long time since I had dealt with an MCB agent;, things might have changed since those days, and there was no reason to poison the well. Also, I had promised Earl and the Boss I'd make nice. That would be the best way to stay in business, after all.

"Do you have a PUFF number?" I asked Agent Beesley as politely as I could manage.

"We'll give you credit for the assist," she replied.

I stared at her, flabbergasted. "But we made the catch!"

"And I arranged its transportation up to North Dakota or wherever." Agent Beesley flashed me that irritating smirk. The *nagualii* wanted to eat it off her face. "Well, Fish and Wildlife is. Unless you want to drive sixteen hundred miles and then file the paperwork."

I was trying to be nice, but Kimpton, being part of that generation of young men who had grown up trusting the system only to get screwed over by them, seemed to be struggling with the concept. "How do you get away with robbing us like that, lady?"

"By the power of this." Beesley opened her windbreaker to show the badge clipped on her belt. Not one of the fake ones for various other agencies the MCB hid behind, but her real one, with the two-headed eagle. "Do you know what this badge means?"

I couldn't help it. "That you make less money than we do?"

Beesley glared at me as she closed her jacket. "Okay, funny girl, you want me to tell the fish cops to turn around and load that thing in your van?"

I sighed. "Fine, we'll take the assist. Who's the owner of the house, anyway?"

"Doesn't matter." The MCB agent's voice had turned frosty. "Call this a win and walk away. You handled it without causing too much of a scene or burning the place down. That's a positive in my book."

I decided to get one last verbal jab in before we left. "Thankfully, nobody said anything about keeping the plumbing intact."

Ignoring Agent Beesley's sputtering confusion, because none of us knew where the water main was and the kitchen was still flooding, I pivoted and walked back to my car.

Kimpton was right behind me, and I could almost feel the unasked questions he had burrowing a small hole in the middle of my back. Even though he was obviously angry at the Fed, he was polite enough to remove his flak jacket and gloves before getting into my passenger seat. He was still soaking wet, but I'd bought this car knowing it would get used for work. Odds were the upholstery would end up seeing a lot worse in the coming months, so there was no reason to fret over it. Still, he made the effort, which was appreciated.

"Only an assist on that damned beaver?" he asked once the door was shut and we were no longer within earshot of the MCB agent. The look on his face told me he was clearly not okay with it but was at least attempting to keep his cool. "It damned near killed Rhino, gored me, trampled Alex, and tossed Justin through a sink, and we get a measly assist?"

"Think long term. We still have the contract with the locals. We're getting paid by them. And the ones in the know will be happy and tell their friends. We knew going in the MCB might cramp our style."

"Fine." Kimpton took a deep breath, as there was obviously something else on his mind.

"Spit it out."

"Look, I'm not one to rock the boat, but what are we going to do about Rhino?"

"What do you mean?" I asked, though I was pretty sure I knew what he was talking about. I'd half expected the conversation to happen, though not so soon.

"He's not exactly checking off too many boxes on the traditional good-leader checklist." It was clear Kimpton was still thinking of me as a lady and trying to phrase that in a gentlemanly fashion.

"As in, he almost got us killed by something ridiculous because he didn't give clear instructions beforehand and instead we rushed in like a bunch of clowns," I clarified.

"Yeah."

Earl said he saw leadership potential in Marco Moss, at least enough to give him a shot at running a team. I trusted Earl. He'd once seen enough potential in me to not gun me down in a dusty Mexican street. They'd described my job as NCO, and part of being a good noncom was running interference for your officer, even when they were being an idiot.

"Rhino's a good Hunter and one tough son of a bitch. He's just new at being in charge. We'll learn from this. He'll figure it out. We all will."

"The way his leg looked he's gonna be figuring it out on crutches."

I turned the key in the ignition and the beast of an engine roared to life. Alright, this Chevy Chevelle didn't have that much raw power, but my idea when I'd picked it was that it wouldn't need as much rationed and expensive gas to get us around the congested Southern California roads as Rhino's big van. I backed up and the cops let us past the roadblock, and we headed down Badillo Street. A quick right had us heading north toward Foothill Boulevard. From there, it would be almost a straight shot back to our headquarters in Pasadena. Given the state of traffic, though, I figured it would take about an hour.

Kimpton fiddled with the radio until Badfinger's "Day After

Day" was playing over the car's cheap speakers. I hadn't bought the thing for its sound system.

After a few minutes of him stewing, I tried a different approach. "You guys might be newbies, but most of you are vets, right? Alex was Navy, you and Justin were over in Vietnam. You know no plan survives contact with the enemy, and that gets even worse when the enemy is a monster. This job is unpredictable."

"'Flexible minds.'" Kimpton supplied the Shackleford family's answer to how best to survive in this business. "But that was just—"

"One of the reasons it's hard to start up a new team is because there needs to be a certain chemistry between everyone before you're effective. We don't have that yet, so we're going to have small missteps along the way." A station wagon cut us off, so I extended my left hand in a universal greeting. Whoever the other driver was returned the gesture in kind. *Ah, California . . .*

"We just got our asses kicked by a giant beaver. We hope we figure it the hell out before we run into something actually dangerous."

So do I.

I didn't say that out loud.

As soon as we pulled into the Gasparyans' lot, Lizz came limping out to greet us, rifle case in hand and a serious look on her face. I didn't bother turning the engine off, and instead popped the trunk and waited for her to load her gear in. Kimpton got out and moved his chair so Lizz could climb into the back seat.

"Rhino's going to be okay," Lizz said as soon as she was settled. "Clean break in the fibula. Cast and everything but no surgery. He's probably going to be out of action for at least two months."

Our first contract and we had suffered a casualty. *Not off to the best of starts.* "Where to, and what're we hunting?"

"Got your map?"

Kimpton popped the glove box, took out the flipbook map, and passed it back to Lizz. She skimmed through the book rapidly before finding our next destination. "Ah, there you are. We're headed for Lake Arrowhead. Get on Foothill and head east."

"But that's where the traffic is. We just came from that way too."

"Covina is much closer than Lake Arrowhead is. It's out in San Bernardino County, in the mountains."

"Ugh," Kimpton grunted. "These boots aren't broken in yet. I hate hiking."

"I waited for you guys. The others are on the way...I can't believe you boys couldn't handle a large, wet, angry beaver."

"Shaddup, Lizz," Kimpton said.

"What's in Lake Arrowhead?" I interrupted Lizz's teasing, figuring I'd let her dig her claws back into poor Kimpton after I knew what the deal was. Not because I was cruel, but it would be good to laugh after our near-death encounter with the *miniwatu*.

"There was a message on the answering machine. I know you thought it was really expensive, but I told you it would pay for itself."

"Lizz..."

"Officially, it was a mountain lion attack." Her tone shifted into business mode. "Only mountain lions usually don't eat half their victims, ya know, and last night was the first night of the full moon."

So much for having a chance to get our act together before running into something really dangerous.

"Shit." Kimpton looked skyward. Through the hazy smog we could see the sun just starting to set. "Traffic is a pain. How long do you think it's going to take?"

"The map says it's only about seventy miles or so."

"So about two hours?" I asked.

Lizz must have missed the sarcasm, because she said, "Ayup, 'bout that."

"It's going to be dark when we get there," Kimpton observed.

"I already called and got two rooms reserved at a lodge up there," Lizz said. "One for the boys, one for the girls."

I was glad Lizz had thought to do that. It beat sleeping in a tiny car. "It's nice to have some experienced hands on a team full of newbies."

"Eh, everyone has to start somewhere. I'm not about to walk through a forest in the middle of the night huntin' a werewolf, though. I've done that before and don't recommend it. I think we should check the body they got on ice at the sheriff's station first to make sure we know what we're dealing with, then go to the scene where they found him to search around."

"Got anything that can help with a werewolf?" Kimpton asked. "Besides silver bullets, obviously?"

"I saw a couple boxes of silver .308 ammo in the trunk," Lizz stated. "I've got my rifle in that caliber. There's more in the van. Plus Rhino keeps a rack of shotguns in his van and a few boxes of silver-pellet buckshot."

Ray had talked about how he someday wanted to get to the point where silver ammo was standard issue for MHI, but right now it was just too expensive to make. Still, we all kept some on hand because there were some creatures that nothing else worked on.

"Wolfsbane?" I looked in the rearview mirror questioningly.

"Ayup, I grabbed enough for everyone. Stuff it in all our pockets and it'll mask our smell."

"Assuming the phase of the moon isn't a coincidence and this isn't something else entirely." Werewolves were pretty rare, and there hadn't been an issue with them in Southern California recently as far as we knew. "Explosives?"

"Dynamite in the van," Lizz answered happily. "This will be fun!"

"I'm starting to wonder if the Boss made the right person our team lead," Kimpton muttered quietly as we continued to move our way through the sluggish rush-hour traffic. I didn't say anything because I couldn't really disagree with him. Lizz had done more planning just now than Rhino had for our *miniwatu* problem. Granted, a werewolf was far more dangerous than an overgrown beaver with a horn.

Team Rhino was definitely off to a rocky start. Hopefully it wouldn't get worse.

The two-hour trip eventually turned into three. While traveling up CA-60 we became hopelessly lost and ended up near Big Bear Lake. Once Lizz got everything sorted out we realized we'd actually missed the turnoff about fifteen minutes before. After swearing enough to make even Lizz blush, I found a gas station to refill the car and headed back down the winding mountain road in the dark. The radio turned to static but Lizz had brought a Creedence Clearwater Revival 8-track tape to keep us awake. As we turned into the wooded valley, the full moon began cresting over the ridge behind us.

"Look, another lake," Kimpton said with a yawn. The adrenaline surge from earlier had long disappeared and the two of us were feeling the aches and pains of our previous call. Lizz, on the other hand, seemed to be reinvigorated after the long and mostly boring drive.

"It's the shape of an arrowhead!" she exclaimed. With the moonlight reflecting off the surface, it really did resemble an arrowhead for a few moments until a new line of pine trees blocked our view. Lizz sat back and sighed happily. "Groovy."

"Groovy?"

"The sixties were nifty," Lizz said. "You kids wouldn't understand."

I almost laughed at that but shooting her down wasn't worth giving up any family secrets. Personally, I struggled to keep up on the slang of the day. "Okay, Granny. Whatever you say."

"Where's this lodge you were talking about?" Kimpton asked. The headlights of my Chevelle were good but not great. I'd gotten used to the city lights. This was the darkest I'd seen it since we arrived in Southern California over a month before. If not for the full moon above us, we could have probably seen the Milky Way.

The Lake Arrowhead community was growing, with numerous houses being built near the water. Luxury homes, larger than most families would ever need, dotted the shore. I was a bit surprised as we drove closer to the lake. There were actual streetlights along this part. The oppressive darkness faded as modern technology fought back.

"If I remember the map right, if we drive into the lake we've gone too far," Lizz quipped. After nobody laughed, she tucked her chin to her chest and scowled. "It should be a two-story building on the left near the shore."

"I think I see it." Kimpton leaned forward in the seat. "Yeah, there it is."

It was one of those cute resort places that were all the rage in the fifties, with a row of rooms looking out over the parking lot and the lake. It had a giant light-up arrowhead on top. It was meant to be a beacon for vacationers, but enough bulbs were burned out or flickering to make it sort of depressing. The lodge had clearly seen better days. Marco's death van was parked out front.

Through the window I could see that Alex and Justin were already in the lobby, both looking the worse for wear. Alex had swapped out his shredded pants with new ones, but probably

neither he nor Justin were too happy about reentering civilization smelling like *miniwatu* musk and poop-covered shag carpet.
Justin was eyeing a stuffed mountain lion that had been posed
near the front entrance. It seemed pretty obvious to me that the
busty girl with the name tag on her tank top standing near him,
talking about the taxidermy, must have been working the front
desk when the incident occurred, and now she was attempting
to flirt. Even if they smelled bad and were dressed funny, both
Hunters were good-looking, physically fit young men.

Alex spotted us and waved when we came through the door.
"Hi, Chloe, guys. Amanda here was just telling us about the hiker
who got killed by the mountain lion last night."

"Oh, you can just call me *Mandy*," she corrected as she gave
me that hostile, *I've marked this man, now back off* scowl of a
woman on the prowl who had just had someone prettier than
her show up. I could have challenged that but declined. There
was no need to cause an incident with hotel staff. That meant
Melanie must have already gone to her room, or was still in
the van—which made sense since it was filled with weapons
and dynamite—because if she were here Mandy would be extra
grumpy at that level of perceived competition.

"How ya doin'?" Lizz asked as she limped forward. "I'm Lizz.
I made the reservations."

"Yes, I gave the keys to Justin," Mandy answered, seemingly
proud she was already on a first-name basis with the boys. "They
were so nice I even waived the two-dollar deposit for the keys."

"Two bucks?" I'd become a lot more sensitive about that kind
of thing since Ray had put me in charge of the team's budget.
"You should waive that because it's highway robbery. How much
are the rooms a night?"

"Doncha worry 'bout it," Lizz drawled, her strange accent
growing stronger. It only became pronounced when she was
irritated. "It's either this or camping."

Which was a terrible idea when there might be a werewolf in
the area. I turned back to the desk clerk. "You know anything
about the hiker who got killed?"

"He's not a local, you dig?" she replied, tearing her eyes off
of Justin for a second to respond. "He was from Los Angeles or
something, I didn't catch it. He was in Room 5. Nice enough guy."

"He was staying here?" I asked.

Mandy nodded. "Yeah. The sheriff took his stuff down to the station to wait for his family to come and pick it all up." She looked around conspiratorially. "Everybody in town is saying it was super awful, like they didn't even find all of him! And there were pieces everywhere. Gross."

"Anybody else checking him out?" Justin asked. "Maybe men in dark suits acting funny-like?"

"Nobody like that. Just you guys," the girl said, before she went back to fluttering her eyelashes at Alex. "So, you were telling me you're some kind of wildlife experts? Like on *Mutual of Omaha's Wild Kingdom*?"

"Something like that," Alex said, oblivious to how into him she was. Even though he had those surfer-boy good looks, he was such a nerd I doubted he'd had much experience with women.

While everybody else started moving bags to their rooms, Kimpton gestured me over to where he was studying the taxidermied mountain lion. It was an impressive specimen, and I had an affinity for cats. Hell, considering the bizarre proclivities of my father, we might even be distant cousins. *Very* distant.

"I grew up hunting these," Kimpton whispered. "They rarely attack people. Maybe if it had been a kid or something, they'd eat one. A full-grown man, though? Maybe mauled, but not eaten, and especially not torn apart like she said."

Lizz's guess was probably correct, then, and if there was a werewolf here, time was of the essence. "After we clean up and change into normal clothes, let's get down to the sheriff's station tonight and see if we can examine the body."

Mandy had overheard that. "Examine the body? Are you with the government?"

"No." I smiled. "*We* actually get things done."

In hindsight, we should have asked for directions. The winding, narrow streets around Lake Arrowhead were a virtual maze and more than once we found ourselves going the wrong way. Our flipbook map was good for the valleys but out here it was terribly out of date. My method of finding our way by getting lost worked much better in the city than out in the wilderness, but eventually we found the sheriff's station.

It was way past normal business hours, so the door was locked, but Deputy Kerr—"it's pronounced like *car*"—Arnold let us in. He didn't know who we were, just that his superiors had told him to help us out.

Deputy Arnold took us downstairs to a walk-out basement. The old, refurbished forestry service station had only been occupied by the San Bernardino sheriffs for a year or so. They had a new building under construction, but it wasn't due to be completed until next year. In the meantime, the sheriff's department had access to large chest freezers for body storage, courtesy of the national forestry service. Normally used for storing animal tissue samples, the largest of them now held the body of one Gerald Larson: avid hiker, photographer, and probable werewolf victim.

"Biggest damn cougar I've ever seen," the deputy said as Kimpton opened the freezer, revealing the sheet-draped lump inside.

Justin looked at the deputy curiously. "You seen it?"

We waited as Arnold coughed and looked slightly embarrassed. "Well, no," he admitted. "But wait until you see the claw marks. Bigger than a bear's paw. If it's a cougar, the thing is monstrous."

I pulled the sheet off, and right away I knew his declaring it *monstrous* was more accurate than he knew.

"Damn." Justin gave a low whistle. "That's nasty."

What was left of the body was a mess. Moving the tattered remains of the blood-caked flannel shirt aside, I leaned in and inspected the body. The wounds on the chest and abdomen, no mountain lion had ever had claws that far apart. There was too much damage to the ribs as well. Almost all of them appeared to be broken on his right side, giving him a very uneven look. That wasn't just clawing, that was striking with each claw having meat-cleaver-level concentrated force. His Levi's corduroy jeans were destroyed, and he was missing his hiking boots. The victim's knuckles were scuffed and coated in dried blood, like he hadn't gone down without a fight, which had probably just made the predator angry. A regular human being would never have a chance against a werewolf barehanded.

The poor guy's face had been partially ripped off. His throat was simply gone. Only the back part of his neck held his head onto his shoulders. Melanie had gone really grey in the face and had to look away, but to her credit, she didn't puke.

Vaya con dios. He'd died hard and if the killer hadn't been supernatural in nature, it might have been one hell of a fight. As it was, our deceased hadn't stood a chance. Werewolves were bastards like that. Tough, fast, regenerated like nobody's business, and would eat you afterward for caloric intake, and Gerald here was probably missing a third of his soft tissue. I vowed right then and there to never, ever end up in a werewolf's belly.

Me and Lizz shared a glance, and she gave me a grim nod. She'd dealt with werewolves before too, and we'd both come to the same conclusion about what we were dealing with here.

"Any missing persons cases around here recently?" I asked because random werewolf attacks didn't just happen. There was always a pattern to them. Werewolves didn't normally arrive in a new territory and immediately start killing lots of people. There would be killings corresponding to the cycle of the moon, mysterious deaths and disappearances, and even pets would be at risk.

Deputy Arnold seemed unsure why I was the one asking questions, but he answered, "Well, we've had a few hikers go missing over the years we never found, and a couple bear attacks here and there up on the peak—or at least that's what we chalked them up to, considering the state of decomposition when we found the bodies."

"Any unexplained murders?"

"We had a B&E turn into a double homicide about three years ago near Big Bear. It was pretty horrific. We backed up the substation in Big Bear for that one. There was blood everywhere. Never did find the perp."

That was potentially very bad news. Newly created werewolves tended to be angry and incautious. They'd do stupid things and tempt fate until someone like us found them and eliminated them. Most werewolves get hunted down within a few full moons of being turned. But werewolves who made it a few years past the change tended to be more cunning and careful, keeping a lid on their bloodthirsty ways, while hiding in plain sight. If that three-year-old murder was our werewolf's doing, then we were dealing with someone truly dangerous.

"Any missing pets?"

"You wouldn't believe how many people bring their tiny little toy dogs up here and then act surprised when something gets it." The deputy chuckled darkly. "We've got coyotes, bears, cougars, hawks, eagles, rattlers...all sorts of things which look at a chihuahua as nothing more than a midday snack."

"Big dogs, horses, livestock?"

"Oh yeah, we get complaints all the time. Animals, we just file a report and forget about it. Missing hikers, we always do a search party, and even call-in aviation units to assist, but sometimes people just vanish. That's how it is in the woods. Last month we had another cougar attack, but it wasn't nearly this bad. Animal attacks chase away tourists, so we were ordered to put it down. A few trackers came up but couldn't find anything. The dogs couldn't follow the scent, so we gave up after a week. It's been quiet until we found Mr. Larson here early this morning. He'd gone out to do a little midnight photography near the lake on the north shore. At least we know what happened to him. We've been having a string of bad luck with tourists getting lost and never found."

"For how long?" Justin asked. It was getting absurd. How did nobody catch any of this?

"I've been stationed here four years, so at least that long."

I tried not to sigh too heavily, because it sounded like there was a werewolf problem around Lake Arrowhead, one that had been brewing for years.

"The attack last month, what was the exact date?" I asked, wanting to know if it was during the full moon, because if a werewolf was transforming on other nights that was a bad sign it might be descending into insanity. "And how damaged was that corpse?"

"Well, on the date, I can't really recall. I'll have to go check the file. But there wasn't a corpse. The girl got bitten a few times, but she managed to run away. She spent a day in the hospital, but then they sent her home."

I pinched the bridge of my nose and tried not to let my frustration show. "Where's *home*, Deputy?"

"I'm not sure. It'll be in the file."

"If you don't mind, I'm going to need those." Not only did we have a live werewolf here in Lake Arrowhead, there was another potential one wandering around only God knew where. Were we dealing with a lone werewolf, as was the norm, or was this one trying to form a pack? That was a nightmare scenario. Nobody wanted to hunt down a pack of werewolves, especially when the leader was a wily older one. There was only one werewolf out there I knew of who wasn't a psycho killer, but Earl was an anomaly. If this werewolf was purposefully infecting others, it was going to cause a bloodbath.

"I'll get them for you."

"We've seen enough," I said, gesturing at the body. The sight disgusted me and pissed the *nagualii* off. It knew what had done this, and felt challenged.

Nodding, the Hunters carefully covered the dead man back up, trying to give him one last moment of dignity. The entire team remained silent until Alex gently closed the top of the chest freezer. I tried to not let my frustration bleed through onto the deputy. This was a death that could have been avoided, but it wasn't his fault. This was the direct result of the MCB forcing those in the know to keep the existence of monsters a secret. I was getting better at sensing my team's emotions, and all of them were agitated to varying degrees.

Back on the main floor of the sheriff's station, it was quiet save for the hum of the lights above. I noticed a large map that had been set on a portable display board near the far wall and went over to look at it. It was a map of the area around Lake Arrowhead. There were colored pins stuck in the map at various spots.

"What's this?"

"One of the other deputies is . . . well, he's an interesting guy. He's taken to tracking odd happenings around the area over the last few years. Deputy Black, Thomas Black. A bit of a nut, actually. Tinfoil-hat sort of guy, microwave brains and whatnot. Good cop, though. But he thinks this cougar has been stalking people and animals over the years. The same cougar, I mean. Like it's the Zodiac Killer. He claims he saw it once, up at the head of Goliath Trail. Only a glimpse, but said it was weird. It was really big for a cat, and looked dark brown, almost black in color . . . and he said some other stuff too, but I figure that was shadows playing tricks with his eyes or something."

There were a lot of pins, all over the place, and they were obviously color coded, but I didn't know what each color meant.

"Can we speak to Deputy Black?" Deputy Arnold seemed like an earnest enough fellow, but he struck me as kind of checked out. Most people simply weren't wired to think of implausible explanations. This map was the work of somebody fixated. Black had actually seen the beast, and you didn't put this much work into cataloging something if you really believed that thing had a reasonable explanation.

"I can call him," the deputy said dubiously. "Only it's his night off."

"If he's put this much work into tracking this thing," Kimpton interjected, "he won't mind getting called in the middle of the night to talk at us."

"Tell him we can pay him a consulting fee if he'd like, for his time." I'd make room in the budget for that.

"Hey, I helped consult too!" Deputy Arnold protested.

Lizz offered him a smile and patted his arm. "You're on duty, Deputy. Otherwise, you'd probably get a few dollars tossed your way."

"Well, that isn't fair," the deputy grumbled as he grabbed a phone from a nearby desk, then flipped through a Rolodex until he found the right number and began dialing.

"Tom? Hey, it's Kerr at the substation. Yeah, sorry to wake you, but headquarters sent some...uh...wildlife biologists or something here about your cougar, and they wanted to speak with you about—Five minutes? Uh, okay. See y—"

Deputy Arnold put the handset back in the cradle, clearly confused by whatever the other deputy had said before hanging up on him.

"He'll be right in?" I asked.

Deputy Arnold nodded slowly. "Yeah. He sounded...excited."

Precisely five minutes later, an old, beat-up pickup fairly skidded to a stop near the front door of the station. A burly, muscular man in jeans and a flannel shirt got out and hurried to the door, a large ring of keys in hand. He was in his forties and had a fantastic handlebar mustache that was almost certainly against department grooming regulations. He fumbled with the front door of the station for a moment before he managed to get the lock open.

"You here about the cougar?" the newly arrived deputy said without preamble. He stuck his hand out at Kimpton. "Tom Black."

"Kimpton Wall. Nice to meet you, but she's in charge." Kimpton sounded amused as he nodded in my direction after shaking the deputy's hand. "That's Chloe Mendoza."

He blinked and looked way down at me. "Oh."

I was unperturbed and used to it. Nobody ever expected the tiny woman who appeared to be in her twenties to be the boss. That came in handy sometimes. Others, not so much. "Nice map. Care to tell us about it?"

"Alright, Ms. Mendoza." I had to give him credit, because Deputy Black adapted well to the idea of a woman in charge and got right down to business. "I've been cataloging every incident that might involve this particular animal." He walked to the stand and began pointing to the pins stuck into it. "Blue ones are missing pets. Dogs, cats, stuff like that."

"That's a lot." Most of the pins were blue, but if there was a pattern there, I wasn't seeing it. "Yellow?"

"Those are the last known location of hikers and campers who've gone missing over the past five years." Deputy Black frowned. "Before then, we only had two people go missing over ten years, total, which isn't a bad ratio considering the number of people using the trails, our terrain, or the weather."

Alex seemed to be tallying up the yellow pins, and there were a lot of those. "Ever find any bodies?"

"A few. The ones with a string from a yellow pin to a red one are last known location and where the body was discovered."

"Cause of death on those?"

"Unknown. Lots of animals had been gnawing on them over the months before they were found, sometimes in places where they probably shouldn't have been able to walk or climb into."

"People do weird things under the effect of exposure," Deputy Arnold pointed out.

"Exposure don't make you lay down in streams, or climb through boulder fields wearing sandals, Kerr. And it sure don't make men jump off cliffs because they're more scared of what they're running away from than the fall."

"Come on, Tom. You don't want to get carried away about this again. You'll catch another suspension. The LT doesn't want to hear any more of your crazy talk."

Only I *wanted* to hear crazy talk. It was my favorite kind. This argument had clearly been going on for a few months. "Hey, Deputy Arnold, you've been a great help. Deputy Black can take care of us from here. We're sorry to have kept you from your regular duties."

"I was just manning the phones, is all."

"You should go back to doing that, then."

Thankfully, he took the hint and left us alone. Some people are just naturally incurious like that and willing to shut up and go along. They make the MCB's job easy.

"Deputy Arnold means well," Deputy Black explained after his colleague left. "They all do. Only I know there's something wrong in these woods now, and nobody wants to listen."

"We're listening now, Deputy," I assured him.

"You might not like to hear what I have to say, Ms. Mendoza."

"Just Chloe is fine."

"Tom." He extended his hand to shake, and it was so dry and calloused it was like picking up a leather boot.

Alex had begun tracing a pattern on the map with his fingertip. "Red pins are human remains, then?"

"That's correct." Tom nodded. "And who the hell are you people?"

"Consultants," Melanie said. "We're experts on wild animal attacks."

That line worked on vapid hotel night clerks, but not suspicious cops. "And I'm Elvis Presley. What're you? Eighteen?"

"Twenty-four." Melanie sniffed.

"The young ones are my grad students," Lizz said. "I'm Professor Yarborough."

"Sure you are. I've talked to every so-called predator expert at every university and zoo in California over the last year on my own dime. How come I've never heard of you?"

"Uh..." Lizz hadn't been ready for that.

I liked the fact that this guy was that dedicated to have done that amount of research. "What made you ask around about this particular cat?"

His eyes narrowed. "Because it ain't no cat. The thing I saw looked canine, not feline. Only there haven't been wild wolves in this part of California for fifty years."

"Level with me, Tom. The other deputy said when you saw it, you talked about it being abnormally large and the coloring being off, but that wasn't the crazy part that got your goat, was it?"

He mulled over revealing his secret. This was an expression that I'd seen before, from people who knew if they told the truth they'd get written off as nuts, but they were compelled to tell the truth anyway.

"It was taller than I am and ran away on its hind legs."

Well, that would certainly get someone's attention. And when none of us reacted to his words incredulously, it was obvious his suspicions deepened that we weren't normal wildlife experts.

"What's the Pinnacles?" Alex tapped an area to the northwest of Lake Arrowhead.

"Mountaintop rock formation. Popular with the city tourists. Lots of people park and camp up there."

"Pretty close to the Rock Camp Forest Station," Alex pointed out, a frown on his face. "What do you say? Maybe two, three miles across the terrain?"

"It's not impassable. There was a company which used to do hiking tours up that way. They'd start out at Route 173 and head north. Base camp there, then go hiking up to the Pinnacles. Not a long hike but it was good enough for the weekenders. They went out of business a few years back."

"What are you thinking?" I asked Alex, but he shook his head slowly.

"Can't explain it now," he said before looking to the deputy. "Is there any way I can borrow your map and the files on these bodies? We're staying at the lodge down by the lake."

"Hell no." He didn't appear so happy about Alex's request either. "This is my case."

Alex probably wanted to save the deputy a visit from the MCB, but I figured he was way past that now, and probably overdue for a visit from them to intimidate him into silence. "We borrow the map and you come with us. We have a van. We won't even have to disassemble the stand or anything. That way, you won't lose your pins. You got a rifle?"

Tom scoffed. "I'm a rural sheriff's deputy. What do you think?"

"Got anything chambered in .308?"

"That's oddly specific. Why?"

"That's the caliber we have for silver bullets."

Deputy Black stared at me for a really long time before saying, "I knew there was something off about this fucking thing, but not *that* off."

CHAPTER 6

We didn't get lost on the return from the substation because Tom showed us a faster way to get back to the lake. It was well after midnight and Mandy the flirtatious desk clerk was nowhere to be seen. I think the guys were a little saddened about that.

Once back at the lodge, we quickly set up the map in the boys' room. None of the pins had fallen out and everything looked like it had back at the station—though I'm almost certain if any had managed to come dislodged, Deputy Black would have remembered where they'd been. The room wasn't very big and had a pair of queen beds and a cot in it, so it was rather crowded. Also, it smelled bad, because even though everyone had showered before going to the substation, their beaver-stank-impregnated dirty clothing was piled on the bathroom floor.

Tom squinted at his map, trying to make sure everything was where it should be. The light in the room was okay, which meant the deputy was overdue for an eye exam. "Like I was telling you, ignoring the animal kills, and looking at just the missing people and bodies, it makes an oval."

"It's a forced concave," Justin agreed, joining Tom at the map. He pointed a finger at the ridges to the north and south. "It's an oval because of the rugged terrain. The valley here runs east to west. This other one is a little more skewed, but it fits."

"You can read a map good, but you don't strike me as country."

81

"Naw, Jack, I'm from Chicago. You spend time patrolling in Nam and you get real good at land nav, or else."

"I can respect that." Tom turned back to his map. "My working theory has been its den is somewhere in the middle, and it ranges out to hunt. The rugged terrain is why there's no witnesses. I bet the lair's up near here somewhere."

"Do you know the area?" I asked.

"Like the back of my hand. The rest of the guys really think I'm into camping, but truth be told I kinda hate sleeping on the ground. It kills my back. But ever since I saw that thing it's haunted me, so I've gone up there every chance I get to scout around. I know every trail now. I've gone in with pack horses for weeks at a time. It's eaten up all my vacation for the last few years."

"Your wife okay with that?" Kimpton quipped.

"She divorced me."

"Oh . . . Sorry."

"Don't be. She was powerfully ugly."

With all that time searching for something that he didn't comprehend, and really wasn't prepared to face, Tom was really lucky he'd not gotten eaten. "The problem is, you were thinking about it like a natural creature. If we're right about this being a werewolf, its lair is probably a house here in town, and it looks like a normal man or woman, until it's time to hunt."

Tom took his time processing what I'd said. "Alrighty, then."

He seemed to take that in stride, so I continued. "I'm not absolutely certain it's a werewolf we're dealing with, though. We've got to keep in mind the possibility it could be something else entirely, like a skinwalker. Area's right for one."

"Jeez, I hope not," Lizz said. "Those things scare me."

"Worse than a . . . *werewolf*?" Tom asked, disbelieving.

"Ayup."

"The timing of the disappearances mostly correlate to the full moon." Alex was sitting on the bed, flipping through the selected case files. "That, and the state of the bodies"—he paused to cringe at a Polaroid of a crime scene—"suggests lycanthrope."

"Lycanthrope?" Tom asked.

"You know anybody local who vanishes for three nights a month, then appears like they've lost a lot of weight after every full moon?"

"No one springs to mind, but I can't say I was on the look-out for that."

Melanie had been going through the files too, and she caught my attention and gave one of the papers a little wave. That meant she'd fulfilled my whispered instructions before we'd left the sub-station. That would be the contact information on last month's attack survivor. Because if she'd been bitten and infected, she'd be changing this full moon. I gave Melanie a little nod and she got off the bed. "Excuse me for a minute. I've got to make a phone call."

Tom didn't even notice her go. "Alright, we need to talk about this whole werewolf thing. Mostly, because, well, werewolves aren't supposed to be real."

"They're real," Kimpton stated.

"Yeah, brother." Justin nodded in agreement. "Real danger-ous too."

"You've seen a werewolf?"

The newbies hadn't, but I raised my hand. "Seen them and shot them." Also was friendly-ish with one, and he'd saved my life and given me a job, but I left that part off, not just for Tom, but for the rest of the team, because Earl liked to keep his secrets even more than I did.

"I hold the all-time company record for the long-range were-wolf kill." Lizz really was proud of that.

"What company?" Tom asked.

"PUFF on werewolves is *nice*," Alex snuck that comment in.

"What's a puff?"

"Look," I cut Tom off brusquely. It was getting late, and frankly I was exhausted. The *nagualii* was really pushing at me. It wanted out, to hunt this so-called predator and show it who was boss. "I know you've got a lot of questions, but you'll just have to be patient and we'll explain everything in more detail tomorrow. It's been a really long day for us."

"We had to wrangle a giant beaver this afternoon," Kimpton said, perfectly deadpan.

"Long story short, we're professional monster hunters. And I mean literal monsters. You know, the kind you hear about in hor-ror stories? Only, you can't go around talking about those things existing because certain elements of the federal government will shoot you if you do. Deputy Arnold said you were a conspiracy nut? Well, this is one of those conspiracies that turns out to be true. Put on your tinfoil hat and buckle up."

Dawn was beautiful in the morning up in the mountains of California. The smog was nonexistent, and the air was filled with the scent of pine. The waters of Lake Arrowhead were still, with just a few wisps of fog drifting up from the surface. It was peaceful, tranquility defined.

It was immediately shattered when Deputy Arnold showed up at the small, family-owned restaurant where Lizz and I had just sat down and ordered breakfast. He was pale and sweating.

"There was another attack last night," the deputy said without preamble, pulling up a seat at the table. "I'm about to head off-shift. The sarge told me to come and let you know. Also, he's pissed off. You people were supposed to be hunting this cougar, not spending a night at the best lodge in town."

This was not the same jovial individual we'd met the night before. I signaled for the waitress to bring him a cup of coffee.

He lowered his voice to a whisper to not scare the other diners. "I just left there. I don't know how it smashed through the front door." Deputy Arnold's hands shaking. "Haven't seen that much blood...didn't know people could have so much."

"Multiple victims this time?"

"Father and daughter."

"Where?"

"North end of town. Outskirts. One of the older homes near Route 143."

"It's getting bolder." Lizz seemed unperturbed, stirring milk and sugar into her coffee. "You say it busted through the front door?"

"Yeah," Deputy Arnold nodded as the waitress poured him a cup. He managed to spoon two scoops of sugar into it without making too much of a mess. He waited for the waitress to leave, before adding, "The inside of the house is destroyed. There's fucking blood on the *ceiling*. How did it get on the ceiling?"

"Who're the victims?" Lizz asked.

"Ronnie and Mandy Calhoun." Deputy Arnold took a sip of coffee. Or tried to, rather, but his hands were shaking too much to drink without spilling. "Pretty young thing. What a waste."

"Mandy. Did she work at the lodge?"

"Yeah, nights."

I winced. That meant we were probably some of the last people to see her alive. She must have gotten off work, gone home, and gotten killed soon after.

"Did you tell Tom?"

"We called out everybody. He's on the way over. There were pieces everywhere!"

"Deputy?" Lizz stopped stirring her coffee. She reached out and touched his hand. Concern was etched deeply on her features. "Deputy Arnold? Did the sergeant tell you to go home?"

"He said to bring you to the scene. Then...I forget."

"Then you're off duty?"

"I think—yes," Deputy Arnold said, nodding slowly.

"Okay, tell you what," Lizz said, standing up carefully and helping him do the same. "Do you have a wife, girlfriend, or a roommate?"

"No. Why?"

"It's nice to have people around when you decompress. Which I can see you need to do. We'll gather the rest of our team and find our own way to the scene."

"Take the main road around the lake west, then right at the second stop sign. There's a lot of squad cars out front so you can't miss it."

"Do you have duty tomorrow?"

"No."

"Good, good." Lizz continued to nod. "Then I'd recommend you proceed to get rip-roaring drunk, until you puke your guts out in your toilet, and then pass out and not have any bad dreams."

"But I don't drink."

"No butts, mister. I'd go light on breakfast if I were you. No point in paying a lot of money for something you're probably going to upchuck later."

Lizz guided him out the door and back to his car. I was starting to suspect that Lizz wasn't in this business because of the nice paycheck, but rather because she genuinely cared about people.

"Mandy seemed like a lovely young woman," Lizz said after returning and sliding back into our booth. "It *is* a waste."

It was also a slap in the face. Any Hunter worth their salt was offended whenever innocents got hurt by the forces of evil, but when it was someone you knew, even in brief passing, that was extra galling. It made you feel guilty, like you should have been able to prevent it somehow. Except that was a pointless path to go down.

"It's escalating." I took a drink of my coffee. "They've documented this before. Werewolves will get into a bloodlust spiral, and it'll just get worse and worse until they're put down."

"Even the monsters who learn how to pass for human for a while eventually lose it and go psycho at some point," Lizz said.

"Not all of them," I snapped.

"Well, ain't *you* disagreeable before breakfast."

The waitress was bringing our food out to us, and the boys and Melanie were out shopping for supplies and wouldn't be back for a few minutes, so I dug in with gusto. I mean, might as well not let a perfectly good stack of pancakes go to waste. We were about to go examine a murder scene, but I'd seen some crazy, horrific things while in the Middle East. What was a single werewolf attack compared to that?

Syrup burns when coming back up. Especially when it's mixed with pancakes and coffee.

"Shit." I spit the last little bit of stomach acid, coffee, boysenberry, and pancake from my mouth. I would never be able to eat either ever again. Just the thought of food caused my stomach to roil dangerously.

"You okay?" Alex asked as he knelt down next to me. He'd gone inside and looked green around the gills as well. Luckily all he'd eaten beforehand was a piece of toast.

"That's..." My voice trailed off. In all my years I had never seen such carnage. It would haunt me forever. I took a deep, shuddering breath and steadied myself. I was a Monster Hunter, and the most experienced one here, damn it, so I steadied my tone. "I've seen worse."

I was lying, of course. I'd never seen anything like that. Mr. Calhoun had been ripped to pieces by the werewolf. There had been entrails dangling from the cheap light fixture in the living room. The ceiling was over fifteen feet high. I had no idea how they had even gotten up there. Had the werewolf tossed them into the air like a child throwing confetti?

It had just gotten worse from there, like he'd played with the body like a dog with a chew toy. I shuddered at the memory as a fresh wave of nausea tore through me.

The worst part was the smell. It wasn't the coppery tang of blood that had gotten me sick, but the musky scent of a werewolf marking his territory. The others had smelled it too, but they weren't the ones with supernatural senses. To me it had been extra pungent and offensive. This werewolf was no juvenile. This was his territory and he wanted the world to know it. The stench was powerful enough to give the *nagualii* pause.

"What do we do now?" Justin asked from the doorway. One quick peek inside had been more than enough for him. *Smart.*

Standing up, I looked at the shattered door, and spit a final time. "We kill this fucker."

Melanie appeared from around the front of the house, walking across the Calhouns' scraggly lawn, and she got a distressed look on her face when she saw that I'd been throwing up. I kicked myself for showing weakness in front of the newbies. I was supposed to be the example.

"Sorry, Chloe. The other body is on the side of the road." She looked toward the darkened house. "Is it that bad in there?"

"Oh yeah," Alex said. "I'd skip it if I were you."

I walked to where the deputies were taking pictures and putting up yellow tape in the front of the house. Normally we wouldn't have access to a crime scene like this, but they'd all be given the same story about my team being wildlife biologists, so we got a pass.

Tom Black was standing there looking downright weary. A big part of that was probably because people didn't sleep very good after somebody dropped a bomb on them like werewolves being real. I'd warned him not to tell anyone about what we'd talked about last night, and since his fellow deputies weren't sending him to the looney bin, he'd listened.

"The paperboy spotted her this morning and called us."

Thankfully, her body appeared to be in far better shape. "May I?"

Tom gestured for the other deputies to get out of my way. "From the blood trail, she got injured inside, probably in the kitchen, but it's hard to sort out because...well..."

"I was just in there. I know."

"Then she ran for it and made it to the road before she fell, probably from the blood loss. She managed to crawl a bit farther before passing out."

I squatted next to Mandy. The poor girl was still dressed like we'd last seen her, complete with name tag, and it was obviously she'd died terrified. She'd been bitten on one arm and her shoulder... The wounds were savage, but compared to what I'd seen in the house, this was downright rational in comparison.

And that damned smell was all over this spot. The werewolf had followed her out here and sniffed around her as she'd crawled across the gravel. He easily could have finished her off, but he'd only bit her and then left it to nature to decide her fate. The werewolf had taken his fury out on the male. That one he'd wanted dead. The female he hadn't. If he'd been a little more careful, a little less brutal, she wouldn't have bled out, but would have lived... infected with lycanthropy.

"Tom, was the victim who got bit but escaped last month pretty?"

"Very much so. Why?"

"We've got big problems."

"No shit, lady. We've got three bodies in two nights," said another one of the deputies. "Some cat expert."

He had no idea. I stood up and started walking rapidly back toward the van, signaling for the team to gather up. We had work to do.

Tom hurried after me. "What's going on?"

"The werewolf is recruiting a pack."

Melanie Simmons surprised—and impressed—the hell out of me.

I'd been on the fence about how suitable she was for this job. Sure, she was smart, but she also struck me as a gentle soul and something of a bleeding heart who always assumed the best in others. In normal society, those were fine traits, except our business depended on us being able to dish out sudden, unrelenting violence with zero hesitation. In training, whenever I'd brought up some new kind of monster, if its evil nature wasn't painfully, glaringly obvious, she had always been the one to wonder if maybe there wasn't some better way to deal with it than just shooting it and collecting the bounty.

Looking back, I think honestly part of my original problem with her was that asking questions like that reminded me too much of the questions the Shacklefords had asked before deciding to spare my life, and I didn't like putting myself in the same category as the nasty things I'd been teaching about . . . which really did deserve whatever Hunters could inflict on them.

Even among my own kind, I was an oddity. Just like Earl was an oddity among werewolves. The vicious killer we were hunting now? *That* was werewolf normal. That was what we needed Hunters to expect. There was no room for kindness or wishful thinking with most of the things we dealt with, and hesitating to pull the trigger in case you'd found the one-in-a-million civilized one was a great way for Hunters to get killed.

I was already responsible for the death of a couple of teammates. I couldn't bear to be the reason for any more. Which was probably why Melanie's Pollyanna nature had rubbed me the wrong way.

Except once I explained to the team my theory that this werewolf had—for whatever reason—decided to start building a pack of his own, and that he had a type—beautiful young women—Melanie had immediately suggested her plan.

"Use me as bait."

"What?"

"Use me as *bait*."

The rest of us shared a nervous look.

"You crazy?" Justin asked.

"This sicko wants a werewolf harem. Use me to draw him out."

"She's definitely nuts," Kimpton agreed. "No way."

"He likes pretty young girls. I'm a pretty young girl." Nobody here could disagree with that obvious fact. Even I had to admit Melanie was a knockout.

"Girl, you're a stone-cold fox," Justin said.

"Thank you."

"And you've lost your damned mind wanting to be werewolf bait."

"Hear me out. Assuming he's a local, I'll put on a cute outfit and go around town today talking about where my campsite is. His last pick died. He'll be looking for a replacement."

"So we parade you around like a piece of meat and hope a supernatural killer shows up to try and bite you?" I snorted. "Brilliant."

"We've only got one more day of the full moon to try and catch him, then we've got to wait a month. And he's been careful up until recently. He might decide all these killings have drawn too much attention and move to a new territory. Tonight is our only shot. And you taught us yourself that when werewolves get ramped up like this, the killings just get worse. He's going after someone tonight. It might as well be someone prepared."

Immediately, Justin, Alex, and Kimpton started arguing with her about how incredibly stupid and dangerous that was. Tom was still too confused to have an opinion, but he struck me as an honorable old-school cowboy sort, so once he caught up he probably wouldn't like the idea much either.

Except everything Melanie said had been on point. I couldn't take her place. I was no slouch in the looks department, but there was the very real possibility the werewolf's superior senses would recognize me for what I really was, and then he'd know it was a trap. *Nagualii* and other shapeshifters tended to avoid each other.

"When you go camping by yourself with a werewolf on the loose, do you want us to put a stake in the ground and tie you up to it, like we're sacrificing a goat?" Lizz clearly wasn't impressed with the idea. "I'd volunteer but I'm old and I don't get the impression he's into short chicks."

"Lizz, did you bring that scope that can see in the dark for your rifle?"

"Of course I did, Chloe. I don't leave home without it."

"You got night vision, Lizz?" Justin was surprised. "That's some high-tech shit right there."

"I picked up an AN/PVS-2B scope back in St. Louis. It'll work well enough in bright moonlight."

"How the hell you get your hands on one of those? We couldn't even get them in Nam."

"Oh, it fell off the back of a truck and I found it in an alley, y'know?"

"Good," I said. "Then we'll pick a spot where Lizz can be on the high ground watching Melanie's campsite, which needs to be in a clearing so we can observe the approach. The rest of us will have to hold back far enough he doesn't sense us."

"Hold up a second," Kimpton said to me. "You can't be serious about going through with this."

"I'm dead serious." And if anyone doubted me, I'd send them into that house to look around to decide for themselves if it was worth it, because I wasn't about to let that happen again on my watch. "You can be chivalrous all you want but everything the damsel volunteering for distress just said is right. If we don't catch him tonight, we might lose him. He could even calm back down after this full moon passes. The murder frenzy would be over, but he'd go back to killing a couple hikers or two a year for who knows how long until we catch him. Or worse, he moves on, and is successful infecting others and we won't know about it until there's a pack of them to deal with."

"The Pinnacles," Tom suggested. "I know a few spots up there that are perfect for what you're talking about. They're in his preferred hunting grounds, and there's some rock formations downwind we could hide in. You got radios so she can call us for backup?"

"We do. And an expert on werewolves taught us that a little wolfsbane on your person can help mask your scent from them."

"I thought you were the experts?"

"Not compared to this guy." And unlike the human experts, Earl didn't have to guess about what worked. "Werewolves can still smell its presence. It just messes with their noses, so he might get suspicious that someone is using it to sneak up on him."

"I think we'll be okay," Alex said. "Wolfsbane, or monks-hood, is officially known as Acontium, and grows naturally in the mountain valleys of California."

"You are such a dork," Melanie said. "Like, the king of dorks."

"Seriously. He should go on that *Jeopardy!* show," Justin added. "We get home, somebody dial up Art Fleming."

Alex shrugged. "I remember what I read. So unless Encyclopedia Britannica is lying, there should be wolfsbane in the air here anyway."

"This is a small town. Everybody's already talking about the last murder. I'd tell the boys to keep it secret, but word will get out about these two new ones no matter what," Tom said. "It won't make no sense for one young lady to be off camping by herself if she knows a wild animal is on the loose."

"That's suspicious, anyway," Kimpton pointed out. "Let me go with her and pretend to be her boyfriend."

Melanie laughed. "Oh, I'd bet you'd like that."

"Hey, I said *pretend*. I'm not making a play. But if we're together in town I can talk a big game about how I'm not scared of no mountain lion, baby, you're safe with me, I'll protect you, that sort of thing. Let the werewolf think I'm dumb and cocky."

Kimpton struck me as kind of quiet and humble, though. War changes people, and I had a feeling that in Kimpton's case, it had left him a lot more reserved and untrusting. "Can you pull off a convincing swagger, farm boy?"

"You're looking at the 1967 Montana state-champion football team's starting quarterback. I think I can remember how to do cocky."

"An extra person might scare the werewolf off, though," Lizz said.

I didn't think so. Lizz hadn't seen the inside of that house. If anything, the presence of another male would probably provoke our werewolf to even greater anger, which hopefully would make him reckless. "When the werewolf strikes, it'll probably be lightning fast, and he'll probably take out what he perceives as the biggest threat first. That'll be you."

"I know," Kimpton answered. "But two sets of eyes are better than one."

I mulled it over, and even though we'd just put in a lot more thought than Marco had for his *just grab the giant beaver* plan, I still wished he was here and calling the shots, because I really didn't like this sudden weight on my shoulders. I was about to send two newbies into serious danger.

"Alright . . . but there's one last thing everybody here needs to come to terms with. This is a werewolf we're dealing with. You might get killed. But worse, if you get bitten, you're going to be infected." Earl had told me that occasionally a werewolf tried to resist the descent into madness and evil, but overwhelmingly they were doomed to failure, and the most merciful thing to do for them was provide a quick death via silver bullet. "There's no cure. There's no coming back. It's a nightmare, and you can count on the fingers of one hand how many werewolves in the history of the world didn't turn into baby-eating killing machines who would make Charlie Manson blush."

"I don't want to go out like that, no siree," Lizz said.

"Don't worry, blood." Justin thumped Kimpton on the back. "If you turn, I'll cap you."

"Thanks, bud. Real comforting."

That was it. We had the bones of a plan. The rest was just details. I handed out assignments and we went to work.

As Melanie and I were walking to my car, she said, "Thanks for trusting me, Chloe. I won't let you down."

"My approval is the *last* thing you need to be worried about right now."

Late that night I was lying on a pile of rocks, looking down at Melanie and Kimpton's campfire. Lizz was a few feet away with a Winchester Model 70 with a starlight scope mounted on it. The gigantic tube was heavy and awkward, but it was a nifty invention that magnified ambient light. It wouldn't work in the pitch black, but on a night like this, with a brilliant white moon overhead, Lizz could basically see in the dark.

So could I, and I did it without the miracles of modern technology. Only that wasn't the sort of thing you bragged about to your fully human coworkers. I avoided doing my cat-eye trick most of the time, because my eyes went from brown to a brilliant turquoise color and my pupils became vertical slits of gold. That's the sort of thing people notice, except right now it was worth the risk, and it wasn't like anyone was going to point a flashlight my way anytime soon.

Lizz hadn't made a sound for hours. The change was eerie. Normally, the tiny woman would talk your ear off, but when she went into huntress mode, she became so perfectly quiet and still that occasionally I wondered if she was still alive. Every once in a while she'd move enough to unkink some muscle or to keep a limb from falling asleep, but she always managed to do it in time with the breeze so the noise wouldn't be noticed.

Despite her telling me that this was no big deal, and she'd done this sort of thing many times, Lizz had to be feeling the pressure. I knew I was. To those kids down there we were their eyes, early warning system, and best hope for survival.

Justin, Alex, and Tom were hidden among the boulders below us. As soon as Liz fired, they'd run straight toward the camp. They were all armed with rifles with powerful flashlights taped under their barrels, and which were loaded with some of MHI's rare and precious silver bullets.

Melanie and Kimpton sat next to the fire, by the blue-and-white tent and a cooler full of beers they'd bought in town today. It turned out Kimpton played the guitar, and decently too. He'd bought one of those too, telling me that it was necessary for the act, so he'd need MHI to reimburse him. I told him if he lived through the night, I'd be happy to.

I could hear him singing from a long way off, but more importantly, so would the werewolf. And it wasn't like the extra noise was going to cover up the approach. You could only hear a stalking werewolf when it wanted you to, especially one this experienced. Kimpton's repertoire consisted mostly of Merle Haggard and Marty Robbins songs. The two of them did a pretty good rendition of "A White Sport Coat and a Pink Carnation." If they didn't get eaten, they could take that show on the road.

So with wolfsbane in our pockets and rifles in hand, we waited, nervous, hoping our werewolf would show, while a tiny-frightened part of me fervently wished it wouldn't. I wanted to kill this werewolf, and then my team could drink that cooler full of beers in celebration, but at the same time I was scared. Mostly for Melanie and Kimpton, but also for the rest of us. Werewolves are unpredictable. If things went wrong the whole team could die out here. Well, except for Rhino, who was still in the hospital, but I bet he'd feel really bad about it.

Hours passed. I couldn't even say how many because moving enough to look at my watch might make too much noise. They got tired of singing, and now Kimpton and Melanie were just talking. They made a convincing couple.

Even with my magic eyes, it was Lizz's science fiction gadget that spotted the werewolf first. I knew something was going on because I could actually hear Lizz suddenly take a breath. I looked in the direction her muzzle was pointed, and sure enough, a shadow was moving through the grass, hunched low and skulking toward the camp. From two hundred yards away, the only thing I could tell was that it was too big to be a deer, and it sure wasn't moving like a person.

Tom had picked the perfect spot for our trap. The werewolf would have no choice but to cross fifty yards of mostly open grass before he could get in striking range. There were no trees big enough to hide it from a bullet.

Lizz slowly, gently, clicked off her rifle's safety.

Suddenly, the shadow stood upright and ran toward the camp. The werewolf was impatient, eager for blood. Lizz now had a moving target.

She exhaled and squeezed the trigger. The Winchester barked.

The shadow spun sideways, but it was still headed toward the camp.

Lizz calmly reached up and worked the bolt, ejecting the case and feeding another silver round into the chamber.

I jumped up and started running downhill.

Kimpton and Melanie had been amped up for hours, and they reacted the instant the sound of the gunshot reached their ears, reaching under their blankets to pull out the shotguns Rhino had left in his van. They knew Lizz was shooting, but not where.

Then the werewolf entered their firelight.

It was tall and lean, with disproportionately long limbs that ended in terrible claws. Its shaggy, canine head was aimed straight at Kimpton as it lurched toward him.

Lizz hit it again.

Then Melanie and Kimpton were firing like crazy, but I was leaping down boulders and lost sight of the action. The boys were leaving their hiding places, dressed in camouflage, faces painted, and turning on their big flashlights as I rushed past them. I was running as fast as I could, which by human standards was incredibly quick. I crossed the scrub-covered ground in no time, heading straight for the campfire, as the flashlights bobbed along behind me.

When I got there, Melanie and Kimpton were standing, shotguns shouldered, still aimed at where the werewolf had been standing a moment ago. Blood had been splattered all over their tent, but none of it appeared to be theirs.

"It went that way," Kimpton said, gesturing with the muzzle of his Browning Auto 5.

I spotted it moving toward the trees and gave chase. A second later, one of the flashlights swung that way, and I heard Tom say, "Dear sweet Jesus," when it revealed the running werewolf to the rest of them for a split second.

There was a lot of blood on the grass. So much I could follow this wet trail in the dark. It was hurt bad, and unlike regular bullets, a werewolf's regenerative powers wouldn't work on silver. He wouldn't be going far. I let my eyes return to normal so my team wouldn't see them glowing in the dark.

Even though everyone was excited, I shouted for them to slow down. The blood loss meant time was on our side, and the last thing we needed to do was to chase stupidly, only to have him be waiting in ambush, or circle around behind us to pick someone off. I turned on my flashlight and took point.

The werewolf only made it another hundred yards running on fear and adrenaline before he fell the first time. There was an obvious spot in the mud where he had gone down, and claw marks where he had used a tree to pull itself back up. This creature had been so careful that it had avoided leaving any tracks for Tom to find for years, but in his haste, the tracks he was leaving were a frightening composite of wolf and man. He had fallen again, going downhill, and had left a long blood smear and clawed handprint on the rock. The run had turned into a stagger, and now he was on his hands and knees.

I spotted the werewolf at the edge of a stream, panting, dying, already reverting back to human form, as mortally wounded werewolves tended to do before they expired. That made covering up their corpses convenient for the MCB a lot of the time.

We approached cautiously, guns up. He looked toward us and snarled, but the bones of his face were already melting and twisting, revealing hints of the human inside.

Melanie aimed her shotgun, but I put my hand on the warm barrel and gently shoved it down. "Silver's expensive. He's done."

Very few human beings ever got to see this kind of transformation and live to tell the tale, so my team watched, transfixed, as the werewolf gradually shrank into a thin, grey-haired man. Claws crawled back beneath fingernails. Bones cracked. Teeth contracted. And now he was just bloody, naked, and pathetic.

He reached down and touched the pattern of weeping buckshot holes in his side and cried out in pain as the silver pellets sizzled. There was a bullet hole through his shoulder and the way it was leaking, Lizz had severed his subclavian artery. A human being would have dropped in seconds, but werewolves were incredibly resilient.

"I recognize him. I don't know his name, but I've seen him around town." Tom suddenly shouted at the werewolf, "Why? Why'd you have to hurt all those folks?"

"There's not going to be a good answer," I told him.

Except then the werewolf surprised me, because I'd figured he was way past being able to speak. "I only wanted to be left alone, but then *she* appeared, three moons ago, commanding me to grow my family. To bring her an army. I was loyal. I did what I was told."

Curious. "Who told you this?"

"The one who'll make you pay."

And then the werewolf sank into the muddy bank and died.

Silver was expensive, but I liked to be certain. "Hey, Justin, hand me your machete."

There was one last thing to do before leaving Lake Arrowhead, and that was have a sitdown with Deputy Thomas Black. Neither of us had slept much the night before, especially after we had taken tissue samples to send to the MCB for our PUFF bounty payment and buried our dead werewolf in an unmarked grave in the forest. When I had finally turned in to catch a couple of hours of sleep, Tom had still been busy reporting to his superiors that the *wildlife consultants* they'd sent had worked out and Lake Arrowhead's killer cougar problem had been taken care of.

He looked exhausted now, sitting across from me in the little diner, but also happier than I'd ever seen him before. Finding out that you weren't crazy was a good feeling.

"So what're you MHI people gonna do now?"

"Head back to LA. Get back to work. The victim who lived, her name is Nicole Varney. The file said she's a student at the University of Southern California and lives on campus."

"Yeah, I interviewed her in the hospital. Nice girl."

That made this so much worse. "I had Melanie call and try to get ahold of her. Nobody's seen her for a few days."

"Oh..." He took a drink of his coffee. "So this werewolf business begins again?"

"Maybe. Maybe not. We don't know if she's infected. She might be lucky." I wouldn't get my hopes up, but there was nothing wrong with letting someone else have that luxury. It was out of his jurisdiction. "We'll look into it."

"Let me know if you need any help again."

I'd already given him the speech about what the Monster Control Bureau would do to him if he ever talked about any of this, but it never hurt to give a reminder. "Remember, none of this ever happened."

"Or G-men will put me in a crazy house, or make sure I have an accident?"

"I'm not laughing. You think you've seen real evil because of your job, and I'm not saying you haven't, but trust me when I say there's a whole world of incomprehensible bad shit out there you really don't want to know about..." I pulled a business card out and slid it across the table to him. "And this is for if you decide you do."

He picked up the card. "What's this?"

"The number on front is our company headquarters, if you ever decide you want to change careers. Our hiring pool is limited to people who know monsters are real, and I think you'd be pretty good at this."

"I didn't do much."

"You did what you could, with what you had, and when the truth came out you dealt with it. That's a rarer skill than you realize."

He stroked his rather impressive mustache. "Well, if you have some problems come up and you need some extra hands, you know somebody who can help without needing a lot of explanations first."

"I might take you up on that. The number written on back of that card is our office in Pasadena if you ever have any other... wildlife problems."

"I'll keep that in mind." Tom took the card and put it in the pocket of his flannel shirt. "Only, I'm content here. I like my job. Though I might take some time off."

"What're you going to do?"

"Anything but camping."

CHAPTER 7

I woke up in a cold sweat.

The nightmare was already fading. Smoking obsidian, and a jaguar who had been whispering secrets to me from across still black waters. Whispering, wanting, pushing me to accept what I am, what I'm meant to be. My lineage and my inheritance. The steady beating of my heart replaced the sound of the *huehuetl*.

The *nagualii* was pressuring me more and more since we'd arrived in Southern California. I really needed to ask Earl how he handled his curse. Werewolves were supposed to be crazier than my kind, yet his self-control was enviable, which pissed me off. I'd had a long time to practice and yet I was nowhere near where he was. There had to be a way to get the damn thing inside to listen to what I wanted.

My bedroom was pitch black because I'd put up really thick curtains. Hunters often worked odd hours and the darkness helped me sleep during the day. I lay there on top of my sheets, breathing hard and listening for danger, but the house was quiet.

I'd just had the same kind of dream that had been plaguing me back in Israel. Every one of those I'd woken up with a sense of unease and a feeling that I needed to go back to America. I'd ignored those promptings, and two good men had died because of it.

Only there was no new prompting now. I felt like I was where

I needed to be, except I felt more anxious than ever before, like something bad was coming. Or something bad was already here.

A figure was standing in the corner.

I always kept a Browning Hi-Power on my nightstand, but by the time I grabbed it, I realized the shape had been a figure of my imagination, merely the last bits of a fading dream. The steel grip in my hand helped bring me back to reality. And thankfully I came to before I put a 9mm bullet through my closet.

Greetings from the Court, child.

The thing in the corner was a fragment of my dream, but that didn't make it any less real.

Damn it. It had been a very long time since I'd dealt with one of the Court's heralds. This one in particular grated on both the *nagualii* and me. "What do you want?"

I bring a gift, and a warning from our great king.

"Old feather snake isn't my king." Not that it would do any good, but I kept the pistol pointed at the shadow, which had now taken on a shape that was vaguely a bird of prey, perched and waiting. I resisted the urge to look at the herald with *nagualii* eyes to see its true form, because it wasn't of this world, and what was seen couldn't be unseen. "I want nothing to do with your kind."

That is your choice. We shall abide.

The bird thing began to fade away, except curiosity got the better of me. The Court's power had waned even in the heart of what once been their empire on Earth. They wouldn't send one of their minions here for nothing. I hoped.

"A warning about what?"

The image slammed into my head so violently that I gasped as it was burned into my mind. Bodies everywhere, rivers of blood, and a red sky filled with winged creatures out of a gibbering nightmare. A maelstrom of death and destruction of what once was the City of Angels. Everything was on fire, a raging inferno with no end in sight.

This is what may be, but what is not yet certain.

Horrified, I tried to push the image away.

The herald seemed amused by my discomfort. Bastard.

That is the warning.

"What's the cause of this?"

She is coming.

"Who? When?"

You have forsaken the Court. To be given such advantage over your enemies, you must freely accept us once more, and only then will we come to your aid.

That wasn't going to happen, and I knew that the Court of Feathers had never considered rivers of blood and piles of corpses to be a bad thing, provided those sacrifices had been made in their honor. "Is she your competition? Why do you even care what happens to this city?"

The Court is above mortal concerns. Our reasons are our own.

"Does my father have something to do with this?"

The usurper remains imprisoned for his treachery. I will consider him no further.

I really was tempted to shoot the messenger, but I didn't know anything about fixing drywall. "Leave me alone."

Our great king has commanded I leave you with this gift, a sign to guide your hunt for this dark master.

A moment of perfect clarity took over. In the darkness, small lights appeared. They spun lazily around, dancing upon the walls, floor, and ceiling. There was a rhythmic beating of a drum in the background. Looking up at the ceiling, there was a new vision far different from the last, spinning and glittering under the constant bombardment of a single light.

It was a slowly spinning disco ball.

The vision faded. The herald was gone.

Seven adults living in a converted warehouse was not comfortable, so I'd rented a cute little house next to the local community college that was walking distance from our HQ as soon as I could. Melanie had family in Monterey Park and was staying with them. Lizz had gotten a place of her own too. Rhino, Justin, Alex, and Kimpton were still living at HQ like it was a frat house, mostly because it was free, but I was going to have to put my foot down and tell them that couldn't last because they couldn't be picking up girls at bars and bringing them back to what was basically a barracks filled with various top secret and/or illegal things without that causing some problems. Not that any of the young guys were going to bring their hookups around Rhino, especially since he was extra surly since he'd broken his leg.

It had been quiet for a few days after we had got back from

Lake Arrowhead. We'd had no luck finding the werewolf's previous victim, Nicole Varney, but on the bright side there hadn't been any unexplained brutal murders in LA during the full moon. Sure, there'd been brutal murders—this was Los Angeles, after all—but they were all *normal* murders. And we couldn't find anything about bodies that looked like they had gotten ripped apart by a pack of wild dogs or anything like that. Some of the first people we had schmoozed and bribed once we'd gotten to town had been the local coroners. They were a great source for tips on potential monster activity.

I filed the Treasury paperwork on our werewolf kill—the PUFF forms had been way less complicated back in the 1940s—and I'd had no choice but to call the MCB and tell them there was a potential new werewolf on the loose. Doing so made me sick, because if the poor girl wasn't infected at minimum the government would make her life miserable and detain her until her blood tests came back negative, but if she was they had more resources than we did and were more likely to find her before she did something awful.

Of course the MCB Agent who answered the phone was rude, but took my information down, promised it would be looked into, and then got defensive when I asked how come the MCB hadn't caught on that the rash of *cougar attacks* at Lake Arrowhead weren't normal and what were they doing with all that tax money anyway? I got hung up on, but at least I'd done my civic duty...not that I'd actually paid taxes in America since Roosevelt had been president.

After that there was the matter of the Court of Feathers visiting me during the night, and how best to broach that subject with my team.

I went to Rhino first. He was in the shop, wrenching on some guns, probably because it was the most useful thing he could do sitting on a stool rather than trying to get around on crutches.

"Hey, Marco, you got a minute?"

He gave me a positive sounding grunt but his focus stayed on his workbench. So I took that as a yes and pulled up a stool next to him.

"I had something strange happen last night, but before I tell you about it, there's some stuff I need to tell you."

"You're only half human and your dad's some kinda Mexican cannibal human sacrifice skinwalker demon thing."

I blinked a few times, then had to look around to make sure that nobody else had been close enough to overhear that, but we had the shop to ourselves. "That's not really accurate on the particulars, but you've got the gist of it."

"Yep." He kept filing away on a piece of metal. "I don't much care, though. Earl said you're alright."

"Earl told you?" *How dare he!* It wasn't like I went around blabbing to the whole company about how he was really Raymond Shackleford the Second, secret werewolf. I vowed to put a bullet in that man's knee someday.

But Rhino shook his head. "Nope. Earl don't snitch."

"Then how—"

"He told me you'd be my second, but for me to shut up and listen when you said something, because you'd been around the block, but also that if you ever got to being weird or creepy for me to call him ASAP."

As much as that annoyed me, it was also pretty fair all things considered.

"Only I got curious, 'cause you didn't look old enough to have done that much, so I pulled the company files, and found another Mendoza, but way too old to be you, except there was some government letter in there from way back when declaring you PUFF Exempt, so I did some asking around, and one of the MCB I knew from New Orleans looked you up."

All these weeks working together and I'd never have guessed Rhino was capable of curiosity. I reached into my shirt and pulled out the silver tag I kept on a chain. This was my *get out of jail free* card, that identified me as—if not a good guy—at least not a bad guy anyone would get paid a bounty for. "Is this going to be an issue?"

"Don't eat nobody, and I don't give a shit."

He was remarkably blasé about it. Say what you will about Rhino, but he wasn't the sort to get emotionally worked up. "Thanks."

"Don't thank me yet. You ain't told me about whatever it is made you want to tell me about what you are yet, so let's hear it, so I can decide if it qualifies as creepifying enough to call Earl or not."

"Well..." The Shacklefords knew *what* I was, but even they didn't know *who* I was. It was one thing to know you're descended from a generic monster, as opposed to a specific entity that had once been worshipped as a god. So I needed to figure out how to put this in a way to not freak anyone out. "I'll save you the long-distance charge. It's probably nothing."

This time Rhino's grunt was suspicious and noncommittal.

So I gave him the vague version. "That world doesn't have much power here anymore. They're just a ghost of what they once were. But sometimes those ghosts can still talk. One of them paid me a visit, warning me that there's some great danger threatening LA."

"You believe it?"

"Maybe. I don't know yet. It was cryptic and they're tricksters and liars. But the messenger talked about *her* being a threat... and it got me to thinking about our werewolf from the other night, where *she* told him to build an army."

That got Rhino to actually look up from his gun parts. "A shot caller."

"String puller, puppet master, whatever you want to call it." It was a rare but not unheard-of phenomena in monster hunting to get some sort of smarter or more powerful creature to manipulate the others for its own ends. "Maybe we've got one up to no good here... or it could just be my ancestors screwing with me because they can."

"They tell you anything else?"

I thought about the closing vision. "It might involve disco?"

Rhino raised one scarred eyebrow. "They're probably fucking with you... but we'll play it by ear."

I was glad he seemed to be putting some thought into this, rather than just going off half-cocked like last time. "Thanks, Marco."

"By the way, good work on that werewolf and handling the team while I was in the hospital."

I'd been handling a lot more than that, for a lot longer than he'd been injured, and I think we both knew it. I just hoped that getting hurt dealing with a threat that was trivial compared to some of the things we'd be expected to deal with had gotten him refocused on being a proper team lead. "It's no biggie."

Except Rhino wasn't in the forgiving mood. "I was stupid, so I'm out of action and useless, and then my team did better without me anyways. Some leader, huh? Ray's probably gonna demote me."

"It's not an ideal start."

"It's a clusterfuck," he stated flatly.

"We've got some kinks to work out," I agreed diplomatically.

While I enjoy monster research, Alex practically lived for it. Our team's self-proclaimed nerd king was more enthusiastic looking up facts about monster than he was killing them. It was one of the traits I'd noticed about him during training. On the so-called "squishy" parts of monster lore—the myth, legends, and rumors—he was unsurpassed. Alex simply had a passion for the topic. If he'd had a degree in something useful, I'm almost certain the Los Alamos team—who handled all of MHI's mad science contracts—would have stolen him in a heartbeat, just like they had Ben Cody, who was probably the only newbie in that class smarter than Alex. Except Ben was the hard-science type, into quantifiable, comparable numbers and facts, while Alex was into the folklore and stories about dark magic handed down by worried *abuelitas*.

Fortunately for me, Alex was a short-time Navy sailor who had barely finished high school, so hadn't rated a second glance from Keegan in Los Alamos. It turned out Alex hadn't struggled in school because the classwork had been too hard, but because he'd been damn-near bored to death and never bothered turning anything in.

"So your mystery voice mentioned a dark master," Alex said as he flipped through one of the binders he had created. Not only was he a compulsive reader and notetaker, he possessed a severe desire to organize and catalogue everything into a color-coded binder system. It bordered on obsessive. "That's a title more than a name, so I'm thinking my red binder. Hopefully, not the black binder."

Ray Shackleford had spent big money for one of those fancy Xerox electrostatic photocopier machines at MHI headquarters, and Alex had put it to work before leaving for California, copying page after page from MHI's library. There were five different colors of binders he used to categorize the different known monsters based on just how dangerous they were.

I'm glad someone convinced the Boss to purchase one of those new photocopiers. Plus, some of those ancient books reacted poorly to being hand copied. I didn't know if MHI had anything like that, but the IDF had some ancient scrolls where we'd learned that machine copies lessened the potential mind-warping evil of certain handwritten texts. Especially the ones written in blood. Those were the worst. A good rule of thumb in this business: if you find an ancient evil tome, don't read it. And if you have to read it for some reason, don't read it out loud. That's how you get demons.

We were ignoring the brown and green binders for now, since those were things like non-PUFF-applicable cryptids, or monsters who weren't really a danger unless cornered, like Sasquatch or pixies. Instead, we concentrated on the yellow, red, and black binders.

The yellow binders were fascinating. There were a lot of monsters in there I'd always viewed as fairly dangerous, but Alex's personal rating system had put them lower. Zombies, for instance, he had them rated lower than gnomes. I couldn't recall a time when a Hunter had died from a gnome attack. However, the list of Hunters who have fallen to zombie bites was pretty long. But who was I to argue with the nerd king's filing system?

The red binder had the traditional big guns—vampires, were-wolves, shoggoths... basically any creature who could take out a fully equipped monster hunting team. Each and every one of them had fat bounties attached. These were the things that were dangerous not only because of their known capabilities, but because there were a lot of unknowns as well. Alex had lumped kappa and kitsunes in there too, not because that was the sort of thing we dealt with often, or really understood, but because of the rumors of what they potentially could do.

The black binder was thankfully the thinnest. These were the monsters Alex had lumped together as potential world enders. The Old Great Ones got a page, not that we knew much about them. Necromancers, even though they were only human, went in the black binder thanks to their ability to create all the nasty yellow and red binder things like zombies, wights, and ghouls. The Fey got a few pages of notes, lumped into various courts ruled by various kings and queens who existed outside our mortal realm. A few gods from ancient mythologies were listed as well, including—I noted—a few paragraphs about the Court of Feathers.

"So *that's* your family?" Alex asked skeptically.

"Unfortunately, yes, but it's not like I get invited to any get-togethers."

I'd had no choice but to bring Alex in on my secret. If there was some mysterious threat out there, he was the most likely one to figure out what it was. That meant giving him the whole truth...or at least most of it.

"I only put the Court of Feathers in my black binder because MHI knew so little of their capabilities. I skimmed through some old books back at the compound and hit the highlights, except I don't know how accurate they are, so my notes might not be accurate."

"Yeah, I got that," I murmured and flipped past the crudely drawn form of a feathered snake. Alex might have a giant brain, but it wasn't wired for quality artwork. "It looks like you've got the basics right."

"They're categorized under Fey on the PUFF tables, but that's more because they've got an other-than-Earthly origin and have been here for a superlong time, than because they've got much in common with the Fey who meddled in European history that we're traditionally used to. They've been here for thousands of years, with whole religions built around them, but we don't know where they're from, or what they really are...though if they can breed with a human and produce offspring, that suggests some sort of biological commonality between our species."

"Ugh...just don't go there."

"Sorry, this is *fascinating*."

Whenever I told someone about my background, I was always nervous about how they were going to take it. Disgust, revulsion, fear...only in Alex's case, he had just gotten obnoxiously excited about it. And part of me felt like I was the hot new exhibit at the zoo.

I pointed at a name mentioned on the page. "That's their herald, but I don't think that's our threat. If they were making a move in this city, I doubt they'd warn us first. I don't think anything in your black binder fits *dark master* the way the voice intended. What about a master vampire?"

"There hasn't been a master vampire spotted in America in ages," Alex said as he went back to the red binder. "I sure hope it isn't a master vampire, Chloe." Alex pointed at one page. "Here's a case from Cuba. Spanish-American War. Lucas Starmount, who'd go on to be the first director of the MCB and in Teddy Roosevelt's Rough Riders, killed the damn thing, but they had to use something like ten *tons* of dynamite to do it. Apparently the thing had four wights and dozens of ghouls protecting it. It was a mess. Lots of soldiers died."

"The only vampires I've ever run across was a nest of babies in Turkey about ten years ago. Local police had noticed an uptick in murders and asked for help. Good thing about baby bloodsuckers is that they're helpless during the daytime. I'm just suggesting the name fits, and a strong-enough vampire could order around other creatures and force them into servitude."

"That'd have to be an insanely powerful vampire." Alex ran his hand through his uncombed hair. The poor kid looked tired. "What about a necromancer? We've got cases of them building an army of the dead."

"Maybe, but how would she order around a living werewolf?"

Alex spread his hands apologetically. "Just an idea. And what about your disco ball?"

I honestly had no idea on that one. I hadn't exactly kept up on musical trends. Benny Goodman was still my jam.

We were interrupted by the phone ringing in the next room. I heard Lizz answer, and from the way she kept her tone really professional, Alex and I perked up, because that meant business might be coming our way.

"Job?" I asked as Lizz walked into my office a few minutes later.

"Job," she confirmed. "Zombies in the Hollywood Hills. There's maybe three or four, but they're supposedly contained at a broadcasting station on top of Mount Lee."

"No danger of them escaping?" Because that's when zombies got really dangerous. It was the multiplying that gets you.

"None. It sounds like a simple cleanup."

"How'd they get there?"

Lizz shrugged.

"I always wanted to go see the Hollywood sign," Alex said.

My first inclination was to just roll immediately, but poor Rhino was downstairs, and it wasn't lost on me that Lizz had reported to me first. "Let's see how Rhino wants to handle this."

"You say so," Lizz murmured, clearly unhappy.

I rushed down to the shop and gave the report to Rhino, whose face was set in his usual frown. "How many you want me to take, boss?"

It was clear he was unhappy with being left behind. However, until his leg was fully healed and he was out of the cast, there wouldn't be much hunting for him. He couldn't be in too much of a bad mood, though, because he'd let Lizz draw a beaver on his cast, though he'd stopped her from adding flowers up and down the plaster. None of the guys had been allowed to even touch it. I was starting to think Rhino was a big old softy for us girls.

"Take Kimpton, Justin, and Melanie. Then figure out what caused the zombies in case that's something we can get paid for killing too."

The rest of the team had heard the commotion and come in to see what was happening. Those three looked excited for the work. Lizz seemed happy to not have to deal with any zombies, because that was a gross, stinky, and unrewarding monster to have to take care of. They were like the plague rats of this business. Alex seemed offended about being left behind, but Rhino told him, "You, find us that girl who might be a werewolf. I don't trust the MCB to not screw that up."

"Who wants to go shoot some zombies and then cut off their heads?" I asked them. Melanie grinned before giving me a thumbs-up.

"I'll drive," she said. "I've got a bigger trunk."

"And a larger back seat," I added. "Shotgun!"

"Cut me some slack!" Justin protested. "Girl, you're five foot tall! I need leg space!"

"Too slow. I'll scoot my chair up, if that'll help."

"Damn it."

The Hollywood sign stands out more than anything else when you're cruising along the freeway. Located on the southern slope of Mount Lee, it can be seen for miles, like a beacon for all those wannabe movie stars coming here from all over the world. It's supposed to be a signal of hope and success for all who gaze upon it. Having spent a lot of hours exploring the seedy underbelly of the area recently, it just reminded me of failure and hopelessness.

We'd been told by the movie company that called us that they had blocked off the road leading up to the station at the peak. A gaffer met us there and filled us in with what the producers had told him, which admittedly wasn't much. What had started off as a film production for a "new and exciting" apocalyptic horror movie had turned decidedly real when the crew had arrived to shoot on location and discovered actual zombies munching on the corpse of the on-site security guard. Panic had ensued, a couple people had gotten eaten, and everyone bitten had been locked inside the chain-link fence where they'd been filming.

Instead of calling the police, though, the movie company had reached out to us.

Which made sense, in a sick sort of way. Movie companies were tighter than the Mossad when it came to keeping secrets. If they'd called the police, it would have been on the evening news. Once it made the news, the MCB would step in, and whatever cover-up story the MCB would order them to use would probably be embarrassing and cast a negative light on their production. Reporters would have been hounding the director and the stars for comment. Lots of companies were already moving away from filming in the Hollywood area, exploring other locales and costing the city millions.

One of the other issues was that C-list movie stars always seemed to get caught up in whatever new-wave religion was the craze at the moment. A lot of times, people with nefarious intent coerce these young, vapid individuals into repeating their mantra and proclaim themselves to be an acolyte of the golden sunset or whatever they called themselves. You see it on the news occasionally when some movie star gets caught up in a real-life cult, though according to Lizz the MCB was really cracking down hard on these. Still, the sea of young people willing to sell their souls for a chance at wealth and fame was really disgusting, and made for ripe and fertile grounds for cult leaders looking for new talent.

Zombies, though? This was something that Golden State Supernatural would have handled, but they were now bankrupt. Fortunately, some studio exec had wound up with MHI in their Rolodex and decided we were the company equipped to handle this, discreetly and quietly.

Three hours had passed since the people locked inside the gate had been bitten. Just like a werewolf's bite, infection was instantaneous and there was no known cure. The average time for a zombie bite to kill a healthy person and bring them back as the ravenous dead ranged from three to five hours. We were a little on the upswing side of the bell curve, but not terribly so, and from what I'd heard Hollywood actors might look great for the camera, but were unhealthy individuals on the whole. Three hours seemed like plenty of time for them to be dead.

It might seem a bit crass to look at it that way, but we all knew the score, even though none of us Hunters liked to talk about it. Shooting a person before they turned was hard. That was the kind of weight you didn't want to carry. Once they died and turned? Shooting them became a whole lot easier. I personally didn't care, but I wasn't about to put that on the newbies. They'd have plenty of chances to do horrible things that would haunt them for the rest of their lives later.

When we arrived at the film site there were several cars and trucks, some trailers, a few tents, and lots of equipment. There was a notable lack of staff for so much stuff, but that was because this wasn't the studio's first encounter with the supernatural, so they'd already known to send away all the potential witnesses. The fewer witnesses there were to intimidate into silence, the less time the MCB would spend interrupting their schedule.

There was a chain-link fence around the station, and on the other side were the zombies. And there were far more of them than we'd been led to believe on the phone. This wasn't some minor outbreak. There were at least ten of them shambling around in there. The studio was delusional if they thought they were going to handle this one quietly.

As we piled out of the car, we were greeted by one of the associate producers for the movie. Introductions went about as well as we'd come to expect from people who had never worked with us before. It didn't help that this guy had the look of a sleazy film producer and gave off a vibe of being an arrogant ass. It was the standard Hollywood greeting when a self-important man looked down on those he considered lesser beings.

"Great," the producer grunted, clearly annoyed. "So this is what's eating up my budget, the famous Monster Hunter Incorporated."

"International," I corrected him. "Nice to meet you, Mister...?"

In spite of the cool morning he was wearing a sweat-soaked, wide-collar shirt open all the way to his navel. The shirt appeared to be begging for mercy from his expansive gut, and he had a horrible combover that did nothing to hide the huge bald spot on the top of his head. His mustache reminded me of two lost caterpillars who weren't quite meeting up at the same spot along his lip. Around his neck was a heavy gold chain that became lost in his chest hair the farther down it went. Not the most attractive specimen around, but since he was a big-shot movie producer, he was probably able to weasel his way into gullible up-and-coming starlets' skirts with promises about making them rich and famous. I was willing to bet he even had a casting couch in an old, ratty office somewhere downtown.

He looked me up and down in a manner that made me want to shower. The predatory look he gave Melanie almost earned him a throat punch. "They send a spook and two slots. Yo, James! I thought you said these guys were pros?"

That made me angry, but it must have really infuriated Justin, because he cleared the distance in a flash, grabbed the producer by his lapels, and hoisted him off his feet. The movie slug looked as overweight as Justin was lean, but Parris Island and the mean streets of South Chicago had made him tough as iron. Justin might not have bulging muscles like Rhino, but the guy was strong.

"The next word out yo mouth better be *sorry*," Justin growled as an accent I'd never heard from him before came out. His eyes were inches from the movie producer's. "If it ain't, I'm gonna toss you in there with the zombies."

"James?! *James?!*" the producer shouted.

Justin's frown deepened and his eyes narrowed. "That don't sound like no apology to me." And he began to drag the whimpering movie producer over to the chain-link fence. Attracted by the noise, the zombies were beginning to shuffle toward the fence in search of their next meal.

"I'm sorry! Jesus Christ, I'm sorry!" the producer sobbed. "Please? Please! I'm sorry!"

"He sound properly contrite to you, ma'am?" Justin asked me, his accent dropping as quickly as it had arrived. The tough street kid from Chicago had disappeared and the respectable, formidable Marine had returned, though the accent hadn't disappeared quite yet.

I failed horribly to hide my smile. "I don't know. He was terribly rude."

"Please, sir! Ma'am! I'm so, so sorry!" the producer blubbered.

Mollified somewhat, Justin released his grip on the shirt, and the producer fell on his ass in the dust. "Your call, boss. Introductions, or zombie food?"

"Let's do introductions. I'm Chloe Mendoza, MHI," I said and offered my hand to the dirty, terrified producer. He reluctantly accepted it and I easily hoisted him to his feet, leaving him clearly shocked at how much stronger I was than I looked. The *nagualii* cheered at the display of dominance. I told it to shut the hell up. "Let's get one thing straight: We want your business, but we don't have to put up with your shit. Spare us the movie mogul bluster. This is what we do, and right now you need us more than we need you. Disrespect my people again, and we walk. Then you can deal with the undead and the government on your own. Okay?"

"Okay," the producer replied shakily.

"You called my office?"

"James did." He was looking at all of us in a new light now. Gone was the arrogant, cocky jerk; standing before us now was some regular schmo who was simply way out of his depth in a crisis, putting on a mask to hide his own insecurities. I'd seen this before from military officers and elected officials. "James knew who you were."

"Can you show us who James is?" I was polite because there was no need to rub salt in the wounds. Justin had kicked his ego so hard it wouldn't reinflate for six months, at least.

The producer led us away from the fence and to a covered area where a handful of men were standing around, nervously watching the zombies. There were multiple cameras angled toward the tower beyond the fence, and a lot of equipment I couldn't easily identify stacked on boxes taller than me. There were a few temporary trailers parked nearby, which I guessed was where the stars were hiding or getting makeup put on. I wasn't sure. I'd never been to a movie set before this.

It was all interesting, but I was there to kill zombies. However, I also knew movie production companies were flush with money, and we could get some long-term contracts out of this little escapade if I played our cards right. Diplomacy would be key here, and I'd promised Ray that I'd remain diplomatic during negotiations. Arrogant and insufferable movie producers notwithstanding, of course.

"James? This, uh, lady would like to speak with you," the producer said after leading us to a man sitting on a lawn chair next to a folding table. On the table was a schedule written in such big, bold letters I could tell with just a cursory glance they were running well behind schedule.

James turned out to be a chubby three-hundred-pound man

with a goatee and a smile. He stuck out his hand. "You're the people from MHI?" Surprisingly enough, he had a British accent.

"Chloe Mendoza," I confirmed. "This is Justin Moody, Melanie Simmons, and Kimpton Wall."

"James Andrew. I'm the director of this film."

"It's nice to meet you, sir," I said as Justin and Melanie both stepped forward for introductions. Kimpton remained in the back, eyes taking in everything but saying nothing. Unlike the other hack, James was unfailingly polite. I chalked it up to a proper British upbringing. Hollywood either hadn't rubbed off on him yet or he was simply a nice guy. I was hoping for the latter.

"The studio didn't want to get the constables involved, and I met a man once while filming in London who said he was from your organization," James said once introductions were completed. "He dealt with some decidedly nasty business involving a... strangler of young actresses, the nature of which Scotland Yard has cautioned that I should never expound on too much in public, if you catch my drift."

"Drift caught, sir." So this guy was read in. *Interesting.*

"So when we discovered this unpleasantness, I decided it was in our best interest to bring in the professionals on this matter."

"We appreciate that. MHI is the best monster hunting business in the world."

"That is what your Raymond Shackleford assured me, despite the protestations of his British rivals." James looked tired, which, given his circumstances, I couldn't fault him for one bit. It must have been a rude and unwelcome shock to discover real zombies eating your fake zombies on set. "We're also in a bit of a pinch here. The studio has authorized me to pay your company ten thousand dollars if you can take care of this by this afternoon, as well as sign a nondisclosure agreement of silence with punitive penalties should said contract be breached."

I did some quick mental math. On average, zombies were good for a few grand a pop, depending on their type. I looked over at the fence, which was now beginning to bow a little under the weight of the zombies pushing up against it. These looked like the typical slow, dumb ones. There were probably more hiding out near the communications tower or possibly in the building itself. Ten thousand was generous, especially when we would file a PUFF on them later and get paid twice.

However, if we could get a contract from this studio, word would get out to the others, and whenever a movie company had a problem, no matter where they were at, they could call MHI. That would lead to bigger paydays and be a much better long-term investment. With the MCB lurking around, an NDA was a waste of time. That was just a piece of paper to them, but if our signing it made them feel better, great.

"That sounds good, provided that you tell your studio what a fine job we did afterward, and that by paying us a reasonable monthly retainer they can save money in the future and keep MHI on-call. We'll guarantee a twenty-four-hour response to their filming locations anywhere in the country."

James cocked his head and looked at me in an entirely new light. "I'd have to contact the studio."

"Of course."

When a young assistant came over and whispered in his ear, James' smile disappeared. "Ah, how fast can you eradicate the problem? The city is beginning to breathe down our necks regarding our permit to film here. It was only supposed to be three days. That was two weeks ago."

"One hour, two tops," I promised. "This sort of zombie is typically slow and stupid. Still dangerous, but only if you're sloppy. Shouldn't be a problem as long as we're careful."

"Just one more thing, young lady," James asked, his smile returning at the happy news. "Would it offend you if we filmed it for our movie?"

"Seriously?" Kimpton asked, speaking for the first time.

"Of course. This is an incredible opportunity for ground-breaking cinema."

"We don't do retakes." I shrugged.

The MCB would never let them keep copies of anything they filmed, so why not? I looked around and saw that the camera mounts were set on tiny little railroad tracks on the ground. Following their path, I noticed they didn't go past the chain-link fence's entrance. "Oh, and sir? We're not going to wait around for your crew to lay down more of that railroad stuff for the camera to roll on."

That seemed to catch them off guard for a moment before the director began nodding.

"Smaller camera, less film on the reel," he said, looking around as the skeleton crew began gathering around him. He pointed at a big dude who clearly looked like he worked out religiously. "You? Boom operator?"

"Yeah?" the man replied.

"Do you think you can carry a rig and reel without tripping, or getting eaten by those nasty beasties over there? While staying close to the young lady here?"

"Uh . . ."

"Yes or no, young man. Time is money."

"Yeah, I can. I think. Yeah, yeah I can do it."

"Excellent." James' grin was infectious. "One take is all we shall get, my dear. Correct?"

"Zombies don't get back up after the way we kill them."

"Splendid!" James clapped his hands, clearly delighted. The change was almost disturbing.

I shared a look with the other Hunters, because we were about to shoot zombies for a real-life Hollywood director and get it all on film. I doubted the Boss would be pleased, but Earl might get a kick out of the absurdity of it all. He was funny like that. Life as a Hunter is never dull, but some things were such a rare occurrence that it was better to beg forgiveness than to ask permission.

We grabbed our gear from the back of Melanie's station wagon. I stole an occasional glance toward the chain-link fence, as I expected it to give way under the increasing weight of the zombies, but whoever had installed that fence had done an outstanding job. It was holding for the time being, and fortunately, wouldn't need to much longer.

Just before we began to kill us some zombies and get paid, James stopped us and handed us a few items from the props department. Frowning, I accepted the bunched-up fabric and eyed it suspiciously. It was a ski mask.

"Are we supposed to be playing terrorists?"

"We knocking over a liquor store?" Justin suggested and grinned.

"When we shoot scenes such as this, it allows us to hide the identities of the stunt men—well, in this case, stunt persons— from the audience." James was downright giddy with excitement. "Then, when the moment is right, she will rip the balaclava from her head, revealing the heroine, and the audience will gasp with delight!"

As fun as this was, I really did need to rain on his parade. "James, you do realize that the government is never going to let you use any of this, right?"

"My dear, if a government agency comes along and asks what it is, we'll simply say it is a skillful blend of makeup and prosthetics. As I said, I've worked with your type before and... how do you Yanks put it? Ah, yes, I 'know the drill,' as it were."

"I can dig it," Melanie said. Kimpton merely shrugged and slid his on.

"Wonderful, my dears! Go kill some zombies. Chop chop!" James saw that I had taken a sheathed machete out of the trunk. "No pun intended! Boom operator? Well, I guess you would be Camera A now. Are you ready?"

"Ready," the former boom operator responded. He was wearing a strange cross harness rig on his chest and a rather large camera was perched upon his shoulder. There was a ginormous battery strapped to his back as well. All told, the contraption had to weigh close to two hundred pounds. Despite its heaviness, it didn't appear to be bothering him one bit.

"My brother, I sure hope these don't turn out to be fast zombies and you have to try and run hoisting that thing," Justin said.

"Good thing I wore my Chuck Taylors."

Flexible mind, strong, unflinching... I made a mental note to keep an eye on this one. If he did well during our clearing of the zombies—and if he ever grew tired of Hollywood—MHI was always hiring.

The zombies were all fresh, and still looked like people. Just bloody, bitten, vacantly staring, obviously dead people. It was sad, but it was what it was. It didn't do any good to dwell on the fact that these had just been living, thinking, feeling human beings a few hours ago. I wondered if James gave that much thought before deciding to just treat them like props.

I turned to my team. Fun and games was over; now it was time to focus and not get ourselves killed. "We've been through this in training. Head shots and anchor shots. Ammo's cheaper than your lives, so make sure they're done before you step over them. Call out your reloads so your partner is covering you. Take your time. Check your corners. Don't forget to look up and down. I'll take off their heads for the bounty samples. We'll shoot the ones through the fence first."

"Miss," James interrupted, sounding a little embarrassed. "Take the heads? Wouldn't that be more suited to someone, ah...more physical? Those poor creatures over there do not look like the rotted sort I've seen in other films. While I've never participated in a decapitation, I'm sure it is not the easiest exercise."

"Don't worry, James. It's all in the wrist."

"Ghastly business," James said as he shook his head.

"You have no idea," I replied as I stuffed a foam plug in each of my ears. Now that was a neat new invention. In the old days we'd just stuffed cotton balls in there. Then I pulled the ski mask over my head. The wool made my forehead begin to itch and it took all of my self-control to not scratch at it with the machete's handle. The others followed my lead, and suddenly there were four well-armed yet nondescript people dressed in fatigues and flak jackets. We easily could have been stunt people ready to film a scene. James really did know his business.

"Ready?"

"Ready," Melanie answered. Justin nodded. I glanced at the cameraman, who gave me a thumbs-up.

"This seems kind of irreverent, but alright." Kimpton sighed. He was the only one who seemed not excited at the prospect of being in a movie—even if nobody would ever see it. Maybe that's what was bothering him. "Ready."

I gave the order. "Let's do this."

"Roll film," James called.

"Rolling."

"Stand by."

"Standing by."

"And...action!"

Melanie turned and immediately raised the Zastava M70 she had somehow acquired while still in newbie training. From a distance of thirty meters she put a round right between the eyes of the closest zombie through the chain-link fence. Its head rocked back as pus-filled brain fluids splashed the others behind it. Remarkably, it didn't drop, so a second shot to almost the same exact spot finished the job. The shambler collapsed to the ground, twitching. All that time out in the desert shooting was paying off.

I heard our makeshift cameraman whistle softly under his breath. "Damn, honey...marry me?"

The gunfire stirred up the zombies and they began pushing harder on the chain link. They made an awful moaning noise, and the metal creaked as it strained under the added weight. Justin and Melanie went to town on the zombies, their rifles barking as they took careful aim between their shots. The cameraman and James moved around behind us, keeping themselves out of the line of fire but still trying to get good angles on film. For a boom operator, he was a born cameraman, it appeared. James was even impressed and, over the distinctive *crack!* of the rifles, kept giving the man direction.

First zombies cleared, it was time to work our way toward the station. Kimpton unlocked the gate, and as we went through my team put more bullets into the zombies that were already lying on the ground. Since we had a moment, I moved in, machete in hand. With each brutal swing I cleanly removed a ruined head from a neck. There was a lot of ichor, blood, and who knew what else spraying into the air. Glancing back, I could see the cameraman was keeping the angle in tight on the scene, though he did look a little green around the gills. James looked equally unwell but neither had puked yet, which was a point in their favor.

I was proud of my team. They were keeping their cool, being professional, making good shots, and communicating. Even though two of them were newbies and one only had a few years on the job, they worked well together.

It only took a couple of minutes to totally clear the fence. No other zombies came down toward the noise, but knowing there might be more up in the broadcasting station proper, we began trekking up the small dirt road to the nearby building. I stopped for a moment and yelled back to the production crew.

"Don't touch the bodies! Don't get any juice on you. Lock the gate behind us!"

I hoped they listened. Even decapitated, some idiot could wander over and get bit by a severed head. That happened all the time. And I didn't think it was possible to get zombified just by getting their ooze on you, but I'd heard rumors of people in China getting infected by drinking pulped zombie brains to try and cure impotence or something, and considering what people put in their bodies these days I wouldn't be surprised if it were true.

The building's front door was closed, which meant little but did suggest nothing had gotten inside. Zombies might be a menace but for the most part they were too stupid to really understand how doors worked. Judging by the lack of cars parked around the building, I was tempted to believe it was empty and call it a day. There was a small, shatterproof rectangular window on the side of the building's metal front door, so I leaned in and tried to look inside. The window was tinted a dark color. I cupped my hands around my covered face and looked in a second time, then hissed, and swore softly.

There were three bodies in the hallway. Their throats had been slashed and strange markings had been drawn on their bare chests. They had been left with their pants on, thankfully. Each of them had once been a fit, attractive man. All three were lying within a dark circle that appeared to have been drawn in blood. Probably their own.

"Ritualistic sacrifice." I had wondered how a zombie outbreak could happen up here, in the middle of nowhere. Now I had my answer.

"How many?" Melanie asked as she covered me.

"Three. Weird number for a sacrifice."

"Is that a sacred number for anything?" she asked.

I shrugged. "Not that I know of."

"What about fairy tales?" Justin interjected as he peeled off his mask. He sent an apologetic look toward James. "Sorry, man. It's hot."

"No, I believe we have the shot we wanted," the director said, waving away Justin's concern. He slapped the cameraman on the shoulder. "Fantastic work, bloody fantastic. Good job, son! Miss? Can we peek inside?"

"One second," I replied before looking back over at Justin. "What did you mean about the fairy tales?"

"It's probably dumb, but you know how fairy tales work. Three wishes from a genie? Three little pigs? Goldilocks and the three bears? Three billy goats gruff? The Boss said once that fairy tales are based on real monster stuff."

"Okayyy," I dragged the word out, uncertain. The best way to warn people about the dangers of monsters was through mediums like myths and fairy tales, but he clearly had something more in mind. "Your parents must have read a lot of those to you."

"Granmama," Justin said. "You think who did this is gone?"

"Probably." I peered back inside, trying to see if there was anything. The bodies of the dead men, outside of their throats being slashed, looked to be in remarkably good shape. They showed no signs of torture from what I could see, and their hands weren't bound at all. The trio might have been drugged, but I'd been told by some unsavory types that using the life force of an individual under the influence could substantially change the effects of whatever dark magic was being harnessed. "We can't be certain until we get inside for a closer look." I tried the door, but it was locked. "Who owns this place, anyway?"

"One of the television stations," James answered. "I could place a call."

"Do that." Then I simply kicked the lock in. It was a sturdy door, but I was motivated and only half human. "Tell them you found their door vandalized."

I nodded toward Kimpton, and he went in first with his shotgun. Justin followed him. But the building was so small that a moment later they called out all clear.

It felt evil inside. And it wasn't just my inhuman senses that picked up on it, but it was obvious the rest of them were feeling it as well. Dark things had been summoned here. Upon examining the bodies and seeing that this was unmistakably some sort of necromantic human sacrifice, I told the others, "We need to call the MCB in on this."

"What? Those bastards...Do we have to?" Melanie asked with a slight whine. She hated the MCB more than any of the others. I never got the full story, only that Earl mentioned something about a brief hospitalization due to intense questioning from MCB agents after her attack had happened. Considering how levelheaded she was, it made me wonder just what the MCB had done to her.

"Yes. Because if we don't, they'll think we were behind this. I want to keep our relationship with them on cordial terms. Sorry, James, NDA or not, the Feds don't mess around when it comes to someone practicing necromancy. They're going to lock this place down until they can investigate it."

"Ah, that's alright. This footage more than makes up for having to move to a new location. I'll show that Kubrick what groundbreaking cinematography *really* means!"

I guessed that Agent Beesley was not happy to see me by the way she almost ran me over in her government-issued black

Plymouth Duster as she pulled up to the Mount Lee broadcasting station. From the sounds of the engine revving violently beneath the hood, she was pissed off that she had missed.

I gave her a friendly wave as she got out of the car. "Agent Beesley. So glad you could join us. Lovely day, no?"

"Ever since your company rolled into town, you've made my life a living hell," she said after slamming the car door shut. It was clear she was angry about something other than not allowing her to run me over. Probably had something to do with the dead zombies, the film crew, and the report of a ritualistic killing inside the locked broadcasting station. My day was going okay, but it was clear hers wasn't, so I decided not to antagonize her. Let's give peace a chance.

"So what's shaking?" I asked her.

"Why is there a film crew here?" Beesley demanded, giving James and the rest of the movie people a nasty glare. They were back on the other side of the fence, pouring bleach all over everything that had gotten zombie on it, as my team supervised.

"They were here first. They called us."

"You know how many people here are going to talk?"

"None," I told her. "They were making a movie up here when the zombies ate some of their crew. They locked the fence, ran away, and called us. That's just a skeleton crew. The director was read in and knew to send most of the potential witnesses home for the day. We took care of the zombies, then discovered three bodies from what looks like a ritualistic sacrifice in that building over there. I called you. I'm just trying to do my job, Agent, and not interfere with yours."

"We're still going to have to warn every single one of them," Beesley grumbled, clearly irritated. For just a split second I almost felt pity for the hatchet-faced shrew. Witness intimidation was one of the messier jobs the MCB had to do. Fighting monsters the way MHI does is straightforward. Dealing with the aftermath, like an MCB agent? I'd rather fight a vampire in the dark than have to do what Agent Beesley did.

...go to the ravine, a terrifyingly familiar voice whispered in the back of my mind. *We must speak.*

I frowned and tried not to let my sudden unease show.

The Court of Feathers had returned, but why I had no idea. This wasn't the same herald as before. This voice was sleeker, deeper, and somehow it felt more secretive. Getting psychic messages from mysterious entities after seeing the end-result of a dark magic sacrifice wasn't how I wanted my day to go. The fine hairs on the back of my neck stood up. I hoped Beesley didn't notice.

She did. "What's wrong with you, Mendoza?"

"I just hacked a bunch of heads off with a machete. What did *you* do for your lunch hour?"

"I ate a tuna salad sandwich. I'd have treated myself to something nicer if I'd known I'd be spending the rest of my day screaming at actors. And human sacrifice? Do you have any idea how much paperwork that takes? Plus, what mundane excuse am I supposed to use for this many deaths?"

"I don't know. Have your guys knock one of the letters off the Hollywood sign and say it fell and crushed them."

She actually seemed intrigued by that idea. "Not too shabby, Mendoza. I did already use the old bus-crash excuse for a mass casualty event this year. Good old construction failures are a classic. Covering up more than a handful of deaths from one incident is a pain. Singles are easy. You know that thing about how one of the leading causes of death is slipping and falling in the bathtub?"

"It isn't?"

"MCB came up with that one," Beesley said proudly. "It explains away *so many* monster attacks. The public bought it so well that I just wish I would've got stock in the company that makes those little flower traction stickers that people put on the floors of their bathtubs before we took it live." She handed me a business card. "Do me a favor: Next time, don't go through the switchboard. I'd appreciate a personal heads-up so I can get a head start."

"Will do. You need me for anything else, or can I leave?"

Beesley waved her hand dismissively and began walking toward the film crew. "We'll be in touch."

I glanced over at Melanie, who was standing by the car, and signaled for her to give me a moment. She didn't seem in a particular hurry to leave, especially after the film's star had left his trailer and immediately begun flirting with her. She had that effect on men, even while she was standing there in blood-splattered fatigues and holding a rifle. If I cared, I might have been a little jealous of her natural beauty. I didn't care, though, no matter what my facial expressions may have suggested.

Looking around the site, I hadn't seen anything I'd describe as a ravine. The south face of Mount Lee looked out over Los Angeles and the entirety of the valley, so technically that could have been considered a ravine, but the voice had to mean something more specific than that. After making certain Beesley wasn't looking my way, I headed back toward the broadcasting station.

More black cars were arriving. The MCB had sent a large contingent to deal with this mess. Shortly, agents would be tromping all over the place, intimidating the film crew and threatening to toss them in a mental ward—or worse, a shallow grave—if they talked about the things they'd seen. They were atrocious at calming survivors of monster attacks, and I'll admit I despised them for it.

Behind the broadcasting station there was a steep drop-off down the hill, and a tiny footpath that led between two rises in the slope. It was the only thing that resembled a ravine. Tall bushes hid it well but there was a lot of trash around the entrance. This place was probably used by teenagers needing a place to drink and screw around. Cautiously, I began making my way down, trying not to trip over the piles of beer cans. After only a few seconds I stopped, because blocking my path was the biggest jaguar I'd ever seen in my life.

The cat was gigantic, muscled, and sleek. It made no sound as it studied me with eyes that were far too intelligent to belong to any normal animal.

This was unexpected and unwelcome, but I couldn't show weakness, because this was the avatar of a very dangerous being. I tried to put steel in my voice. "Jaguars aren't native to this region. You're kind of conspicuous. Change."

The jaguar turned its head back and forth, inspecting the body, before the creature *melted* into something smaller. In the blink of an eye it was a regular housecat now, though the spotting on it was still very much a jaguar. I noted that it was missing one of its back legs.

"Tezcatlipoca."

"I bid you greeting, daughter," the cat replied, dipping its head slightly.

"Don't call me that," I growled in a low, dangerous voice. "I'm the product of your crimes."

The cat flicked his tail and stared at me with golden eyes. If my comment bothered the avatar thing, it didn't show on his feline face.

"How'd you escape the Court's prison?"

"This is merely an aspect of my greatness. I remain imprisoned beneath the sixth house. The sun is high now. Though summer approaches, night will spread again."

My father was a cryptic alien *thing*. He was also an incredibly powerful and dangerous entity that could obliterate me on a whim, so I tried to remain calm and choose my words carefully. "Why are you here?"

"Why are *you* here, daughter?"

I ground my teeth together and said nothing.

"You fled to the land eastward, away from my gaze. I am lord of the north, and to the north you have returned. You were compelled to come back to your people."

California was north of his old stomping grounds, but his current jurisdiction consisted of some extradimensional prison cell for his crimes against his own kind. Had those promptings I'd felt in Israel to bring me here been Tezcatlipoca's doing?

"My affairs are none of your concern."

"You are mistaken."

"Why'd you call me?"

"Time is short."

"Then talk," I snapped, which wasn't careful, but he and I had some issues.

"The pathetic sacrifice you found here is the work of the being the Herald dispatched by the Court of Feathers warned you about. Except the Herald twists his words." Tezcatlipoca's avatar's tail was flicking back and forth in the dirt, as if agitated. "Their mouth is a bowl of lies. The Court knows precisely what threatens this land."

"What's this *dark master*, then?"

"You seek wisdom, child? I will gladly help you...for a price."

Screw that. "I ask you for nothing. I offer nothing. I pay nothing."

"Then I shall only speak what I give freely. The Court of Feathers is concerned because this being has recruited some of their former soldiers. Dangerous things, yet the Court cowers, waiting, hoping mortals will do their work for them. The Court hides the truth from the worlds, so they may prove their neutrality later, after time breaks and the great chaos awakens."

That made no sense to me. Time breaking? Time can't break.

That's not how physics worked. It sounded stupid. Then again, I was standing behind a building that had been used in a ritualistic ceremony to create zombies, speaking to a cat avatar of my dad, who was an extradimensional monster once worshipped as a god. My life was strange like that.

"When the great war comes, sides will be chosen. The Court is weak now, egg without yolk, bone bereft of meat. Fearful, they will wait to see which side is stronger before declaring their loyalty. Their hesitancy shall be their demise. Only that is not your war. That is the war to come, and great it shall be. The Chosen who will break time has not yet been born. That war will have a new generation of champions. Your war begins now."

"I see," I lied. This was all news to me. But then, monsters are always talking about some war or prophecy or Chosen One. It was kind of their shtick. "You'd like a big war, wouldn't you?"

"As would you. You do not need to pretend meekness with me. Your heart yearns for conflict. You want to slash the arteries and see their blood freed. Through hostility, comes beauty."

My hands curled into fists. "Your ways aren't my ways."

"So you claim." The cat dipped his head. "I see you now carry the token of your slavery, and the symbol of the book god." I wore two things around the chain on my neck: my silver PUFF Exemption tag; and an old Star of David that had been given to me as a gift on a freighter out of Europe. My hand went there unconsciously, as the cat spat, "Weakness."

"I chose a religion that has survived everything the world could throw at it. Your religion ended up in the trash bin of history."

"You rebel against your true father like a petulant brat. The conquistador god may have been victorious over the empires who paid sacrifice to the Court, child, but our realm has been destroyed many times before, and with each age we return, greater than before. Your world only gets one chance... Ironic."

I had never heard a house cat chuckle before. "What's so funny?"

"It amuses me that one of the same men who crushed my kingdom will return in time to attempt the same to yours, only now the conquistador flies the banner of an older, crueler god. However, as I have said, that is not your war. Your war is now."

"Yeah, thanks for all that cryptic prophecy stuff. Why are you here?"

"Preparations for battle," the cat avatar said as he began to groom a paw. "The Court cowers. Tezcatlipoca does not. They are shadows of their former glory, filled with bitter vanity. They expect chaos to win. I told them they are fools to placate such an entity. My rebellion was why they placed me in chains."

"They threw your sorry ass in jail because you broke their laws," I snapped as my temper flared. "There's supposed to be a truce between mankind and the Court. You broke that when you attacked my mother and created me."

It was impossible to read the emotions of the cat avatar of an ancient god, but for a brief moment, I thought Tezcatlipoca looked disappointed in me. "You know nothing. The Court has deceived you."

"We're done here, drought bringer. Don't ever contact me again."

Suddenly, the placid housecat was gone, and the ferocious jaguar had returned, only now it was tall enough we were standing eye to eye. The beast showed me his fangs and snarled.

I snarled back.

"Such insolence... You remind me of your mother."

I resisted the urge to pull my pistol and start pumping bullets into the creature, but then half a dozen MCB Agents would come running to see what was happening and find a PUFF Exempt half human having an argument with a giant talking jaguar, and that would be a whole big thing.

The jaguar's lips hid his fangs. "Trust the Court at your own peril. When you are most desperate, they will offer aid. Their offer is a trap. They would enslave all *nagualii*."

I snorted. "Oh, like whatever you have to offer is better?"

"I am not a god who requires slaves. I am a father who will protect his family. Farewell for now, my daughter."

And with that, the jaguar turned to smoke.

I stood there as the avatar drifted away on the silent wind, until it was just me standing alone in a ravine filled with garbage left behind by teenagers.

The Court of Feathers was probably trying to manipulate me somehow. I had to agree with my father on that one. However, all the other stuff was up in the air about being truthful or not. Tezcatlipoca, after all, was not known for his straightforward trustworthiness. He was feared and reviled for a reason.

When I turned around to start making my way back up toward the broadcasting station, I was surprised to see Kimpton and Justin standing there, dumbstruck.

Oh shit.

Hopefully they hadn't caught too much of our exchange.

"What the hell was that?" Kimpton asked.

"Uh...It's complicated."

"A motherfucking tiger the size of a horse just said you were his kid!" Justin shouted. "I'd say that's pretty fuckin' complicated!"

"First of all, keep your voice down. Second, jaguar. Not a tiger. Huge difference."

"He turned into a cloud and floated away, Chloe!"

"I'll explain in the car."

CHAPTER 8

We found a pay phone at an old gas station on Franklin and called in to HQ to give them an update on our status. Lizz answered on the first ring.

"MHI, this is Lizz."

"It's me," I stated. "Fifteen zombies bagged. Got samples for them all. Good PUFF, no injuries on our end. We had a different problem come up, though. Can you get Alex?"

"Sure, hang on," Lizz said. Her voice became muffled over the line. "Alex! It's Chloe!"

He must have been sitting nearby because it was less than thirty seconds before she passed the receiver over to him. "What's going on, Chloe?"

"Pay attention because this is going to be a lot to take in, so I only want to say it once." I was about to really put the Shackleford family mantra of *flexible minds* to the test on this one. "The zombies were a side effect of some kind of ritualistic sacrifice made within the broadcasting station. Afterward, the avatar of Tezcatlipoca appeared to me and said it was the work of the thing we were trying to figure out earlier."

"Tezcatlipoca...the Aztec war god?"

"Among other things. But anyway, I'm pretty sure whoever told our werewolf to become a recruiter and now these zombies are from the same source. Think black binder, not red binder—or

129

maybe red binder, but something really top-tier bad. We need to figure out what this ritual was supposed to do." I tried to describe the symbols I'd seen etched upon the victim's skin from memory, but it was really hard to describe something so vile. I'd taken pictures but would need an opportunity to get the film developed. I was grateful the symbols hadn't hurt my brain just trying to look at them, like things from the Old Ones did. Once I finished describing the scene, Alex was silent for a moment.

"If Tezcatlipoca—like, the actual big guy himself—was there, wouldn't that suggest the sacrifices were for him?"

"Nope. Not his style. Their hearts hadn't been plucked out."

"How do you know there's not—"

"Because he's my father, okay?"

"Uh ... That's ..." Alex trailed off, but to his credit, he was exactly the kind of person the Shacklefords had in mind when they'd come up with their mantra. "Alrighty, then."

"Keep that to yourself. Well, I guess you can tell Liz and Rhino, but nobody outside the team. The guys and Melanie just found out."

"How'd that go over?"

It had been an extremely awkward car ride. You couldn't have cut the tension with a chain saw, it was just too thick. "We'll talk more about that later. Focus on the sacrifice for now, because I've got a bad feeling this thing is just getting warmed up."

"Okay, there were three victims?"

"Yeah. Justin thought there might be some sort of fairy-tale angle to that."

"And to think he calls *me* a dork. Someone always has a meaning behind their ritual. You and I perform rituals every day."

"No, I don't."

"Yes, you do," he argued. "You wake up, brush your hair and teeth, get dressed, get coffee—black, no cream ..."

"I see your point," I grudgingly allowed. For a second, I'd gotten defensive because I thought the whole ritual thing was meant to insinuate something about my father. "What does this have to do with the sacrifices?"

"Routines are powered by belief. Whoever used the three men believed three was the right number, that it was very important to them. Since it made zombies, clearly there was some real power to it. I'll dig into what I've got and call Alabama to see if they've got any ideas, but if Justin's gut is right, our monster's probably European."

"Why there?" I asked.

"That's where all the best fairy tales involving the number three originate. I'll see what I can do. Anything else?"

Considering the bomb I'd just dropped on him, it was impressive he'd ask. "That's it for now."

"You're in Hollywood, right?"

"Yeah, at a gas station near Echo Park," I said, looking at the pumps, which all had red rags hanging from the handles. The oil crisis was getting worse and fuel was running short at a lot of stations. "No gas here, though."

"You're not too far from USC's campus. The girl who got bitten by the Lake Arrowhead werewolf went to school there. You can see if the MCB's been there yet. Or, since the full moon's passed, see if any other students are missing. Might be some dead college kids out there we need to find. Or even another baby werewolf to track down and kill. Remember, her name is Nicole Varney. I put in a call to student services already. They confirmed she's still a student there but won't give a dorm room number over the phone. Are you presentable?"

I looked down at my gore-soaked shirt. Most of the zombie blood and ichor had ended up on my vest and gloves, but enough had managed to slide through the gaps to make my shirt resemble a Jackson Pollock piece. Before getting covered in gore, it had been one of the few short-sleeve buttoned shirts I could find that wasn't made from that nasty synthetic polyester stuff. I probably could have sold it now for a few grand if I could convince the buyer I was a famous painter. "I have some clean clothes in the trunk."

"It'd probably go smoother if two girls who look like they're in college ask around for her," Alex suggested. "You know, concerned friends who were in her English lit class with Professor... Clark?"

"How do you know what class she has?"

"I snagged a course catalogue from all the local colleges when we first got here," he explained. "Did you know that in major cities, a huge percentage of monster attacks happen on campuses? Crazy, right? Anyway, Professor Paul Clark teaches English Literature at USC. Lit 101, 102, 201, and 202. It makes sense that she would be in one of his classes at some point, since you need a minimum of twenty-four English credits to earn an undergraduate degree."

The man was too smart for his own good. "Good work, Alex. Thanks."

"I'll keep digging," he said. "Good luck."

I hung up the pay phone. The gas station had a bathroom we could change clothes in. Hurrying back to the car, I told the others what the plan was.

It seemed that Melanie had accepted the news the best, but then again, she'd not seen Tezcatlipoca for herself. The other two were still kind of shaken. It was one thing to hear about the avatar of an ancient being, it was something entirely different to be in its presence, and both Kimpton and Justin were still looking a little shell-shocked. A creature like that didn't look like much, but you could just tell by the vibe they gave off that mortals were puny and insignificant to them. I'd dealt with those things before so I was used to it.

At least they didn't seem mad at me. Or, too mad at least. Kimpton was kind of guarded anyway, but he'd slowly been warming up to me while we'd been working together. Only he'd barely said a word since my explanation, so whatever closeness we'd built was probably gone forever. Justin still seemed baffled and incredulous, like I was trying to sell him a bridge or something.

"You guys okay?"

"I don't know. Are we?" Justin asked. So much for the bridge.

"Come on, Justin. I'm the same person as before. Give me a break."

"That seems like the sorta thing you'd tell your team."

"Like anyone else goes around bragging about stuff from their past they're not proud of? You ever tell the others why you had to enlist or go to prison?"

"I was young and dumb and stuck up a liquor store," Justin snapped. "There. But that ain't the same. I didn't ever know my pop, but I'm damn sure he never ate anybody's heart."

"Always with the human sacrifice." I didn't have time for this nonsense, and we could sort it out later. Grabbing our spare bags from the trunk, Melanie and I went into the bathroom for a quick wash and change. It was tiny and designed for only one person at a time, but we made do with the space we had. There was zombie gore all over our pants, and though we'd ditched the vests already, our undershirts had some residue on a few of the exposed parts. Those went into a trash bag as well. I wasn't a fan of flared pants and waist-high belts, but it was all I had packed.

"Stupid," I muttered and quickly buttoned up my blouse.

Melanie was already dressed and putting on makeup. "Let's go see some college boys!" she said excitedly. Somehow the extra clothing she'd packed seemed designed to get as much attention as possible from the opposite sex. It only took her a tiny bit of effort to look perfect. Even her hair looked good. Mine looked like I'd been wearing a ski mask and sweating while chopping up zombies.

"That's just not fair."

"Please," she said, dabbing her lips with red lipstick as she looked into the mirror. "Aren't you an Aztec princess or something? Jealousy is very unbecoming."

"So you're okay with all that about me being only half human?"

Melanie puckered her lips. "Eh. I'll be honest, I don't even know who that guy is supposed to be or why he's a big deal. History wasn't my best subject. Do you have any...magic powers?"

"Kind of. There's downsides too." Except I really didn't want to get into a discussion of the *nagualii* ways in a gas station bathroom. "Big advantages that'll help the team are that I'm a lot stronger than I should be for my size, and my body is much more resilient than normal, which means I age slower too."

"So that's why you had so many experiences to talk about in training. Kimpton just thought you were exaggerating and making stuff up."

"Yeah...I'm sure this revelation will make him feel so much better around me."

"How old are you, anyways?"

"I could be your grandmother."

"Seriously?" Melanie scoffed. "Then you extra shouldn't get bitchy about me getting to be prettier than you for a *few* years." She checked her hair again. "Let me enjoy this."

I told very few people my secret, and even fewer took it this nonchalantly. "So you're really okay with who I am?"

"Sure. You run the team, I get the boys."

"What?"

"You never noticed? Wow." She rummaged around inside her giant purse, looking for something in particular, before pulling out a large eyeshadow kit. She handed it to me. "Add some blue eyeshadow."

I rarely, if ever, wore makeup. Not because I felt I was too naturally attractive or anything, but because I enjoyed sleeping in. Applying makeup meant getting up early. I'd rather spend that time being languid, or if I absolutely had to wake up early, drinking coffee. Lots and lots of coffee.

"College girls are all wearing blue eyeshadow and red lipstick now, and we want to fit in," Melanie explained. "Also bright red rouge on the cheeks, but not with your complexion."

"What do you mean, my complexion?"

"You look too Mexican."

"No shit." My mother had been from Oaxaca. I suspected I inherited her looks, but it wasn't as though I could remember her, though, since she'd died during childbirth. "Of course I don't look like Marilyn Monroe."

"It's a good thing too," Melanie said as she inspected her hair one last time in the mirror, then blew herself a kiss. "One dumb blonde on the team is more than enough."

She was far from dumb but I knew her well enough now to know she was simply fishing for a compliment. There was absolutely no way I was going to give her the pleasure. I left her hanging for a few moments, pretending I didn't hear the comment until she grumbled under her breath about how I was the worst teammate ever.

"Well, there's always Alex," I added insult to injury. "He's blond."

She huffed a little before cracking a small smile. "We've worked together long enough I feel like I know you. We're chill, Chloe. Don't worry about the boys. They'll come around. Let's go find a werewolf."

If there was a contest to see which Hunter was more nonchalant about something that most people would think insane, I wasn't sure if the winner would be Alex Wigan or Melanie Simmons. It might be a tie.

It took a while before we managed to find a parking space. Even on a Friday afternoon, parking on campus was a nightmare. I tried to imagine what it was like on a Monday morning and shuddered. Saturday night demolition derby at a car show had more grace than college kids trying to find a parking space right before class.

Most kids couldn't afford a car while living on a campus but this was USC and, more importantly, Los Angeles, where it seemed like every kid who attended a fancy university somehow had the financial means. Plus, nobody walked in LA. Unlike cities back east, Los Angeles was a sprawling mess. Their bus system was rudimentary, they didn't have a subway like New York, and their streets made no sense as they bounced from city to city.

Except Foothill. God bless that street.

"What do you want us to do?" Kimpton asked, looking around. He sounded even grumpier than before, if that was possible. "This isn't the best neighborhood, you know."

He was right. Despite USC being one of the largest and most exclusive private colleges in California, it was smack-dab in the middle of what could loosely be called the ghetto. The neighborhood wasn't completely gone yet, but there were parts that even I would be leery to walk through in the middle of the night. I'd seen safer neighborhoods in various slums throughout Egypt.

"Make sure no one steals my car," Melanie said as she got out.

Justin leaned out, frowning. "Girl, who'd wanna to steal your crappy station wagon?" he called after us.

In spite of the neighborhood around it, USC had a rather nice campus. There were trees everywhere and actual green spaces, and there was an energy here that I hadn't felt anywhere else in Los Angeles to date. It was simple youthful exuberance all tied into hopes and dreams of what the future might hold. The sensation was a stark contrast to the rest of our day. Zombies might be the company's bread and butter when it came to paying the bills, but they were still nasty.

The Bovard Admin Building was one of the most notable places on campus, mainly because it was one of those weird structures that only happened in the middle of Southern California. A massive three-story brick edifice, it had an imposing entryway and looked like a mash-up of Spanish mission and Eurotrash. It was probably the oldest building on campus and, judging by the state of the paint someone had slapped on sometime in the last decade, was in the most need of repair. The architecture was interesting, but the place clearly needed some work. That was sad. Considering what they charged their students, I was a bit surprised the sidewalks weren't paved with gold.

Melanie led the way inside, and unerringly guided us to the proper room we needed to go to without getting lost or turned around once. She'd been asking about my supernatural gifts earlier, but she had the sense of direction of a homing pigeon. In some past life she must have been an elf tracker, though there was no way I would ever say that to her face.

Luck struck twice in the span of five minutes. Instead of an old, crotchety secretary I'd been expecting to try and lie my butt off to in order to get the information we needed, there was a young man manning the admin desk. Melanie, smelling blood in the water the same way a shark does, moved in for the kill.

"I'm soooo embarrassed," she cooed and leaned *way* over the desk, her low-cut blouse giving the boy more than an eyeful. If she'd done that around a cop she would have been arrested for indecent exposure. And frisked. "My best friend in the whole wide world hasn't been to class in ages, you dig? She got a new dorm room and didn't even tell me where it was at! Can you help me track her down?"

"Please?" I added, leaning over as well, because sometimes Melanie brings out the *nagualii*'s competitive nature.

His eyes flickered between the two of us, but it was painfully clear Melanie was the center of his entire universe at the moment. I let her have the victory. I'm classy like that. "Uh, well, I'm not supposed to..." His voice trailed off as Melanie reached out and, with one perfectly pressed-on red nail, ran her fingertip across his forearm.

She gasped as she wrapped fingers around his thumb. "Oh, my...Do you work out?"

The girl was a force of nature. He stood no chance. It really wasn't fair.

"I can...yeah...uh...what's her, ah, name?" The guy was practically choking on his tongue now. If she kept that up he was going to pass out, or worse.

"Nicole," Melanie answered. "Nicole Varney."

"Ah, okay, let me see." He began flipping through the pages. After a few moments of distracted searching—Melanie was smiling and twirling her hair, and she was so good at flirting I was beginning to wonder if it really was just an act—the poor guy finally found the entry. "Varney, Nicole. Von KleinSmid Memorial Hall, Room 257. Once you're out the front door here, go north. There's a plaque in front. Can't miss it."

"Thank you, sweetie." I swear the woman was part succubus or something. "Oh, and can you not tell anybody that we're on our way over? We want to surprise our friend."

The boy stammered a goodbye but we were already halfway out the door. As soon as we were out of the admin building Melanie's persona shifted. One second she was a college student hitting on an admin clerk. The next? The flirtatious blonde was gone and the hard-core Monster Hunter had returned. It was eerie.

"What're you carrying?" she asked me.

"My Browning Hi-Power and three magazines," I replied as we walked along one of the narrow paths toward the large cluster of buildings that had to be the dorms.

"Any silver bullets?"

"Duh," I replied. I'd gotten one box of ammo silver plated. It was expensive, but effective on werewolves. Not as effective as Rhino's silver buckshot, though. It sure would be nice if Ray could get a reliable company-wide supply going for silver bullets, because it was a pain paying for them out of your own pocket.

Melanie got a concerned look on her face. "What if she's eaten her roommate or something?"

"Someone would have heard the screams, right?" Though I'd never been in a college dorm before. If the walls were made out of cinder block or something similar, it could potentially muffle most loud noises.

"Or smelled the mess," Melanie added after thinking about it. "It's been a few days since the full moon and it's been warm."

This area of campus seemed newer than the rest and was a beehive of activity, even though it was Friday afternoon. Several buildings were under construction, and there were crews of workers making noise. There was also an abundance of young and hot students walking around, which explained why Melanie was only getting cursory looks and not the full-on tongue wagging she was used to. I knew she was used to being the center of attention. When it didn't happen, like now, it clearly bothered her.

Call me old-fashioned, but everyone's shorts—boys and girls both—were far too short.

We found the dorm and went directly to our suspected

werewolf's room on the second floor. By unspoken agreement we avoided the elevator. It wasn't like we were expecting a werewolf to change inside one or anything like that, but the city had suffered enough rolling brownouts the past few weeks that neither of us felt like getting stuck in a metal box.

As we walked up the stairs, Melanie asked, "If she's home, how do we want to do this?"

"We'll play it by ear. If she's bloodthirsty and insane, we'll probably have to shoot her and work it out with the cops afterward. If she's rational, I want to ask her if she knows anything about this monster recruiter."

"What if we can't tell if she's infected or not?"

"Then that's Agent Beesley's problem, and we'll call her to handle it."

"I really hate this. Killing monsters is one thing, but this is just some poor girl. It hardly seems fair."

"It's not," I agreed. "But the better we do our job the less people like Nicole get hurt."

We found Room 257 easily enough. There was a chalkboard mounted on the door to write messages and whatnot, and someone—probably a guy—had drawn a stick figure with giant breasts, with "Nicki's Knockers" written below. Because some boys, it seemed, never left high school, no matter how much money their parents paid to get them out of the house.

After two knocks, the door opened to reveal a mousy-haired girl in a bathrobe and thick bifocal glasses. She squinted at us suspiciously, which meant she couldn't be a werewolf, since the lycanthropic curse would have corrected her vision. Plus, when a new werewolf changes back to human they usually look like they've lost too much weight too quickly, and this girl seemed comfortably plump.

"Yes?"

"Is Nicole around?" I asked.

"She said she needed to get away from campus and left a week ago. Said she'd be back yesterday but I've not seen her. Got excuses from her professors and everything. Is something wrong?"

Your roommate was bitten by a werewolf and might have eaten somebody, but I didn't say that. "We just haven't seen her around and were wondering if she was okay." I snuck a glance inside the dorm room, and it looked precisely how I'd imagined a college dorm room to be, except this particular one was neater than expected. Everything was tidy and organized. It was much cleaner than our HQ.

The girl seemed a little troubled. "What do you mean, 'okay'?"

"Well, last time I saw her she seemed a little...off," I lied, wondering how she would respond.

We got lucky and the roommate opened the door all the way and motioned for us to come inside. Once in, she shut the door and sat down on the edge of her bed and began to spill everything.

"Nicole met some guy at a party, then they went hiking up at Lake Arrowhead a month ago." She kept nervously tugging at the edge of her robe while talking. "When she came back, she was different. I don't know how to explain it. There was an edge to her, like she wasn't the cool, easygoing girl I met last semester. Like she's messed up, you know? She just wanted to go party and stuff after she got back. I think she might be on dope, but that's not like her."

"You two been roommates long?" Melanie asked as she picked up a framed picture sitting on the desk. It was of her and a girl I assumed was Nicole in a photobooth setup.

"Just this year. Our freshman year, we both had roommates who were a little wilder than we were okay with, so when we put in our preferences this year they put us together. We clicked, you know? Everyone always called us N-squared. Nicole and Natalie. We were going to get an apartment next year and stay roommates until we graduated."

"That's a good picture of the two of you." Nicole was an extremely pretty girl, which was probably why the werewolf had picked her.

"It was at a sorority party at Christmas," Natalie said. "We hadn't really thought about joining, but everyone knew the Sig Delts throw amazing parties, so we went. It was okay, I guess. That's where she met that guy. I think his name was Corwin."

As far as we knew, the werewolf up at Lake Arrowhead had been a weirdo kook living in the mountains. If he was trying to form a pack, prowling across college campuses looking for prospects was a good way to do it. Irrational young adults, uncontrollable urges already, then throw in a rebellious streak, and you've got a very fertile ground for that sort of thing.

It also made me wonder whatever happened to poor Corwin. Probably one of those missing hikers they never found. Something to talk to Deputy Black about. I handed her my card. It was a simple business card with MHI on one side and my name and our office number on the other.

"What's MHI?" she asked.

"That's where I work. I don't have a phone in my apartment. If I'm not in class, I'm at work. Easier just to reach me there. My coworkers take messages and my boss is fine with me getting personal calls there. When she comes back, can you call me?"

"Does she go anywhere else for fun?" Melanie asked.

"She's been going to clubs lately," Natalie said in a low voice. "A lot of them. On weekends she hasn't even been coming back here until late Sunday night. She's *changed*."

You have no idea, I didn't say.

"With her getting weird, did any . . . cops ever come by? Men in suits? Or maybe a lady detective?"

"No, nothing like that. Do you think Nicole is in trouble with the law?"

I was just suspicious why the MCB, with all its resources, hadn't sent somebody by to follow up on a potentially deadly threat. Unless they'd picked Nicole up somewhere else and that was why she'd never come home. "Probably not. Thanks, Natalie."

"Want me to tell her you were here, when she comes back?" the young girl asked.

"Don't worry about it. She's got my number. You just give me a call. If she wants to ring me, she knows where I'm at."

"Oh. Okay."

"Hey, it's probably just a phase," Melanie tried to comfort the other woman. "She'll come around."

"Thanks."

"Let's go, Mel," I said exited the dorm room. Before we walked away, though, I looked at the chalkboard for a moment. It was juvenile and made me angry. A newly created werewolf might see that, get angry, and go on an absolute tear through the dorm, killing dozens of unsuspecting innocents. There was no reason to add fuel to the fire. "Mind if we erase your chalkboard? Stupid boys . . ."

"It's the girls, actually," Natalie said in a morose voice. "They're jealous of Nicole so they pick on her."

"Jealous?" Melanie asked, intrigued.

"She's really smart," the girl clarified for us. "And she's super-cute but doesn't act like it. So they pick on her because she's really quiet and never stands up for herself. Bitches..."

I wiped the chalk off the board with my hand. The poor girl had been picked by the werewolf to be his second, to help him guide his eventual pack. She'd had no say in the matter. He was lucky he was already dead because I really wanted to hurt something.

Predators always go after the meek, whether it's monsters preying on humans or mean girls picking on the nice ones. It's been that way since the dawn of humanity. It sucked, but it was a part of life.

It was almost certain Nicole had been bitten judging by what the sheriff's report had said, and from what Natalie was saying about the personality changes and odd behavior, she'd probably been infected, so things were going to end poorly for her. At least she had the smarts to get away from the college during the full moon, so she had that going for her. Unfortunately, new werewolves had little if any control over their ability to change. Even if she understood what was happening to her, and was trying to control it, any little thing could trigger her rage, and then people would die.

Outside, the sun was beginning to set and the construction workers were packing it in for the day. The campus was quieter, but there were still students walking around on the paths. The trees cast shadows in unusual parts of the campus and the tall buildings blocked the sun. The quaint, hope-inspiring campus I'd marveled at earlier now deemed a little more sinister, darker. I shivered in spite of the warm air.

"I thought having something to show around to identify her might be handy." Melanie reached into her giant purse and pulled out the photo of Nicole and Natalie that she had stolen. "Do we need to call the MCB about this, Chloe?"

"We should, yeah," I confirmed. Saying it out loud made me feel like crap, though. A sweet, innocent young girl had her future taken away because of some asshole with a god complex. The more I thought about it, the angrier I got. "That's assuming they haven't already found Nicole and made her disappear."

We found the nearest pay phone, I dropped in a quarter, and dialed Agent Beesley's direct line. Luckily she was still in the office.

"Beesley."

"It's Chloe Mendoza, from MHI."

"Oh hell. I spent my whole day screaming at entitled movie morons. You should have heard the weeping when I confiscated all their film. I can't believe you let them record you, dumbass."

Agent Beesley was as surly on the phone as she was in person. "I can't stop regular people from doing anything, Agent—that's *your* job. But that's not why I'm calling. You said you'd appreciate a personal heads-up next time, so that's what I'm doing."

"What now, Mendoza?"

"I already called this one into the MCB, about how the Lake Arrowhead werewolf might have infected someone else, but we've looked into it, and I'd move her from suspected to probable."

Beesley was quiet for a moment as she shuffled papers. "I don't have anything about that."

"I did what I was supposed to and reported it to your office. Tell your guys to get their shit together. Her location is unknown, and it sounds like she might be on the prowl. I was just calling to make sure you hadn't already liquidated her."

"*Liquidated?*" Beesley sounded aghast. "The MCB aren't the monsters, Mendoza."

"Sorry, take care of, disappeared, whack, whatever you call it." If only Beesley realized what my last job had entailed, she'd understand I wasn't trying to be offensive. My responsibilities had been to deal with the supernatural, but that had only been part of the Kidon's mission. Sometimes governments just quietly make problematic people go away. I didn't have to like it, but it was what it was. "I just need to make sure MCB hadn't already handled the issue before we wasted our time searching for her."

"We're not that bad at paperwork. I can assure you that nobody in this office has *liquidated* any werewolves recently. I'll look into it."

"Alright. Thanks." It was odd that the MCB would drop the ball like that, but it wasn't my problem. I hung up the phone and turned back to Melanie. "It sounds like Nicole is still out there."

"This sucks," Melanie said.

"Hey, you should be happy."

"Why should I be happy?"

"You get to go club-hopping on the company's dime."

"What?"

"Didn't you hear what Natalie said back there? Nicole's changed. She's club-hopping, going to discos, partying. She's probably got a newfound feeling of power and invincibility, ultimate freedom out there in a sweaty meat market. If she's going to lose control before the full moon, it'll probably be in that kind of environment." And then I recalled the vision given to me by the Court Herald and the slowly turning disco ball. "Shit."

"What?"

"I'm used to my family lying to me. Them telling the truth scares me. This is all connected, and I don't like it."

CHAPTER 9

Los Angeles is a huge sprawling mess spread across five hundred square miles, and that's not counting the smaller cities right next door that always get lumped in with the metro area. There had to be thousands of discos, bars, and nightclubs, plus who knew how many underground establishments that would never be discovered by anyone except for those "in the know." The club scene here was more secretive than the MCB. The City of Angels was the Wild West when it came to discos. We were going to need a lot of luck to find Nicole before the body count started to rise.

Why hadn't the MCB already been looking for her? Natalie had said no one else came around to ask about her missing roommate, and it was clear the witness intimidation program—also known as the MCB—hadn't spoken to her yet. If the sheriff's department had called us about Lake Arrowhead, then surely they'd told the MCB too, and it shouldn't have taken me to tell them that the cougar attacks were really suspicious. The Feds were supposed to be more astute than this, and Ray had assured me that they were even more militant than the last time I'd worked with them. Agent Beesley might be a pain to deal with, but she struck me as efficient and ruthless. Taking care of a newly turned werewolf that they had police records on should have been handled ASAP.

The next day, we met to talk about our missing college student. Finding her was what we would concentrate on whenever we weren't actively working some other case, and there hadn't been any new callouts since the zombies. We decided that every night we'd split into teams and hit various nightlife spots. We made copies of the photo Melanie had stolen, so at least we'd have something to show around to all our contacts.

Rhino had a surprise for us. He had managed to snag a police radio for each of our vehicles. We could use their emergency channel if needed, which could come in handy when we needed to pass a message back to base. This was really nice because I was always out of quarters when I needed to use a pay phone. I think part of this new project was that Rhino was still mad at himself for getting his leg broken, and at least doing the installs would make him feel useful, but I sure wasn't going to say that to the poor guy.

While we talked about our werewolf search, eating doughnuts the Gasparyans had brought us and drinking coffee, I could tell that there was another topic looming, and we really needed to have it out. The silences were awkward. Justin kept looking at me like he was expecting me to shape-shift and start eating people.

Surprisingly, Rhino actually read the room for once, did his job, and took charge.

"Alright, we need to clear the air about something. Some of us already knew Chloe was PUFF Exempt. Some of you found out the sudden way."

"That would've been nice to know before," Justin said.

"Get over it, kid. If that's the weirdest thing you see in his job, you'll have gotten real lucky."

Lizz raised her hand. She actually seemed excited to talk about it. "Ooh, ooh, since this is in the open now, I got questions."

"Here we go again." I took a sip my coffee before launching into the usual answers. "No, I'm not a cannibal. No, I'm not a *were-jaguar.* Silver doesn't work on me. Yes. I can change form, but I rarely do, because it's a miserable experience. I save that for when there's no choice because that part is dangerous to others. I'm not a lycanthrope. It's totally different. I don't care about the full moon. I'm not going to flip out and lose control. It doesn't work that way. I have to specifically want to change. And no, I will not do a demonstration for you."

Lizz slowly lowered her hand. "Well, that covered most of mine!"

Alex raised his hand. What was this raising-the-hands crap? Were we back in the classroom?

"Practically speaking, what kind of biological differences are we talking about?"

"I like long naps in the sunshine."

"No, I mean like pragmatic stuff, like . . . *powers*."

"I can seduce men and mind-control them with my voice."

"No way!"

I sighed. "That's a siren, you idiot. Of course I can't do that. Pragmatically speaking, I've got better-than-human physical abilities, I'm hard to kill and I recover quickly. If I'm ever badly injured, don't take me to a hospital, just let me sleep it off. I'm serious about that. My vital signs just confuse doctors. And I can see in the dark about as well as Lizz's scope thing. The downside is that I have a horrid extended family."

"And an insatiable thirst for blood?" Lizz asked.

"No."

"Just checking."

"Try not to sound so disappointed."

"Sorry."

This was the most I'd talked about being a *nagualii* in a very long time, and frankly I found it exhausting. "That's it, guys. I'm not that odd. I'm pretty boring. I'm the same person you've known since training. The only thing that's different now is my father showed up."

"Tezcatli-motherfucking-poca," Justin said. "That'd be like Kimpton's dad was Jack the Ripper or Adolf Hitler and he kept his trap shut about it."

"He's not," Kimpton stated flatly. "For the record."

Those were the two Hunters I was the most worried about. Rhino was too jaded to care, I think Melanie still thought of me as a regular person, Alex appeared to find the whole thing fascinating in an academic sense, and Lizz seemed to find my background *quirky*. But Justin was suspicious, and Kimpton I couldn't get a read on, but he already seemed to have trust issues.

"Well, Ray Shackleford and Earl Harbinger both vouch for me. Take it or leave it. I don't care." I got up from the conference table and grabbed one last doughnut from the box. "We've got a werewolf to find."

✦   ✦   ✦

We'd been searching fruitlessly for a week when something odd happened.

That night, Melanie was dressed to kill, with the sort of dress you'd see on a cover of a magazine. Gold was definitely her color, though I'd never seen any color on her that didn't work. There was a little bit of envy, because I sure couldn't wear a dress like that straight off the rack. Kimpton looked rather plain next to her in his powder blue shirt and tight white pants, but still cut a rather dashing figure.

Lizz and I decided to go the opposite route and maintain a low profile. We had our body armor and gear in the back seat of my car just in case, but otherwise it was hip huggers and dark shirts. We weren't exactly trying to be inconspicuous, but if a werewolf spotted us and recognized us for what we were, it made no sense to be in a glitzy dress and heels you can't run in. The flashy girl gets attention. Attention means the flashy girl gets eaten first. While I don't want to be eaten at all, if it came down to it, I'd rather get picked last for a midnight snack.

Lizz had given me a pair of pants with strange bumps in the knees to wear. When I rapped my knuckles on them, they gave off a distinct sound beneath the fabric. I was curious and inspected the inside. She had taken some rubber padding and sewn it into the material as well. I looked over at her and noticed her pants were similarly made.

"Padding. I hate kneeling down on pavement and hurting my knees. Those younger hunters might not care now about their knees, but I don't want to be using a cane when I'm forty."

I wanted to say something about her leg and its current condition but decided against it. She probably knew she was only a few years away from the hated cane already. There was no point in being a bitch about it. Plus, it was a pretty neat idea.

Since we weren't dressed up or anything, we were actually able to get started on our search while Melanie and Kimpton were still getting ready. Justin and Alex were planning to stay back at base and keep Rhino company. Before we left, we did a radio check and discovered it was working perfectly. Rhino, immensely proud of his installation instructions, actually smiled. With all his scars it was positively ghastly, but at least he was in a good mood. That counted for something.

Pulling out of the garage, we turned and headed toward

Glendale. I wanted to avoid Chavez Ravine, since there was a baseball game tonight and it would cause a lot of traffic. That meant heading directly west first, then south. It would dump us out on the north end of Hollywood. From there it was simply cruising Sunset Strip until we either spotted the girl or called it a night.

Melanie and Kimpton would be doing something similar, except they would be looking inside all the clubs. Given the lines that were expected outside some of the trendier clubs, I wondered how they were going to manage to get into more than two. I was sure Melanie would find a way, but other than bribery for the bouncers guarding the doors I doubted they would get much searching done. I applauded our superior search methods.

After a couple hours of absolutely nothing, we changed tactics and decided to simply park near Mann's Chinese Theatre and walk around the block. Lizz was not a fan of the idea, but it wasn't like this was a large block. Plus, it would allow us to get a closer look at the lines. There were at least seven disco halls on this block alone, and every single one of them looked like it was packed. Plus, my gut was telling me that we would strike pay dirt if we tried this. However, Lizz trusted my gut about as much as she did three-week-old Chinese food, so it took a little more convincing to get her to walk with me.

We strolled slowly around the block, looking at the people in lines to get into the clubs while trying to remain inconspicuous about it. There was a strange discordance while we made our way along Sunset Boulevard. LA is a strange place, flashy and scummy at the same time. We could see the glitz and glam of the people dressed to the nines, while just to the side and in the shadows were clusters of eyes watching us warily. They were a part of the city's massive homeless numbers.

A small percentage of them probably weren't human. One thing they harp on during newbie training is the propensity for monsters to hide among the homeless. Sometimes they're PUFF-applicable, legit predators, but others it's something harmless and trying to stay hidden. I heard rumors that there was an entire tribe of Orcs living in a hobo encampment once and nobody even looked twice at them. Lots of monsters use our own preconceived notions against us as camouflage. It's always a good idea to remain wary. The street bum you might be trying to ignore could be sizing you up as dinner.

We passed hundreds of people, but no Nicole. Occasionally, we'd make conversation and show the copy of her picture and ask if anybody recognized her—and the only reason we could get away with that was neither of us looked like cops—but if anybody had seen her they didn't speak up. Sad part was, we weren't the only ones desperately showing pictures of a missing person to total strangers, in the hopes of finding somebody. It was moms and dads looking for their teenage kids, or family members looking for the one who'd gotten hooked on drugs or decided to run off to become a movie star. LA simply devoured people like that, and nobody really batted an eye. It was sad, and just one more reason why I was growing to detest the dark underbelly of this city and the lifestyle it encouraged.

Something strange caught my attention as we walked past the front entrance of a club. The design of the building was unusual, almost gothic, so it seemed out of place. It must have been a popular place because the line to get inside was huge. But the thing that caught my eye was that in the filthy, trash-filled alley next door was parked a dark-colored sedan, and there were two figures inside, both of whom were watching the crowd intently. I cocked my head slightly as I recognized Agent Beesley. I didn't know who the man in the passenger seat was, but I pegged him as another MCB agent by the suit. I had no idea what they were doing out here in the middle of the night.

"Hey, Lizz. I think that's our MCB agent on stakeout."

"Ah, it is old hatchet face. Wanna go see what they're up to?"

Ignorance killed the cat. Curiosity was framed. So I sauntered over to Agent Beesley's car. They spotted us. The man appeared confused. The look on Beesley's face could have frozen an ocean. Grinning, I rapped my knuckles on the driver's-side window. Beesley rolled it down and I could almost see her wrestling with the idea of simply shooting me to make me go away.

"Good evening, Agents."

"What do you want, Mendoza?" Beesley demanded.

"Just wondering what MCB is doing outside a disco on a Friday night," I replied as Lizz leaned against the front fender.

"Watch the paint," the male said.

Lizz smiled sweetly at him. "It's not like you guys worry about a little ding in your fleet cars. Oh, this one's cute. Is he spoken for, Beesley?"

"How's your night going, anyway?" It was clear we were interrupting something, and I was really hoping that they were watching this particular place because our werewolf was inside. "Find any good monsters lately?"

"Nothing as interesting as the one that beat the shit out of your boss," Beesley snapped back. "He couldn't handle a single angry beaver. Boys, am I right?"

Say what you want about Beesley, but she was spunky for an MCB agent. "Marco's such a klutz. Great smile, though, what with all his scars and everything. So, what're you guys doing? We're innocently minding our own business out here tonight, club-hopping and trying to pick up some hapless guys for wanton times of indescribable fun."

"Oh really?" Beesley eyed my outfit suspiciously before her eyes moved to my oversized purse. "I'm sure that's filled with nothing but makeup accessories and prophylactics, right?"

"Of course," I agreed. It actually contained my Hi-Power, extra mags, a flashlight, a sap, and my butterfly knife because it was cool, and it intimidated Alex that I could flip it around without cutting myself.

Beesley didn't seem too concerned by my blatant lie. It wasn't as though I were waving the knife around in public like a lunatic, terrifying all the people around us. For an MCB agent, she was only mildly annoying. I'd met worse in Israel. "Well, I'd hate to interrupt your whoring and debauchery. Good night, Mendoza." She began rolling up her window.

I put my elbow on the window so it would be harder to crank. "So you guys are just sitting here in a dark alley, enjoying burgers and shakes while watching the night pass by uneventfully, then?"

"You're very good, Mendoza. You should be a private detective. But we're all out of burgers and shakes now, so you should go."

"Got him," Beesley's partner suddenly blurted out, his eyes locked on the entrance of the nightclub. "The tart's with him again."

Beesley sat up straighter in her seat and I was all but forgotten in the span of a heartbeat. I turned to see who he was talking about and nearly ripped my eyes out of their sockets, because exiting the nightclub was a creature straight out of a nightmare. With huge, batlike ears protruding from its misshapen head, fangs that extended past its bulging lips, piercing yellow eyes with black dots in the center, and a shock of white hair, the beast was hideously ugly.

I expected screaming and people fleeing in terror at the sight. What I got was a crowd of people absolutely fawning over the monstrosity that was holding hands with a well-built, middle-aged but normal human man. And everybody was acting like this was completely normal.

Rubbing my eyes to make sure I wasn't hallucinating, I stared harder at the monster. I wasn't losing my mind. The thing was there, wearing a sparkling designer dress over its lumpy pink body, and all the clubgoers were eagerly trying to get its attention somehow, despite it being the ugliest damned thing I had ever seen in my entire life.

Lizz looked away from the thing, clearly unbothered by it. She must have noticed the expression on my face because she immediately asked, "Are you okay?" I wasn't retching just yet, but it was a close thing. Clearly there was something going on I was missing.

"Bad tamales," I lied and risked another glance in the direction of the club's entrance. The *thing* was still there but the effect had lessened somewhat the longer I looked. It was like the hideousness dissipated the longer I stared. Either I was going insane or my senses were becoming duller. I couldn't be certain which.

Lizz, though, recognized the man who was walking closest to the creature. "Hey, isn't that MCB's regional director?"

I shifted my gaze from the monster to the man walking next to it. "Yeah, that sure looks like Special Agent in Charge of California, David Orwig, doesn't it? Isn't he the big guy in your building, Beesley?"

"Yeah," she admitted grudgingly.

"Who's the thing on his arm?"

"She's just some piece of eye candy," Beesley said, defeat in her tone.

"Eye candy?" I asked, flabbergasted. "That?"

"She's a fashion model or something out of Europe," Beesley replied, actually sounding a little defensive of her boss. She looked at me suspiciously. "You jealous or something? What does it matter to you?"

Son of a bitch... I turned away from the agents so they wouldn't see my eyes change color, and used my *nagualii* sight.

Sure enough, there was powerful magic emanating from the duo. The air around the entire block seemed to be pulsing with magic. The sheer weight of the glamour was palpable. Refocusing on the ugly *thing*, now I could see a stunningly beautiful woman. It made my eyes itch.

"She's a hag," I muttered.

"Naw, everybody says she's aloof, but that she's actually very charming once you talk to her," said the other agent.

Only I'd meant it literally. Hags were born of both Fey and of the Earth, which meant they had some Fey abilities, like glamour, but lacked others. Like me, they were a hybrid being, so which powers they would inherit was unpredictable. They ranged from dangerous, to super-crazy dangerous, to *fuck this noise, call in the tac nukes*. They were more of a European problem—where the Fey had a longer history of carelessly consorting with humanity—than here. Since hags weren't usually spotted in the US, I didn't even know what their PUFF status was. It had to be astronomical since it was technically Fey, after all.

We really didn't know how many Fey courts there were, only that there were several that intruded into our world at some point to meddle in human affairs, and that most of them hated each other and were continually at war. A Fey court could bring lots of death and destruction to us, but humanity could bring extinction to the Fey. There was some kind of long-standing truce between our two species, the details of which were foggy now, but everybody knew the Fey were extremely dangerous and not to be messed with. Which made this hag hanging on the arm of a high-ranking MCB agent all the more disturbing.

The only reason I could imagine a hag hitting on an MCB agent with that much glamour was for something nefarious, or disgusting. Probably both. It made me sick thinking about how poor, unsuspecting SAC Orwig was going to bump uglies with the ugliest.

That also made me smile, just a tiny little bit, on the inside. I am a bad woman sometimes.

The hag's magic was clearly fooling both of the MCB agents, as well as Lizz. I hadn't realized I could see through something like that before, but I'd never dealt with a creature who could fling around glamour like a party girl did glitter, so I never would have guessed it didn't affect me like the others. Just one more helpful thing I owed to my deadbeat father.

Terrific.

The hag broke away from her adoring crowd long enough for Orwig to talk to the valet, who got some car keys from the booth and ran toward the parking lot. Beesley immediately tensed and started her car.

"Why are you tailing your own SAC?" I asked, because I was going to have to decide real fast whether to warn her about just what she was dealing with here. There could be one hell of a situation if things went sideways. Even though the hag wasn't a true Fey, it was still plenty powerful enough to wreak havoc, especially in a crowded place like this. There was also the fact that Beesley would probably blame all of the casualties on MHI.

"Seriously, Mendoza, fuck off." And since I'd stood upright to get a better look at the hag, Beesley successfully rolled her window up.

I struggled for a moment. Werewolf, or hag? Which didn't take long for me to decide. The werewolf hopefully wouldn't be a danger until the next full moon. The hag, on the other hand, was a crime against nature right now. If it was influencing the MCB and they didn't know, this was something I would need to report in to Earl and the Boss as soon as I could.

There was no way the government car had enough space to perform any sort of U-turn, which meant they expected their boss to head out onto Sunset and would follow.

"Beesley, wait." I rapidly knocked on her window again. "That woman is dangerous."

Only she studiously ignored me because the valet had returned with a red Porsche. SAC Orwig opened the door for his lady friend, helped the bat-demon thing from another dimension in, then went to the driver's side. They were leaving in a hurry. Poor Orwig was grinning like he thought he was about to score.

I kept knocking. "Damnit, Beesley. She's a monster. She's Fey." Except Beesley apparently didn't hear what I was saying, and she flipped me the bird as she pulled out after her boss, clearly annoyed that I was interrupting some private MCB business.

Not wanting to miss out on a potentially gigantic PUFF bounty, I grabbed Lizz by the arm and started dragging her back toward where I had parked. Lizz just trusted me, hurried, and didn't ask questions, because she's awesome like that. A short U-turn across the nearly empty street and we were quickly on Beesley's tail.

"What's going on?" she asked once we were on the road.

"That fashion model is a hag."

"Like hag hag, like she's a bitch? Or Fey hag?"

"Fey. And *ugly*."

"Okay," Lizz said slowly. "I don't know much about that one."

"Predatory, carnivorous, clever, totally malicious, and likes to play with their food. They live a long time, and the older ones learn how to use crazy amounts of evil magic. Super dangerous, but *huge* bounty."

"Great. What're we doing exactly?"

"We're going to follow Beesley as she follows the hag," I told her.

"What happens if the hag splits off?"

"We stick with the hag," I decided, not really giving two shits about the sexual predations of an MCB regional boss. Let Beesley deal with that.

"Are we going to be in some sort of crazy-assed gunfight involving cars?" Lizz asked, sounding a little worried. "I don't want to be in a gunfight after some crazy car chase, okay?"

I scoffed at her. "A gunfight in Hollywood? This isn't the movies. This is real life."

She sounded uncertain. "What about the werewolf?"

"The next full moon is a month away. We'll get her before then." And then it hit me. "If the local agent in charge is under Fey influence, he could be corrupt, and covering things up, working for this dark-master thing."

"You suggesting he's on the take?"

Lizz hadn't seen just how profoundly gross that bat-woman thing was. "He's on the something."

I grabbed the radio. "Base, this is Hunter Two," I said, clicking the handset once I was finished.

"Go," Rhino's voice seemed extra gravelly over the radio.

"Got a lead on a monster, Lizz and I are following now. Will radio for backup when needed."

"Confirmed monster?" Rhino sounded a little surprised. "The werewolf?"

"Worse," I told him. "Hag."

"There hasn't been a hag seen in decades," Alex cut in, so excited that I could just imagine him wrestling the radio handset away from Rhino. "Where are you guys?"

"Sunset Boulevard, near Mann's Chinese Theatre. Be warned: MCB agents are already on scene, but are...doing something else."

I clicked off the mic and frowned as I thought about it. What *were* the MCB tailing their own SAC for? Beesley hadn't acted like she was on bodyguard duty. She was spying on him, not protecting him. And then I remembered how she'd reacted when I'd followed up about my report on Nicole, and Beesley had been surprised that she'd not been told about it. Beesley struck me as rather driven. She had probably looked into it and discovered that it had been Orwig who had squashed my report.

"I think Beesley thinks her boss is dirty, and I bet she's doing her own unofficial investigation."

"How dangerous are hags?" Lizz asked.

"Big range of danger. All bad, but the really bad ones are *really* bad. They're half Fey, half human, all hideous."

"Aren't you half Fey and half human?"

"Yeah, but my mother was human. Hags are what you get with a human father and a Fey mother. *Totally* different."

"Uh-huh..." Lizz, who normally preferred to shoot from range, had come prepared for up close and personal, and out from under her blouse came a rather impressive .357 Magnum revolver. I hadn't thought Lizz was big enough to hide something like that. She opened the cylinder, made certain it was loaded, and then put it back in the holster. Because of how I was dressed, my gun was in my purse. Which wasn't ideal, but I'd put trying to blend in ahead of function. Apparently Lizz didn't have that problem.

"Don't get too close, Chloe. We don't want to get spotted. Or too far, and we'll lose them."

"I know what I'm doing." Working with the Kidon had taught me the art of surveillance. If you followed a car directly behind them at the same speed, you're sure to get noticed by a suspicious driver. Since I've never met a Fed who wasn't suspicious, I wasn't going to follow Beesley in an obvious manner. Instead, I changed lanes to stay on her right and two car-lengths behind. I fluctuated my speed a little and even let a few cars come between us when they needed to turn.

I was also keeping an eye on the flashy red sports car Orwig was driving. I was pretty sure Beesley knew how to tail someone, but there was always the possibility she could lose him. This was Los Angeles, after all. Traffic was normally pretty bad. Tonight, thanks to it being after midnight, it wasn't too harsh for the moment, but if Orwig got onto the 101 and put the hammer down in that thing, we'd probably lose him. Even on a Friday night it was precariously balanced between being a road or hell and purgatory.

"You concentrate on driving, Chloe. I'll keep the boys updated on where we are."

Once again, we got lucky. Orwig kept his sports car on Sunset Boulevard heading east, out of Hollywood until he turned into the area of town known as Little Armenia. Not entirely sure where we were at, I kept on Beesley's tail. Lizz, though, seemed to know our location.

"We're near Silver Lake Reservoir. Nice neighborhood. Upscale. Not Malibu, but pretty close." She reported street names over the radio as I kept an eye on our surroundings.

It seemed rather scenic and nice, which was odd considering we were still in the LA basin. The area was hilly and the streets narrow, far different from what I was used to dealing with when it came to driving around the rest of Los Angeles. Even Covina had wide roads, and the city had barely a fraction of the area this had.

It was weird watching someone watching someone else. It made for a strange game of cat and mouse, except in this case the mouse was a creature that could rip us apart in a matter of seconds and the cat was a well-armed sociopath from a heartless federal agency. I couldn't decide if the cheese was poisoned or explosive.

I checked my wristwatch. It was almost one in the morning and the streets were very quiet. I had to hang back much farther than I liked, but Beesley would be sure to notice us here. The Porsche stopped at a nice two-story home overlooking the reservoir, so I stopped on a nearby hill and killed the lights, a hundred yards from where Beesley parked and did the same.

The house was really big. I figured that must have set him back a pretty penny. When I mentioned this to Lizz, though, her face became serious.

"I betcha that's why Agent Beesley is following him. Fancy cars, fancy house, government salary."

"MCB agent on the take from supernatural forces? Selling out mankind for money? That's . . . disturbing."

"Probably why Beesley's watching him, though. Trying to find out who he's working for."

"She acted surprised about Lake Arrowhead," I pointed out.

"What if the SAC knew but hadn't told anybody else about this werewolf trying to build a pack? That makes no sense."

"Just means more work for the MCB if there's a pack of them running around," I agreed.

"But if someone else told him to keep it quiet, like say his hag girlfriend, who works for some dark monster thingy who's also powerful enough to be recruiting werewolves and raising zombies and who knows what else, who also happens to be scary enough to worry a Fey court like your feathers people—"

"Court of Feathers," I corrected.

"Whatever. Somebody who rivals them. At first glance it looks like the Fey might have control over the Los Angeles MCB. That could be bad."

"Understatement of the year right there, Lizz." I got my binoculars from the back seat and settled in to wait. It appeared Beesley was doing the same thing we were. "Think we should go talk to Beesley?"

"And risk her getting angry at us? Or spooking the hag? Oh, heck no. I say we camp, tell spooky stories in the dark, and wait for our friends with the van full of guns to get here."

It was better than anything I could think of, so we hunkered down and waited. About thirty minutes later, Agent Orwig left the house and began walking back to the Porsche. There was no sign of the hag.

"This might not be his place," I suggested. "Looks like he's leaving."

"He could be innocent and just be thinking that he's gotten lucky with some high-end model."

She hadn't seen the bat-faced thing. There was nothing lucky about that.

"Follow him, or stay here?" I asked, but it was a rhetorical question. "Stay here. Hope Beesley follows her boss so the MCB aren't around to complicate things. And kill us a hag to collect a big old bounty."

"Before we kick in some rich lady's door, are you sure you saw what you saw?"

"Yep."

"I'd hope so, Chloe, but we followed her to *her house*. It's not like we caught her murdering people. This seems kinda..."

"Premeditated?"

"Yeah. What if she's PUFF Exempt, like you?"

That was a valid point. We were extreme rarities, but maybe there was a perfectly innocent explanation for why a senior MCB agent was hanging around with a supernatural predator with crazy illusion powers. Probably not, but maybe.

"Gimme the binoculars," Lizz said, so I handed them over. "Something's wrong. His car's rocking."

"Ew."

"No, look." She handed them back.

I sighed and peered through the darkness. In spite of the suburban nature of the neighborhood, there wasn't much illumination. However, Orwig had parked directly beneath one of the few streetlights, and sure enough the Porsche was shaking. There wasn't just one form in the car, but two shadowy shapes, and it looked like they were wrestling. The movement grew more violent with each passing second.

"Wait...there's something in there attacking him! Radio it in!"

I started the car, shifted into gear, and floored it. We had realized what was going on and reacted faster than Beesley had, but their headlights turned on as we sped past. I slammed on the brakes and stopped right behind the Porsche. I grabbed my pistol and bailed out of the car, thankful I'd not worn heels.

Beneath the lonely streetlight, the little red sports car was shaking violently and I could hear shouting coming from inside. Whatever was in there was doing a number on Orwig. I reached the car just as the screams abruptly cut off and so much blood hit the back window that it was like somebody inside had thrown a bucket of red paint.

The rocking stopped. The car was still.

That much blood that fast, it must have ripped Orwig *in half.*

I raised my 9mm and it suddenly felt really inadequate in my hand.

"Lizz, grab the shotgun from the trunk."

My heart was hammering in my chest. Even though I was only a few feet away, there was so much blood coating the windows there was no telling what was still inside the car.

The MCB car stopped right behind me, and I heard the

doors open, but I didn't dare risk taking my eyes off the threat to look back.

"What are you doing here, Mendoza?" Beesley asked as she ran up beside me.

"Saving your butt, apparently," I snapped in reply.

Then Beesley saw all the blood, exclaimed, "What the hell?" and she pulled an old GI .45 from a holster on her belt. "Hang on, Orwig!"

"I think your SAC is dead."

"I've got to check." Beesley's hands were shaking so badly that I could hear her gun rattling. "Cover me!"

Beesley was brave. Stupid, but brave. I heard the *chu-chunk* of a shotgun being pumped, so I knew Lizz was ready. I moved toward the passenger side so Lizz would have a clean shot. Beesley, however, was already heading for the driver's-side door.

"Wait for your partner!"

"He's on the radio calling for back—" Except then something kicked the Porsche's door so hard it flew right off. The door nailed poor Beesley and it still had enough energy to fly across the street. The MCB agent dropped like a sack of potatoes and didn't move.

Me and Lizz both started blasting. Bullet holes and buckshot patterns appeared in the metal. Glass shattered.

The monster must have ducked down behind the seats because I couldn't see anything in the shadows. It couldn't be very big if it could hide that well in a car that small.

By some miracle the flying door hadn't removed Beesley's head from her shoulders. I could see she was still breathing, but there was a lot of blood. She was alive for now, but if she kept losing blood at this rate it wouldn't be for long.

The monster launched itself through the broken rear window, right at my face.

It was like getting sucker-punched in the forehead by a bowling ball. Before I could even register pain I found myself sailing backward.

I landed heavily on the pavement and barely had time to recognize that something was on top of me. Teeth snapped at my throat, but I brought the Browning up and reflexively fired. The creature screeched and rolled off. I scooted backward until I hit the curb.

My attacker was scurrying on all fours beneath the street-light, still painted red by Agent Orwig's blood, maybe five feet tall counting the tail. It was like someone had crossed a monkey with a gecko or stuck four hairy limbs that ended in all-too-human hands onto the body of a snake, and that was all the time I had to comprehend what I was dealing with, because it was coming back around to bite my legs with its baboon face filled with dagger teeth.

I kicked it away, then Lizz blasted it with the shotgun. Meaty green chunks flew out the side of its body, spinning it sideways. I cranked off what I thought was a few more rounds, only to be surprised when the slide locked back on an empty mag because I'd already burned through thirteen. I reached for my purse for a spare, only it wasn't there. I spotted my purse in the gutter, lying atop leaves, twigs, and an oil stain. There would be no saving it. My bag was probably ruined. In the back of my mind I mourned the death of my favorite purse, which considering what was going on right then tells you just how hard I'd hit my head.

Lizz slammed another round of buckshot into the thing, which rolled it over, but it popped right back up, and left a trail of green blood in its wake as it ran toward the fallen form of Agent Beesley. I also rolled over, dragged my purse from the gutter, and grabbed another mag. Lizz kept shooting.

I thought that maybe the thing was going to finish Beesley off, but the clever little bastard slithered behind her, nudged her unconscious body upright at the waist and hid behind her, using her as a human shield.

It was only then that I noticed something about the strange monster that I'd not seen before—that its tail ended in another humanlike hand, which was really freaky, and got more so as that tail shot out way farther than I'd have guessed was possible, to snatch up Agent Beesley's dropped handgun. The muzzle swung my way.

I flung myself behind the Porsche as the monster started shooting wildly. "Duck!"

The monster was using Beesley as a hostage, its skinny body mostly hidden behind the unconscious agent, while its super-prehensile tail stuck out over her head, firing blindly in our direction. Sometimes life wasn't fair.

I looked over to Lizz crouched behind our car, hurriedly

shoving more shells into the Ithaca riot shotgun. She cringed as a bullet clanged off the engine block. "What is this thing?"

I risked a glance over the Porsche's hood, to see that the Beesley's gun was empty. "Out of bullets!"

The monster tossed the Colt, dumped Beesley, and ran toward the lake, crazy fast. Lizz and I both popped up and started shooting. It got hit a few more times, and flopped over, but kept crawling.

"I got this." Lizz ditched the shotgun, pulled her .357, cocked the hammer, braced her arms across the hood, and smoothly nailed the monster square in the back of the head. Green brains squirted and it went down, barely inside the circle of light.

My ears were ringing, but I think it was quiet. One of the monster's rear hand-leg things was twitching, but barring magic or some weird regenerative powers, I was pretty sure Lizz had killed it for good. *Wow.* My head hurt and the world was spinning. It hadn't been very big, but that thing had hit like a truck.

I threw my purse strap back over one shoulder and got shakily to my feet. Nothing was moving at the hag's house, but that was another menace we still had to worry about. Moving around the sports car, I got to see what was left of the Orwig, and the gecko thing had torn the stuffing out of him. The Special Agent in Charge had been dismantled. The coroner was probably going to have to use an air hose to blow the bits of him out of the air-conditioning vents.

"I'll check on Beesley." I started in her direction.

"The boys are almost here," Lizz said.

That reminded my poor traumatized brain that the MCB had been calling for backup too. "Where's Beesley's partner?" And I turned to look just in time to see the second—totally different—monster crouching atop the other agent's obviously dead body. And by obvious, I mean really obvious, even in the dark, what with him being decapitated and all.

The newcomer saw me staring, and stood upright, and unlike the first thing that had been lean and wiry and quick, this one was hulking and thick, and it started my way with a lumbering gorilla walk.

When it got into the headlights, I couldn't believe my eyes, because the agent wasn't the only one missing his head. The thing probably would have been seven feet tall, if it had a regular skull, only its body just kind of stopped at the very broad and hairy shoulders. But a lack of a head didn't keep it from seeing me, since it clearly had eyes—black and unblinking—in the top of its chest, and it still had a mouth...a gigantic, snarling, snaggle-toothed maw where its belly should have been.

Lizz saw it too. "Nuh-uh. Nope. Fuck that."

I'd never seen one in person before, but from that rather unique description, this had to be an Ewaipanoma—a headless Amazonian ogre—which meant we were in deep shit.

The grunting, slobbering monstrosity was coming my way. "Lizz, get in the car and go." I lifted the Browning, aimed for where I hoped its heart should be—right between the eyes—and started shooting. I was unable to tell if the 9mm even did anything to it, but I think the end result was it only became angrier. It bellowed loudly and charged, its heavy footsteps reverberating up my spine. The monster ran past the unconscious Beesley, barely missing stomping on her as it aimed for me.

A fool would have made a brave, final stand, protecting the downed MCB agent. I wasn't that stupid. I ran.

Instinct told me not to run down the street, because even though this thing was so dense with muscle it had to weigh a ton, it would be quick in a straight line. So I got the Porsche between us. The Ewaipanoma was fast as I feared, but it cornered like a Corvair with flat tires and tripped over its own feet trying to slow down. It tumbled across the sidewalk and onto the hag's front lawn, taking out a pink flamingo lawn ornament and one of those cheap bird fountains in the process.

The headless ogre picked itself up off the grass, the broken beak of the plastic flamingo stuck to its chest fur, and it began circling after me around the car. It viewed me as the biggest threat since I'd shot it multiple times. Mission accomplished. That would give Lizz a chance to escape and regroup when help arrived. I just needed to stay ahead of it until then.

Except I should have known Lizz wouldn't abandon me, and she laid into it with her hand cannon. "Leave her alone, ugly!"

Only Lizz didn't know what we were dealing with, or that Ewaipanoma were legendarily difficult to kill, and we'd not packed any elephant guns. Her .357 Magnum bullets just flattened and bounced off its magic hide.

I sprinted over to where Beesley lay and grabbed her by the wrist. Crouching down, I hoisted her over my shoulder. She was the kind of lady who preferred weight lifting to manicures, so she was heavier than she looked. This was one of those rare times I was thankful I wasn't fully human, and supernatural strength was a nice bonus in situations like this. Carrying Beesley, I ran back toward our car. "Drive, Lizz, drive!"

The shaggy creature was snarling now, its stomach-mouth frothy, and drool running down its belly. I don't know what levels of anger this particular monster could feel, but if I had to guess I would say it was the next step past slobbery rage, into frothy homicidal berserker mode.

Lizz had gotten in the driver's seat. I reached the passenger side and was trying to figure out how to get Beesley and me in before the ogre got here and stomped our guts out, when Lizz shouted, "The engine's dead!"

And then I remembered how the first monster had managed to hit our car with its crazy tail-driven mag dump. It must have gotten lucky and hit the battery or something.

"Go to the MCB car." Lizz ran for it. With Beesley over one shoulder, I turned back and shot at the ogre, doing the same thing as before, trying to keep a vehicle between us as a barricade. One of my bullets chipped a belly tooth and it roared. If I thought it was angry before, the hatred this thing must have felt toward me now could have powered a thousand suns, and it began chasing after me at a rate far faster than I thought possible. Then it really ruined my plans when it reared back with one stump leg, and kicked my car so hard that it spun sideways. I narrowly avoided getting clipped. There really wasn't any reason for me to hang around anymore so I did what any sensible girl would do and ran for my life.

Luckily, the back door of the MCB sedan was unlocked, so I was able to pull it open and toss Beesley inside. I jumped in after her. "Go! Go!"

Lizz appeared at the driver's-side door, panting. "I hate running!" She barely gave the decapitated agent a second look as she tossed her shotgun inside and stepped over his body. There was blood pooled on the bench seat but Lizz didn't even care. She was so tiny she looked like a little kid sitting in the driver's seat. It would have been ridiculous except for the monster trying to kill us all. I shot it right through the window. A 9mm is super loud inside the confines of a car.

Luckily, the engine had already been running but Lizz seemed to be struggling.

"Just drive!" I shouted as I grabbed a fresh magazine from my bag.

"I told you I don't like driving!" she screamed back.

The monster slammed into the side of the car, desperately trying to get at us. The rest of the windows shattered, and a massive hand came through the window, searching for me. Glass stuck to my bloodied clothing. It caught hold of my sleeve. Its beady chest eyes were looking at me, and the gaping maw was only a foot from my face. It had horrible, rancid breath and was dragging me toward its scary, flat chomping teeth.

I pulled back and thankfully my sleeve ripped off. I used up the rest of the rounds in my second magazine, and that must have stung enough that it momentarily pulled back.

I reached over the seat, grabbed Liz's shotgun, shoved the muzzle out the window, and fired a round of buckshot right into one of its eyes.

The Ewaipanoma screamed so loud that if it hadn't broken all the windows already that might have done it.

"Go!"

"I'm trying!"

"It's an automatic! Pull the level down and step on it!"

"I know how, I can't fucking reach!" And I realized Liz was scrunching down so awkwardly because she was trying to find the gas pedal, and the dead MCB Agent must have been really tall. It wasn't like she'd had a chance to adjust the seat.

"Are you serious?" I turned the shotgun back around, leaned over the seat, and stabbed the gas pedal with the smoking muzzle. That wasn't exactly a precise move, and the rear wheels squealed and created a cloud of rubber smoke.

The monster must have sensed we were trying to escape because the damned thing bit my door and wrenched it off the hinges. Turning, it spit the metal out the same way a ballplayer would sunflower seeds. It reached for me, but the tires had finally found purchase and we were going forward. The monster took a swipe and his impossibly strong fingers scored deep gouges across the rear paneling. I heard a loud *bang!* from the rear. I looked back to see chunks of rubber flying, and immediately realized the thing had caught the tire, causing it to blow out.

The car was moving at a decent speed now but there was no way Lizz—who really was a terrible driver—would be able to handle it for much longer. I let off the gas as the rear began sliding to the left. The car continued to slide and Lizz panicked, overcorrecting the steering wheel to the right. This had the opposite intended effect and we went into a spin, which meant Lizz's short legs then missed the brakes, and we hit the one fucking tree on the block.

We were probably only doing forty by then, but that collision would have thrown me against the door. Only I didn't have a door anymore. So I got tossed out.

In the movies they always show the hero leaping from the vehicle, rolling on the pavement, and coming up without so much as a hair out of place, ready to continue the fight against the army of villains in pursuit. Entertaining, sure. Realistic, oh no. For one, it's probably a stuntman jumping from the car. Two, the reel was probably sped up a little to make the car appear to be moving at a much higher speed. Because realistically, you're gonna get hurt.

What should have happened was me losing all my exposed skin as I slid across the pavement, broken all my teeth, probably an arm or leg as well, and maybe some ribs.

It's what would have happened to any normal human being.

Sometimes it's nice to not be normal. I like to claim that I always land on my feet, but not doing forty.

I hit hard on one shoulder, bounced, smacked my head on the ground *again*, somehow landed on my knees, and slid to a stop. The pain was intense, almost causing me to vomit from the sheer, sudden intensity of it, but I'd gotten off easy. Sure, I had a concussion, but at least those knee pads Lizz had sewn in there for me had worked great!

The monster began stalking toward me now. I knew it could smell my blood, my injury. Monsters are like that. Any weakness, any injury, and they go into predator mode. Before it had been lashing out, trying to hurt us. Now, with fresh blood in the air and a seemingly helpless victim, it was savoring the moment before the kill.

Boom!

A .357 fired directly over my head to hit the monster in the shoulder.

Dang, Lizz was tough, and not about to let some little thing like a car crash slow her down. Another bullet hit the monster in the chest, right between the eyes. That was good shooting considering we were now in the dark.

Except we weren't.

I blinked, feeling stupid. The light was from oncoming head-lights. The monster didn't seem to notice there was something larger and decidedly more dangerous coming up from behind it.

I should probably move.

Rhino's van seemed larger than anything else I had ever seen in my life, and even though everything hurt, and I was feeling rather dizzy and sluggish, I staggered up and somehow managed to get out of the way.

An unearthly scream filled my ears as the lower half of the monster was pulverized by a few thousand pounds of a fast-moving van. Blood and fluids splashed everywhere on impact.

The van's engine coughed, sputtered, then died.

Inside the van, someone was shouting. Dark clouds of smoke erupted from the front as a fire started in the engine compartment. The Ewaipanoma was trapped under the front tires, still alive, but not reacting well to the fire. The rest of my team climbed out of the back of the van in a hurry.

A puddle was spreading along the ground from the back end of the MCB Plymouth. It took me a second to recognize a new smell. *Gasoline.* The van had wound up only a few feet away.

Oh, that was bad.

I forced myself up and stumbled to where Beesley was still in the back seat unconscious.

"The door's bent!" Lizz shouted. "I can't budge it. I can't get her out."

The head injury and near-death experience must have lowered my inhibitions a bit, because the *nagualii* was right there waiting for me to ask for help, and I tore the twisted metal wide open with my bare hands. Lizz just stared at me in shock as I hoisted Beesley out.

I carried her away as the puddle reached Rhino's truck, soak-ing the monster's fur. It raged and thrashed and was even making some progress trying to lift the van off itself, but not for long. I didn't know how big the explosion was going to be, but as a rule of thumb, the farther away the better.

Then Kimpton was running alongside me, warning, "There's dynamite in the van still."

Where'd he come from? I kicked the running up a notch.

My team stopped what felt like a safe distance away, and I was glad to put Beesley down. She was still breathing, so I sure hoped all that effort hadn't been for nothing. I collapsed to the ground with the worst headache ever, while the stars spun in circles overhead.

Alex knelt next to me. "Are you okay?"

"Ha!"

"I think she's in shock." He gently moved himself into position to cradle me so I wouldn't hurt myself further. Fingers probed through my hair. "She's got a bad head injury."

Alex was either stronger than I thought, or I had lost some weight, he maneuvered me so easily. He also smelled surprisingly good. I nuzzled my cheek on his chest, which caused him to squirm uncomfortably.

"*Hola, chico,*" I purred into his chest. Or was it the *nagualii*? "*Eres muy bonito.*"

"I think she's really concussed!" Alex added loudly. "Not making much sense. Lizz?"

"We got everyone here," Justin shouted in reply. "Keep your heads down. Van's gonna blow."

As if on cue, the flames from Rhino's engine met the fuel on the ground. I watched with mild euphoria as the fire spread, rapidly heading toward the destroyed gas tank of the Plymouth. The monster's screams were becoming more and more desperate.

"Oh, Agent Beesley's going to be *mad*," I laughed and closed my eyes. My head was spinning, probably from all the blood loss. Or the head injury. When did I hit my head? Weird.

"Just wait until Rhino finds out what we did to his van," Alex said.

Mercifully, just before the world blew up, I passed out.

"...biggest explosion I've ever seen in my life," a voice was saying as I came to. Everything looked fuzzy and it took me a moment to realize I was no longer in the middle of the street being attacked by monsters. Glancing around, I recognized the bunk room at HQ, and from the sunlight coming through the window, it was the middle of the afternoon. The speaker continued, unaware I was awake. "Glad you remembered those explosives were in the van before the fire hit, or I don't think any of us would've lived!"

"Rhino's still furious about his van blowing up, though," Melanie said from somewhere to my left. She stepped into my field of view. "Hey, look who's finally awake."

"Your healing ability is amazing!" The first speaker turned out to be Alex, and he looked relieved to see me awake. "If not for the whole 'my father is a monster' thing, this seems like a pretty neat thing to have."

"The van blew up?" I asked, rolling my neck to see how badly I was injured. It didn't feel too bad, mostly sore. My back wasn't throbbing with pain, so either I was on the good pain meds or it had healed. Perhaps both.

"Alex blew up his van," Melanie corrected.

"That was only partly my fault." Alex sounded sheepish. "I mean, it's not my fault the box full of explosives was unlabeled. Melanie remembered, though, and we got away before they went up."

"Agent Beesley?" I asked.

"Alive but in the hospital still," Melanie answered. "Lizz is okay. Because an agent died, the MCB said they want to question you."

"I'm not even sure what happened," I admitted, and honestly, everything was rather blurry. "How long have I been out?"

"A day and a half," Alex helpfully provided. "But like you asked, we didn't take you to the doctors. We've been taking turns watching you. Let's see, what else...? A three-car accident is pretty easy to explain, so MCB was actually happy about that."

Melanie handed me a cup of water, and I took a big drink. I would've preferred coffee. "What about the hag?"

"Lizz told us everything you said, but she thought we shouldn't tell the MCB. If Beesley and her partner were suspicious her boss was crooked, then who knows who else might be involved?"

Melanie gave me the plastic container with Rhino's codeine pills in them. I popped three of them in my mouth, and washed them down with the rest of the water. "Good call."

"But we know when they were checking the neighborhood to see if there were any witnesses, that house was empty. It's a vacant rental."

That made no sense. "Did she lure Orwig out there just to have him killed? If she had him under her control, why? We've got to talk to Beesley."

Alex and Melanie shared a look, and Melanie said, "Sorry, Chloe, she's in a coma. They don't know if she's going to pull through or not. She doesn't have Aztec princess powers."

I closed my eyes. "Shit." I should have stopped her, taken charge, done something to keep her from rushing in, not that Feds ever listened to people like us. "That's on me."

"Not from what Lizz told us," Alex said. "We don't even know what the monsters that attacked you are, and their bodies got burned in the fire."

"The big one was what's called an Ewaipanoma. They're native to the Amazon."

"I thought so!" Alex seemed proud of his correct guess. "But it was hard to tell off Lizz's description, what with it being pretty dark, and her trying not to die. They're terrible things, but extremely rare and never seen in the US."

"They were sometimes used as foot soldiers by the Court of Feathers in their glory days, though," I muttered, recalling Tezcatlipoca's words about how our mystery threat was recruiting monsters. "Which means the little thing with the tail hand that ambushed Orwig was probably an ahuizotl."

That seemed to make Alex's day. "Those are the ones who hide in rivers, crying like a kid drowning, and when someone rushes over, sees the little hand sticking out of the water, and goes to help, it drags them down and drowns them, just out of spite."

"That's mean," Melanie said.

"Ambush predator, and the little shit packed a punch too," I said, as I gently touched the wicked lump on my head. "Good PUFF on both of those, I take it?"

"Yeah, I'll have to look it up, but it's a nice payday." Alex nodded, smiling now. "Not bad, Chloe. Not bad at all!"

"I'll go tell everybody you're okay." Melanie got up to leave.

"More important, tell them that that his hag has to be our big bad monster that the Court of Feathers was warning me about. *She* is coming. And our crazy werewolf was taking orders from a woman."

"Are hags powerful enough to do that?" Melanie asked.

"Oh, yeah. They can be. Recruiting monsters and co-opting the federal monster cops at the same time? She's dangerous and up to something."

"I'll warn them," Melanie said as she left.

Once we were alone, Alex seemed really hesitant about something. "Hey, so, uhm..." He scratched the back of his neck. "While you were injured, you said something to me...about..."

I remembered, but I feigned stupidity, because frankly, I'd been knocked stupid. Yes, Alex was a very attractive young man. However, I was a very old, moderately attractive half human who kept the potential romance side of my life totally locked down, not even sorta open to exploration. Relationships with colleagues were complicated anyway, and I was extra complicated, with an incomprehensibly different background and life experiences and a whole lot of baggage that I wasn't going to inflict on any poor Hunter. The downside was that I was a workaholic with no social life, so the only men I ever got to know were my coworkers...so basically I was a nun...with the occasional meaningless liaison every decade or so, over the last half a century, which I'd tried to forget about afterward.

I'd dealt with Mrs. Robinson situations before. It got easier over time.

"I'd just got brained and everything was blurry. I don't remember what I said. I apologize if it was something dumb. Let's just forget it ever happened and never ever talk about it again. Cool?"

"Yeah, totally cool..." I couldn't tell if Alex was relieved or disappointed, but whatever it was he was quick to move on. I'd been told that even though I have a young face, I've got old eyes, and luckily that scares most potential suitors away. "This whole situation, I mean with the MCB SAC, it feels like it's connected to the werewolves, the human sacrifices, and the warnings from your relatives, like there's something strange afoot and it's all connected. Why did two monsters who are native to Mesoamerica assassinate a senior MCB official in California? While he was out on what appeared to be a date with a Fey creature? Was it her doing? Because if the hag wanted him dead, she had plenty of other ways to do it that wouldn't draw attention from the MCB. Even powerful monsters avoid attracting the government's eye. Or did someone else send the assassins? If so, who? The Court of Feathers maybe? But why?"

That was too many questions for a headache this bad. I yawned, feeling like I could sleep for another two days. "We'll figure it out. Tell the MCB I'm still brain damaged. I'm going back to sleep now. Wake me up tomorrow."

CHAPTER 10

Two days later, I found myself sitting in the interrogation room of the regional office of the Monster Control Bureau, staring across a plain steel table at the biggest man I'd ever seen in my life. He wore a scowl on his ugly face and his gigantic fists looked more comfortable punching things than filling out paperwork. He sported a dark suit and one of those clip-on ties that were all the rage. I wasn't sure how he found a suit big enough for those shoulders. His hands were massive and looked perfect for choking the life out of someone.

I don't intimidate easily. I especially don't get intimidated by regular humans.

This dude wasn't regular.

There was a second agent in the room who did almost all the talking. He was also seated across the table, with the big one next to him. Agent Travis Stewart acted like a decent enough sort, though I'd seen too many movies with scenes similar to this. Stewart was the good cop, and the scowling hulk to his left was the bad cop. Stewart might have been handsome in his youth, but stress and time were treacherous bastards, and now he looked worn down, getting wrinkled and grey. I'm pretty sure the unintroduced agent had never been considered handsome. *Scary* would be a more apt description.

"Chloe Mendoza. Part nagual, part human. United States

citizen, naturalized in 1935." Stewart read from my file. "Looking good for an old woman."

"Thank you."

He continued "PUFF Exemption earned by voluntary service on Special Task Force Manticore during World War II. Interesting. What'd you do there?"

"That's classified," I said sweetly.

The big one grunted. It sounded like an agreement.

"You were later granted the Israeli equivalent to a PUFF Exemption. I didn't know that was a thing. How'd you end up there?"

"I liked the weather." There was no reason for me to volunteer any information on how I ended up in Israel in the first place, or what I'd done afterward. I suspected there were elements within the US intelligence community who might have an inkling, but apparently the spy department didn't talk to the monster hiding department. Earl knew why I'd gone, and for him I might give some details about some of the ops I'd participated in that led to my recruitment by the Kidon. But these guys? Screw them.

"Some people in my office have insinuated you might be working as a clandestine foreign agent."

"You got me. I've infiltrated Pasadena to steal America's cutting-edge secret technologies, like linoleum. Come on, Agent."

"I'm trying to help you, Ms. Mendoza. Your interference in an MCB internal affairs investigation may have cost the lives of two agents," Stewart said as he opened another manila folder and began flipping through pages. "Special Agent in Charge Orwig, as well as Agent Jacob Latrell. Agent Erin Beesley is still in the hospital."

"Is she going to be alright?"

"She's awake, but will have a long recovery, and might be looking at a medical retirement. Time will tell. That's three capable agents removed from the equation, with no good explanation for why a PUFF Exempt creature who has spent the last few decades working for a foreign power was even there. So explain to me why I shouldn't just turn you over to Agent Franks for a more thorough interrogation."

So that's the big guy's name. "It wasn't my fault. We were after something else when we ran into Beesley."

"What, pray tell, would that be?" Stewart asked, leaning back in his seat.

"A werewolf, which I've repeatedly reported to the MCB. Then I spotted the Fey."

"Fey don't just waltz around letting anybody see their true form," Stewart pointed out.

He was a sharp one. I'd have to be careful around him. "I saw through her glamour."

He went back to the first file. "That wasn't disclosed as one of your abilities when you applied for your exemption. You realize withholding information on an exemption application is a serious offense, right?"

"I've never seen a hag before. This was a new experience for me."

"You're lying," Franks growled.

I blinked at him, surprised, as that had been the first time he'd uttered a word the entire time we'd been here. The menacing aura around the guy compelled me to be a little more forthcoming.

"I've learned I can see through some creature's illusions, sometimes, if I'm really paying attention," I clarified, striving to sound more honest and less combative. It wasn't like I'd known I could see through that level of glamour before the hag showed up. "Since we were looking for the werewolf, I was definitely using all my senses to find her. That's how I spotted the Fey. I'll be happy to update my exemption paperwork with that detail."

"Of course, because you're a proper law-abiding mostly human citizen . . . So why wasn't this potential new werewolf not on your original report to us?"

"I don't know why Nicole wasn't on your report, because she was on mine. That sounds like an MCB problem. And when I told Beesley about it afterward, she sounded surprised. My take is that someone in your LA office left that part out on purpose, and maybe, just maybe . . . Naw. You don't want to hear my *crazy* theory."

Stewart sighed and crossed his arms. He was half the size of Agent Franks but looked fairly tough and had clearly been around the block a few times. "Let's hear it."

"The MCB failed to notice that a series of *cougar* attacks and missing persons cases, spanning years, had werewolf written all over them . . . because somebody in this regional office didn't want it noticed. None of your agents ever went to check it out."

"How do you know we didn't?"

"Because if the deputy who had made it his life's work to

catch the damn thing hadn't been talked to, then either nobody has, or you guys really stink at your job. Beesley—who strikes me as honest and nosy—looks into it, and next thing I know we find her tailing her supervisor...who just happens to be on the arm of a nefarious, mind-controlling, string-pulling, fairy-tale creature. What a coincidence. Somebody suspicious might think the LA MCB is compromised by monsters. Including the MCB, which is why you two out-of-towners are here to investigate them."

"What makes you think the two of us are from out of town?"

"Because if *that* was local"—I gestured at Franks—"Beesley wouldn't be so overworked trying to intimidate witnesses."

Franks grunted what sounded like an agreement. Stewart had to grant me that one. "We're from Washington. Is there anything else you want to tell us about this *theory*?"

"No. That's pretty much it."

Franks scowled but said nothing. Stewart clearly wasn't buying it, but I wasn't lying. I was leaving some things out, but that's different from lying. Stewart looked to Franks, like he was a giant ugly polygraph machine, but Franks nodded, and that seemed to satisfy Stewart I was telling the truth. I wasn't sure what was going on in Franks' brain but the hamster in the wheel must have been getting tired.

"I can neither confirm nor deny any internal MCB issues, but Agent Franks and I look forward to getting this matter cleared up."

Probably meaning they were going to see who other than Orwig had been tainted by the forces of evil, and then remove them. Permanently. I actually felt a little bad for the other local agents, because Franks struck me as a *shoot first and don't ask questions* kind of guy.

"Good," I stated. "Since there's probably a baby werewolf running around getting ready to rampage at the next full moon we really need to find, can I go now?"

"Oh, there's just one last small thing to clear up," Stewart said. I tried not to grumble too loudly as he continued to flip through his notes. "What is your relation to the Court of Feathers?"

I blinked. *How did the MCB know about those clowns?* "None. Well, I mean, I know who they are..."

"Are you, or have you ever been, a vassal of the Court?"

Well, *that* was weird. Time to be honest. I shook my head. "No, never."

"Have you had any contact with them recently?"

"Uh," I swallowed, suddenly nervous. "*They* contacted *me*."

Stewart looked up from his notes. His expression could be best described as bland. It made every hair on my neck stand up in alarm. "Go on."

"They sent a messenger, who claimed to warn me that something—not them—was threatening this city." My eyes drifted back over to Agent Franks, and I couldn't help but wonder how many different ways he could rip someone's arm off and beat them to death with it. I coughed and continued. "A so-called dark master. We're investigating."

"Why do they care?"

"I don't know."

"Why you?"

"Distant cousin, I guess."

Franks grunted again, and from his unblinking glare I couldn't help but think he wanted to use me as a hand puppet. Which was a mental image I didn't need dancing around in my head.

"If any member of the Court of Feathers reaches out to you again, you are ordered to report any and all contact to the MCB immediately." Stewart's tone was cold and flat.

I opened my mouth to speak but stopped after Franks grunted, and that time I could have sworn it was an angry grunt. Swallowing, I meekly nodded.

My PUFF Exemption gave the MCB leverage they could apply on me whenever they wanted. Israel was similar, but at least there once you earned your exemption they treated you like a human being, and not just some expendable thing they could bully and threaten. I hated this part. I felt my temper begin to rise a little and squashed it, hard.

"Since Agent Beesley's down and your SAC is dead, who exactly would I report to?"

"Me." Agent Franks crossed his arms and I swear his biceps made the seams of his jacket beg for mercy. The guy probably ate barbells for dinner.

"Agent Franks and I will be in town until a new Special Agent in Charge of Los Angeles is assigned."

"Okay, goody," I muttered, really not looking forward to working with tall, dark, and brooding.

✧　　✧　　✧

It took over three weeks before everything was cleared up with the MCB. Agent Franks was a bastard but unless I screwed with him, he pretty much left me alone. Since I didn't have a death wish and nobody from the Court tried to contact me, I was only required to call in weekly, which consisted of me talking and him saying little to nothing until he got bored and hung up on me. My guess was he really hated dealing with this petty stuff, so I tried to keep the calls short and to the point. It seemed like he preferred it that way. Or not. I didn't know or particularly care.

With the full moon approaching, we all suspected our werewolf would be making an appearance. Assuming there weren't some half-eaten bodies out there nobody had found yet, we'd gotten lucky the last time. I figured Nicole had driven herself out to Death Valley or someplace equally secluded and stuck around there for three days during the last full moon. That was my assumption since there hadn't been any gruesome unexplained murders. Nicole had done the world a small favor by hiding from us so well.

If she could keep that up long term, and leave mankind alone, I'd be rooting for her. Experience demonstrated that almost never worked out.

We'd kept up our club-hopping search. Only now our primary target was a werewolf and our secondary, a hag. Stewart wasn't exactly forthcoming, but he did tell me that there'd been no sign of Orwig's lady friend since the incident. Still, Melanie enjoyed herself, since we were footing the bill.

The nightclub we'd seen the hag outside of went out of business two days after we'd spotted her. That sort of thing happened all the time in Hollywood, but it meant we were starting from scratch. Beesley had said she was supposedly some kind of model from Europe, but you'd be surprised how often nonsense like that got tossed out about mysterious pretty ladies in LA. Half the self-proclaimed *European countesses* here were actually girls from Ohio or Kentucky who'd tried to make it as actresses and failed.

It had been an interesting couple of weeks. The nightlife side of the city's culture was a cocaine-fueled, nonstop party that would have made Dionysus blush. It was drastically different from what I saw in the daylight. America had changed a lot since I'd left, with a big chunk of society getting disillusioned and saying to "hell with it" thanks to Vietnam. This country was so changed from the one I'd left that at times it was barely recognizable as the same place.

Los Angeles was the epitome of this attitude. The problem was, I didn't know if this growing disgust at the culture was because of how much things had changed, or if the *nagualii* was influencing my opinion, hoping to turn me into a vengeful killing machine. I really hoped it was the former. If the *nagualii* was beginning to influence my emotions too much, I was going to have to talk to Earl.

The odds of me enjoying said talk were about zero.

After Lizz and I had nearly gotten killed, Rhino had decided that search parties of three would be safer than pairs. I'd disagreed, as three groups would cover more ground than two, but Rhino had been adamant. Since his leg was still in a cast, he got to bitterly stay at HQ manning the radio and answering the phone, so I think the decision was mostly to help him feel like he was still useful and in command. I really felt for the poor guy.

That night it was me, Lizz, and Melanie working as a team. We were all dressed to the nines, three single ladies out on the prowl. Or at least, that's the image we were trying to project. If anybody had checked they would have been surprised to discover the amount of weapons a woman could pack.

Cruising through West Hollywood, we weren't just looking for suspicious activity. This was Southern California, after all. There was a lot of stuff that could be considered suspicious if one didn't know any better. There were street performers who looked like monsters, monsters who were actual humans, and everything in between was out and about. There was so much pent-up energy in the city I was surprised it didn't explode. Hunting for something suspicious would have turned me into an alcoholic in short order. Or a chain smoker, like Earl.

We didn't even know if the hag was still here, or if she'd just been passing through. Fey were ugly but they were fascinated by beautiful things. The lore about hags said they liked to prey on and torment pretty people, and the only other place we'd seen her had been a club, and there was no shortage of pretty in places like that. The problem was, if the others ran into her while out looking for Nicole, they might not even know. I seemed to be the only one immune. Judging by how Lizz had perceived her, her glamour was good enough to fool even somebody experienced.

We passed a few clubs where the crowds didn't seem big enough to warrant closer inspection. For all we knew, Nicole could be a thousand miles away by now. Our best guess for the hag was, being Fey, she'd want the best-looking specimens, which meant bigger crowds and better men to choose from. If the club wasn't packed, it wasn't popular, which meant the hag wouldn't get whatever it was looking for. Fey were creatures of habit and rarely changed their methods. If the hag was hunting, it wouldn't change despite knowing we were onto it. One of the few perks about going after something of this caliber.

That night, we stayed close to the area we'd spotted the hag the first time, hoping that she might stick to familiar territory. Just because the original nightclub was now shuttered didn't mean she'd move to an entirely new location. Alex had suggested this, because from his reading whenever Fey were hiding among humans they were prone to be just as territorial as any natural predator.

As we passed Mann's Chinese Theatre and turned onto North Orange Drive, something caught my eye. It was a tiny little club by all appearances, but there was a long line stretching halfway down the block. Every man was dressed to impress, but oddly enough I couldn't see very many single women in the line. There were a few couples, though. I wondered if this meant the bouncers were letting in a lot of women and holding back the men, to keep it from becoming nothing but a stagfest. Glancing up at the sign above the door, I nearly slammed on the brakes as I saw the name of the place.

SIREN'S LAST CALL.

"Oh, you've got to be joking," I growled.

Melanie, riding in the passenger seat, noticed the name and chuckled darkly. "That's a good omen."

"It's worth a shot," Lizz added. I circled around the block, looking for a parking spot. I got lucky and found a space with a busted parking meter. Lizz leaned between the front seats of the car and brushed her curly hair out of her face. I handed her one of my spare headbands from the glovebox and she slipped it on. Bedazzled, she continued. "If I were an alien bat-monster thing who seduces and eats people, that's the sort of place I'd get drawn to."

"That's so morbid," Melanie said.

"Ayup, it's nothing but false promises and honeymoons until someone decides they're hungry and wants a midnight snack."

"Focus," I told them. "We're here to find a werewolf."

"And let hot men buy us drinks!" Melanie exclaimed.

"And let the *attractive ones* buy us drinks," I allowed. It wasn't as if we couldn't afford to buy our own, but for some reason, martinis always taste better when someone else is paying for them.

"Just don't leave with any of them until Chloe can give them the once-over to make sure they're not a Fey in disguise," Lizz added mercilessly. "There could be a whole herd of them in town!"

"Herd?"

"Pod. Tribe. Whatever."

It was Melanie's turn to sigh in exasperation now. "I'm not planning on leaving with anybody, Lizz. We're on the clock."

"Right, right," Lizz waved her hands in the air. "You've never gone home with a cute guy before, like last week?"

"I'm not a slut!" Melanie protested. "It was one time, and nothing happened!"

I must have been on a different search team that night. "What happened now?"

"Right, you guys went back to his place and . . . what? Read poetry? Studied nuclear physics? Ayup, that's what happened."

"It was my place, actually," Melanie sniffed and crossed her arms. She seemed a little offended. "And we played Parcheesi."

"Sure ya did."

"We did!"

"Right."

"That's all we did!"

"No, really. I believe you."

I gently banged my head against the steering wheel and prayed for strength. Children. They were all children. The *nagualii*, for once, agreed.

It was going to be a long night.

As we approached the front door of the disco, I noticed many of the men in line were looking the three of us up and down with very interested expressions on their faces. Melanie, who was tall, leggy, and blond, drew most of the attention. I knew I looked exotic and mysterious, which garnered a good share of appreciative looks, while Lizz, even with her limp, cut a very striking figure with her strategically applied makeup and a very slinky red dress. Shiny bedazzlements were in, and we fairly sparkled as light danced off our outfits. The shimmering effect had been Melanie's idea, because in theory if we were dazzling people with our clothes, they'd be less likely to notice our eyes suspiciously tracking everything around us.

It was a clever idea. The Kidon had trained me to be more subtle, relying on stealth over misdirection, not being seen at all, or if you had to be seen, be totally unnoteworthy. This was the opposite.

The bouncer didn't even slow us down as we strolled up to the front door and skipped the line. That wouldn't have worked if we'd gone with my original instinct, so points to Melanie there.

I overheard somebody asking one of the bouncers if "the Mistress" was going to be here tonight. Which caused me to share a nervous glance with Lizz. Normal club owners didn't call themselves the Mistress. At least not in public—well, that might not be true. This *was* West Hollywood, after all. I'd heard about pleasure dungeons and other... things. I might be reading too much into the name, but I'd been extra paranoid lately.

The entrance led down a set of stairs, through a doorway, into a surprisingly big space. I could see a dazzling array of lights dancing across the walls and ceiling. It was packed, a sea of humanity struggling to let off steam after a frantic work week. There was an indescribable frenetic energy around everyone that made me dizzy. Maybe I was just old, but music had gotten louder. Taking a deep breath, I followed Melanie and Lizz through the buzzing room.

Inside, the melodic tone of George McCrae's "Rock Your Baby" filled our ears. The slow, rhythmic dance beat caused our hips to sway. It was powerful, mesmerizing. I suspected if I was a werewolf sowing her wild oats, or a hag wanting to prey on the young and virile, this was the kind of place I'd want to be.

"I'll go get us a table," Melanie said as she slid between two men who had appeared from somewhere nearby. "You boys should buy us drinks." And they followed her like lapdogs, not even giving Lizz or myself a second glance. If not for the real reason we were here, I might have been offended.

"How does she do that?"

Lizz was clearly annoyed. "Ugh. Because she's tall and blond, with legs that go on for days."

Our teammate was hot. No amount of grumbling would change the fact, but Melanie had already found us a good lookout position. The table was also on a slightly elevated spot where we could look out over the dance floor, and a few dummies to flirt with would keep away the rest of the lounge lizards.

"Overachiever," Lizz complained as we moved through the crowd to where Melanie was already seated. She gave up the stool with the best view for me, since I was the only one who could see through the glamour of the Fey, it made sense for me to have the best seat. Unfortunately, this put Lizz with her back to the dance floor, which left her displeased.

"These are the Charleses," Melanie introduced us to her two new loyal followers, then laughed coquettishly. Both men smiled widely, completely smitten, as she laid on the dumb blonde routine a little thick. "Can you believe they're both named Charles? What are the odds?"

"What are we drinking, ladies?" one of them asked.

"Apple martini," I said.

"Water," Lizz grumbled.

I quirked an eyebrow at her. I knew she was irritated at getting ignored by the men, but I hadn't realized just how mad she was about it. We needed to blend in. She caught my look and sighed. "Fine. Gin and tonic."

"Charles? Would you be a dear...?"

"Right away!" both Charles chirped in unison and scurried off, leaving the three of us alone for a few moments. Once they were out of hearing range, Melanie turned a basilisk gaze on Lizz.

"What is your problem? We're supposed to be undercover!" There was no danger in anyone overhearing Melanie, since the speakers were about as loud as a jet engine. "Water? Might as well act like you've got a badge on you. I wouldn't be surprised if someone thought you were a narc."

"Just once I'd like to play the dumb blonde routine and have the boys fawn over me," Lizz complained.

"You're not even blonde!" Melanie threw her hands into the air. "You know what? Fine. The next time we go out, I'll pretend to be a foreign exchange student who doesn't speak English and you can do all the talking for me."

"Drinks are here," I warned them as the two Charleses came back with about a dozen drinks on a circular tray. Apparently the dynamic duo thought buying us extra at once would increase their odds of getting lucky. I didn't think they knew what they were getting themselves into. I momentarily felt a little pity for the boys' wallets.

The martini was actually decent, the glass chilled, and even Lizz's mood perked up after sipping her drink. The place had the sort of *je ne sais quoi* that would make it very trendy and popular in a hurry.

As the night went on, the Charleses were replaced by a Mark and a John, followed by a trio of college students we didn't even bother getting the names of, and then a tall, handsome guy I thought I recognized from a TV show who called himself Dirk. Melanie smiled, flirted, and gave out wrong numbers for them to call her—except for Dirk, who got her actual phone number and a kiss on the cheek. I had to give her some credit—she was doing her job of distracting the men while I continued my scanning. Even if Lizz wasn't happy about it, she hid it well by pounding her drinks like a sailor on shore leave. I had no idea where she was putting it all.

I got asked to dance a few times. I always said no. You can't really watch a crowd while you're dancing, plus, I had absolutely no idea how. And disco was way out of my wheelhouse, though part of me was tempted to try, but it was a tiny stupid part, so I told it to shut up. Despite hundreds of people coming and going, I never saw anyone who looked like Nicole's picture.

It was around midnight when I felt a change come over the club. It wasn't sudden or anything, but a gradual buildup of energy that made the small hairs on the back of my neck stand up. I couldn't see anything different and yet it was there—in the midst of the writhing bodies under the blacklights and disco ball was something I'd never felt before. It wasn't precisely fear, but similar. A few moments passed before I finally realized what the sensation was: terrible anticipation.

At precisely twelve minutes after midnight, the hag appeared in the midst of the gyrating men and women. One second there had been an empty spot on the dance floor, the next there was a horrifying creature who was not of this world among them. The wide, bat-like face of the Fey was hideous atop the body of a withered scarecrow with a beaded dress hanging off its weird limbs. Her jerky motions looked more like a seizure than a dance. The hag's glamour was so strong, though, that nobody else really noted its sudden arrival.

I let the illusion take hold for a second so I could get the layperson's point of view. The spell was powerful enough that the image everyone saw was that of a tall woman with a shapely figure and dark hair. Her eyes were alluring, and her body language practically screamed European wealth and aristocracy. Now it looked like she could dance too, making every move accentuate her figure in a manner maximized to draw attention. She craved the attention, the worship. There was no doubt about it. She knew precisely what she was doing to the men surrounding her. Plus, the blue shimmering dress left absolutely *nothing* to the imagination.

I let my eyes refocus, and the awful leering bat thing returned.

"She's here," I told Melanie and Lizz as I nodded toward the dance floor.

"Who's here?" a strange man who had gotten a little close to Melanie asked, clearly confused. He wasn't nearly as good-looking as anybody else in the club, was older than the rest, and also dressed a little more conservatively than what was appropriate for a disco.

"Ah..." I hadn't really expected to need an answer for something like this. "The...pretty one."

Lizz and Melanie looked that way, and from their knowing reaction, they clearly saw who I meant. Odds were, she was as stunning to all the regular people as she was hideous to me.

"Oh, you're talking about the Mistress," the man said as he followed my gaze. "Stunning, isn't she? Vera Chatelaine. Retired model and entrepreneur. She owns this club."

"You know her?" I asked.

He nodded eagerly. "Well, yes, I do. I'm her accountant."

Of course a Fey creature wasn't going to lower herself to counting coins. She'd have lackeys for that. We were fortunate said lackey had stumbled into us.

"What's she like?" I batted some eyelashes his way, which was unnecessary, since he was completely smitten with Melanie and therefore a font of information.

"Amazing, simply amazing. Of Romanian and French descent,

her family emigrated here before the Iron Curtain went up." He coughed slightly, his skin flushing as Melanie casually stroked his bicep before he continued. "Her family was wealthy. She inherited everything when her parents died in a plane crash. Horrible business. Has a few properties around the valley. Recently started searching for a more permanent place to settle down, though."

"Does she own a lot of clubs?" I asked.

"No, this is the only one so far."

"Does this place make a lot of money?"

His eyes sort of glazed over then. "This business is financially sound," he replied in a dull, monotone voice. The look on his face cleared up instantly afterward.

Paydirt. He'd been enchanted to answer that exact question, in case someone came around, snooping for information on our hag. I was willing to bet a dollar she'd done it herself. All Fey were inherently magical creatures, but their power varied. By all accounts, hags clouded or controlled minds.

You clever bitch, I thought as I turned my attention back to the awful thing twitching and jerking its way across the dance floor. She was intermingling with the other dancers, but had turned her predatory eye onto a particularly hunky young man who was moving drunkenly next to her. I don't think he even realized she was there yet. He was like a seal with a great white coming from the depths below. But when a slow song came on, then he noticed the striking creature dancing very, *very* close to him. She turned him around to face her with but a touch, and I had no doubt she'd picked her dinner for the evening.

His jaw went slack and his eyes glazed over. Undoubtedly he believed he was staring into the lovely dark eyes of some goddess who had deemed him worthy to ascend her heights. If we didn't do something quick, that poor dude was dead, and the hag would have scored her next meal.

"Shit," I muttered as I realized what was going to happen, and that we couldn't just start shooting in a room with hundreds of witnesses. I looked toward Melanie but she was keeping our friendly accountant busy. There was no way I could approach—the Fey would smell me for what I was in a heartbeat. And once she knew she was being followed, she could just disappear, and set up in some other town. Which left one other option.

"Psst. Lizz. Go act like that guy is your boyfriend. Get pissy and cause a scene. The hunky guy dancing with—yeah, him. Get him away from her."

"But—"

"Do it! We can't tip her off who we are, but if she takes him out of here, he's a dead man."

Lizz's eyes widened but she nodded. Sliding off the elevated chair, she sauntered onto the dance floor, making her way through the dancers with ease. For someone with a bad leg, she knew how to disappear in a crowd. I watched her progress until she reached the hag and her ensorcelled target.

For a moment I wasn't sure how Lizz was going to handle this, but I shouldn't have worried, because our veteran hunter had everything under control.

Lizz waited for the quiet instant after the song ended and *crack!* The sound of her palm striking the man square on the cheek was surprisingly loud. Many heads turned to stare as Lizz began screaming at the poor dummy she had just slapped with all her tiny might. For a woman shorter than I was, she was shockingly strong.

"Five minutes! I was only gone for five minutes!" Lizz was in full-on drama queen mode, her fists clenched into tight balls as she stared up at the tall, good-looking dude, who looked like he was waking up from a dream and was really confused what he was doing there. "I was in the bathroom for five minutes and I come out to find you dancing with this *whore!*"

Oh, Lizz was good. I wanted to give her a standing ovation. There wasn't an actress in Hollywood who could have topped this performance. She grabbed him by the shirt and began dragging him off the dance floor and toward the door, still screaming at him about *wait until we get home* and *how could you be such an ass.* She was calling him every name in the book, including some I was pretty sure she made up on the spot. He was clearly dazed and had absolutely no idea what was going on, which was a combination of a mind-control hangover followed by Lizz slapping the snot out of him.

The hag watched the duo depart, and I could see the deep frown on her real face. She licked her fangs, but she made no move to stop either of them as they left the club. I had a hunch that after she'd picked her target, she'd expended a bit of energy to ensnare her prey and now she would need some time to recover.

Serves you right. It looked like our hag wasn't going to be getting her dinner tonight and it was plain to see—for me at least—that she wasn't happy about it. I glanced over at Melanie and the accountant, and both of them were watching the scene too. Melanie was trying not to laugh while the accountant had a pained expression once more.

"The Mistress isn't going to be happy about this."

"Looks like the party's over," Melanie said as she squeezed the man's arm. "Thank you for a lovely time, Paul."

"It's Phillip."

"That's what I said," she said cheerily and hopped off the chair.

I kept us to the far wall, trying to stay as far away from the hag as I could while still keeping an eye on Lizz. She might not know the guy she was manhandling, but she looked like she had a lot of experience in this regard and was doing just fine. I took one last look toward the hag as we ascended the stairs. *I'll be seeing you soon*, I promised.

We walked out into the warm summer night, Melanie right on my heels.

Outside, we found the still-confused man standing next to the bouncers, both of whom were not quite sure what had transpired downstairs and were trying to mollify his confusion. In spite of the late hour, the line to get into the club was still long, and a few of the guys we'd seen earlier were still there waiting, hoping against hope they'd finally get let inside. Judging by their desperate pleas and out-of-style clothing, tonight was not going to be their night.

I don't think they realized how fortunate they were. The hag was truly something else.

"Where'd your girlfriend go?" I asked the man Lizz had rescued from the hag.

He looked down at me, then over at Melanie before giving her a flirtatious smile. "Hey."

Apparently Lizz hadn't slapped him hard enough. Rolling my eyes, I grabbed his chin and redirected his focus back on me. "Hey, focus. I asked you a question."

"The tiny girl with the bum leg?" he asked, still confused somewhat. He wasn't used to women manhandling him. Tonight was his lucky night, apparently. "She took off that way." He pointed toward where I'd parked our car.

I patted his cheek and thanked him before setting off to chase down Lizz. In spite of her leg and claiming she was slow, the tiny huntress was fast and already at the car before we caught up to her. Once we did, though we could see her laughing.

"That was *so groovy!*" she practically shouted. I'd never seen her so excited about anything other than shooting before. She was bouncing like a child on Christmas morning. "I've never gotten to do that before! I've dated lots of guys who deserved it, but *damn* that felt real good!"

"Okay." I unlocked the doors and Lizz climbed into the back seat as I moved around and got into the driver's side. "The important thing is you had fun."

Once Melanie was inside, we began strategizing. "So what now? We go in guns blazing?"

"I'm not sure. We'll have to figure that out. Is this her lair? Or does her fake identity have a home somewhere else? It would be better to hit her someplace without so many innocent bystanders. Either way, for something this dangerous we're going to want all hands on deck."

"So, what about the rule 'do not sup with the Fey'?" Lizz asked as she leaned back in the seat and closed her eyes. Her previous excitement was still there, but it was clear the alcohol was finally beginning to affect her. *About time*, I thought. She'd drunk enough to kill a Russian tug boat captain. "Is she going to own our immortal souls now because we drank her booze?"

"She's not pure Fey, and this isn't her realm, and Fey don't do souls. Plus, somebody paid for it," I responded as I shifted my car into gear. "We should be good."

"I was right. It's probably good you didn't just get water. Those are free," Melanie said. "That could be construed as the Fey giving you a gift."

"You're such a rules lawyer."

Melanie shrugged. "We need to call Rhino and the guys, but then what?"

"Everyone's favorite game show: Stakeout."

Both of the women groaned in unison.

CHAPTER 11

Before we could deal with the hag, we got another call. Southern California was definitely heating up.

Something had woken up while construction workers were digging up the earth to add new rides at an amusement park up in the Santa Clarita Valley. A worker had been killed before the creature slipped back beneath the ground. Per the new contract MHI had with the county, we were obliged to deal with it.

Given the description of the monster in question—"a large, snakelike *thing*"—we'd need all our capable Hunters for this one. Which meant Rhino, still nursing a broken leg, was stuck back at headquarters, still angrily manning the radio. Since they'd blown up his van, we didn't have as much hauling capacity as before so we took three cars. The next biggest trunk belonged to Alex's beast of an Oldsmobile, so he got to transport the explosives. I told him to pray his deathtrap didn't get rearended on the way to the job. My black Chevelle was next, so I got the extra guns, ammo, and a bag of grenades, just in case. Kimpton's little car didn't offer much cargo space, but got better mileage than Melanie's station wagon, so the duo rode up together. Justin still wasn't speaking to me much, and after one exploding car incident too many this month, Lizz didn't want to ride in the Oldsmobile of death. So Justin accepted his fate of riding with our excitable nerd for the hour-plus drive. Once we all had maps and directions, Lizz climbed into my car, and our convoy headed northwest toward the Santa Clarita Valley.

Justin had mostly avoided me since the incident behind the broadcasting station at Mount Lee. I knew he was freaked out by my father's avatar—and really, who wouldn't be? Everybody had taken it differently, but for whatever reason Justin was acting like I'd somehow betrayed them all. We needed to trust each other for this team to work. If Justin couldn't have faith in me to watch his back during a firefight, then he wasn't going to be focused on killing monsters and staying alive. We'd been busy, but I really needed to talk to him one-on-one after this job was done. We needed to have it out or one of us needed to transfer to a different team.

Kimpton wasn't as bad, but he had been suspicious to start with. It was like he went through life expecting everyone to let him down anyway. There was a lot of anger built up in the poor kid. My guess was that most of it was left over from Vietnam. He'd come back from the war completely disillusioned, spit on, abused by people he'd thought were his friends before he'd been drafted. It boggled my mind why anyone would blame the soldiers. If anything, they should be blaming the ones who sent them there in the first place, but... people are strange.

Dealing with people is a lot more complicated than monsters sometimes.

It was a long drive, so I hashed out plans with Lizz. She was great for bouncing ideas off of. Though she hated the fact that I'd had to call the MCB to tell them we'd found the hag. More specifically, I'd had to tell Agent Franks. Killing the thing and collecting the massive bounty should still be our responsibility. But if they found out I'd hidden that from them, MHI would have been in deep shit with the government. Besides, this meant somebody else could keep an eye on Siren's Last Call while we were hanging out at amusement parks.

Santa Clarita Valley was unincorporated territory still, but there were housing developments going up around the south end of the valley. It was a pretty barren place overall to live, but if one could appreciate the aesthetic beauty of rugged California before it was settled, this area would be ideal. Given the current sprawl of Los Angeles and how fast the population there was growing, I figured it wouldn't be but ten, fifteen more years, tops, before the Santa Clarita Valley was nothing but homes and strip malls, and the cities to tax them.

Alex's enthusiasm must have been contagious, because cresting the hill and spotting the large, rainbow-colored tower off in the distance got my heart pumping a little. There was something neat about a place designed to create joy and laughter for people of all ages. Sure, I was an old, jaded monster killer, but that was just kind of neat.

We weren't supposed to go into the park itself. According to Alex, there weren't a lot of rides done yet, and the problem was in the area that was still under construction. We were directed to a rear entrance that took us behind a large hill, away from the main park. Due to the "accident," the park hadn't opened for the day just yet, but apparently delays happened all the time and the park visitors were still patiently waiting to get in. The line wasn't superlong, but it was still a decent crowd out at the main gate.

We parked where we were directed, well out of sight of the witnesses, and my team started kitting up.

"I wonder why nobody's chasing those people away?" Melanie asked.

"It's probably something small enough they just assume we'll handle it fast, and then they can open like normal and start making money," Alex answered.

"That's optimistic of them." Melanie pulled her long, blond hair back into a ponytail, something I'd not seen her do before. Seeing my interest, she explained. "Dinner plans. If this takes too long, I won't have time to shower."

"Nobody'll say anything about you smelling like gunpowder or anything?"

"I'll just say I went out into the desert and did some shooting for fun. Some guys find that hot," she replied before looking at the surrounding hillsides. "Eh. It's almost desert here."

Just then, a burly man with an unshaven face walked over to where we were gathered. He looked around at us, the skepticism clear on his rough features. He'd clearly been expecting something a little more... military. After a moment he sighed.

"You the hunter folk?" He looked especially close at tiny Lizz as he asked this.

"Yeah," I nodded and stuck out my hand. "Chloe Mendoza. Nice to meet you."

"I don't know why, but I was expecting a lot of men with even more guns," the foreman admitted as he shook my hand. He had remarkable calluses, which told me quite a bit about his work ethic. Probably a good boss not afraid to do the work he asked his people to.

"Don't worry, sir. We've got plenty of guns. We try not to drag them out until we know what we're dealing with."

"Sheriff said you handle this stuff a lot." When he caught sight of Justin and Kimpton, I could see the foreman relax a little, as if these were the *real* hunters of the group. It made the client feel better to see some seriously tough-looking dudes, and it made me a little irritated at Rhino for being stupid and breaking his leg, because that man looked like he'd killed one of everything. Things would be a lot easier if he were around. Maybe.

For a moment, I was reminded just how well Special Task Force Manticore worked together during World War II, and how nobody had ever doubted our capabilities. It'd been almost all men in my unit, except for me. Nobody ever looked at them and wondered when the pros were going to show up. Of course, when one of your team members was a massive half ogre who looked like he could toss a Sherman tank a hundred yards, not a single person dared question your viability in combat.

"So what's our critter?" I asked, shaking off the memories.

"Big, black thing with lots of teeth, was burrowed underground," the man said with a wave of his hand. "Scariest damn thing I ever saw. Ate five of my crew before we bailed on the site."

"Five?" They'd only said one on the phone. "We were told it hadn't moved since. Is that still the case?"

"Yeah. I think it's taking a nap."

"Big, dark-colored, underground, lots of teeth, sleeps while it digests. Alex ain't the only one who can read a book," Justin said. Ignoring me, he glanced over at Kimpton. "Five bucks says it's a grinder."

"Five dollars?" Kimpton looked over at his friend before nodding. "Sure, why not?"

"Seriously doubt it's a grinder, Justin," Alex interjected. "I wouldn't make that bet."

"You know what? Let's make it ten, since the nerd thinks I'm wrong," Justin said.

"Naw, I'm good with just taking your five," Kimpton stated. "You're on."

"Afraid of losing ten bucks?" Justin egged him on.

"I'm worried you don't have ten to lose," Kimpton countered. "You'll need the gas money. If you can find a station out here that has some, I mean."

"I'm telling you guys, grinders aren't native to California," Alex said.

"Neither are Ewaipanoma except we blew up one with the van. Fine, five bucks."

"You're on," Kimpton stated, and they shook on it.

Alex shrugged. "Don't say I didn't try to warn you."

"Anyway..." I cut them off and turned back to the site foreman. "Can you take us to a spot where we can see the thing without getting too close?"

"Sure. That way." The foreman gave us directions but didn't want to go with us. We went through the back gate and up a steep hill. Lizz had problems keeping up, so Justin hung back and volunteered to carry her gun case. On the way up, Alex and Kimpton were gawking at all the rides they could see in the distance. A tram car on tracks looked impressive until I realized it was nothing more than a people mover leading to the top of the hill. One of the shops along the path was barbecuing chicken nearby and it made my mouth water. I'd forgotten to eat anything that morning except for some gas station coffee, which should have been illegal to sell since it was more like molasses in a cup than anything else. Lizz had finished two cups of the stuff and proclaimed it the best coffee she'd had in weeks, which caused me to make a mental note to get my friend some psychiatric help. Or new taste buds.

Straddling the top of the hill was the large, rainbow-painted tower we'd seen when we first arrived. The forestry service used towers this like as fire watch stations all across the state, though they fell into disuse as the sprawl of Los Angeles reached them. The park had kept the foundations after purchasing the land and proceeded to build their giant tower on top of it. The height allowed for a complete view of the entire Santa Clarita Valley, as well as parts of the San Fernando Valley in the distance. It also gave us an unobstructed view of the construction site where the monster was.

Once we were up at the top of the hill—with Lizz swearing the entire way—we quickly spotted what had caused the call in the first place. I used my binoculars to get a better look at the monster below. I felt a little bad for Justin. I passed the binoculars over to Alex, because if anybody would recognize the precise species we were looking at, it would be him.

"Holy crap...that thing is *big*." Alex whistled. There was a huge smile on his face as he handed the binoculars to Justin. The former Marine peered through them and started to frown. Alex continued. "That's not a grinder, though, is it? Justin? Any comment? Nothing? Hey, Chloe? I'm pretty sure the thing which *clearly* isn't a grinder is big enough to swallow a car whole."

It was a snake. Probably the biggest damn snake any of us would ever see in our lifetimes. It was thicker than the steel beam it was wrapped around. Looking at its head, Alex wasn't exaggerating, and it probably could fit a car in there. At least a compact. Maybe. It was hard to tell from here—with it being coiled around itself instead of stretched out, I guessed it had to be eighty or a hundred feet long. That was one big snake.

"You sure it's not a grinder?" Justin adjusted the focus on the binos. It was clear he was stalling. "Aww, come on. The foreman said it was a giant black thing with lots of teeth. It's only got two fangs. And that's *not* black. I'm black! That ain't even a dark brown! It's...warm beige, maybe!"

"How much we getting paid for a giant snake?" Lizz asked.

"The PUFF always depends on the type and size of the giant serpent." Alex got a thoughtful expression. "That one looks like a rattlesnake. See the tail? I bet when it rattles the noise could shatter our eardrums. Like standing next to a million tambourines going off at the same time. Given its size? I'd say mid five figures, easy."

"Not too shabby," I replied, except we'd not been prepared to deal with anything quite like this. "How do we kill it?"

"Oh, I've got just the thing," Alex said, rubbing his hands together. He looked positively gleeful, which made me nervous. "If I use up all the explosives in my trunk, I don't have to worry about driving them home!"

"Let's not forget the important thing here," Kimpton said as he stuck his hand out. "Pay me, sucker."

"Can't believe I lost five bucks." Justin opened his wallet and passed a crisp bill over to Kimpton, who accepted it in stony silence. There might have been a slight smile on his face, but since he was always gracious in his victories, it was probably just the sun playing tricks on my eyes. "That's some bullshit right there."

"Focus, boys. Lizz? Can you put a round through its head and kill it so Alex doesn't accidentally blow up half the state?"

"Maybe if I had some sort of anti-tank weapon. It's an easy shot, but the skull on that thing has to be thicker than anything I've ever seen before. My little old bullets are just gonna annoy it."

"What happened to the 90mm we had in inventory?"

"It was in Rhino's van," Kimpton said.

Oh yeah. Oops.

"I brought enough explosives to kill the thing," Alex assured me. He looked a little too eager to play bombmaker. This made me doubly nervous, because in my experience, guys who really wanted to blow things up that badly were one slipup away from vaporizing themselves and their city block. "I mean, I brought enough to take down a building or three. Let me blow it up, Chloe. Please?"

"I know you brought enough," I acknowledged. I wasn't ready to give in just yet. "What about fire?"

"And burn down half of Southern California in the process?" Melanie said and shook her head. "Look how dry the brush is. Those new EPA feds are annoying and *love* whining and fining."

"Can the National Guard call in some sort of training exercise and use artillery?" I continued to ignore Alex and instead asked Justin. He stared at me in stony silence before shrugging. As much as Justin was upset with me, a Marine always knew the mission came first.

"In a few days, maybe," Lizz answered. "Calling in something like that is MCB territory. They'd have to do it. And at that point they just cut us out and we don't get paid at all."

"What about a *little* bomb...?" Alex whined. "Kimpton, back me up here. You were a demo guy!"

"How much dynamite did you bring, anyway?" Kimpton asked.

"Ten ten-pound cases."

"I can't believe I rode with yo crazy ass," Justin muttered.

We were running out of options. Oh, what I wouldn't give for my old contacts in the IDF right now. One phone call and I could call in an airstrike. No more snake. If we left to get bigger weapons, the serpent might have moved on. Or eaten more people. Or slithered halfway to Los Angeles. *That* would be a sight. Santa Clarita Valley wasn't very populated, but there were civilians nearby. A snake this size could be seen all the way from I-5 if it started moving. And the reason we got these jobs was because our clients knew we offered a fast and discreet service.

Kimpton had taken the binoculars. "Damn. That's one fat snake. I wonder how it tastes?"

"Ew!" Melanie grimaced. "You're *so* gross. You'd probably eat octopus."

"*Adobong pusit* is really good. I mean, it's squid and not octopus, but you should try it sometime," Kimpton added for good measure, pushing his hair out of his face.

"Eww!"

"How the hell that putz not recognize a snake when he saw one?" Justin asked, still grumpy about losing his five dollars.

"A bomb, Chloe. Just a small one. Think about it," Alex continued to beg. "Please?"

"*Enough,*" I snapped, because I'd noticed the snake was starting to move. The need to kill something was strong in my heart. War drums, beating. *No.* I shook my head. We needed to kill this thing, and fast.

I looked over at Alex, who had the face of a hopeful little boy on the first night of Hanukah.

"Okay, blow it up."

"Sweet."

"Blow up the *serpent*, and not the entire park!"

"Fine, Mom. Sheesh."

"And no secondary fires either."

"Oh, come on!"

"Alex and Kimpton can put together a bomb, but how do we intend to deliver it?" Lizz asked.

"I . . . got an idea," Justin said, his eyes drifting back toward the barbeque shack.

Watching Alex and Kimpton work together to build a bomb was like mixing an overly complicated drink—one part giddy schoolboy, one part seasoned professional who wanted to keep all his fingers, stirred—not shaken—with a hundred pounds of high explosive, five buckets of chicken gizzards and blood splashed around, and one borrowed golf cart, courtesy of the park staff.

Alex's constant giggling was kind of disturbing.

I went off to hammer out some of details with the site foreman, who was still so angry about his employees getting eaten that he said he'd be happy to deal with any bomb damage. In fact, if we made a big enough crater, they could amend the plans and put in a lake. Fuck that snake.

When I came back, Justin was having a quiet conversation with Melanie away from the others. They didn't hear my approach, and with my better than normal hearing I caught some of what they were saying. Melanie was much easier to listen in on, since her voice kept rising and falling as she grew more irritated with him.

"I don't care what you think. Earl Harbinger trusts her. Rhino trusts her. Lizz trusts her. So you need to trust her."

"No, I don't."

"Yes, you do," Melanie countered hotly. "There's no way we can function as a team if you don't."

"Then she shouldn't have lied to us."

"Gah! She didn't lie, she just didn't volunteer everything about herself. Big difference. Omission isn't lying."

"You sound like a lawyer... stop dipping in my Kool-Aid."

"Hey, guys." I interrupted their conversation from far enough away to be polite. They both looked over at me. Justin was clearly bothered still, while Melanie seemed mad at him. Great. My amazing teambuilding skills had done one heck of a job... tearing it apart. Not for the first time did I silently blame Marco for all of this, because if he'd been here, he would have squashed this before it got to this point. Maybe.

Or not.

"We're just sorting a few things out," Melanie replied. I nodded slowly as Justin threw his hands up in disgust. Turning, he walked away. She didn't bother trying to stop him, so I let him go.

Meanwhile, the giant serpent seemed to be enjoying the warmth of the metal support beam it had curled around, the earlier violence and destruction apparently forgotten while it snoozed after its midmorning snack. The hole it had emerged from was right in the middle of the excavation site. I idly wondered which ride was going to be put in here. From the looks of the beams, it was a big one.

Where had this damned thing come from? Giant snakes were weird and rare. It could have been hibernating underground for centuries. Luckily for us, there weren't any special rules pertaining to these things. Were they magical? We had no clue. My working theory was that they were just big, dumb reptiles. They weren't protected. Fish and Game wasn't going to make us sedate it and drive it to North Dakota. When Hunters found one, it was shoot, shovel, and shut up.

Which, frankly, was rather refreshing.

Lizz had taken position on top of a row of nearby porta potties, her rifle trained on the head of the giant serpent. It was highly unlikely that she would be able to kill the thing, but if it moved she could possibly take out its eyes and blind it. Considering how tough these things were, I didn't have much faith there. Plus, being blind might cause it to thrash and panic, which could cause more harm than good.

Alex and Kimpton worked surprisingly well together. I'd expected more machismo or posturing between them, but Alex took a back seat to Kimpton's real-life expertise when it came to the bombmaking, while the latter listened to Alex's book learning when it came to odd monsters and how to properly kill them.

Alex had pointed out that most rattlesnakes were ambush hunters, which meant they'd be lazy and wait until something stumbled in its path. It would bite them, then follow slowly along until the prey dropped dead from the venom. To encourage our giant serpent to eat the bomb the crazy duo were making, Justin grabbed buckets of guts, blood, and bits from the park's food shacks. It had to have looked suspicious as hell, as they had no idea what was going on in the construction zone, but those employees had been told to shut up and cooperate. He'd used that nasty mess to paint the golf cart.

It was good thinking on Justin's part, and I told him so. He simply grunted and carried on with his gruesome work. I watched in silence for a few moments before I decided I needed to say something.

"I'm sorry."

He paused in the midst of applying chicken gizzards to the hood of the golf cart and looked my way. The anger was still there, but he did his best to keep it from showing on his face, even though it burned through in his eyes. "Okay?"

"Look, I've been dealing with this for a long time. Not everyone reacts in a good way when they find out. The more people I tell, the harder it makes my life. I felt that it was easier to work with you guys first, and get to know the team, instead of making it complicated. I guess that was a bad call. So again, I'm sorry."

"Alright."

"Look, Justin, I'm trying to apologize here."

He didn't reply, instead focusing on his gruesome task. I left him to it, because if I stuck around with his bullheaded stubbornness it probably wasn't going to end well for either of us.

I checked on Lizz, who looked rather comfortable on top of the porta potties. If the smell of the johns and our sacrificial golf cart were bothering her, she wasn't letting on. I knew she'd seen some shit while in St. Louis, but her blasé attitude toward this kind of thing had a calming effect on me. My frustration toward Justin faded as we spoke.

"Ya think we could talk Ray into buying me a proper elephant rifle on company funds?"

"Earl did send us with a bazooka."

She tilted her head slightly. "I never needed anything bigger than my regular trusty old rifle in St. Louis. But then, we never had a giant rattlesnake show up. Undead, sure. City was full of them—ghouls, wights, hordes of the dang things."

I'd only run into a wight once. The idea of them being a common thing gave me chills. "How's the snake?"

"Snoozing still." She checked it through her scope again. "Looks pretty content. I hope it didn't get full on the construction crew and doesn't want the blood cart."

A few minutes later, Alex called out, "We're ready."

I looked over at the converted golf cart and grimaced. While Alex and Kimpton had gotten the bomb secured into the back, Justin had painted blood flames on the front of the golf cart. He'd also used a nailgun he'd found somewhere to pin on some chicken wings and trash bags filled with other disgusting things.

Unfortunately, Justin decided he really wanted to share.

"When the snake bites it, all that blood and gizzards'll pop open and give it a treat. When the bomb goes off, the treat gets spicy."

"I hope it does more than that," I told him as I gave the other boys a look. They seemed almost too pleased with themselves, which made that little spot in my guts tingle nervously. The sensation was similar to the *we're going to die* feeling I always got when plans were about to go sideways. The others must have shared my apprehension because nobody replied. "Are we far enough back?"

"We *should* be out of the blast radius," Kimpton said before frowning, and ticking off numbers on his fingers. "I think."

"If y'all excuse me, I'm gonna hide behind something more solid." Lizz quietly slid down from the porta potties. Shouldering her rifle, she and I moved farther away from the site without another word. Alex, after consulting quietly with Kimpton, joined us.

There was a heavy construction excavator nearby that I took refuge behind. Lizz climbed up into the abandoned cabin for a better view. It was open air, so she took her rifle along, just in case. "This is gonna be great."

It was almost as if Earl had purposefully given me a gang of extremely violent children. We were going to have a talk the next time I saw him.

"All set," Kimpton called out as he finished taping the steering wheel of the golf cart in place. He'd prepositioned it so the front end of the cart was pointed directly at the snake. The road down was more of a dirt path, but it was straight and led almost directly past where the serpent was. Given the immensity of the beast it would be a miracle if he missed. He was using a cinder block to hold down the gas pedal.

The engine of the golf cart didn't sound like it had enough power to make it to the snake, much less carry all the weight from the bomb, but the guys had faith in their tiny kamikaze vehicle of death.

"Clear the cart," Kimpton instructed. He had a radio detonator, and there was a nice, long spool of wire ready to be played out as the cart moved toward the snake. That way if one method failed, we had a backup.

With a final check to make certain the cart was lined up properly and the spool of wire prepared, Kimpton gently set the cinder block down on the gas petal. The golf cart immediately lurched forward and began slowly making its way down toward the snoozing rattler. Kimpton was watching the spool of wire carefully.

Closer. *Closer.*

Kimpton extended the antenna on his first detonator.

"We've got its attention," Justin informed us. "Look."

The giant serpent's head had slowly lifted off the ground and was watching the golf cart lazily cruise along in its direction. I really wished we'd picked one with a little more get-up-and-go, but a Hunter worked with what they had. A few pieces of chicken fell off during the transit, but the two most important parts of the plan appeared to be intact still: the bag of blood and guts on the top, and the giant makeshift bomb.

The sound of a million angry hornets filled our ears as the snake's tail began to shake rapidly. Its tongue flicked out to taste the air. The buzzing grew loud enough to hurt my ears. Alex began to swear.

"What's wrong?" I asked.

"It thinks it's in danger," he explained. "They don't use the rattle when hunting."

"Will it bite the cart?"

"Oh yeah," Alex confirmed. "It just won't eat it."

"Damn."

"Yeah."

"I can time it to blow when it bites the cart," Kimpton said, holding the detonator in his hands.

"Ever seen a snake strike before? They're fast, almost faster than the eye can see," Alex stated, a frown on his face. "I've got no idea how fast this one will be."

We all stared at the golf cart as it rumbled merrily along, completely unconcerned or aware of its fate. Timing was everything. Too early, and the blast might not be close enough to kill the snake. Too late, and its strike could disable the bomb.

"Shit, shit, shit." Kimpton put his finger on the button.

The buzzing sound somehow grew even louder. Even though we were a good distance away and wearing ear protection, it was bad enough that I could feel it in my teeth. It was a good thing we'd demanded that the nearby area be evacuated, because everybody within miles had to be hearing this.

The snake's strike was fast, but not nearly as fast as I'd expected it to be. It was still quick, though, and considering it was bigger than a city bus, something that big flinging itself was absolutely terrifying. Fortunately, our brave little golf cart was inanimate or else it would have screamed in fear and tried to run away.

The snake's bite completely destroyed Justin's giblet bag. Blood sprayed as each of the two-meter-long fangs punctured through the plastic roof of the golf cart.

Kimpton hit the button.

Nothing happened.

The ride must have jostled something loose. The electric engine of the golf cart gave a high-pitched whine before giving up the ghost. The wheels stopped turning and our bomb package delivery system was officially dead. I could hear something sizzling, and it took me a moment to realize the snake's venom was so highly corrosive it was eating away at the plastic of the ruined cart.

"Plan B!" Kimpton squatted down next to the spool, took the bare ends of the wire, and struck them to a waiting battery. He looked up hopefully, and when it still wasn't exploding, said, "Oh shit."

Lizz was watching through her scope. "The strike knocked the wire out! The wire's on the ground."

There wasn't a Plan C, beyond shoot it a whole lot, but before I could give the command to open fire on the snake and hope for the best, Justin shouted at Melanie.

"Lighter! Give me your lighter!"

"What?"

"*Fucking lighter! Give!*" he shouted as the sound of ten thousand angry hornets rose once more.

The snake, clearly irritated, also seemed a bit confused by the sudden turn of events. The long tongue of the serpent kept flickering in and out as it struggled to grasp why the golf cart it had bitten was still there and not running away. It struck a second time, with similar results—only this time there were more golf cart pieces flying around in place of drumsticks and gizzards. The giant head reared back for a third strike but it hesitated, confused. The horn of the golf cart gave a sad little beep as a drumstick slid off the roof and landed on the steering wheel. The snake hissed at the sound.

Nobody ever said giant serpents were particularly smart.

Melanie tossed her lighter to Justin, who snatched it out of the air as he ran, his eyes frantically searching for something, until they locked onto the porta johns. Sprinting over, he grabbed the latch on the closest door and yanked it open, then fumbled around inside for a moment before backing out, holding a large roll of toilet paper.

I realized now what he was going to try...and just how stupid it was. There was zero chance a flaming roll of toilet paper could be thrown to hit the golf cart from such a distance. Unfortunately, I was wrong again, since Justin had no intention of simply throwing a flaming roll at the golf cart and hoping for some luck; instead, he started running toward the damned thing.

"Fire's not gonna work!" Kimpton shouted at us, his voice barely audible to me over the thunderous and constant buzzing. "Stick the wire back in the cap!"

"Wait! Stop!" I shouted at Justin, except there was no way he could hear us over that damned rattle, and he continued running toward the bomb, and the dude was *fast*. "I'll fix the bomb. The second we're clear, hit it!" Swearing up a storm, I went after Justin. This was an incredibly bad idea.

Justin hauled ass downhill, sliding to a stop about twenty feet from the golf cart. That close the buzzing from the rattler had to be absolutely deafening. He flipped the Zippo open and tried to light the roll of toilet paper, only the damned lighter wouldn't light. Catching up with him, I considered the paper for a moment before deciding it was a waste of time. Kimpton knew what he was doing, so if he said setting it on fire wouldn't work, it wouldn't work. The wire needed to be reattached. But would it blow up the moment I did it?

No idea. It didn't matter. The snake was super pissed and moving, so it was kill it now or a whole lot of innocent people were going to be in danger. The snake had to die.

Steeling myself, I sprinted past Justin to the fallen detonator line. The snake's wide head turned and it looked at me, tongue flickering in and out as it tried to figure out what the hell was going on. Dodging left to right, I tried not to stay in a straight line in case the serpent decided to try and take a bite out of me. I was faster than most, true. But was I faster than the RV-sized rattlesnake?

"Stupid fucking lighter!" I barely heard Justin bellow in frustration somewhere behind me.

The line had landed only a few feet away from the ruined golf cart. I kept a wary eye on the pissed-off snake while I snatched it out of the dirt.

When working with the Kidon, one learns many interesting

tricks to the trade. Killing monsters was, after all, their real forte. However, the one thing I'd actively avoided was bombmaking. Honestly, it scared me. "Elegant bombs for inelegant beings" might as well have been their unofficial motto. Sure, I always appreciated the end results. The bigger, the better. Especially when dealing with the myriad crop of monsters that always popped up in the Middle East. But building one? Not my cup of sachlav.

However, Kimpton and Alex's hasty bomb wasn't that complicated, and even I could see exactly where the cord had fallen out. The question remained: would it blow up when I stuck it back in?

There was no time like the present to find out. "Justin, get down!"

I reattached it...and didn't blow up.

Hooray.

The angry snake just looked down at me unblinking, like, *Are you fucking kidding me?*

Justin came running up to me, Zippo in one hand and toilet paper in the other, looking absolutely ridiculous. I opened up my mouth to yell at him for his own stupidity but instinct shrieked at me that the snake was striking. I threw myself against Justin, taking us both out of the way as the massive head whistled past. Fangs dug a trench in the ground where we'd just been. Venom squirted out. Oddly enough, it smelled like cucumbers.

Justin and I both scrambled to our feet and ran as the snake's head lifted, bits of dirt and gravel raining from its mouth onto us. We needed to find someplace safe from the blast so Kimpton could hurry and nuke this thing.

I spotted the original snake hole the same moment that Justin did. We shared a look, and immediately made a break for it. The snake, clearly confused by potential prey running *toward* it, reared up higher, and we were in its shadow.

Deep inside, the *nagualii* pushed against my control in eager anticipation. It loved when I was in dangerous situations. The likelier I was to die, the more I needed it, but I'd rather die than let the monster out. One day the *nagualii* might win, but today wasn't going to be that day.

Legs pumping as fast as they could go, we got away from the cart, and dove into the hole just as the snake's body came crashing down. It slammed into the earth, only we were still falling. And oh shit. Falling.

Flailing into the dark, we suddenly hit the ground. I landed on my feet and rolled. Justin belly-flopped, and the only reason he didn't break bones was that the ground was remarkably *squishy.* It wasn't like diving into a pool of water. More like Jell-O.

Hot, sticky, wet...Jell-O.

Laying there gasping, I looked toward the light above, except it was immediately blocked by the head of a very angry super snake, which was probably wondering what we were doing inside its *house.*

Kimpton must have pushed the button.

There was a thunderous roar. The ground shook, and we were instantly covered in a shower of falling dirt and snake blood.

The two of us lay there, eyes closed, breath held, as we got splattered and pelted.

The ground beneath us was soft but at the same time, hot. Absurdly hot. I inhaled a mouthful of dust and began to cough uncontrollably. There was so much dust and blood and chaos that I had no idea what was going on anymore.

My eyelids cracked open. It should have been pretty dark this far down the snake hole, but light was streaming in from above, because the explosion had made the hole even bigger, caving it in around us. Then I realized that most of me was buried in soft dirt, and I began to thrash, trying to get myself free.

I had a vague recollection of where Justin had landed, and when I looked over, he was totally buried beneath under at least a foot of dirt. "Shit!" I got myself free, rolled over, and started digging desperately. My fingernails hit chest, and then I traced that up to his neck, found his head, and started trying to shove dirt out of the way so he could breathe.

Justin came up gasping like I'd just saved him from drowning. "Jesus!"

"You okay?"

"Yeah!" He wiped the dirt from his eyes, looked up, and blinked. "That was a bigger drop than I thought it was gonna be."

"What the hell were you thinking? Flaming toilet paper?"

"Woman, we needed to kill the snake!"

Somewhere above us, the rattle noise started again. One problem. It wasn't dead.

The rattle was so loud that we could barely hear the gunfire as the team opened up on it.

"Come on." I got to my feet. Luckily, the snake hole wasn't a vertical shaft, and there was enough of an angle we could scramble back up it. The ground beneath my boots felt very unnatural—soft, but not too much give, like we were standing on a water bed. Which caused me to have a terrible thought. What exactly had broken our fall?

Justin must have been wondering the same thing, because he pulled the crook-neck flashlight off his flak jacket, and aimed it farther down the hole. "Are them eggs?"

The shaft we were in kept going down and opened up into a larger chamber. The eggs were everywhere, embedded in some kind of gelatinous snake goo. There had to be over sixty man-sized eggs down here, embedded in the weird nest. Each egg was oblong in shape and white but seemed to pulse with life. Then I realized the texture on the wall immediately around us was actually skin. The giant rattlesnake had shed and used that to pad its nest. Bones—some human, some not—stuck out at seemingly random points.

One of the eggs moved on its own.

"Screw this. I'm out." And Justin started climbing.

Up top, the snake was severely injured but *pissed*. There was a new crater in the ground where the golf cart had blown up, and chicken and snake chunks everywhere. A random tire was rolling away, partially on fire. With the threatening golf cart dead, the snake was heading for the next most menacing thing, which was apparently the humans shooting it with rifles. It was slithering away from me and Justin, straight up the hill toward the others.

Alex, Justin, and Melanie were firing as fast as they could, but it didn't even seem to notice the bullets. The snake was slower than it had been before, and was leaking blood by the gallon, but it was going to reach them in a matter of seconds. They needed to run. Why weren't they running?

Except then I realized the big construction excavator we'd used for cover earlier was rotating. I didn't know anything about heavy equipment, but this thing was like a big crane on tracks, and at the end of the arm were giant scooping jaws. That scoop stopped—bouncing on its cables—directly over where the snake was rushing at my team. A loud *twang* echoed as the crane thing released and the scoop fell to the ground.

Tons of steel hit the snake right on the head.

Its skull must have gotten smashed, but even better it was driven deep into the ground. The rest of the body began to twist and thrash, crushing everything nearby, but its head was pinned. The rest of it hitting the ground over and over made it feel like we were in an earthquake.

Everybody kept shooting. For me and Justin, our rifles were still up top, and I very much doubted a 9mm or a .45 would even sorta make it through that level of snakeskin, but we pulled our pistols and joined in anyway. It felt good to be doing something. The rest of the team treated it like a pincushion.

The golf cart explosion had done a number on the snake, and it was squirting blood from a bunch of lacerations, so it wasn't quite strong enough to wiggle out from under the scoop, but it was furiously making progress. Except the more it pushed the steel jaws to the side, the more it dragged down the huge cables, and as it dug itself free, those got wrapped around its wounded head. The entire crane began rocking back and forth as the snake thrashed.

Lizz leapt out of the crane cabin, just as the entire thing toppled.

The crane arm came down on the snake. A large dust plume erupted from the impact. Blood splashed everywhere. And I mean *everywhere*. The entire construction site got coated in a fine mist of snake.

The violent thrashing was done. Thankfully, that awful rattling had stopped. A loud hissing sound filled the air as the snake exhaled its final breath. Now it was just postmortem twitching.

We still shot it a few hundred more times, just to be on the safe side.

When we were a hundred percent sure it was dead, my team approached the body.

"Son of a bitch!" Kimpton kicked it in the head for good measure. "I just did laundry."

"I think I got snake in my mouth," Alex added, looking a little queasy. He eyeballed one of the snake's now-exposed fangs. "Hmm...I wonder what's the going rate on giant serpent venom? Is there a black market for monster remains out there? You'd think there would be."

I gave Lizz a thumbs-up, impressed, as I hadn't realized she could jump that far, considering how much her leg bothered her.

She was clearly in some pain from it, though. That was the worst of our injuries, though, and in exchange we had just pulled off one hell of a kill.

"Chloe..." Justin interrupted the celebration before it could get going. "What about the eggs?"

"Eggs?" Melanie asked. "It was a momma snake?"

I led them back toward the hole. It was like Justin and I both felt like we had to be the ones to handle it—a little unfinished business. Alex was the only one excited enough to climb down with us. Everybody else was happy to stay at the top after I'd described what was down there.

I was no giant herpetologist, but these eggs were clearly fertilized and looked damn-near ready to hatch. If there were dozens of these things slithering around, the MCB would probably carpet-bomb Santa Clarita into the Stone Age if we didn't do something.

"Think this slime will burn?" Justin palmed the borrowed Zippo, his expression grim. "It feels really oily and this old snake skin is super dry. We just need something to start a fire with."

Something gently bumped my foot. I almost screamed in terror but managed to keep it to a sharp inhale. Looking down, I saw the roll of toilet paper resting there against my boot. Somehow it had managed to survive to eventually roll perfectly into the depths of the cavern without losing one sheet of single-ply to end up precisely where we needed it at the most opportune time.

Sometimes when weird, unnatural things like that happened, I was tempted to accept it as the blessings of Tezcatlipoca. Because my father worked in mysterious—and creepy—ways. But we'd probably just been fortunate and I could chalk it up to clean living and hunter's luck.

Scooping up the roll, Justin eyeballed the eggs before flicking the lighter. It lit easily this time, the flame bright in the darkness. "Oh, *now* you work."

"I really hope those eggs are flammable..." Alex murmured.

Turns out, they were. *Extremely.*

The hole was still smoking—as was the newly created crater—but things had calmed down. The foreman and a few other high-ranking park employees who had been in the know had come out to see how bad the damage was once it was safe. Somehow,

Lizz had bummed a bag of ice off one of them and was sitting on the tailgate of a pickup truck, icing her knee.

"Good job on that crane. How'd you know what to do?"

"I just guessed how to use the controls. Proof that God loves fools, drunks, and children," she declared. "Pure instinct."

"Bullshit."

"Okay, sure, maybe my uncle owned a construction company and I may have ridden in one of these before. But instinct sounds cooler."

"Well, good call." We really should have come up with a Plan C before going in. I'd almost pulled a Rhino.

Some of the braver employees approached the snake, but they were hesitant, as though it might rise up and swallow them whole at some random moment. But Melanie was still eyeballing the dead serpent suspiciously and herded them away from it. Rightly so, in my opinion. The snake might be dead but it was still dangerous. The fangs, for example, were longer than I was tall, and wickedly sharp. I was pretty sure the venom sacs inside the rattler's mouth had to be big as a Saint Bernard, and whatever they were filled with was so caustic it had melted plastic.

Kimpton was having a rather animated discussion with one of the park employees. Curious, I ambled over to listen.

"Dunno yet," the man replied to Kimpton with a shrug.

"Come on. Rattlesnake is delicious. It'll be great with a dry rub."

Judging by the outfit and apron, I was betting this was the guy who ran all the cook shacks Justin had raided, and he was looking over the dead rattler with calculating eyes. After a long pause he began to nod, and in a slow, South Texas drawl, he said, "Yep. I can probably barbecue that thing."

Before I could tell them they really shouldn't try to harvest ten thousand rattlesnake steaks, the MCB rolled up in their typical subtle manner. Five cars, each filled to the gills with armed and angry federal agents, parked in a half circle around our dead snake.

With Beesley gone, Agent Stewart appeared to be the man in charge now, and he went straight to where I was sitting. "Sitrep, Mendoza?"

I gave him the fast version. He wouldn't care about details. And then because I was trying to keep the MCB off my back, I helpfully provided him with the pertinent stuff to make his job easier. "Five dead construction workers. Eight other witnesses that I know of, and I believe all of them are currently here. Nobody outside of the immediate vicinity saw it as far as I know, but you'll need a cover story for the noise, because that rattle was really loud."

"Thank you, Ms. Mendoza." He put his hands on his hips and looked around. "Construction accident clearly. Crane collapse. The noise was from the resulting high pressure gas leak. The gun shots were oxy-acetylene tanks from the cutting torches exploding. Five workers were crushed or caught in the blast. Very tragic."

The site foreman must have realized Stewart was the big-shot government man, because he came over and said, "That's not what happened here. We were digging and hit a giant monster that came out of the ground and started eating us."

"Wrong. Giant monsters are imaginary," Stewart declared, even though we were fifty yards away from a dead one. "Only crazy people say otherwise."

"Who is this asshole?" the foreman asked me.

"He's from the government."

"What part?"

"The not-fucking-around part," I answered, dead serious.

Stewart patted the foreman on the shoulder in a very patronizing manner. "This is nothing more than a tragic workplace accident involving the crane tipping over when one of your crew improperly balanced it."

"That's . . . that's not how it all went down!" the foreman protested. "That big-assed snake *ate* my crew!"

"Construction accident," Agent Stewart proclaimed, eyeing the agitated site foreman critically. "Tragic workplace accident. Happens all the time on construction jobs. Isn't that right?"

"But—"

"Fight me on this and the paperwork will say it was your fault. You'll get your license pulled and never work again," Agent Stewart told the innocent man. "Go with the official story and keep your business. Argue, and lose it. Don't worry, I'll give you and all the other witnesses the official story. Then I will be watching for the rest of your life, and if you fail to stick to the official story, I will happily ruin your reputation, bankrupt you, foreclose on your house, and put you in an insane asylum. Don't make this more difficult than it has to be. Your call."

The foreman stared long and hard at the MCB Agent before swallowing his angry words and nodding. I felt bad for the guy. Dealing with the super-secret agency always left a bad taste in the mouth, especially when it came to covering up the deaths of people who worked for you. "Yes, sir," he finally managed to not-quite spit out. "Workplace accident."

"And you." Agent Stewart turned and looked at me. "I'll have my secretary send you the PUFF claim number."

"Eggs, too?"

"Eggs?" he asked.

"About sixty of them. Fertilized and about to hatch, if that makes a difference. They're in that hole."

He paled a little at that. Agent Stewart didn't like going underground, apparently. "Eggs too."

"Great. Where's your partner?"

"Franks is occupied elsewhere."

I assumed elsewhere was in a sniper's nest outside the Siren's Last Call. "How's Beesley doing?" It wasn't like we were friends or anything, but Agent Beesley and I had fought a monster together. Well, sort of. I'd carried her over one shoulder while I'd fought a monster, but there was always a special bond forged between girls during a gunfight.

"I'm surprised you care," the MCB agent stated. "She's doing better, but she's not very communicative yet, so we've not been able to get her side of the story, if that's what you're worried about."

"Actually, I'm a decent human being—"

"Half," he corrected.

You fucker, I didn't say. "Half-decent human being who just wants to know if Beesley's going to be alright."

Stewart relented. "It appears she'll recover, but it'll take time."

"Thanks." Beesley might be a pain in the ass MCB agent, but she seemed like she had a pretty good head on her shoulders, all things considered. As competent as she might be, though, I'd never let her on my MHI team.

"Why is that man in the apron taking a meat cleaver to the snake?" Agent Stewart asked, looking past me.

"I think he's the head cook, and they're going to butcher and barbeque it."

"*What?*"

"You need to get rid of the evidence, right? Park guests will eat any sort of meat as long as it's smoked and tastes good. Besides, it's just a big, dumb snake."

"They can't *eat* it," Stewart snapped. "It could be something more. You haven't even tested it to see if it's radioactive! It could be diseased. What if it's eldritch cursed? Or magically tainted? Consuming magically tainted snake flesh? That might be how snake people are created!"

"Is that actually a thing?"

"Not that I know of, but I don't feel like trying to cover up an outbreak of food poisoning too. You there! Off the snake!"

CHAPTER 12

Stakeouts are dull. There's no other way to put it. Every minute feels like five, and hours crawl by in a painful manner. You can't read a book or magazine or anything because you don't want to lose track of time and miss the person you're looking for, so you're stuck listening to the radio. Except the radio drains the car battery, and eventually you have nothing but idle conversation to pass the time with. It's doubly horrible when you have to stay night after night while everyone else takes turns rotating out. Since I was the only person who could actually see through the hag's glamour, I had the luxury of sitting in the car for hours on end.

After returning from the amusement park, I barely had enough time to shower and swap out gear before I had to turn around and head out to Hollywood to try and spot the hag, and that's what I had been doing fruitlessly ever since.

The others got to keep looking for the werewolf, and I was jealous. My life now consisted of boredom, staring, and chitchat with whoever I was partnered up with that night. I'd change cars and positions to keep from sticking out, but it was always at some vantage point on the same block in sight of the Siren's Last Call. It did no good for the rest of my team to watch for the fashion model, because if a hag could create one fake identity, she could create more.

It was midweek so the club would be quiet until the weekend.

215

Hags were supposedly nocturnal, and our assumption was this was her lair. Except if we kicked in the door and went in, and we were wrong and nobody was home, then she'd bolt and we'd never catch her. So we would have to wait until I spotted her, then act.

Lizz and I were on the first night, and she's always a hoot to hang out with. She had stories from her days back with the St. Louis team that had me rolling in stitches. The Gateway City might not be the most active area when it came to monsters, but since they responded to everything from Indianapolis to Kansas City and all the way up to Minneapolis sometimes, there were some crazy things that popped up from time to time, often caused by people messing with magic or necromancy. Bored Midwestern teenagers were a perpetual danger to society.

When Melanie took her place, we'd had a nice talk. The girl had really grown on me since training. My initial take on her had been way off. Sure, she was softer than most Hunters, but she wasn't squeamish. It turned out she had wanted to go to law school, and do the strong, career woman thing, and was still thinking about trying that after socking away a few years of nice Monster Hunter paychecks. But then she spent the rest of the night talking about how jealous she was of her older sisters who'd settled down and how cute their babies were. Yeah, girl, life is complicated.

The next night, up first was Kimpton, who really is a sweet guy, but outside of killing monsters and pro baseball, his conversation skills were surprisingly limited. He mostly kept to himself, taking catnaps and running out to get food when we needed something. He never once brought up meeting my family, and I kind of felt like he'd gotten over that. Not being a baseball fan much myself, we mostly sat in silence while watching the hag's nightclub.

It was Justin who showed up to take the midnight-to-dawn shift. I was surprised to see him here, since he'd done so much avoiding me over the last few weeks. He walked up with two coffees and a bag of snacks, knocked on the passenger window to make sure we were awake, and then climbed in the back seat before Kimpton could get out to leave, which meant he probably had something to report.

"What's up, guys?" He passed me one of the coffees.

"Isn't that other one mine?" Kimpton asked.

"Naw, you get to go home and crash. You don't want strong stuff. This shit'll keep you awake all night. Before you go, though, no luck finding the hag's accountant. Too bad Melanie never got his last name. But we got hold of the paperwork and this club's owned by a shell company that's owned by another shell company. I don't know all the details, but Rhino was complainin' about Swiss bank accounts and shit like that."

"So our hag's got money, and that accountant she brainwashed is pretty good at his job." I sipped the coffee, and Justin wasn't kidding about it being strong. It also tasted like licking a tire. Thankfully, Justin handed me some Sweet'n Low packets. "Anything else?"

"With the full moon coming up fast and being on the lookout for two different monsters at the same time, Rhino broke down and called 'bama to see if they could send some temporary help."

Normally I'd be prideful enough to take offense at that, but we still hadn't seen any sign of Nicole, I was stuck here for eternity, and Rhino was on crutches. "Who?"

"The Boss's brother, Leroy. He got some big contracts to negotiate for us out here anyway, so we'll pick him up at the airport tomorrow. You know him?"

"That's one Shackleford I've not met," I said. "I hear he's good, though."

"Good? Cat's a legend."

"I heard he once killed a wendigo single-handedly," Kimpton said.

"No way." I snorted. Earl, maybe. A regular human beating a wendigo by themselves? Wasn't going to happen.

"Someone said that President Ford personally offered to appoint Leroy as head of MCB," Justin said. "Only he told the president straight to his face that whole outfit should be disbanded in shame and their office space turned into something honest and dignified, like a whorehouse."

Kimpton laughed. "You know, after what happened to my unit in Cambodia, the MCB offered me a job? That's how they recruit agents. Just like MHI talks to survivors, MCB tries to keep it to people who are already in the know, only it's military and government types. They said I'd shown I had skills, and did I want a job? And this was barely five minutes after they'd threatened to make shit up and court-martial me and throw me in prison if I ever talked about what I'd seen. Can you imagine?"

"Same thing for me, kinda," Justin said. "Marines run into some freaky weird shit in the jungle. They say that's Top Secret and they'll kill us if we blab, dig? Thing is, I didn't get a fancy federal job offer out of it. Uh-huh. I wonder why? You ever seen a Black MCB agent?"

Come to think of it, I hadn't. "Beesley was the only woman I know of."

"And probably the last, after she damned near got her head taken off."

"Don't feel bad, man, we get paid a whole lot better than those assholes. Now I'm going home." Kimpton opened his door and got out. "Don't have too much fun."

"See you, brother." Justin took his place in the front seat, closed the door, and held out the bag of snacks. "Pork rinds?"

I was terrible at staying kosher, but I already had one god grumpy at me, so I should probably try to stay square with my adopted one. "Naw, I'm good."

And then we sat there for about ten minutes of awkward silence, watching a nearly empty street. It was so dead it wouldn't have surprised me if a tumbleweed had blown through.

"Kimpton's a good dude," Justin said out of nowhere. "Solid."

"I agree."

"It takes him a while to warm up to people. It's because of what happened to him after he got back from Nam." Justin kept eating. "I bet he was a cool customer before that. Had faith in his country, pledged allegiance to the flag, apple pie, all that bullshit. So him and all his friends getting used and abused and treated like shit and killed, all while nobody seemed to care if they lived or died, then getting spit on and called a baby killer when he got home... You see why he's slow to trust folks now."

"What's your deal, then?"

He chuckled. "I got spit on *before* I left. When you expect the worst, you don't let your guard down. I rarely get surprised."

"I bet finding out someone you thought of as a friend was the daughter of a bloodthirsty Aztec god was quite the surprise."

"It's a kick in the nuts." He brushed crumbs off his shirt. "Ain't gonna lie."

"So why'd you volunteer to be here tonight?"

"Rhino threatened to beat my ass with his crutch if I didn't take a turn."

I laughed. "I knew he'd catch on with the leadership thing eventually."

Justin laughed too. "Even crippled in a cast, that mother-fucker's scary."

Luckily, Justin brought other snacks too, so I reached over and grabbed a bag of potato chips. "I can't believe you were going to try and set a hundred pounds of explosive on fire with toilet paper."

"Improvise, adapt, overcome."

"I've heard that before as improvise, adapt, *survive*."

"I might've slightly underestimated how fast I could get to cover. Or, how likely the snake was to bite me in half...Which, by the way, thank you for saving my life."

"*De nada.* You'd do the same."

Justin mulled it over. "Yeah, I'd probably try. So it's kinda pointless me being an asshole to you in the meantime...We cool?"

"We're cool."

One reason I loved this job, Monster Hunters tended to be honorable people.

The next night's first shift I got Alex, and I couldn't get him to shut up. He also brought snacks and had plenty to talk about, mostly regarding mythological beings from history and his personal theories of how monsters became intertwined with these myths. It might have been a fascinating conversation but at this point I was stir crazy and easily annoyed. Staying up night after night, watching a club from a distance wasn't exactly fun. To be fair, Alex's book smarts were interesting, and I did learn a lot about how mermaids were not manatees like everyone claims these days. Sailors might be imaginative, but even they weren't that desperate.

"Sailors aren't so drunk and stupid we're going to mistake a sexy, clam-shell-bikini mermaid for a big honking manatee."

"I'm just saying that I've seen drunken sailors hit on man-nequins in storefront windows."

The Siren's Last Call was only open from Thursday evening to the early hours of Monday morning, which left three days during the week for the hag to clean the place up. Or, conversely, do whatever it was that hags did. In fact, with the exception of the night when Agent Orwig was killed, we had never spotted the hag outside. It was irritating when a monster wouldn't show its ugly face so we could just kill it.

I'd floated a few ideas to the team but without any way to test them, we were going on the assumption that the hag was simply living in the basement. Considering we couldn't find any current plans on the building at either the county or city planning commission's office—and those bribes hadn't been cheap—we were shooting in the dark with this thing.

MCB had been useless. They knew what we knew, but they were playing their cards close to the vest. If they were keeping an eye on this place too, they were way better at being unnoticed than we were, because I'd not seen any of them.

Hollywood after midnight was actually quiet during the workweek—not completely asleep, but there was definitely less going on. There were a lot of bums wandering around, but this was to be expected wherever the police didn't patrol as much, and I rarely saw them here. Some of the homeless had stolen shopping carts from a nearby grocery store, and it was sad to see them shuffling around with all their life's belongings gathered together in a simple little cart.

Two of them were working their way down the sidewalk toward us, picking cans out of the gutter to sell. They were bundled up in coats, hoods, and hats, probably because it was the best way to carry every bit of clothing they owned.

"Man, that's messed up," Alex said.

"Do not—I repeat, do not—give them any money. If they knock on the window, ignore them."

"Charity's a good thing, Chloe, and we're going to get more money off that snake bounty than these guys have seen in their lives."

"You want to feed the pigeons, don't do it on company time."

"That's cruel."

I had worked undercover in the underbelly of Cairo. He had no idea no idea what cruelty looked like. "I had this same conversation with Melanie. We're on a stakeout. You give them money. They'll come back, and their friends will come back, and then the crowd looks suspicious, and the target will know we're here." I'd already had to chase off a couple of guys who wanted to squeegee the windows. "Don't make my life more difficult than it already is, Alex."

"Alright...Hey, I think whoever is in that car is checking out the club."

Sure enough, someone had pulled onto our street and slowed to a suspicious crawl in front of the nightclub. The headlights were coming our way.

"Duck."

He did, and I scrunched down in the seat too, so I could barely see outside. I'd parked in the shadows. So many streetlights had been burned out that had saved me from having to use the BB gun I had stashed in the trunk for bulb busting. Destroying city property was better than getting spotted by a hag.

It was a muscle car, and from the noisy rumble it had a gigantic engine. Though I could only see the shape of the driver, from the sheer mass of him and that big square head, I knew right away who it was. Somehow, despite me trying to hide in the dark, I had a suspicious feeling that he'd seen me anyway, but he kept driving.

"Well, hello, Agent Franks."

"Is that the big scary one you were telling us about?" Alex asked from beneath the dash.

"Franks makes Rhino look like Lizz."

"Why do you think he's here? Hey, if the hag was seducing Orwig, maybe she found a new MCB agent to ensnare! That would explain why the MCB hasn't just raided the place."

I didn't know Franks hardly at all, but from what I'd seen I doubted very much than anybody or anything had ever *ensnared* that man. Watching in my side mirror, I saw that Franks stopped in the street about a hundred yards away, then backed into an alley. I lost sight of his car, but the headlights shut off, so he'd parked.

"I'm going to go see what he wants. Stay here and keep an eye on the nightclub."

"Okay. Be careful, Chloe."

When I got out, it was unseasonably cold, so I stuck my hands in my pockets, and started walking toward the alley.

The car was a turquoise Dodge RT with white racing stripes, and though I wasn't a car person, from the way the engine was so big it had to stick out through a hole in the hood, I got the feeling this thing was very fast...and also not a government-issue vehicle.

Agent Franks had gotten out and was clearly waiting for me.

He was still in the very-inappropriate-for-a-stakeout suit and tie and was unwrapping a sandwich. I think his dinner might have been a thick pastrami on rye, but I couldn't be certain in the dark. At least, my stomach thought so, because it reminded me I had been munching on the terrible treats Alex had brought with him and I'd not eaten a proper meal in days. Alex was a terrific Hunter but the boy had a sweet tooth that dentists were going to pay their mortgages off with.

Being from the office that controlled my exemption status, Franks could make my life miserable, so I tried to keep it polite. "What can I do for you, Agent Franks?"

Ignoring me, he shoved almost half the sandwich in his mouth and started chewing. I'd seen dogs with better manners. I waited patiently as Franks seemed to contemplate shoving the second half in his mouth before he swallowed and deigned to give me an answer.

"Your job."

"If you didn't notice, I'm trying to do my job. What are you up to, then?"

"You don't need to know."

It was too late in the night for this, and I was too weary and hungry to keep up the polite act. "Why are you being such a prick?"

He seemed to think this one over between bites of his sandwich, and I was beginning to wonder if he was trying to come up with an answer that would irritate me the most. Most MCB agents I could charm, or at least get them to answer a few questions before chasing me off. Franks, however, seemed immune.

"Alright, if that's unanswerable, then how about this? I told you about who Orwig was with before he died. Hags are deadly fairy creatures. I told you where we last saw her. Right over there, and why we think she's the owner. Why isn't the government rousting the place?"

He scowled, which told me he had wanted to kick in that door. "It's complicated."

"Why?"

"You don't need to know."

"Really? You can't even tell me that?"

Agent Franks shoved the last of his sandwich into his gaping maw, chewing noisily as he mulled it over.

"Is there any question you'll actually give me a straight answer? Good sandwich?"

He shrugged. The guy was as communicative as Rhino on a good day. I don't know what it was about people who preferred to communicate in as few words as possible, but it was starting to piss me off. The *nagualii*, though, was calm and quiet. Which...was unusual.

"Oh wait, don't tell me. I don't need to know. Sandwich quality's a matter of national security. That's classified too, isn't it? Nice car, Franks. Yours? Oh wait, don't tell me—I don't need to know, it's classified."

While I went off, Franks held up a Styrofoam cup and loudly sucked from the straw.

"I've not seen you guys for days. What's MCB doing here now? Wait, I think I got this—it's classified. Is that a soda or tea you're drinking? Let me guess. *Classified.*"

He paused and looked at me, a curious expression on his face. If I didn't know any better, I could have sworn he almost smiled. Something I said must have been funny to him. Or he just had indigestion from eating his sandwich in three bites. There was no way to be certain with the man. I was beginning to have a serious dislike for the hulking brute of an agent, even more than I had for the average MCB agent.

"Shut up and listen." He tossed the now empty cup on the ground. "MCB can't touch her. This hag's got diplomatic immunity."

"She's a hag! They're dangerous and super evil! Even if she's from some court the government has cut a deal with, she was obviously meddling in MCB business, and it can't have been for any good reasons!"

He nodded, like, *No shit, Sherlock.*

"Who made that stupid decision?"

"Classified." And it almost seemed like he enjoyed saying that, because it was one word while *you don't need to know* was five. It was like I'd given him a helpful suggestion on how to save four whole words a day.

"Hang on...That's why you're here like this. Your hands are tied. Mine aren't. Until MCB gives MHI the official word to back off a particular monster, as long as they're PUFF applicable, we're weapons hot."

Franks said nothing.

"Holy shit, you're off the government reservation, aren't you, Franks? You know this thing's a menace as much as I do, so you're going to slow-roll the on-the-record orders for us to leave it alone, so the private sector contractors can kill it for you and save you the red tape hassle."

Franks shrugged his massive shoulders and began walking back to his car.

"Can you at least confirm if this is her lair, and I haven't been wasting my time?"

"She'll be beneath the club during daylight." Franks got in the car and closed the door, but his window down. "You'll need to access an *eskrathidor*."

"What's that?"

Franks stuck an envelope out the window, and I took it. "You've got twelve hours before getting ordered to back off." He started the engine, and it was so loud, that I reflexively put my hands over my ears. If that car got more than a mile a gallon I would have been stunned. "This conversation never happened."

Franks drove away and left me alone in the stinky alley.

I opened the envelope and inside was a single sheet of paper. With Franks' car long gone it was too dark to read, but I was curious enough I let my eyes shift so I could at least see what it was. It appeared to be the typed MCB case notes and a summary of an interview with the still hospitalized Agent Beesley, time stamped tonight, about what she'd found out investigating their deceased SAC.

Well, this is interesting. Our hag was probably the city-destroying threat the Court of Feathers had warned me about, and she was somehow politically connected enough that she could get someone to pressure the MCB to back off, even though this case involved Fey, werewolves, human sacrifice, and dead agents. Any of those things would normally be enough to send the MCB on a rampage.

With the clock ticking and a lot of work to do, I hurried back toward my car.

I heard glass breaking. Then a gunshot echoed through the empty street.

"Alex!"

With my eyes still changed, ahead of me I could see that one of the two bums we'd spotted picking cans out of the gutter had fallen into the street. The other one was violently pulling

Alex out of the passenger-side window. He was struggling and yelling, but got dragged out and hurled to the sidewalk, where I lost sight of both of them.

I drew my pistol and sprinted toward the car.

The one Alex had shot was getting back up, and though I had mistaken it for human earlier, with its hat and scarves knocked off, this thing clearly wasn't. What I'd taken for malnourished skinny was actually dangerous wiry. It was wearing fingerless gloves, but those weren't fingers sticking out the end. Those were claws.

The bum heard my rapid footfalls approaching and turned to growl at me. The mouth opened, revealing a tongue that was a cross between a knife and a suction cup.

Blood fiends are nasty things, twisted and deformed. Shorter than the average human, they have a reddish tint to their skin that becomes more prominent the more recently they'd fed. Judging by how white this one was, I'd say it must have been on the verge of starving.

I didn't even slow down. I just raised the Browning one-handed and started popping off shots. I'm no master pistolero, especially shooting on the move, but I made up for that in volume. A couple bullets missed, but a few others hit.

Puffs of filth flew off the fiend's dirty coat. It screeched, fell to all fours, and ran down the street, trying to get away.

Alex's shouting had stopped.

"Hang on!" I went around the trunk of my car, gun up, rushing stupidly. I should have slowed down, checked the blind spots, but a fellow Hunter was in danger. The *nagualii* warned me Alex wasn't the only one in danger. The second blood fiend was nearby and radiating hunger. The heavy stench of coppery blood filled the air. The monster was feeding.

I found them on the sidewalk. The blood fiend's claws were holding Alex down, feeding on him through the little mouth protrusions in its hands. It had been so starved and distracted by feasting that it either hadn't heard the gunfire, or simply didn't care.

"Leave him alone, you bloodsucker!"

The blood fiend looked up at me and hissed. It released Alex and started to stand up, hands spread wide, like, *What are you gonna do about it, bitch?* The tiny lamprey mouths in its palms were opening and closing and dripping Alex's blood.

It stumbled when I put two in its chest, but quickly recovered and charged.

Instead of trying to meet the monster head-on, I used its momentum against it, caught it by the coat, and flung it against my car, hard enough to dent the door. I was furious. The *nagualii* was furious. And when I hurled the fiend across the sidewalk and into the light pole, it bounced off the iron with a bone-snapping *clang*.

They hadn't been expecting something like me.

Except the second one had circled back, run up the hood of my car, and tried to leap onto my back. If I'd not heard its shoes hitting metal, it would have gotten me, but I ducked and turned, and it hit the concrete where I'd just been. I fired, but at a really bad angle, only hitting it in the leg. As the blood fiend hissed and retreated, I lined up another shot, and this one struck its shoulder and clearly punched out the monster's back. An unearthly shriek of agony erupted from its throat.

Both fiends were upright, but they were trying to get away, awkwardly scrambling from the bullet wounds and broken bones. All of my instincts screamed at me to chase them. When prey runs, the cat takes it down.

Alex moaned.

It was their lucky day. *Run, you little bastards.* I rushed to Alex's side.

There were circular bites on his chest, arm, and neck. Blood was flowing freely. If I didn't do something soon, he was going to die. "Hang on, Alex. You're going to be okay."

Alex couldn't even say anything. He just kept his hand pressed against his neck, eyes wide, terrified he was going to die. It looked like he might be right.

"Just keep pressure on there."

I rushed back to the car, yanked open the door, and grabbed the first aid kit. I spilled Alex's bags of sugar snacks in the process.

"Okay, get your hand out of the way." Only I didn't even really need to say that because he'd already passed out. I ripped open a bandage and got that on his neck, because that looked to be the worst of his injuries. Alex groaned weakly. My night vision is difficult to describe in human terms, in that I could still see colors, but everything was more greyed out. Even then, I could tell Alex was deathly pale. A few more seconds and it would have sucked him dry. I had to get him to an emergency room, fast. There was one only a few blocks from here.

The blood fiend had managed to pulled Alex out of the car but thankfully hadn't taken him far. Dragging his limp body along the sidewalk, I hoisted him back into the seat. He was a lot heavier than he looked.

The next hour was frantic and jumbled. I was barely tracking anything going on around me. Alex's heart stopped minutes after he arrived in the ER, so the nurses performed CPR on him while hooking him up to a few machines. I told them not to give up on him because he was stubborn. They told me to get out of the room.

I called HQ from a hospital pay phone. Lizz had been in tears but I'd told her I thought everything would be okay.

When hospital staff came to update me, they told me that a doctor had managed to suture his jugular vein. That was all they had for me, and no idea if he was going to live or die.

A couple of beat cops arrived after the intake nurse had called them, suspicious because it looked like someone had tried to slit Alex's throat. I told them we'd been attacked by a couple of transients with knives. They wanted to know what the two of us had been doing in Hollywood at that hour, as if we'd brought this upon ourselves.

I suppose, in a way, we had.

Luckily, Kimpton and Justin arrived, and they were in the state of mind necessary to run interference with the cops, and direct them to speak with somebody in the know, who'd tell them to shut up and accept our *bum with a knife* story at face value.

The rest of the team got there a little while later, including Rhino walking on his crutches. We sat in the waiting room all through the night, hoping to hear something, anything. The emergency room staff were polite but firm in not letting us go back to see him. Justin paced angrily around the waiting room while Melanie simply sat next to Lizz, holding her hand. Nobody looked at me. I don't think they blamed me, but at the same time I'd been distracted by Agent Franks and hadn't been expecting to be ambushed by blood fiends. They might not have blamed me, but I sure did.

I passed around the notes Franks had given me. In her

interview, Agent Beesley said she had been suspicious that Special Agent in Charge Orwig was on the take, and she had evidence that he had covered up several monster incidents in the LA area over the last few months. Her theory was that some powerful entity had her hooks into him and other important political figures, in order to avoid attention while it put together some kind of monstrous operation in the city. From the cases Orwig had squashed, she suspected this force was an alliance consisting of renegade Fey, werewolves, a necromancer, some miscellaneous undead, and...a pack of blood fiends.

There was nothing else we could do except wait. It felt like the longest few hours of my life.

Rhino wasn't the waiting type, though, and I'd never seen him this mad. One of his Hunters was hanging on by a thread, and we knew where the ultimate culprit was sleeping, and we had just one morning available to murder the bitch. He told me he'd call me when it was time, and then he went to work.

Just before sunrise a surgeon came out, and the way he hadn't wanted to look any of us in the eyes told us the news wasn't good. Alex was alive, barely, but he had lost so much blood that they weren't sure if he was going to pull through or not. He told us to pray because it was in God's hands now.

Good idea, only I had a different, angrier god in mind to talk to.

CHAPTER 13

I don't remember leaving the hospital, or the drive through Hollywood. One minute I was in the ER waiting room at Cedar Sinai, hoping for news of some sort, the next I was driving up a dirt road toward the Hollywood sign. My subconscious had taken the wheel while my mind was in turmoil. Alex was critically injured. He could even die. Sweet, goofy, nerd king Alex... brilliant, young, and entrapped by some monstrosity playing games with us. We were supposed to be hunters. Right now? I felt like the hunted.

It was supposed to have been an easy stakeout, to watch and see who came to visit, and to try and confirm if she was actually home. Nothing more. We didn't even have a battle plan ready yet. My hands gripped the steering wheel so tightly if I wasn't careful, I could bend it.

Predawn gray began to change as daylight crept incrementally closer. Fate had led me here. Or I had been pulled. Either way, this was the one entity I knew who would know the answers.

There would be a price. There always was. This time, though, I was willing to pay it.

I'd lost team members before—with MHI in the old days, with Special Task Force Manticore, and most recently with the Kidon. Each wounded or dead comrade hurt me just as much as the last, and this was no exception.

The difference now, though, was this one felt *personal*. Something had sent the blood fiends after us, and it was probably

229

my fault. Or, in a roundabout way, the Court of Feathers was
to blame. It had been their Herald, after all, who passed along
the stupid warning in the first place. Blame could also be laid at
my father's feet. Maybe if he had been more forthcoming with
his information, Alex wouldn't be in the hospital. Or perhaps
Tezcatlipoca didn't think one mere mortal dying warranted much
concern. Lots of Hunters end up dead or crippled in this business. It was just that dangerous.

The cloud cover overhead matched my mood. It was the typical hazy, polluted morning that had plagued the area the past
week or so, threatening to rain but not quite doing so. It was
enough to block out the sun and keep the temperatures down,
but nothing else. I would have preferred the rain. At least rain
gives life. Too much could kill, but that was how life was with
all things. While Tlaloc—a distantly related cousin worshipped
as a rain god once upon a time—wasn't as vicious or sadistic as
some of the other members of the Court, he was still a monster.

I stopped the car near the repaired fence of the broadcasting
station, which looked good as new. If I hadn't known better, there
would have been no way to tell a zombie outbreak had happened
up here. The MCB had done a tremendous job at hiding the evidence, and I'd never even heard a thing about it on the news.
They'd even brought in fresh sod and laid the squares down to
hide the gore stains on the old, dead grass.

Looking out across the valley, in the early hours of the morning Los Angeles was a strange, forlorn place. The daytime was
always filled with the hopes and dreams of the aspiring people
looking to make it big in a city that cared not a whit for them.
At night, the same people partied hard to release the stress of
the day, to cleanse their emotional palates from the rigors of
life. It was more alive then but bereft of its soul. Or perhaps the
corrupted soul was more on display?

These hours between, though? The gray hours. They were
indescribable. The life and energy was gone, replaced simply by
a sense of exhaustion. The longer I looked out over the sprawling, seething mass of civilization, the more I could see that the
city was tired and dying. This place should have died long ago,
when it burned bright with hope and wonder, and not after
falling into such squalor. It was only a matter of time before
civilization devoured itself here, to become a parody of life. The

city would consume the innocents the same way it had almost snagged Alex, and had our missing werewolf, Nicole. Civilization here needed to be cleansed, lanced like an infected boil. It was a sprawling, uncaring rot of existence. The old ways were better, cleaner. Bone and flame, tribal instincts, fighting tooth and claw to survive. My kind had been rulers of old, humanity nothing more than livestock to be kept, fed, and slaughtered.

I shook my head, irritated.

"Shut the fuck up," I whispered at the monster within. The *nagualii* always struck when I was down, feeding off my depression and sadness to try to exert more influence over my mind. "I need to think. Go away."

Civilization was *not* a blight on the world. The world was a place worth living in. We had come a long way since living in caves and harnessing fire. This was humanity's moment, not the monsters who lived in the shadows and hunted like craven cowards. What lay dormant beneath the oceans in some dreamless sleep needed to fucking *stay* there, and I would do everything in my power to make damn sure of it.

Feeling a little calmer now that the *nagualii* part of me had been silenced, I moved to the back of the building. The grass here hadn't been replaced, but there hadn't been a need. The zombies had focused on the front entrance of the gate, where the living had congregated. The back was nothing but scrub bushes and a few small pine trees.

It was fairly easy to find the ravine. I looked up into the sky, watching the red light atop the tower blink steadily for a few moments before I started descending. The path was narrow. Instead of stopping near the top and hoping the avatar would find me, I went farther down, searching for a spot where I could sit, unseen, and simply think and meditate on things. Somewhere to let my mind dwell on the good memories.

A small bluff along the trail about halfway down was the perfect spot. There wasn't much trash here, and judging by the poor condition of the trail it wasn't used much, if at all. I could see both the San Fernando Valley to the north and the Los Angeles basin to the south. I could even make out the towering skyscrapers of downtown Los Angeles. Turning slowly, I spotted the old Griffith Park Zoo down below. Alex had been severely disappointed to learn, when we'd first set up shop here, that it had been shut down a few years before. He had a strange fascination with giraffes. Roller coasters, ancient mythology, and giraffes. The boy was *weird*.

This spot would do.

I sat cross-legged and faced east. Far in the distance I could see the first rays of light cresting over the San Gabriel Mountains. The clouds didn't let much of the light through, but it was enough. Sunshine always felt better than the dark. Light meant hope, which meant life. The rising sun chased away despair, and though I knew evil existed in daylight as well as dark, it felt manageable during the day. Even with the clouds hiding it, the light was out there, waiting. The good memories needed to be honored. The bad ones could wait their turn.

"The poet breathes life into the void, creating beauty of nothing," a familiar voice whispered from the nearby bushes. "The scholar explains what beauty is but cannot create. Balance is made and maintained."

"Tezcatlipoca."

"Light heralds my arrival, daughter."

I opened my eyes and found the avatar sitting on a small rock directly in front of me. The three-legged housecat this time instead of the menacing giant jaguar, except this time the cat was cloaked in black smoke. Looking out into the LA basin, the smog obscured my view. The tall buildings of downtown had been swallowed by the pollution. It was another glorious day in Southern California. No wonder the god of smoke and obsidian seemed to like it here.

"Of what do you wish to speak, child?"

Right to the chase, then. Even he must have known I was hurting. A welcome change of pace. I took a deep breath. "I need your assistance."

"You did not ask for the Court's assistance?" the cat avatar thing asked. I swear it looked smug, as though it had always known this day would come. So much for him feeling sympathy for my aching soul. Asshole.

"The authorities here are aware of the Court of Feathers and have said if they contact me, I have to report it," I told the truth as I eyeballed the avatar. "You, as stated in the past, are no longer part of the Court."

"Truth," the cat nodded knowingly. "I am imprisoned, outcast, bereft of title in their eyes. I am no longer of the Court. This is clever of you to lie without lying. Such is our way."

"I don't trust them," I added. "Or you either, really. But I don't have time for their riddles now. I need answers. I suspect you'll give them to me, as long as you feel it benefits you."

"The Court's truth is its own. It is not yours. I am Tezcatlipoca. You are of me. My truth is your truth."

"But at what cost?" My palms were sweaty. He'd been trying to "collect" me for decades, and I'd always managed to resist him. Only a fool thinks they can play with fire and not get burned. You can't weasel your way out of deals with ancient beings forever, no matter how clever you think you are.

"A birthright has no cost, child."

"Nothing is free."

"The Daughter of Smoke seeks counsel? What father would deny such? Beyond counsel requires action. Action has cost." The avatar chuckled. "Heed me or not, you will do as you will. About what shall I counsel you? The fate of the scholar child of the sea, who lies in the building of the sick, bitten upon his throat?"

"Yes." I swallowed as a lump grew in my throat suddenly as Alex's face appeared in my mind. "He's a strong man. Smart. A good friend, and better human being."

"Spare me your tears," the avatar said. "It is unwise to show weakness in the presence of a predator."

"Like I give a shit what you think."

The cat flicked out its little claws and examined them. "Ah, but I care about your success."

"As long as it benefits you."

"You may despise me, yet you are not fool enough to disrespect me," the cat avatar told me as I felt the raw power behind his words. Like him or not, Tezcatlipoca was an incredibly potent force. Even locked away in an extradimensional prison he could direct things and exert influence on lesser beings. Twisting the features of the avatar beneath the cat's face ever so slightly, just to demonstrate that within those golden eyes lay something horrific and old, ancient in this world and the next. Maybe not evil, but definitely not good. I felt myself drowning in those eyes, struggling to breathe in the expansive *nothingness* of it all. He pulled back. Time returned. Shivering, I pulled my arms across my chest. It did little for the chill.

"Give your request before I change my mind."

I hurried. "I need information about the enemy we face today."

"You seek power and dominion over your enemies?" The cat seemed to perk up at that, since he represented a god of darkness and violence. "Finally."

"No. Only information."

"Child, all information is *power.* Your scholar ally who waits at the doorway to Mictlan understands this. Why can't you?"

Mictlan was the Aztec underworld, *where the obsidian knives are creaking.* "Will Alex live?"

"He shares your new desert faith, thus his fate is not my decision to make. As for the knowledge you seek, I am banished from the Court, yet trusted allies within it relay information to me which could be beneficial. Those who would trade in secrets and shadows have not forgotten our debts. *All* our debts, large or small."

I nodded. "So you have spies."

"My allies have spies," Tezcatlipoca corrected. "Your enemy is a very capable foe, more so than you realize. If you challenge her forces with what you have today, you and all your allies will certainly perish." I believed him too. He might withhold the truth—lying by omission—but when he answered so directly it was usually true. "If I were to aid you in this battle, your triumph is not assured...for she is near, and I am far...but it is possible."

"Your cost for assisting me in this battle. Name it."

"You," the cat avatar replied, as if that was the most simple and obvious thing in the world.

"In what way, me?" I'd expected something along those lines—fealty, servitude, or whatever—but for him to come out and directly say it was disconcerting.

"Within the span of a few generations, the north will have its vengeance. The Court of Feathers claims to be neutral in the war that is coming. I do not believe in this so-called neutrality. Cowardice will unmake the world, unbind the natural order of things in favor of chaos. I have grown fond of this realm. If all the humans are dead, they cannot worship me. The Court believes it can wait, like a condor looking for scraps of morsels after the kill, but all that will be left is rot and ruin. This I shall not tolerate."

"What's all that Court politics got to do with me?"

"When this time comes and I summon you, you would serve as my willing weapon, to help me reclaim what is rightfully mine. I would allow you to unlock your full potential, with power beyond your mortal comprehension. And after our victory over Disorder, you would be royalty within *my* court... if you so choose."

"Nope," I told him. "That's way too open-ended of a deal."

"I see." The avatar flicked its tail, displeased. "You would rather be an assassin slave to mere humans than a princess in your father's kingdom?"

"No deal." I crossed my arms, scowling as I stared at the avatar. Tezcatlipoca stared back, unblinking, for many minutes before it heaved a sigh more befitting a god than a domesticated housecat.

"Your stubbornness is tiresome."

"Thanks."

"That was not meant to be a compliment."

I sure took it as one. "I won't be cornered into your fee. I choose my own path. If that means we work together someday, so be it, but it'll be because I think it's the right thing to do, not because I got forced into it by some agreement open to your interpretation."

I'd clearly annoyed Daddy Dearest, but he wasn't feeling murderous enough to smite me just yet. The avatar cocked its head to the side, seemingly amused. I didn't know cats could smile like that. It was unnerving. "Do you have any further questions, child? Before you rush off to your near inevitable doom?"

"What can you tell me about this hag in particular?"

"The lands of the conquerors are overripe and rotted. Many fell beings dwell within this realm. She has soldiers and magic. Your hag is old, yet not nearly as ancient as her master. Like me, she is supposed to be trapped. And like me, she has found a way to escape."

"Agent Franks mentioned us having to access something to get to her."

"Do not consort with... Franks. He is not what you believe him to be."

Oh, was my father trying to warn me away from bad boys now? But I let that go. "How did this hag get imprisoned?"

"Do you know the legend of King Owiyot?"

I did, actually. It was one of the few I'd picked up while at the orphanage in Oaxaca. The nuns there weren't really big on fairy tales, but there'd been one sister in particular who seemed more attuned to the weirder aspects of our world, and she loved to tell us the myths of kings long past, those who ruled in the name of the old gods, before the arrival of the conquistadors had upended their entire world. For the better, if you ask me.

"I do."

Tezcatlipoca's avatar scowled. "Speak your understanding."

"Once there was a great king of the Acjachemen tribe," I began, pulling what I could remember from my childhood memories, which were actually pretty happy, until the locals had decided I was a witch and that they needed to burn me. "His name was Owiyot. He loved his people, and they him. Except his rivals were jealous of how much he was loved, so they conspired against him, portraying him as cruel. They turned his people against him and cursed him. Owiyot led a war against his enemies but failed, because they had allied themselves with a foul creature from the Distant Lands and the being poisoned the king. With his last act before dying, the king vanquished the creature."

"Your legend is wrong. It was not vanquished," Tezcatlipoca explained patronizingly. "With the aid of a mighty shaman, it was imprisoned."

Tezcatlipoca was making too much sense. My father was many things—some sort of alien, godlike monster being at the top of that list—but he was always reticent with his information. He was worse than an old miser handing out alms to beggars. Offering me so much freely made me more than a little suspicious.

"Is the monstrosity the hag?" I asked, though I was fairly certain the answer was yes.

"Asking questions you already know the answer to is unbecoming of a child of this House."

"Then how's it getting free?"

"Sacrifices in the beauty of the flesh, the blinded eyes, and the devourer of life. Once they all are made, the creature will be able to break free of its prison at a certain time and place."

"What?" I asked. The cat turned and looked toward the broadcasting station, like I was stupid. Ah yeah, the zombies. Those had been a side effect of the leftover necromantic rituals. I could have slapped myself in the forehead. "The human sacrifices are designed to let her out. And she was out and about before that... I bet those earlier sacrifices were some of the things Agent Orwig covered up for her."

"Once fully free, you will lack the strength necessary to kill her, and she will serve her master well."

"Pretty sure cluster bombs and napalm will fuck her night right up."

"In this realm they will not. She must be thwarted before her ascension, or not at all."

"Well, isn't that just peaches... Wait a second. You knew all this before. Orwig was covering for the hag. She wouldn't have him killed by two monsters who are native to South America. You've got allies on the Court still who owe you debts. *You* did it!"

"The child is wise," the avatar stated, as if it should have been obvious to me from the start. Which it should have.

"I almost got killed! Lizz almost got killed! Beesley's still all messed up and her partner got his head yanked off!"

The housecat just looked at me like, *So?*

The more I thought about it, the worse it became. The first time we'd crossed paths with the hag, she'd lost her corrupted MCB agent. My clever ruse to have Lizz distract it from feeding on the young man must have tipped her off further. When I'd left Alex alone, the creature had already known we were hunting it and had struck first. His injury was my fault because I had made a foolish mistake—I'd underestimated it.

The *nagualii* was pushing hard to be released, to hunt down and kill the threat, but the prospect of my other half roaming the streets of the city was a terrifying one. There was no way I could let it out. Ruthlessly, I shoved it away. The monster could never gain full control.

"You were picking this fight, with or without us!"

"I did not send you there that night, child. That was your decision alone which brought you to that place. It is your destiny that you fight on the same side as mighty Tezcatlipoca. The *ahuizotl* knew not who you were. If you had not killed it, I would have to, for striking one of the royal line—even unwittingly—is a great crime."

The golden eyes of the cat glowed in the midday light. I could feel the power of the creature through the gaze. Peering into the depths of my soul, I felt naked and exposed. The waves of his *unnaturalness* washed over me. I felt the raw power of something *more*. It made me ill. This was no simple monster. Man's worship in centuries past had given Tezcatlipoca power. Hundreds of thousands of souls, possibly even millions across the years, given willingly in his name. It made me want to cower, to hide. I did neither. This would be seen as weakness, and a *nagualii* could never afford to be weak. I stood strong and withstood the power behind the gaze. Somewhere deep within the swells of insanity and darkness, I could almost feel my father's approval.

It was not something I'd ever wanted and could do without having again.

"I can see you are set on your path. You will make war against your enemy today, regardless of the futility of it. Without my aid, you will surely perish, but you will not accept my terms."

"I guess we're at an impasse then, huh?"

"No. I will give you this gift."

A shadow passed by. I heard a whistling noise in the air and looked up to see a gigantic buzzard flying overhead, carrying something in its talons. The bird let go, and a black object fell, flipping through the air. It was a knife, and it landed point down in the sand, directly between me and the avatar.

"Take this. While you wield it, you will be able to enter your enemy's prison. There, you may defeat her."

The knife's handle was made of white bone, but the blade was something else entirely. I thought it was black iron, but that couldn't be right since the material appeared to have *grown* organically from the bone.

"It is known as the Black Heart of Suffering."

Ominous. "No, thanks. I already told you I'm not paying your price."

"There is no price. This is an inheritance." The cat turned and sauntered off into the weeds. "Besides, it is not mine to give, merely to return. It belonged to your mother."

What? That made no sense. My mom had been a poor innocent farm girl who'd been preyed upon by a malevolent ancient thing. "What do you mean, belonged to her?"

"It is not for the father to tell the story, but for the daughter to remember it." With that, the cat walked into a cluster of bushes nearby, and disappeared, leaving me all alone on Mount Lee once more.

"Oh, fuck you too, Dad."

Hesitantly, I reached down and picked up the little knife. The blade seemed to swirl when I looked at it, like it was made out of super compressed smoke. I hated to admit it, but as someone who knew her way around a knife, this thing was really comfortable in the hand.

As I was making my way back toward my car, I heard Tezcatlipoca's voice as a whisper on the wind. "There are many prisons between the worlds. They should remain closed. Tell your allies this: If the doors to prisons are to be flung open, they must be prepared for what follows."

"I hate this mystical bullshit," I said to no one, because I could already tell he was gone back to wherever he'd been entombed. My father had just given a warning if I'd ever heard one. However, I wasn't certain if it had been directed at me in particular, or something I needed to pass along to someone else. Regardless, I needed to get back to my team, who were probably wondering where I'd gone.

First, I had to go and check in on a friend. Then, it would be time to hunt.

CHAPTER 14

Time was against us. We needed a plan but without Alex, I worried we might be floundering a bit as a team. The newbies were still in shock. They'd gone through training with Alex and had formed a very tight bond with him. Melanie and Kimpton were handling it as best they could but I could tell they'd been hit hard by him getting seriously hurt. Rhino was clearly bothered but he was doing his best to be stoic about everything. This was the most emotion I'd seen from him our entire time working together. Lizz, on the other hand, got her crying done already and was set to roll on the hag. Justin, I didn't know, because he was at the airport waiting for Leroy Shackleford's flight to come in, but he was tight with Alex too.

Me personally, each time a friend got hurt or killed, it stung and sucked, but I knew that the best way to honor them was to go kill more monsters. And we had a very narrow window to do that before the MCB came down on us like a ton of bricks. If we hit the hag after they told us to back off, MHI would be looking at fines, and Team Rhino would be looking at prison.

Back at headquarters, I told my team almost everything my father's avatar had said to me. Even though the guy who was the most sensitive about my background wasn't even here right now, I was mostly an open book. I told them I'd cut no deals, but got a supposedly killer knife. I didn't mention the bit about it having belonged to my mom, because that sounded way to outlandish to be accurate.

Franks had told us to look up an *eskrathidor*, but sadly our smart guy who was into that kind of thing was occupied barely hanging onto life, so the rest of us were bumbling around, making long-distance calls to other teams to ask if they knew what that was.

After checking and packing our equipment, we gathered in the conference room to do one final rundown. We'd be on the move within the hour. We were also using Lizz's nifty answering machine to screen our calls, because that way if it was other Hunters calling us back, we could pick up, but if it was the MCB telling us to leave the club alone, we just wouldn't answer and then we could play stupid later. Plausible deniability.

The only building plans we had managed to snag from the county commissioner's office of the club were hopelessly out of date. It was built beneath a multilevel structure, and the dance floor we had been on was the old storage cellar, which had been excavated and rebuilt to be its own business sometime after the Korean War. Sadly, it had been modified a lot since then. Kimpton had tracked down one of the contractors, but all he could tell us was that what had started as a warehouse area with lots of little cubby holes had been turned into a maze of rooms all connected to one central location: the dance floor.

Luckily, Melanie's sense of direction translated well into going over architectural plans, and she remembered how the place was laid out a lot better than I did. "Yeah, that's the dance floor, alright. Only these walls are all gone. This cubby over here? That's where the bartender was set up. Bathrooms were two different rooms here and here. We sat about here." She pointed at a seemingly random spot on the blueprint. "I could see there were hallways here, and here, but don't know where they lead. And a doorway here... and there. But they never opened so I don't know where they go."

I had no idea, but I trusted Melanie's judgment. "Okay, so we're pretty certain the entrance to the hag's prison is somewhere in the club."

"Makes sense," Rhino said. "Assuming your jaguar dad is legit."

That could go either way, but we proceeded with the hope Tezcatlipoca wasn't conning me somehow, and came up with a rushed plan of attack, and how we would sweep and clear the place.

"What sort of prison do you think this is?" Kimpton asked, leaning forward across the table.

"Bubble pocket dimension, more than likely," Lizz declared as she entered the room. "I just heard back from Cazador. That thing Franks told you is an elf word."

"A bubble what now?" Kimpton asked.

"A bubble from a different reality, stuck onto ours somehow," Rhino explained. "Two different places existing in the same place at the same time. Usually with some kinda magic portal to go between them. Size ranges between a broom closet to something you could play football in." Our commander may have looked like a lunk, but he'd been around the block and knew a thing or two about this business. "I hate weird magic shit."

"Ayup," Lizz agreed with Rhino. "Finding the entrance to that is gonna be hard if it's camouflaged. Earl said they can be hidden in plain sight, or downright obvious."

"Anybody have any personal experience in dealing with something like this?" I asked the group. They collectively shook their heads in the negative. I'd never seen one in person either. "Melanie, skim through Alex's binders for anything about that or anything else that might be some kind of interdimensional prison, you dig?"

"On it."

"We're down a man, but we've got to work with what we've got." Rhino was reasserting his command authority in our time of crisis. "I called the Seattle team, but there's no way they can make it in time. Next closest is New Mexico. Same story. They'll be here in time to take over if we fail."

"There should be a Vegas team," Kimpton grumbled under his breath. "We're on an island here. Bad defensive position. Phoenix, Vegas, and LA would form a nice triangle. Think of the business we'd drum up and still be able to watch each other's backs."

"Complain about it later to the Boss. Focus on the problems we got now," Rhino said with his command voice, because clearly the beaver incident had been humbling and educational for him.

"Yes, sir."

"Justin's on his way back with Leroy. Luckily, he was already on the red eye. While you were gone, Chloe, Lizz called that deputy from Lake Arrowhead to see if he wanted to come help."

"What?" I looked Lizz's way. "Tom Black's not a trained hunter."

"He's a trained cop. He's already shown us he's got a cool head under pressure. He found out monsters are real and handled it fine...and too late, he's already on his way and will meet us there."

"I didn't like that she involved a citizen *without asking me first*," Rhino muttered. "That's against company policy unless it's an extreme case. That's how you get friendly fire incidents."

"I told him we found who was ordering his werewolf to attack folks, and he didn't hesitate to jump in. If Deputy Tom gets killed, I'll feel super guilty. In the meantime, we need somebody to watch the door if we draw attention, and he can at least flash a badge to make the looky-loos go away."

Lizz had a point there. The club was in a basement, but we'd be making a lot of noise. "We've got a couple city works contacts who will take bribes. I'll see if we can get the street shut down for road work," I suggested. "That way if it spills out into the open we can keep the collateral damage down."

"Already handled that. There's going to be a"—Lizz made quote marks with her fingers—"*broken water main* there in about forty-five minutes."

It was nice working with professionals.

Someone honked a horn in the Gasparyans' parking lot. Kimpton went over and looked out the window. "Justin's back. That must be Leroy with him."

"Good." The timing of his visit was fortuitous. I didn't know Leroy, but I very much doubted there had ever been a Shackleford who wasn't worth their weight in gold on a hunt. That family had just been born to fight and had the experience to match. "Alright, guys, any questions?"

There were none. They all had their assignments. Every single one of them had a determined look on their face. I hadn't needed to worry about them holding up after Alex had gotten hurt, because Team Rhino knew what was at stake here. I glanced at the wall clock. Time was wasting. We had work to do.

"Get to it," Rhino ordered. We all started off to grab our gear, but Rhino coughed to get my attention.

"What, boss?"

"I don't like that Lizz is inviting park rangers or whatever the hell he is to the party, but having somebody else to watch the street means I can go in with you." He tapped his leg cast. "Come help me get this off."

"Marco—"

He cut my protest off. "I can't help if I'm stuck here. I'm sick of that shit. This one's personal. Everyone fights. No one quits."

According to the docs, he was supposed to have it removed in two weeks anyway. I hoped that wouldn't make much difference, but then again when I was a kid if somebody broke their leg, they simply tied a splint on the thing and hobbled on it until it healed.

"Damn it, Mendoza, I really need help cutting this thing off. Please?"

The fact that Rhino was using complete sentences and asking nicely told me just how serious this was. "I'll grab a saw."

We met our new arrival in the parking lot, and I had to admit Leroy Shackleford was a good-looking dude. Tall as his brother but lean instead of thick, Ray was built like he lifted weights. Leroy ran marathons. If I squinted a bit, it was like I was looking at a taller, handsomer version of Earl Harbinger. Rhino limped over to him, shook hands, then provided quick introductions.

"Nice to meet y'all. Now, I hear there's some killing needs to get done."

"You in, boss?" Rhino asked.

"Damned right, I am. I flew out to negotiate the final deal with your movie company lawyers." He looked toward me. "Mendoza, right? Thanks for impressing the studio people, by the way. Big potential there."

I shook his hand too. "It was only some zombies."

"They said it was your quality customer service. But the lawyers can wait. Killing a hag sounds far more appealing than golf."

"A Shackleford golfs?" I asked incredulously.

"I had to learn. It's the fashionable way for millionaires to negotiate nowadays. I got pretty decent at the game, but between you and me, a golf course is a waste of a perfectly good rifle range."

I'd never seen a Shackleford dressed in a tailored suit and Italian shoes before either. They were so pragmatic the fancy clothing seemed downright unfitting on one of them. Apparently Leroy seemed to think so too. "Anybody got something I can wear instead of this frilly nonsense?"

"We've got an extra kit inside," Kimpton said.

"You happen to have a spare MG-42 or M-60 lying around? I don't usually pack machine guns on business trips."

"Right this way, sir." Kimpton led him toward the office.

When Leroy was gone, Justin said, "Riding over with him, all I can say is that dude's a badass."

"Uh-huh," Melanie agreed as she twirled one finger through her hair. "Is there a Mrs. Shackleford?"

"There was once," Lizz stated flatly. I'd known Lizz could harbor a grudge but this was a level of hate I'd seen her save for monsters. "Only she turned out to be a coldhearted, money-grubbing, mean-as-hell manipulative shrew, who decided she hated Hunters and wanted nothing to do with us. She took their kids and left him. One nasty divorce later and now he doesn't even get to see his sons."

"So you're saying he's single now?" Melanie asked.

"Oh, calm down," Lizz said.

"Just playing."

We handled last-minute prep, and hashed out the long list of things that could go wrong. We didn't know what we were up against. We didn't know what kind of defenses would be in place. We didn't even know what kinds of magic the hag could do, or even how to find her hidden chamber. To say there was a lot of nervousness would be an understatement.

Leroy came back a few minutes later, kitted up and looking like a proper Shackleford. I was surprised to see he was wearing an eye patch now. I'd had no idea he was missing an eye.

"The usual eye is a realistic fake, but it tends to pop out in a fight and I hate when it rolls around getting scratched up," he explained. "Though I do wear the eye patch to negotiations if the client seems like they'd be impressed with the whole *man of danger* look. If the patch might scare them, I plug the fake eye in."

"Smart."

"Contract negotiation's a science." Leroy tapped the side of his head. "Psychology, Mendoza."

Judging by how fast MHI had been expanding, apparently he was pretty good at it too.

"Alright, Team, this one's for Alex. Saddle up." Rhino spun one meaty finger in the air. "We'll meet at the club."

CHAPTER 15

We rolled up to the nightclub about twenty minutes before noon. Our cars converged on the front entrance in the alley simultaneously. Nearby, men dressed in city utility uniforms had blocked off the alley from all other traffic, including neighboring streets, and parked large vehicles in strategic positions to shield everything from prying eyes. Even Hollywood Boulevard had traffic restricted down to a single lane going both ways.

Lizz hadn't told me how much of a bribe she had paid, but seeing it in action, this was going to be a serious kick to the old budget.

As we piled out, a pickup truck that had been waiting down the street pulled in behind us, and Tom Black got out, dressed in jeans and a flannel shirt, like he was about to go turkey hunting. Only then he reached back into the cab and pulled out a riot shotgun and a bandoleer of shotgun shells and ran our way.

"Is that your cop newbie?" Leroy asked.

"Yeah," I told him. "Tom's got a good head on his shoulders."

"I hope you've got his full name written down somewhere, so if he dies we can find his next of kin to send them the check."

Deputy Tom heard that as he was approaching. "What? I even get paid for doing this?"

Leroy grinned. "I like this guy. New guy, you follow Lizz."

"Gladly. I've seen her shoot."

"He should stay and guard the entrance," I said. "He's not been through training. That's company policy."

"Yeah, I wrote it," Leroy replied. "My gut right now overrules it. Everyone makes entry, then we'll reassess."

I'd learned a long time ago not to argue with a Shackleford about how to conduct a monster hunt. That family were as much creatures of instinct as I was.

Rhino surveyed his assembled force, looked toward the gigantic building, and made the final call. "We're on. Chloe's squad on the front door. Mine on the back. Let's go." He took a gigantic sledgehammer with him in case the back door lock was stubborn, and started limping toward the alley. His weakened leg had to be killing him to put weight on it like that but he was too tough to show any pain. "If this goes sideways, don't hesitate to burn this place to the ground. You understand?"

Everybody shouted in the affirmative, and then headed for their assigned area.

We only knew of two ways in, and we were stacking four Hunters on each one. We didn't know much about the layout other than what me, Lizz, and Melanie had seen, and the out-of-date blueprints we had were a guess at best. Ideally, we'd hit a place this big with a dozen Hunters to sweep the interior fast while more controlled the perimeter, but you work with what you got, and Franks' ultimatum had screwed any chances of getting help here in time.

I strolled nonchalantly to the front door, with Justin backing me up, followed by Lizz and Deputy Tom.

We stopped at the door and waited, because it would take Rhino, Leroy, Kimpton, and Melanie a bit longer to get into position. I knew from our past trip here the stairs went down at a steep angle. At the base was a hallway with no doors or anything that dumped onto the dance floor. The other team would be entering through the fire exit into the hall by the storage area. Then both teams would work our way toward the only door Melanie had seen marked PRIVATE, which on the plans looked like it would be a warren of small rooms in the very back.

"I'm still kinda fuzzy on what's going on here," Tom said. "What's our rules of engagement?"

"If it ain't human, shoot it," Lizz said.

"If what ain't human?"

"Well, that's the conundrum: We don't rightly know. Probably blood fiends—think red-colored goblins with vampire hands—and who knows what else. The big bad bitch we're after is probably either gonna look like a supermodel or a devil-bat critter. That's probably who was telling your werewolf to make more werewolves. But anyways, don't bother to shoot the bat model because that buckshot probably won't do nothing, and just let Chloe stab it with her dad's magic murder knife instead. Got all that?"

Tom blinked slowly. "Not really, but sure."

All of us were trying to stand in a way our guns wouldn't be too visible from any passersby, though the broken water main cover story kept traffic—or anyone walking by—from seeing much. According to Agent Franks' letter, at four in the afternoon our twelve-hour window would expire and the government would get involved. We needed to make sure that didn't happen until the hag was dead. I checked again to make sure the Black Heart of Suffering was in the leather sheath on my belt. Luckily, I'd found one that fit it pretty well, and with a strap around the bone handle, I wasn't going to lose it. I had a Galil rifle and my Hi-Power. Justin had his AK-47 slung over one shoulder, because he had a big pry bar in his hands to use against the front door.

Except I paused and tested it, and sure enough, the front door was unlocked. Of course, if there was a carnivorous, human-sacrificing Fey and her blood-drinking servants in here, they'd be happy for random people to blunder in during the week. Transients looking for places to sleep or even would-be burglars would all end up as food. Justin shrugged, put the pry bar back on his pack, and got his Kalashnikov ready.

We were amped up, and had enough ammo, guns, and explosives to take out a small Caribbean nation. We were just waiting for the signal from Rhino.

The fire escape door getting smashed in was loud enough we all heard it. The other squad was on the move. I threw the front door open. There was nobody in the entryway where the bouncers had been. Taking a deep breath to steady my nerves, I descended the stairs.

The near silence within the nightclub was disconcerting. The only sound I could pick out was the faint electrical hum of a few lights that had been left on. Lizz flicked on the rest of the lights as we went. We all had flashlights ready in case the monsters killed the power, but until then, light was our friend.

An odd rhythmic, hissing sound started in the shadows below.

I'd heard something nearly identical last night, when the two blood fiends had ambushed Alex. An angry growl erupted from my chest, deep and primal.

I heard a second blood fiend, then a third. Our entrance had woken them up. Now there were so many of them that it sounded like we were descending into a nest of snakes worse than the real one we'd recently been in. Apparently there was a blood-fiend convention on the dance floor. I sniffed the air but the overpowering smell of stale booze, cigarette smoke, and other things I couldn't easily identify overcame my senses. I felt my pulse race—not in fear, but anticipation. Because I already knew this was going to be one of *those* fights.

I reached the bottom of the stairs. If Melanie's memory was correct, Rhino's team would be reaching the back of the disco hall in the next few seconds. We were at the front. Between us it sounded like there was an entire pack of feral blood fiends hiding in the big dark space.

Except it wasn't dark for long, because when the other team passed by the control booth, one of them must have gotten the bright idea to turn everything on.

Suddenly it was floodlights, alternating strobes, and disco balls spinning. In the center of the dance floor was what had to be *dozens* of blood fiends gathered to feast on several dead bodies. The monsters jerked upright, nightmare faces contorting into fearful surprise.

The weird strobing effect of the lights, combined with the disco ball hanging above the dance floor, made everything seem slanted and off-kilter. There were curtains hanging from the ceiling, sparkling silver things that shimmered and reflected the mostly naked, emaciated creatures below. The corpses on the floor had been people once, but the fiends had practically ripped them to pieces in their eagerness to feast on their blood. It wasn't nearly enough to feed so many creatures, so the hag had to be keeping them here, miserable and starved.

The speakers started to blare Billy Preston's "Outa-Space."

"This must be blood-fiend hell," Justin whispered.

Blood fiends were normally ambush predators who didn't like straight-up fights, but the hag had kept these things so famished that the instant they saw us, they were so overcome with hunger, they charged.

"This is for Alex!" I flipped my rifle's selector to full auto and let it rip. Justin was right next to me, roaring and working the AK back and forth across the dance floor.

The skinny monsters were hammered with bullets. Chunks of starvation-pink meat got blown off bones. Blood squirted. One nearly flanked us before Tom put a round of buckshot into its belly. He fired again as fast as he could pump the action and the next shot took the top of its skull off. Fiends tried to crawl over their dead compatriots in order to escape. Some of them ran for the back exit—

—only to have Rhino's team open fire on them too. Leroy had a belt-fed, and the thunder of an M-60 is astoundingly loud indoors.

The pack of fiends was caught in the center of a deadly X. And since the two who had put our friend at death's door were in there somewhere, *no mercy.*

These monsters had clearly never gone against real Hunters before, and the sudden carnage shattered any bravery they might have possessed. The only thing on their mind was to flee, but there was no escaping our wrath. They served the hag's bidding and now would die because of her. It was the perfect symmetry of life.

Fiends ran for the bathroom. A couple of them even made it into the ladies' room. Kimpton ran over and tossed a hand grenade through after them. The resulting explosion knocked the door off the hinges and caused a rain of dust to fall from the ceiling. Another fiend vaulted over the bar to try and hide on the other side, only to have Rhino methodically work a shotgun over the whole bar, each blast blowing a gigantic hole through the wood and shattering glass on the other side. The shelf holding all the bottles came crashing down.

Blood fiends are remarkably resilient, though, and even getting hammered with bullets, some of them were closing. Justin and I had run dry at about the same time, but one of them was still upright and rushing us. I went for a new magazine, but Justin stepped forward and smashed it in the face with the butt of his AK. It flailed back and slid across the hardwood on its back. I dropped the bolt and stitched a burst of 5.56 rounds from its pelvis to forehead.

I hadn't known fiends could climb, but some of them were making their way up the curtains. We shot those too. Some of the floodlights exploded. Melanie put half a dozen bullets into one fiend with her Colt Commando before it dropped, tearing down the sequined curtains behind it, like a parachute that had failed to open.

They hissed, they crawled, they fought, but in the end the blood fiends did what all good monsters did when MHI came calling: they died.

Our gunfire tapered off. The floor was covered in fiend blood, body parts, and brass shell casings. The smoke and dust began to clear a little. The ventilation in the club wasn't the best but it was at least working a little. Even at just a few thousand bucks a pop, that was a whole lot of PUFF bounty lying there. Alex would be pleased.

"Well." Rhino looked around at the pile of blood-fiend corpses. Somehow blood had even gotten on the disco ball. It wasn't nearly as glittering as before. We'd done a number on the monsters and hadn't even been so much as scratched. "That was easy."

Of course, that was when the werewolf came crashing through the drywall and damned near ripped Rhino's arm off.

The big man didn't even have a chance to react before blood fountained outward, painting the ruined wall. Rhino started screaming in pain once it dawned on him his wrist had been slit wide open. The werewolf hit the floor, spun around, and claws slashed through the air to rip more of Rhino's arm open.

It was right in front of Rhino. I didn't have a shot.

The werewolf snarled, blood dripping from its claws, and started toward its next victim. Kimpton reacted and fired from the hip, but at such close range it was nearly impossible to miss. The steel-jacketed rounds punched clean through the werewolf. It howled, twisted sideways, and backhanded Kimpton across the flak vest. The blow put Kimpton *through* the wall.

Rhino stumbled backward a few feet before shock leveled him. Groaning weakly, he slumped against the opposing wall. *Now* I had an angle.

But so did Lizz, and she was a better shot. She struck it repeatedly, and in a flash the werewolf had gone back through the hole it had come from.

"Load silver if you've got it!" Leroy shouted, because of course we'd not been wasting the rare stuff on mere fiends. He didn't have a belt of silver for the M-60, but sufficient volume worked too, and he moved to a position where he could cover both of our fallen hunters.

"Can I have some of that?" Tom asked.

Liz shoved her hand into one pocket and handed him a handful of shotgun shells. Tom began feeding them into the magazine tube like it was the most important task in the world, right then, and it probably was.

Melanie found a metal rod about a foot long lying on the floor, remnants from some of the piping in the wall the werewolf had just crashed through. She grabbed a strip from one of the tacky silver curtains hanging from the ceiling and ripped it down. Tying the sequined rag just above Rhino's elbow, she used the rod to tighten it until blood stopped pumping from the stump. "Stay with me, Marco," Melanie said as she twisted the bar in her hands. "We'll evacuate you to the hospital."

"I ain't going nowhere."

"You've lost a lot of blood."

"I've got extra." Lying on the floor with his back against the wall, Rhino took a few deep breaths. "Would somebody please shut off that godawful music?"

Leroy glanced over at the sound system area, and absolutely leveled all the sound equipment with a burst from the machine gun. "Better?"

"Thank you..." Rhino composed himself and used his words. "As nice as your curtain rods are, Melanie. I've got a real tourniquet in my med kit."

"Sorry, boss," Melanie said as she reached for the pouch. "I got excited."

"Give me a second to get this faucet pinched off." Rhino pulled his shotgun over and pumped it one-handed. "Track it down. I'll bring up the rear and cover us."

Rhino was one *tough* motherfucker. For a moment, I almost asked him if his dad had served during World War II in a special unit before deciding against it.

Kimpton came stumbling back, covered in drywall dust, and from the way his vest was shredded the only reason the werewolf hadn't flayed him to the bone was the flak had slowed the claws down. But he looked like that hit had rung his bell.

"You okay?" I shouted.

"I'm fine." He dropped the mag of regular ammo from his

Colt and pulled a twenty-rounder from his back pocket that had a stripe of silver paint on it. With silver-plated bullets loaded, Kimpton watched the walls in case the werewolf decided to make another sudden entrance.

My squad moved their way, stepping over blood fiend bodies. "I think that was our missing college student."

"Shit," Lizz spat. "Nicole didn't maul anybody last month during the full moon. What if it was because the hag managed to keep her caged in here somehow?"

The whole time we'd been looking for her, she might have been with the hag the entire time? And had she changed on command during the middle of the day when we'd broken in? The prospect was scary. If a hag could exert that much influence over a newly created werewolf from her prison, then there was no telling what she could do once she was free.

"Don't borrow no trouble," Justin muttered as he looked around the room. The werewolf had made one hell of a disappearing act. "Stick to the mission. Take out the hag."

He was right. With silver, we could kill a werewolf. The hag was the real threat.

"Melanie, Tom, stay right next to Rhino. The rest of you on me. Let's go," I ordered automatically. Leroy outranked me, but he was a sharp guy who knew he was an outsider while the rest of us were used to working together. He wasn't about to mess with that dynamic.

Justin took point this time. The werewolf had burst through from a storage room, which was empty now. On the other side was a long hall. We quickly moved down to where there was a door marked PRIVATE. Justin kicked the flimsy interior door in, and I swept in after, gun up and ready to fire. It was dark inside, so I blinked hard and when my eyes opened, they were the glowing eyes of the *nagualii*.

This had to be the accountant's office. There was a cluttered desk with an electronic typewriter on it. There were graphs and numbers on the wall, none of which made any sense to me. In the corner was one of those fake plastic plants that were all the rage. It looked like a peace lily. On the desk there was a picture of the accountant, his wife, and three daughters. I remembered him hitting on Melanie. Asshole. Cute kids, though. However, there was no sign of the werewolf.

I turned back to tell the others that, and Justin jumped when he saw my eyes. "Shit!"

"Clear. No werewolf. Sorry."

"Naw, we still cool. That cat-eye thing is just some freaky shit, is all."

Lizz, being the smart one, walked in and flipped the light switch on.

Something strange caught my eye. There was a map of the area on the wall, and several locations had been circled in red marker. Inside one of them was the broadcasting station near the Hollywood sign where I'd talked to Tezcatlipoca. I bet if we checked those other spots, we'd find traces of other human sacrifices, probably covered up by Agent Orwig.

"Check this out." Lizz had picked up what appeared to be an actual stone tablet off a shelf. "What language is that?"

I glanced over. "Nahatl...Put that down!" The last thing I needed was somebody on my team trying to read bad magic.

Leroy walked to the far wall and looked at it curiously. His head tilted sideways and he frowned. "There's a seam." He ran one hand over it. "This isn't right. This is a secret door. There's probably a hidden latch mechanism somewhere in here. Check the filing cabinets."

Justin smashed a hole in the wood paneling with the pry bar.

"Or that works too."

The wall smoothly slid open to reveal a passageway—brick, pitch black, and sloping downward. Now that certainly hadn't been on the old blueprints. "Where do you think that goes?"

"Bet you a dollar it leads to the hag," Lizz said.

"Not taking that bet...It bends to the left. I can't see where it goes," Justin reported.

"Want to toss in a grenade?" Kimpton asked hopefully.

"No," I answered instantly. "There might be hostages or something back there. What if the hag made a feeding pit, like vampires do?"

"Good point," Kimpton said. "That was the best way to handle tunnels in Vietnam, though."

"How you wanna to do this?" Justin asked.

"I'll take point," I told him. He grunted and moved to the side as I pulled out a flashlight. I had my father's eyes, but the rest of the team was out of luck. Either the hag had been too cheap to install lighting in this part or, more likely, the things that frequented this part didn't need lights to see in the dark.

After the bend, there was a fork in the tunnel. One fork went down, while the other was back level with the dance floor. From the fresh blood smear on the wall, that was how the werewolf had come at us before, and that was probably Rhino's blood.

"Which way?" Lizz asked.

"Down," Leroy and I said at the same time, because we were both feeling the same thing. The hag would be at the bottom of this.

I listened to make sure that Rhino, Melanie, and Tom were still behind us, and, satisfied they were, kept going down. I didn't know how the hell Rhino was still on his feet.

Shining the light around the corner of the dark hallway, I could see it went down farther before making another left. We were on a downward spiral. It was brick-and-mortar construction, and for some reason I guessed 1930s, like a Prohibition era bootlegger tunnel, but I really had no idea and it could have been built last year. There were cobwebs above, but the floor was surprisingly free of them. It was clear that something came through here quite a bit, since I could see the worn path through the dust.

As we kept corkscrewing into the ground, I came across a prison cell. It was a small room, with heavy steel bars for a door, and it stank of werewolf. There were several sets of shackles on the wall.

"She was going to use this werewolf to create more," Leroy said.

I didn't like cunning monsters. Blood-fiend hunger, werewolf fury, those were predictable. A monster who could plan, anticipate human responses, and have contingencies was a terrifying prospect. I don't know a single monster hunter out there who had ever gone toe to toe with a high-ranking Fey solo and survived. I'm sure they were out there but if anyone had succeeded, they were awfully quiet about it. For good reason too, since Fey Courts were notoriously vengeful things.

Tom made it around the corner to join us, with Rhino leaning on him for support. Our team leader didn't look good, but he was too stoic to actually show any pain. Melanie was walking backward behind them, ready to mow down anything that was following us.

"This thing's breeding werewolves?" Tom asked, having apparently overheard us.

"Yeah...she's turning innocents into killers. This is the evil you've been fighting against all these years, and you never even knew it," Lizz said. "I bet you never imagined anything like this when you started sticking pins in a map, huh?"

"Not even close," Tom muttered. "Let's finish this."

A bit past the steel bars was a man lying facedown on the floor. I approached carefully, and as I did so, he moaned. The rest of my team got ready to shoot just in case it was a trap. I rolled him over with my boot and shined my flashlight in his face. It was the accountant Melanie had flirted with when we'd scouted this place. He coughed up a bunch of blood. I pointed my flashlight down...the damage was horrendous. His stomach had been pulled open and his guts were hanging out. There were clear bite marks all over him. He was dying but wasn't quite dead yet. If he survived, we'd have another werewolf on our hands. That would not do.

"She said she'd protect me," the man whispered hoarsely. "The Mistress said she'd protect me from her pets."

"Bitch done lied to you," Lizz said.

I didn't feel pity for him, not in the least. He knew what he'd been working for, even if he had lied to himself about it. Magical befuddlement only works for a time, and after that you're sticking around because you want to. You don't work around this level of evil and remain ignorant of it for long. Then I thought of the map and tablet in his office.

"You weren't just serving as her accountant. You were her *priest.*"

"She is divine."

Leveling my pistol at his forehead, I said, "Do not sup with the Fey." I had nothing for him, but I did feel a momentary twinge of sadness for the man's family before I pulled the trigger.

Over the ringing in my ears I could make out the growl of something big and scary. The werewolf was around here somewhere, stalking us. A slight shiver of fear crawled up my spine. I hate being the hunted.

"That's coming from below," Justin said.

Nicole knew where we were and since none of us had planned on the werewolf being here in the club, nobody had thought to bring wolfsbane with us. Even with the powerful aromas wafting throughout the club, she could track us easily. Their noses were supersensitive, far better than mine was, and astronomically better than a human's. Werewolves were stronger, faster, and tougher than *nagualii* were as well. Life just isn't fair sometimes.

The werewolf of Lake Arrowhead had had a god complex and been relatively easy to kill. For all her being new, this one seemed sneakier. She had already ambushed us once and was clearly circling around somewhere, preparing to get us a second time. A clever werewolf was worse than a psychotic one.

Moving farther down, my stomach felt a little queasy. Even over the stench of the werewolf I could feel a difference here. Out on the dance floor of the disco hall it had been filled with the smells and feeling of the living. Here? Not so much. There was something deeply and profoundly wrong here. Shaking my head, I tried to get a grasp of just what my gut was warning me about. My head swam and my mouth grew dry.

I remembered feeling like this once before, but it had been a long time ago, at the orphanage in Mexico. There was the influence of a higher power here, and it was the opposite of a sanctified place. The *nagualii* was pushing hard to take over, knowing my control was slipping. I needed to breathe, to relax.

"Are you okay, Chloe?" Justin asked, as he sensed the change. He seemed to be doing fine, as was everybody else I could see. Whoever had constructed this dimensional prison had made it so that if any unnatural thing like me drew near, it would be incapacitated. Or worse, changed.

"I'll be fine." I gritted my teeth and carried on.

The corkscrew tunnel opened into another room, only this one wasn't made of bricks. They were great big stones, and every one of them appeared to be intricately carved. The room was big enough that my flashlight couldn't reach the back wall, so I waited for Rhino and the others to catch up. Once the gang was all here, we went through.

In the center of the room was a rectangular altar, just big enough to hold a human body, which I was positive wasn't a coincidence. On the other side of the altar from us was an ancient stone statue of a being I recognized.

"Oh shit."

"That looks Aztec," Leroy said as he shined his light on the squat, bat-headed thing, with its wings spread wide.

"It's not. That's Camazotz, the Mayan death bat. Worshipped

by Mayans. The Court of Feathers doesn't give a shit who worships them, or what. But the names are important."

"Another relative of yours?" Justin asked.

I tried not to take that as an insult. "No, but I bet the hag is related to him. This place is set up to honor a descendant of Camazotz's line."

"What's Camazotz's deal, anyway?"

"He's a lord of night, death, and sacrifice."

"Ohhh..." Justin said slowly. "Did you guys ever think about having any pleasant deities?"

"Yeah. When I converted to Judaism."

The werewolf moved in the shadows behind the statue, growling.

"There she is."

Every gun swung that direction, but Nicole was merely a distraction.

The hag had already had time to use her to infect more werewolves. *Four* more of them, in fact, and they all came flying at us from the shadows, blurs of hair and teeth.

"Motherfu—" Lizz started but it quickly turned into a scream of pain as a werewolf struck.

We all started shooting, only this time we had loaded silver.

Swinging flashlights and muzzle flashes created an effect similar to the disco ball and strobes above.

"Lizz!" It was like the werewolf had instinctively picked out the smallest and weakest from the herd to attack. Except the repeated *boom* of her gun told me she hadn't died, and the werewolf yelped as she took a piece out of it.

After the smallest, instinct said target the wounded, and one werewolf almost made it to Rhino. He lifted his shotgun one-handed, and put 12-gauge silver buckshot pellets right through its open mouth to blow out the back of its skull.

Had it been five experienced werewolves, we all would've been dead in seconds. But with these four new creations—and this was probably their very first time changed—we had a slim chance.

I looked back in time to see a sleek werewolf shrugging off a whole bunch of bullets as it leapt over the statue of Camazotz, claws extended right for my face. I yanked the trigger on my Galil, but the werewolf plowed straight into me, knocking my rifle away. We both came up superfast, and it was only by my inhuman reflexes I avoided its tearing claws. It was so close I went for my knife instead of my handgun.

When my fingers landed on the Black Heart of Suffering, the bone was cold as ice, and when I drew it and slashed, instead of splitting werewolf throat, the magic blade cut the world in two.

CHAPTER 16

I was no longer in the room of stone. The altar, my team, and the werewolves were gone.

Knife extended, I spun around, trying to figure out where I was. Somehow, I was in a dark, steaming hot jungle. Unseen animals hooted and insects chirped. Sweat immediately formed on my brow.

It was as if the magic knife had sliced through reality, and I'd fallen out the other side. It felt like I'd been instantaneously transported to another continent, except this had to be the hag's domain. Though it didn't really have the right *feel* of belonging to her.

My team needed me, only I couldn't find my way back. It was like the slash through reality had sealed up behind me. Swinging the little magic knife at it again did nothing.

Surrounded by gigantic trees and thick leaves, I didn't see or hear any immediate threats, so I crouched down and tried to get my bearings, still breathing hard from the werewolf fight. "This is really weird," I muttered and frowned, because the words sounded wrong in my ear, flat and hollow. It was as though someone had slapped earmuffs over me and then dumped me into the water. Everything about the place was off.

This place was real, but not right. There was no other way to explain it.

Gradually, I realized the problems. There were stars overhead, millions of them. It was more like they'd been painted on the inside of some kind of dome. The plants were alive, but they didn't feel vibrant and natural, more like they'd been planted like a garden. It was so hot that I'd immediately begun sweating, but it felt more like I was under a heat lamp than the natural humidity of a jungle. Listening carefully, the animal noises seemed to be on a repeating pattern. Everything was fake.

This wasn't a jungle. It was a terrarium.

The *nagualii* was crouched in the back of my mind as usual, only in this place it was almost as if I could see it there waiting, like a heavy black smoke floating just outside the edge of my peripheral vision.

I could hear water flowing nearby. Looking around, I spotted the culprit. A stream cut through the bushes, so I got up and followed it up to a rocky cliff, where it turned into a shimmering waterfall. Below was a lake and a tiny valley. It was scenic and hauntingly beautiful. In other circumstances I might find it charming. However, if killing the hag meant burning it all to the ground and salting the earth to ensure her demise, then so be it. I just needed to find some gasoline and a lighter.

I checked to see what equipment I had left. I'd lost my rifle, but my Browning Hi-Power was holstered on my belt, along with four extra mags. I wished that I had packed some hand grenades. I still had the Black Heart of Suffering, so I returned it to the sheath. Carefully, because I really didn't want to cut myself with a magic knife that looked that scary unnatural. It couldn't be good for you.

With my *nagualii* eyes I continuously scanned for any sign of the hag as I climbed down toward the clearing. There appeared to be some kind of mound or structure in the middle, so I figured that was as good a destination as any.

I found a trail along the waterfall heading in that direction. There were footprints in the dirt. Something flickered at the very edge of my eyesight. Turning quickly, I thought I saw movement between the trees.

"You are not supposed to be here." The voice sounded close, but the way things were twisted in here it could have come from anywhere.

You're telling me . . . "Show yourself."

A *thing* leapt out of the bushes to land in the dirt, kicking up quite an impressive cloud of dust for something as short as it was. I was at least a foot taller, but it was twice as wide as I was. Whatever the creature was, it was *ugly*. It was sort of human shaped, but with spiky fur, a pig snout, and gnarly tusks. He was wearing armor made out of animal hide and carrying a spear that ended in an obsidian shard. I caught a whiff of a very musky odor.

"You dare carry devices made from cold iron into this place?" I could tell he was sizing me up the same way I had him.

He must have been talking about my gun. The aversion to metal meant this thing was probably Fey, just like the hag. I didn't know if he was an ally, enemy, or neutral. Despite looking like a bipedal javelina, the armor appeared to be in good shape and that little spear looked remarkably dangerous.

"I need these tools because I'm here to destroy a hag."

His pig snout nostrils snuffled as he got my scent. "You should not be here, Daughter of Tezcatlipoca."

"Where is *here*?"

"A place long forgotten beneath Ilhuicatl-Nanatzcayan, where an heir of Camazotz has been condemned to spend eternity for her crimes. What is your name, Child of the North?"

"Yeah, no way." Names had power with the Fey. There was no way I was about to let Pigface know what my real name was. I wasn't taking any chances with this.

"You are not allowed here, Yah-Noway, heir of Tezcatlipoca."

Unimaginative. Definitely Fey of some kind. "Where's the hag?"

"She is wandering her prison like a proper little inmate. Why would a *nagualii* such as yourself want her? Your kind and hers have no quarrel."

You have no idea just how wrong you are, I thought. "She's not been condemned here for eternity very well if she's been sneaking into my world and causing trouble."

"Impossible. It is inescapable." Pigface seemed immensely proud of this declaration because he puffed his chest out and grinned, which was a horrific sight.

"Yeah, so was Alcatraz," I muttered, looking around.

"Your kind doesn't belong here." Pigface said, frowned around his massive tusks. "You must leave."

"Can't," I half apologized. "I need to kill the hag first."

"The *ch'aglessi* is not yours to kill." He angrily snorted. "She is to remain imprisoned here. She must serve her sentence in full."

"She's going to escape!"

"There is no escape."

"Are you stupid?" Now I was getting angry. "Have you even heard a word I've said? She's already been sneaking out, she's going to escape into my world permanently soon, if I don't stop her. Help me kill her or get out of my way."

"Then those shall be your final words," Pigface said and hurled his spear at me.

I barely had time to lean to the side as the spear flew through the air where my head had just been.

Pigface let out a furious terrible screech. I wasn't about to give him a second chance at killing me, so I drew my handgun and squeezed the trigger.

Luckily, ammunition still worked inside the pocket-dimension terrarium. The round smacked into the pig-guard's armor and bright purple blood flew out. He snorted in surprise and pain, then staggered and fell face-first into the dirt.

The single gunshot echoed across the area, seeming to be far louder than it should have. Somewhere in the distance, there was another pig shriek. And another, and another calling out in reply. The screams were distorted and twisted, a haunting sound designed to strike fear into the heart of man. The rest of the guard force had been alerted to my presence and were probably on their way to skewer and skin, then after they were done with all of that, go ahead and kill me.

Pigface was lying there, perfectly still. He was still breathing, though.

"Are you dead?"

"I am wounded," the guard growled. "I will heal and return to duty. Eventually."

"Good!" I meant it too. Even though he'd tried to kill me, I had no ill will toward Pigface. He was just trying to do his job. "I only want to kill the hag."

"You do not understand this place, Yah-Noway. There is no death here. The lords of death have forsaken this realm so that the suffering of those banished here may be eternal. All who dwell inside are forever beyond the grasp of Mictlan."

That put an all new spin on the concept of life without parole.

The pig shrieks were getting closer. "So your friends aren't going to murder me?"

"They cannot."

"Oh, good."

"Instead they will rip you apart and scatter your bits so you will spend eternity in endless disassembled suffering."

"I think there's been a misunderstanding."

"Tell that to the others," Pigface muttered as a dozen more guards appeared atop the waterfall. The squat little javelina men began angrily shaking their spears over their heads when they saw me.

I squeezed off shots as fast as I could and pig guards started going down. One little guy went tumbling over the waterfall. I'm no Annie Oakley, or Lizz for that matter. Normally, I'm at best a decent shot. However, in that moment every bullet I sent hit exactly where I meant it to. It was like I couldn't miss.

But there were a whole lot of angry guards coming this way fast, and as if to prove what the first one had claimed was true, no matter how many of them I dropped, they were absolutely fearless and not worried about dying. Some of the little bastards jumped off the waterfall just because it was faster. And there were more coming! I was going to run out of bullets long before they ran out of bodies.

There were pig men right behind me, and it turned out that they dropped to all fours when they ran, and they were *fast*. More of them jumped out of the bushes ahead of me, wielding wooden clubs embedded with obsidian chips. I gunned them down too. The Browning's slide locked back empty, so I dropped the spent mag and shoved a new one in.

And for the first time, I saw something that really scared them. One of the guards chasing me screamed in terror when it saw the empty magazine on the ground, and threw on the brakes, skidding on its rear end, trying desperately to stop, but its momentum caused it to bump into the mag.

The *steel* magazine.

There was a sizzling pop, the smell of burning bacon, and that pig guard reacted like a human being catching 220 volts, jerking and twitching until he broke contact, and then he squealed and ran for his life.

It was said different kinds of Fey were vulnerable to iron to various degrees. Steel was an alloy of iron and carbon. Apparently that was close enough for this particular Court.

Despite that one getting fried—and it apparently being a whole lot worse sensation than lethal gunshot wounds—the rest of the guards were too dedicated to give up. Spears were flying all around me. There was grunting and thrashing in the bushes as they ran after me on all fours, only to pop up and take swings at me with their razor clubs.

Somehow I stayed ahead of them. This place was affecting me. Making me faster. Or maybe it wasn't the place itself, but rather who owned it. This was closer to my father's realm than I'd ever been, and I was stronger because of it. I sensed a spear flying for my back, turned, snatched it out of midair, and, still spinning, used the shaft to smack a leaping pig man ten feet in the opposite direction. Instead of throwing it back, I kept this one. It might come in handy.

Only they didn't care who I was or how many of their asses I kicked, they were going to keep at it until I was in pieces. Until, that is, I reached the center of the realm, jumped over a row of low stones, and ran into the clearing. Then the shrieking, grunting, and spear throwing suddenly stopped.

It was sticky hot, and I was out of breath, so I was glad they'd given up—but why? Spear in one hand, pistol in the other, I turned back to the pig mob, and gasped, "You done?"

One approached the edge of the clearing but stopped just shy of the stones. The creatures were pretty much identical looking, but from the position of the bullet hole in this one's armor and the purple bloodstains on his spiky fur, I was pretty sure he was the first one I'd met.

"We do not enter the prisoner's lair."

"How come?"

He pointed his stubby little fingers toward the mound, which actually turned out to be a low stone building that was just overgrown with moss and vines. Only it wasn't the structure he was gesturing at, but the piles of gnawed-on bones. From the size, shape, and tusks, these had once been other pig guards.

"I thought you said nothing could die here."

"They are devoured. Not dead."

That took a second for me to process. "Oh...damn." That was a grim way to spend eternity.

"You are fierce, Yah-Noway, Daughter of Tezcatlipoca. You understand now you cannot slay her in this place, so we will allow you to leave in peace. Go now, before her attention is drawn."

"Tempting as that offer is, piggy, she's sneaking into my world somehow, and you guys can't seem to keep her locked up, so I've got to find a way to stop her before she escapes once and for all."

"You think you can stop me, *nagualii*?" a haunting voice called out from somewhere nearby. Every single hair on the back of my neck stood up. "I am old blood. You are new. Your kind is nothing to me."

The pig guards all squealed in fear and disappeared back into the jungle. They sure talked a big game about handling their prisoner, until she was actually present.

"Whatever you say," I replied as I looked around the clearing. There was no sign of the hag anywhere, but I could feel an evil presence.

Well, it was more like multiple evil presences, because the *nagualii* spirit was poking around at the edges of my mind, as if coaxing, *Let me out. This is beyond you. Let me handle this.*

I told that wicked part of myself to shut up and back off. I had this under control.

In the dirt in front of the stone house was a fire pit, which suddenly erupted into a massive bonfire, making the already miserable heat even worse.

There was a shadow crouched inside the stone house, so dark that even my eyes couldn't make it out.

"It took centuries clawing at the mortar of this prison before I discovered a crack, and decades more scratching away until my voice could be heard on the other side. I found minions, and then I found a mighty ally. Weary, I rested my bloody nails, and let them chip away the prison walls from the other side for me." She reached one hand out of the shadows to scratch the floor, and it was the gnarliest claw I'd ever seen: six-fingered, with hooked talons long enough to butcher a cow. "I have enjoyed my small measure of freedom. I am eager to return in full. Your world is soft and ripe to feed upon."

Goading a Fey wasn't ever a smart thing to do, but I was out of options. "Your jailers claim nothing can die here, but what do you say me and you test that out?"

"Why do you wish to be my enemy, Daughter of Tezcatlipoca?

We are both outcasts, forsaken by the Court of Feathers. They abandoned us. Made us less than we could be. Cut our horns and snapped off our fangs. They are gods no more... yet, we could be."

The hag slid out of the shadows and into the firelight, bat-like and twisted, even more disgusting than she had been the first time I spotted her outside the club with the MCB chief. Only now, even hunched over inside the house, she had to be seven feet tall.

"Pandora has offered me my own Court, with dominion over your city of angels. Join it."

"Pandora?"

"A different kind of goddess," the hag whispered. "She who denies hope, and brings sickness, perversion, and evil into your world."

"Is she another refugee from the Court of Feathers too?"

The hag scoffed. "Pandora is of no Court. She is of Earth, but older than the conquistadors' cross god. She was there when your desert church members were still slaves to the Court of Ra. I have pledged fealty to her."

The Herald had warned me that *she was coming*, and I'd taken that to mean the hag... "You mean, there's something out there *worse* than you?"

The hag had to duck to get out of the doorway, but then she drew herself up to her full impressive height, and spread her tattered wings, towering over the bonfire. "Am I not sufficient, cousin?"

I had my pistol up and was firing before she had finished speaking. Bullets punched into her bloated, disgusting body. She rushed me, straight through the bonfire, so fast I was barely able to recognize she was attacking before she was on me.

She struck at my gun, and when the steel touched her arm, flesh sizzled and cracked, but she still managed to knock it away, and the Browning went bouncing through the dirt. I thrust the obsidian spear into her hairy side, and from her reaction, the reason the pig men were armed with obsidian was that it actually hurt her.

This realm made me faster, but apparently that worked on her too, and she'd been here a whole lot longer. Her wings beat around my head, slamming into and disorienting me. Something cracked painfully in my chest and I flew backward. On Earth that hit would've sent me tumbling, but here, I instinctively twisted my body and landed on my hands and knees, still ready to fight.

The shaft of the pig spear was really narrow to suit their stubby little fingers, but the wood seemed incredibly dense, and I thrust it at her bat face, slicing open her wide nose. She swatted the spear away, and it clattered against her stone house.

The hag launched herself at me like a missile, engulfing me in her terrible embrace, sinking her claws into my flak jacket, and then her wings spread wide and we were soaring upward at a dizzying speed. We were a hundred feet up in a few heartbeats, heading straight for the illusion of stars.

The bitch intended to drop me!

This does not seem like being in control to me, the *nagualii* spirit whispered.

"Shut up!"

This high up I could see the entire dimension, and that it was a circular bowl of jungle, with absolutely nothing on the outside. I struggled to reach my magic knife, but that arm was pinned. My other hand was free, though, so I jammed my thumb into her eye and ground it deep, trying to pop it.

She let go of me.

Instead of dropping, I got two handfuls of bat fur and held on for dear life.

Off-balance, the hag flapped and spiraled downward.

Her joints bent unnaturally to allow one of her legs to reach up and slash my hip with her toe claws. When one of my hands let go, she screeched in triumph.

Only I wasn't slipping. I'd needed that hand to draw the Black Heart of Suffering. I pulled myself upward and slashed wildly at one of her beating wings.

If the obsidian had stung her, the mystery blade rocked her fucking world.

The hag screamed as her wing was sliced in half and then both of us were twirling toward the ground. She slashed me across the back. I stabbed her in the gut. Then we hit the dirt.

It hurt unbelievably. No cat was landing on its feet after that trip.

I would have, the *nagualii* insisted.

Gagging, I tried to sit up, only to have a gnarled, hairy foot kick me in the face.

My head snapped back from the blow. I stabbed with the knife, but she caught me by the wrist, and jerked it back so hard my elbow popped. I cried out in pain and lost the knife. She sank her claws through my flak far enough to split skin, picked me up, and threw me against the stone house. I bounced off and ate dirt.

Her hot, rank breath washed over my face as she leaned in close to me. I could hear the hunger in her tone as she began whispering in my ear. "Pork flesh is bland. It's been far too long since I've eaten something exotic like a *nagualii*. Your kind are a delicacy. I do crave something...*different*. I will eat you piece by piece, leaving your brain for last, so you can have understanding of the entire experience."

We can be stronger together, the *nagualii* spirit begged. *I do not want to rule, merely help.*

"No!"

A rough, sandpaper-like tongue licked my bloodied face. "Delicious!"

I tried to roll away but she pinned me down with her knee, grinding my broken ribs. I screamed. She laughed.

Time seemed to slow down. The *nagualii* was desperate. She didn't want to die either. I was scared to death and there was no one else here to hurt, so instead of fighting the power in my blood, I could let it run free.

But there had to be rules!

The *nagualii* understood.

Surprisingly, it was as if in this place outside of the real world, the *nagualii* and I could actually understand each other for the very first time.

I warned her not to break the rules.

Agreed.

A blood oath was made.

I felt my limbs lengthen and gain strength as the change came over me.

The previous times I'd let the *nagualii* take hold of me, I'd lost all sense of control. I'd just been along for the ride. My thinking mind got shoved to the back as the predator went into full monster mode. However, this place was so different that, as I changed, I remained me. I became the monster but stayed human. For the first time I saw her face, and she saw mine.

She was glossy fur and savage fangs. Everything about her was sleek and dangerous.

You are stronger than you think, the monster whispered.

For the first time in my life, I wasn't scared of her. The *nagualii* would either respect me, or be locked away, forever.

We can be stronger, together.

"We only fight evil. We never hurt innocents again."

The hag was confused when I said that. "What?"

Let's kill the evil, then.

When the hag went to lick the other side of my face, I was ready, and grabbed her gigantic, forked tongue, crushing it in one fist with unexpected strength.

"What's wrong? Cat got your tongue?"

The hag's eyes widened as she tried to pull back, and as soon as her weight was off me, I spun my body, but kept hold of her tongue, and kicked her with both boots, ripping her nasty tongue right out of her head.

As the hag vomited black blood all over the clearing, I got up and tore off my flak. The heavy, awkward thing was just slowing me down. Then I sprang toward the magic knife. It had landed twenty feet away, but I reached it in one bound and snatched it from the dirt.

The hag was reeling in circles, both of her hands pressed against her ruined mouth, so she never even knew I was coming until I'd landed on her back, wrapped one arm around her neck, and went to stabbing with my long claws.

She threw me off and fell on her hands and knees, scrambling to flee. She made it a few feet before I bit her on the calf and dragged her violently back so I could stab her some more. Her unbroken wing flew up and smacked me away.

I landed on my feet and immediately circled, looking for an angle to pounce.

The hag surged upright and realized that she was no longer fighting a human with some extraordinary abilities, but the living daughter of a blood-soaked war god. She tried to speak, to beguile me with her cunning words, but I'd already taken her lying tongue. Served her right.

Determined, she came at me again, claws extended. I cut her wrist, spun beneath her arms to slash open her belly, rolled between her legs, splitting one tendon along the way, and then rose behind her to strike at her remaining wing. The magic knife ate through the hag's flesh like it was hungry.

The hag swung wildly for me, but I ducked under it, jaguar quick, and the knife rose with me, opening her from pelvis to throat. Unspeakable things came squirting out.

That should have killed her, but nothing could die in this place. She staggered back, reaching for me, and I struck off her hand. It went flying into the jungle. When her other hand reflexively flew to the stump, I sliced that one off at the elbow.

Things might not die here, but I could make sure they were never in any danger of escaping ever again, and I would make certain that it hurt along the way.

I don't know if the hag could read minds, or maybe it was the savage, fanged grin that split my jaguar face that enabled her to guess what I was planning to do, but she fled in a panic then. She made it all the way back to her hut before I picked up the pig spear and hurled it with *nagualii* strength. It struck her through the heart and slammed her back against the wall, pinning her to the stone.

I pounced onto her a moment later, hitting so furiously that the entire house collapsed around us.

Picking myself up out of the dusty wreckage, I found the hag still pinned by the spear like an insect in a collection. The spawn of Camazotz didn't give up easily. She tried to claw me with her toes. In response I lopped both of her legs off at the knees.

In my defense, even a cooperative *nagualii* is incredibly bloodthirsty.

Slowly, things seemed to return to normal. My savage half, gleeful at being able to let loose, was happy to subside. I felt my body weaken, and, laws of physics be damned, become smaller and lighter. Within a few seconds I was just Chloe Mendoza again, except covered in hag blood and missing most of my clothes. All the aches and pains of the beating I'd taken before the change returned as well, which was some agonizing bullshit.

The hag was alive, but broken and limbless. There wasn't any part of her that hadn't been ripped by the magic knife. Except she couldn't die, and for all I knew, she might still somehow be able to recover from this and threaten Earth again.

"Hey, guards!"

A moment later, there was some grunting and snuffling in the brush, and the stubby pig men appeared, approaching the border warily. They were a whole lot more deferential now.

"You summon us, Princess Yah-Noway?"

"Earlier, you threatened to pull me apart and scatter the living parts across this realm."

I'm pretty sure the speaker was the original I'd met, and he seemed a little bashful about that threat now. "Apologies. That was before I knew how pure the blood of the Drought Bringer was within you."

"I just need to know if that would actually work on her, and if they all stay alive. They're not going to grow new ones like a gecko's tail, right?"

"That is correct."

"Good." I gestured at the limbs I'd severed. "Then scatter these."

The pig men seemed confused by that request, snuffling at each other, but then they oinked excitedly as they realized what I was doing. "The witch will continue to live. Our purpose remains."

"Yeah, she just won't be hunting any more of you for sport without her arms and legs. You're welcome." I scooped my Browning off the ground, dusted it off, and went over to where the hag was still struggling against the skinny spear she was impaled on.

She glared at me with unbelievable fury and tried to curse me with a mouth that couldn't operate properly. It was difficult to decipher the sounds now, but I was pretty sure she was telling me that we weren't done, and she'd find a way back to the real world, mark my words, and so on.

"Oh, you thought I was done. I might have called this good enough, only you sent those fiends to try to murder Alex." I held up the steel pistol, so she'd get a good look at it. "That makes this personal."

When the hideous bat thing realized what was happening, she started to thrash even harder, but it was too late. I slid the end of the spear shaft through the Browning's trigger guard, and let the pistol drop onto her chest. When the metal hit, flesh sizzled, and the hag convulsed, pinned beneath it.

And it would stay like that until the steel rusted away, which I guessed in this realm would take a *very* long time. She wouldn't be trying to invade Earth again anytime soon.

Exhausted, wheezing, and in terrible pain, I walked back over to the guards.

"You're not going to try to stop me from leaving, are you, Pigface?"

"I will show you the way back to your home, Princess," he replied. "Please do not tell your father of my earlier rudeness."

I found myself back in the secret chamber beneath the nightclub, standing a few feet from the statue of Camazotz. The first thing I heard was the death whine of a werewolf, far more high-pitched than a regular human could hear.

Since I'd appeared out of thin air, I damn near got shot by my justifiably jumpy teammates. Multiple guns swung my way, but cooler heads started shouting, "Whoa! Whoa!" or "Hold your fire!"

Melanie lowered her rifle. "Chloe! You just vanished. We thought you were dead." Then she saw the sorry state I was in. "Are you okay?"

"I'll live." The sudden temperature drop from the artificial heat of the pocket dimension caused me to shiver uncontrollably. "I was sent to the prison."

Rhino was lying on the floor next to a nearly headless werewolf. "Is it over?"

"The hag isn't coming through anymore," I said, dodging the question slightly. What I'd done to that monster was worse than death. It was torture—constant, unending. I didn't know if they would approve of what I'd done, but they hadn't been there.

I looked around and counted five very dead werewolves in various states of dismemberment. Everybody on my team looked beat up, but they were all here and alive. They should have been triumphant. Why'd everyone look so melancholy?

"What's wrong?"

"Guys? I think... I need your help," Lizz muttered as she limped slowly my way.

She was looking down at her arm. Justin shined his flashlight that way so we could see better. A large chunk of skin and meat was missing from Lizz's bicep. It was a horrific mess, but worse, embedded deep in the exposed muscle was a single, razor-sharp tooth that had broken off sometime during the fight.

My heart began hammering in my chest.

Poor, sweet Lizz had been bitten by the werewolf.

"Oh no..." I covered my mouth, horrified. "No."

The entire team was staggered. Even Tom the new guy understood what this meant, because we'd explained it before our hunt at Lake Arrowhead. Werewolf clawings were hit or miss, but if you were bitten, their saliva was in the wound, you were infected, period.

"Nope, not gonna be a werewolf," Lizz muttered as she stumbled over to me.

I reached out and caught her in my arms, and held her as she gently slumped to the floor. I cradled her head on my lap and wept. Lizz was my friend.

Despite Justin sticking her with the morphine from his med kit, her pain was obvious. The claws of the werewolf had punctured through her flak jacket multiple times, and the heavy vest was probably the only thing holding her insides in the right place. Her arm had nearly been torn off at the elbow. She was in agony, only it would all be healed. She would be fine, but everyone else would be in danger. She would become the very thing she hated.

Leroy approached, squatted next to her, and put one gentle hand on her shoulder. "You might be able to handle it."

"We know that ain't gonna happen."

"It's been done before."

"I know. One out of how many?"

Leroy nodded sadly. "Yeah... There's that."

"Fuck that. I ain't gonna hurt innocent people."

"I'm sorry, Lizz," I whispered, tears in my eyes. "What... what do you want me to do?"

"Take care of it now before I go crazy." Lizz's unusual accent was thicker than normal as she started to drift off. "Let me go out while I'm still me."

"I can't kill... no. There has to be another way."

"There's not. Smarter folks than us have looked," Lizz reminded me.

It was true. The curse of the werewolf was passed through the bite. Even if we'd cut her arm off one second after it happened, it was too late. The next full moon she would change into a feral killing machine.

"Suicides go to hell. I need you to do it for me. I can't."

"I didn't know you were Catholic."

"Lapsed."

"Ah."

"Yup." Then she winced. We could all see Lizz was in terrible pain. It was a tough choice for her but she was unyielding. My team member was proving once more how much stronger she was than I was. So much potential there to be more than just a teammate. Given enough time, we could have been as close as sisters. Now? I'd never get to know. Everyone was gathered around, devastated, either staring at Lizz, or off into space.

"I'm not big on long goodbyes. Could y'all give me and Chloe some space?" she asked.

Rhino nodded solemnly. "You heard her." And he began herding everyone else toward the exit. Melanie broke down sobbing.

Kimpton held out his .45 for me.

"Better be silver bullets in there," Lizz muttered. "Don't wanna be coming back."

"No, ma'am, you taught us too well for that," Kimpton said. "Bye, Lizz."

I hesitantly took the pistol from him.

"Love you kids," Lizz called after them. She waited until she was sure they were gone like she'd ordered. "Quit being a wimp, Chloe."

"I—"

"Do it!"

I kissed her bloodied forehead. "I'll make sure Ray puts your plaque up on the wall."

"Damn right you will."

There was a fever in Los Angeles. A poison had been spreading, hidden in the shadows. Our job was to fight the darkness, and casualties were expected. I'd just never thought it would be Lizz. She had been steady as a rock the entire time.

I didn't look in her eyes. I couldn't. Everything was blurry. Stupid tears. I wiped my eyes. My soul protested, crying out in anguish for me to show compassion. *Only this* is *compassion*, the *nagualii* assured me.

"*Sic transit gloria mundi*, Lizz," I whispered to her, then pulled the trigger.

The world was oblivious to what we'd just done for them.

Somewhere out in the City of Angels a creature older than Judea was on the prowl. It was my job to kill this thing with extreme prejudice, but part of me wanted to walk away, to let the party boys, the club goers, and C-list Hollywood stars be dinner to the monsters they unknowingly worshipped. And for the first time, I really understood why the Boss and Earl were nervous about my returning. They feared I'd grow to hate and resent the people I was supposed to protect.

It wasn't their fault. The powers that be kept them ignorant, supposedly for their own safety. My duty was to keep the bad things so scared of people like me they'd remain in the dark.

I might be a monster, but I wasn't an evil one.

The vision of this city in flames stuck with me, and I knew that fate was still a possibility.

There was one lead. Thanks to the hag, I had a name.

Pandora.

Nobody had said anything about Lizz as I'd walked out of the club. There were no words that could make me feel better. I felt defeated and wondered if it was worth it. The fighting, the struggle. Losing loved ones. Justin had carried her body. He'd said she didn't weigh hardly a thing.

Half of us had to go to the hospital for something. Rhino would be lucky to not lose his hand. Deputy Tom went home, but I doubted he'd stay there for long. You couldn't just go back to work in the normal world after what he'd seen. Leroy had declared he'd be sticking around for a bit, as it looked like we could use the help.

At the hospital, Alex was still unconscious. The doctors were unsure of the prognosis, but he was a tough kid, and I had faith he'd pull through. As soon as he was awake, I was going to start picking that big old brain of his, because we had a new monster to find.

Hope wasn't lost. I wasn't just a human woman, but *nagualii*. For the first time ever, my two halves had worked together... and honestly, it felt *good*. I didn't know if I could replicate that in the real world, but I couldn't live my life in fear. My kind existed to *cause* fear. *Nagualii* were older than written language. There were pictographs of creatures like me in ancient caverns warning man of how dangerous we were, long before he'd invented the wheel.

Pandora. Pretentious bitch, wannabe Greek poseur. I might only be a half-breed, but my father had been worshipped as a *god*. I wasn't just going to track her down to protect this thankless city, or to pay her back for Lizz and Alex, I intended to hurt her so bad that my blood-soaked ancestors would smile in approval, and the lesser ones tremble in terror.

I was really looking forward to that day.